Red Spider

Red Spider

Sabine Baring-Gould

NONSUCH

First published 1887

Nonsuch Publishing
Cirencester Road, Chalford, Stroud, Gloucestershire, GL6 8PE

Nonsuch Publishing (Ireland)
73 Lower Leeson Street, Dublin 2, Ireland

www.nonsuch-publishing.com

Nonsuch Publishing is an imprint of NPI Media Group

For comments or suggestions, please email the editor of this series at:
classics@tempus-publishing.com

British Library Cataloguing in Publication Data.
A catalogue record for this book is available from the British Library.

ISBN 978 1 84588 359 1

Typesetting and origination by Nonsuch Publishing Limited
Printed in Great Britain by Oaklands Book Services Limited

CONTENTS

Introduction to the Modern Edition

What curate in an industrial parish in the North today would dare to single out a millgirl and have her sent to a place where she could learn to speak in an educated style and then marry her? What local council would allow a squire today to rebuild his house in a Rhenish style as did Baring-Gould in Lewtrenchard? What vicar and Diocesan Advisory Committee would allow a squarson to remove tablets from other churches and put them up in his own, as Baring-Gould did at Lew?

John Betjeman

Sabine Baring-Gould was undoubtedly one of the most prolific and versatile writers of the Victorian age. There is no definitive bibliography of his works, but it is clear that his oeuvre is extensive, numbering well into the hundreds. He was also a man renowned for his somewhat unconventional lifestyle, behaviour and opinions, as well as the diversity of his interests; he has also, until recent times, failed to receive the recognition that his vast contribution to literature clearly merits.

He was born in Exeter in 1834, the eldest son of a land-owning family possessed of estates in Lewtrenchard, west Devon. He had a rather unsettled childhood, much of which was spent travelling throughout Europe with his family as his father sought to relieve the boredom of a life in which his career had been cut short—he had worked with the East India Company until a carriage accident abruptly brought about his early retirement. Despite little formal schooling, the young Baring-Gould managed to complete his education at Cambridge, where he became well known for his eccentric ways and his anti-establishment views. After taking holy orders in 1864, however, he became a curate in Horbury, Yorkshire. There he met a young mill-girl named Grace Taylor, who, in a now unsurprising act of unconventionality, he decided to marry after first sending her away to be educated. Their forty-eight-year marriage ended only upon Grace's death in 1916, and during this time the couple had fifteen children, fourteen of whom survived into adult life.

Baring-Gould had returned to his family home in Devon in 1881, where he was content to take up the role of squire and parson of the small parish of Lewtrenchard. Here he spent the greater part of his life caring for the welfare of his parishioners, raising his large family, and continuing to travel as he had once done as a child.

Baring-Gould's principal pursuit, aside from his other responsibilities, was the writing of that prodigious amount of literature. He was ranked as one of the most popular novelists of his day, though his work did extend to a wide variety of non-fiction books, pamphlets and magazines, on subjects ranging from archaeology, theology and history to folklore, travel guides and biographies. He was regarded as an authority on these subjects, his *Lives of the Saints*, in particular, becoming a standard theological work of reference. He is often recognised for his composition of the famous hymn 'Onward Christian Soldiers,' the popularity of which surprised him, as he apparently jotted it down in only a few minutes. It was certainly not regarded by him as amongst his greatest achievements; indeed, his self-proclaimed most important work was the collection of the folk songs of Devon and Cornwall, published in 1889 as *Songs of the West*. This endeavour occupied him for a total of twelve years, during which time he toured the length of the two counties, visiting the old people who knew the songs best, in their homes and in the fields. The originality of the work can be attributed to the personal approach Baring-Gould took to it; he approached the people as his friends and his equals, and gave it the subtitle 'A collection made from the mouths of the people.' He was not always able to include every original word, as some were considered unsuitable for publication, but he endeavoured to modify them while remaining true to his sources where possible. The book, which ran to four volumes, was the most ambitious of its kind, and has come to be regarded as invaluable for the legacy it has provided for folk revival singers in this part of the country. Appreciation of his achievement can be seen in the present-day societies dedicated to the study of his works, as well as in the folk festivals which are held in his name.

Baring-Gould wrote thirty novels during the course of his life. They were usually inspired by his travel through a particular area and, as a result, the stories were often placed firmly in the context of their settings, with a great deal of local colouring. They tell dramatic, exciting tales of smuggling communities along the south Devon coast; of passion and obsession in the wilds of the Essex marshes; of a love triangle steeped in the romance and customs of ancient Dartmoor. All are filled with highly original and memorable characters who find themselves in extreme, yet realistic, situations.

Baring-Gould's fascination with local lore is demonstrated to its fullest in *Red Spider*. In this work he takes up the folk legend that a red spider will spin money in the pocket of he who secures its services. Interwoven with an exploration of this myth is a more traditional tale of moral virtue and pride, of friendship and the boundaries of loyalty in a world of temptation. What emerges is a finely drawn portrait of a time and a people, in which the differences of culture and manner are affectionately preserved, and their deeper similarities to the mores of today are brought to light. Baring-Gould provides, through this wonderful tale, a window into the past and a mirror through which we can recognise ourselves, as is the case with all true classics of literature.

PREFACE

FIFTY YEARS AGO! HALF A century has passed since the writer was a child in the parish where he has laid the scene of this tale.

There he had a trusty nurse, and a somewhat romantic story was attached to her life. Faithful, good creature! She was carrying the writer in her arms over a brook by a bridge elevated high above the water, when the plank broke. She at once held up her charge over her head, with both arms, and made no attempt to save herself, thinking only of him, as she fell on the stones and into the water. *He* escaped wholly unhurt, owing to her devotion.

Many years after, the author read a little German story which curiously recalled to him his nurse and her career. When a few years ago he revisited the scenes of his childhood, he thought to recall on paper many and many a recollection of village life in the south-west of England in one of its most still and forgotten corners. So he has taken this thread of story, not wholly original in its initiation and has altered and twisted it to suit his purpose, and has strung on it sundry pictures of what was beginning to fade half a century ago in Devon. Old customs, modes of thought, of speech, quaint sayings, weird superstitions are all disappearing out of the country, utterly and for ever.

The labourer is now enfranchised, education is universal, railways have made life circulate freer; and we stand now before a great social dissolving view, from which old things are passing away, and what is coming on we can only partly guess, not wholly distinguish.

In revisiting the parish of Bratton Clovelly, the author found little of the outward scenery changed, but the modes of life were in a state of transition. The same hills, the same dear old moors and woods, the same green coombs, the same flowers, the same old church, and the same glorious landscape. The reader will perhaps accept with leniency a slight tale for the sake of the pictures it presents of what is gone for ever, or is fast fading away. Coryndon's Charity, of course, is non-existent in Bratton parish. The names are all taken, Christian and sire, from the early registers of the parish. Village characteristics, incidents, superstitions have been worked in, from actual recollections. The author has tried to be very close in local colour; and, if it be not too bold a comparison, he would have this little story considered, like one of Birket Foster's water-colours, rather as a transcript from nature than as a finished, original, highly-arranged and considered picture.

I

The Brothers-in-Law

HEIGH! FOR A BADGER-SKIN WAISTCOAT like that of Hillary Nanspian of Chimsworthy! What would not I give to be the owner of such a waistcoat? Many a covetous glance was cast at that waistcoat in the parish church of Bratton Clovelly, in the county of Devon, on Sunday, where it appeared during public worship in a pew; and when the parson read the Decalogue, many a heart was relieved to learn that the prohibition against covetousness did not extend to badger-skin waistcoats. That waistcoat was made of the skin of a badger Hillary Nanspian had himself drawn and killed. In colour it was silver-grey graduating to black. The fur was so deep that the hand that grasped it sank into it. The waistcoat was lined with red, and had flaps of fur to double over the breast when the wind lay in the east and the frost was cruel. When the wind was wet and warm, the flaps were turned back, exposing the gay crimson lining, and greatly enhancing its beauty. The waistcoat had been constructed for Hillary Nanspian by his loving wife before she died.

Hillary Nanspian of Chimsworthy was a big, brisk, florid man, with light grey eyes. His face was open, round, hearty, and of the colour of a ribstone pippin. He was, to all appearance, a well-to-do man. But appearances are not always to be trusted. Chimsworthy, where he lived, was a farm of two hundred acres; the subsoil clay, some of the land moor, and more bog; but the moor was a fine place for sheep, and the bog produced pasture for the young stock when the clay grass land was drought-dry. Hillary had an orchard of the best sorts of apples grown in the West, and he had a nursery of apples, of grafts, and of seedlings. When he ate a particularly good apple, he collected the pips for sowing, put them in a paper cornet, and wrote thereon, 'This here apple was a-eated of I on—' such and such a day, 'and cruel good he were too.' (*Cruel,* in the West, means no more than 'very.')

The farm of Chimsworthy had come to Nanspian through his wife, who was dead. His brother-in-law was Taverner Langford of Langford. Taverner's mother had been a Hill, Blandina Hill, heiress of Chimsworth and it went to her daughter Blandina, who carried it when she married to her Cornish husband, Hillary Nanspian.

Taverner Langford was unmarried, getting on in years, and had no nearer relative than young Hillary Nanspian, his nephew, the only child of his deceased sister Blandina. It was an understood thing in the parish of Bratton Clovelly that young Hillary would be heir to his uncle, and succeed to both Langford and Chimsworthy. Taverner said nothing about this, and took no particular notice of Hillary junior, but, as Hillary senior and the parish argued, if Taverner does not leave everything to the young one, whom can he make his heir? Hillary was a warm-blooded man. He suffered little from cold; he liked to live in his shirtsleeves. When rain fell, he threw a sack over his shoulders. He drew on his cloth coat only for church and market. He was an imposing man, out of his coat or in it, big in girth, broad in beam, and tall of stature. But especially imposing was he when he rode to market on his white cob, in his badger-skin waistcoat turned up with crimson. The consciousness that he was, or ought to be, a man of substance never left him. His son Hillary would be a wealthy yeoman, and he—he Hillary senior—was the father of this son, this wealthy yeoman prospective. On this thought be puffed himself up. Considering this, he jingled the coins in his pocket. Boasting of this he drank with the farmers till he was as red in face as the lappets of his waistcoat.

Adjoining the house was a good oak wood covering the slope to the brook that flowed in the bottom. Fine sticks of timber had been cut thence, time out of mind. The rafters of the old house, the beams of the cattle-sheds, the posts of the gates, the very rails ('shivers,' as they were locally called), the flooring ('plancheon' locally), all were of oak, hard as iron; and all came out of Chimsworthy wood. An avenue of contorted, stunted limes led to the entrance gates of granite, topped with stone balls; and the gates gave admission to a yard deep in dung. The house was low, part of cob—that is, clay and straw kneaded and unbaked—part of stone laid in clay, not in lime. In the cob walls, plastered white, were oak windows, in the stone walls two granite windows. The house was shaped like the letter T, of which the top stroke represents the stone portion, containing the parlour and the best bedroom over it, and the stairs. The roofs were thatched. There was more roof than wall to Chimsworthy, which cowered almost into the ground.

At the back of the house rose the lofty bank of Broadbury, the highest ridge between Dartmoor and the Atlantic. The rain that fell on the Down above oozed through the shale about Chimsworthy, so that the lane and yards were perpetually wet, and compelled those who lived there to walk in wading boots.

In shape, Broadbury is a crescent, with the horns east and west, and the lap of the half moon lies to the south. In this lap, the nursery of countless streams, stands Chimsworthy, with a bank of pines behind it, and above the black pines golden gorse, and over the golden gorse blue sky and fleecy white clouds. The countless springs issue from emerald patches of bog, where bloom the purple butterwort, the white grass of Parnassus, the yellow asphodel, and the blood-tipped sundew. The rivulets become rills, and swell to brooks which have scooped themselves coombs in the hill slope, and the coombs as they descend deepen into valleys, whose sides are rich with oak coppice, and the bottoms are rank with cotton grass, fleecy and flickering as the white clouds that drift overhead.

Chimsworthy had originally belonged to the Hills, a fine old yeoman family, but the last of the Hills had carried it by marriage to the Langfords of Langford. How it had gone to Hillary Nanspian by his marriage with the daughter of Mrs. Langford has already been told.

Langford had been owned for many generations by the Langfords, once a gentle family, with large estates both in Bratton Clovelly and in Marham Church, near Bude in Cornwall. Nothing now remained to Taverner but the ancestral house and the home estate of some four hundred acres. Chimsworthy had been united with it by his father's marriage, but lost again by his sister's union with the Cornishman Nanspian.

Something like twenty-four months of married life was all that poor Blandina had; and since he had lost his wife, Hillary had remained a widower. Many a farmer's daughter had set her eyes on him, for he was a fine man, but in vain. Hillary Nanspian had now lived at Chimsworthy twenty-two years. His son Hillary was aged twenty.

Langford was a different sort of place from Chimsworthy, and Taverner Langford was a different sort of man from Hillary Nanspian. Langford stood higher than Chimsworthy. It was built on the edge of Broadbury, but slightly under its lea, in a situation commanding an extensive and superb view of Dartmoor, that rose against the eastern horizon, a wall of turquoise in sunshine, of indigo in cloudy weather, with picturesque serrated ridge. The intermediate country was much indented with deep valleys, running north and south, clothed in dark woods, and the effect was that of gazing over a billowy sea at a mountainous coast.

Not a tree, scarce a bush, stood about Langford, which occupied a site too elevated and exposed for the growth of anything but thorns and gorse. The house itself was stiff, slate and with slate sea walls, giving it a harsh metallic appearance.

Taverner Langford was a tall, gaunt man, high-shoulders, with a stoop, dark-haired, dark-eyes, and sallow-complexioned. He had high cheekbones and a large hard mouth. His hair was grizzled with age, but his eyes had lost none of their keenness, they bored like bradawls. His eyebrows were very thick and dark, looking more like pieces of black fur glued on to his forehead than natural growths. He never looked anyone steadily in the face, but cast furtive glances with which, however, he saw vastly more than did Hillary with his wide grey-eyed stare.

Taverner Langford had never married. It had never been heard in Bratton that he had courted a girl. His housekeeping was managed by a grey-faced, sour woman, Widow Veale. As Hillary Nanspian was people's churchwarden, Taverner Langford was parson's churchwarden. The Reverend Mr. Robbins, the rector, had appointed him, at the Easter vestry five years before the opening of this tale, because he was a Dissenter. He did this for two reasons: first, to disarm Langford's opposition to the Church and secondly, to manifest his own tolerance—an easy tolerance that springs out of void of convictions. The two wardens were reappointed annually. They and two others acted as feoffees of an estate left in charity for the poor. They let the land to each other alternate years at a shilling an acre, and consumed the proceeds in a dinner at the 'Ring of Bells' once a year. The poor were provided with the scraps that fell from the feoffees' table.

Taverner Langford was respected in the place and throughout the neighbourhood, because he represented a family as old as the parish church, a family which had once owned large possessions and maintained some state; also because he was an exceedingly shrewd man, whom no one could overreach, and who was supposed to have amassed much money. But he was not a popular man. He was taciturn, self-contained, and shunned society. He drank water only, never smoked nor swore; with the farmers he was unsociable, with the labourers ungracious, in all his dealings he was grasping and unyielding. Dishonourable he was not; unscrupulous he was not, except only in exacting the last penny his bargains.

Hillary Nanspian's presence was commanding and he was fond of his glass, smoked and swore; the glass, the pipe, and an oath were all links of good fellowship. Nevertheless, he also was not a popular man. In the first place he was a foreigner—that is, a Cornishman; in the second, he was arrogant and boastful.

The brothers-in-law got on better with each other than with others. Each knew and allowed for the other's infirmities. Towards Taverner, Hillary bated his pride; he had discretion not to brag in the presence of a man to whom he owed money. Hillary was a bad man of business, wasteful, liberal, and careless of his money. He had saved nothing out of

Chimsworthy, and, after a run of bad seasons, had been forced to borrow of his brother-in-law to meet current expenses.

Taverner and Hillary were not cordial friends, but they were friends. Taverner felt, though he did not acknowledge, his isolation, and he was glad to have his brother-in-law to whom he could open his lips. Knowing himself to be of a good old gentle family, Taverner kept himself from terms of familiarity with the farmers, but he was too close with his money to take his place with the gentry.

There was one point on which Hillary was irrationally sensitive; there was also a point on which Taverner was tender. Each avoided touching the delicate and irritable spot in the other. Once, and only once, had Nanspian flared up at a word from Langford, and for a moment their friendship had been threatened with rupture.

Hillary Nanspian was, as has been said, a Cornishman, and the rooted, ineradicable belief of the Devonians is that their Celtic Trans-Tamarian neighbours are born with tails. The people of Bratton Clovelly persisted in asserting that Nanspian had a tail concealed under his garments. When first he entered the parish rude boys had shouted after him inquiries about the caudal appendage, and he had retaliated so unmercifully that their parents had resented it, and the chastisement, instead of driving the prejudice out, had deepened it into indelible conviction. 'For why,' it was argued, 'should he take on so, unless it be true?'

He was annoyed at church by the interested attention paid to him by the women and children when he seated himself in the Chimsworthy pew, and when riding to market, by the look of curiosity with which his seat on the saddle was watched by the men.

The only occasion on which the friendship of Langford and Nanspian threatened a cleavage, was when the former, whether with kindly intention or sarcastically cannot be determined, urged on Hillary the advisability of his publicly bathing in the river Thrustle, one hot summer day, so as to afford ocular demonstration to the people of the parish that they labour under a delusion in inserting the prolongation of his spine. This proposition so irritated Nanspian that he burst into a tempest of oaths, and for some weeks would not speak to his brother-in-law. Though eventually reconciled, the recollection of the affront was never wholly effaced.

The sensitive point with Taverner Langford was of a very different nature. Not being a married man he was obliged to engage a housekeeper to manage his dairy, his maids, and his domestic affairs generally. His housekeeper, Mrs. Veale, was a vinegary woman, of very unpleasant appearance. She managed admirably, was economical, active, and clean. The mere fact, however, of her being at Langford was enough to give rise to some scandal. She was intensely disliked by all the servants on the farm and by the maids in the house.

'Why don't Mr. Langford get rid of the woman, so ill-favoured, so sharp-tongued, so unpleasant, unless he can't help hisself?' was reasoned. 'You may depend on it there's something.'

Taverner was touchy on this matter. He broke with Farmer Yelland for inquiring of him flippantly, 'How goes the missus?'

Langford detested the woman, who had a livid face, pink eyes, and a rasping voice; but as scandal attached to him with such a creature in his house, he argued: How much more consistency would it assume had he a better favoured housekeeper!

'Moreover,' he reasoned, 'where can I get one who will look after my interests so well as Mrs. Veale? If she be bitter to me, she's sloes and wormwood to the servants.'

II

The Money-Spinner

A LITTLE SPARK WILL BURN a big hole—a very little spark indeed was the occasion of a great blaze of temper, and a great gap in the friendship of the brothers-in-law. Langford possessed this disadvantage: it lay so high, and was so exposed, that it lacked cosiness. It had nowhere about it a nook where a man might sit and enjoy the sun without being cut by the wind. Broadbury was the meeting-place of all the winds. Thither the wind roared without let from the Atlantic, and to the back of it every tree bowed from the north-west; thither it swept from the east with a leap from the rocky crests of Dartmoor, sparing the intervening park-like lowlands.

Chimsworthy had no prospect from its windows; but it stood at the source of an affluent of the Tamar, and beyond its granite gates, across the lane that led up to Broadbury, was a stile, and beyond the stile a slope with a view down the valley to the setting sun and the purple range of Cornish tors above Liskeard, Caradon, Boarrah, Kilmar, and Trevartha.

On Sunday evenings, and whenever the fancy took him, Taverner Langford would descend Broadbury by the lane, cross the stile, and seat himself on a rude granite slab on the farther side of the hedge, that had been placed there by one of the Hills—it had been the 'quoit' of a great prehistoric dolmen or cromlech, but the supporters had been removed to serve as gateposts, and the covering-stone now formed a seat. On this stone Taverner Langford spent many an hour with his chin on the handle of his thorn stick, looking over the wood and meadows and arable land of Chimsworthy, and scheming how money might be made out of the farm were it profitably worked. He noted with jealous eye the ravages caused by neglect, the gaps in the hedges, the broken roofs, the crop of thistles, the drains bursting many yards above their mouths, bursting because their mouths had not been kept open. The farm had been managed by Taverner's father along with Langford, and had been handed over on Blandina's marriage, in excellent condition, to Nanspian and had gone back ever since he had enjoyed it. This angered Langford, though he knew Chimsworthy would never be his. 'This is the sort of tricks to which young Larry is reared, which he will play with Langford. As the bull gambols, so capers the calf.'

Hillary did not relish the visits of Taverner to the Look-out Stone. He thought, and thought rightly, that Langford was criticising unfavourably his management of the estate. He was conscious that the farm, had deteriorated, but he laid the blame on the weather and the badness of construction of the drains—everything but himself. 'How can you expect drains to last, put down as they are, one flat stone on edge and another leaning on it aslant? Down it goes with the weight of earth atop, and the passage is choked. I'll eat a Jew without mint-sauce if a drain so constructed will last twenty years.' Chimsworthy could never go to Taverner, what right then had he to grumble if it were in bad order?

When Langford came to the Look-out Stone Hillary soon heard of it, and went to him in his shirt-sleeves, pipe in mouth, and with a jug of cyder in his hand. Then some such a greeting as this ensued:

'Trespassing again, Taverner?'

'Looking at the land over which I've walked, and where I've weeded many a day, with my father, before you was thought of in Bratton Clovelly.'

Then Hillary drew the pipe from his lips, and, raking the horizon with the sealing-waxed end, said, 'Fine land, yonder.'

'Moor—naught but moor,' answered Langford disparagingly.

'No cawding of sheep on peaty moor,' said Nanspian triumphantly.

'No fattening of bullocks on heather,' replied Taverner. 'It is wet in Devon, it is wetter in Cornwall.'

'Wetter! That is not possible. Here we live on the rose of a watering-can, pillowed among bogs.'

'There are worse things than water,' sneered Langford, pointing to the jug.

'Ah!' said Hillary in defence. 'Sour is the land that grows sour apples and sour folks.'

'Heaven made the apples—they are good enough. Man makes the cyder—which is evil. Thus it is with other good gifts, we pervert them to our bad ends.'

This was the formula gone through, with slight variations, whenever the brothers-in-law met at the granite seat. A little ruffle of each other, but it went no further.

Hillary Nanspian was a talker, not loud but continuous. He had a rich, low, murmuring voice, with which he spoke out of one side of his mouth, whilst he inhaled tobacco through the other. It was pleasant to listen to, like the thrum of a bumble-bee or the whirr of a winnowing fan.

The eyes closed, the head nodded, and sleep ensued. But every now and then Hillary uttered an oath, for he was not a man to wear a padlock on his lips, and then the dozing listener woke with a start. When that listener was Taverner, he uttered his protest. 'The word is uncalled for, Hillary; change it for one that sounds like it, and is inoffensive and meaning.'

There was much difference in the way in which the two men behaved when angered. Hillary was hot and blazed up in a sudden outburst. He was easily angered, but soon pacified, unless his pride were hurt. Taverner, on the other hand, though equally ready to take umbrage, took it in another fashion. He turned sallow, said littler and brooded over his wrong. If an opportunity offered to resent it, it was not allowed to pass, however long after the event. One evening the brothers-in-law were at the Look-out Stone. Hillary was standing with his foot on the block on which Taverner sat.

'I'll tell you what,' said Nanspian, 'I wish I'd got a few thousands to spare. Swaddledown is for sale, and the farm joins mine, and would be handy for stock.'

'And I wish I could buy Bannadon. That will be in the market shortly, but I cannot unless you repay me what you have borrowed.'

'Can't do that just now; not comfortably, you understand.'

'Then what is the good of your scheming to buy Swaddledown? A man without teeth mustn't pick nuts.'

'And what is the good of your wanting Bannadon when you have as much as you can manage at Langford? A man with his mouth full mustn't take a second bite till he's swallowed the first.'

Then neither spoke for a few moments. Presently, however, Hillary drew a long whiff, and blew the smoke before him. Slowly he pulled the pipe from between his lips, and with the end of the stem pointed down the valley. 'It would be something to be able to call those fields my own.'

'That would be pulling on boots to hide the stocking full of holes,' sneered Taverner. Hillary coloured, and his eyes twinkled. 'There is no picking feathers off a toad, or clothes off a naked man,' he muttered; 'and if you squeeze a crab-apple you get only sourness. If I were not your brother-in-law I shouldn't put up with your words. But you can't help it. Sloes and blackberries grow in the same hedge, and their natures are as they began. Older they grow, they grow either sweeter or sourer.'

'Ah!' retorted Taverner, 'out of the same acre some grow wheat and others nettles.'

'It is all very well your talking,' said Hillary, putting his thumbs in his waistcoat arm-holes, and expanding. 'You, no doubt, have made money, one way or other. I have not; but then, I am not a screw. I am a free-handed, open man. God forbid that I should be a screw!'

'A screw holds together and a wedge drives apart,' said Taverner.

'I don't know,' said Hillary, looking across lovingly at the Swaddledown fields, 'but I may be able to find the money. My credit is not so low that I need look far. If you will not help me others will.'

'How can you raise it? on a mortgage? You cannot without young Hillary's consent, and he is not of age.'

'Luck will come my way some time,' said Nanspian. 'Luck is not nailed to one point of the compass, brother Langford. Don't you flatter yourself that it always goes to you. Luck veers as the wind.'

'That is true, but as the wind here sets three days out of four from the west, so does luck set most time towards the thrifty man.'

'Sooner or later it will turn to me.'

'I know what you mean. I've heard tell of what you have said to the farmers when warmed with liquor. The wind don't blow over a thistlehead without carrying away some of its down and dropping it where least wanted. I've heard your boasts, they are idle—idle as thistledown. Do you think you'll ever succeed to Langford? I'll live to see your burying.'

'My burying won't help you to Chimsworthy,' retorted Hillary. 'My Larry stands in your way. Heigh! I said it! The luck is coming my way already!' he exclaimed eagerly. He put down his foot, placed both palms on the slab of granite, and leaned over it.

'Not a moment before it is needed,' said Taverner 'You've had some bad falls, and they'd have been breakdown tumbles but for my help. I suppose you must let Swaddledown go; it's a pity too, lying handy as the button at the flap of your pocket.'

'She is coming my way as fast as she can!'

'What, Swaddledown?'

'No! Luck! Look! running right into my hands. The money-spinner!'

'The money-spinner!' Taverner started to his feet. 'Where? Whither is she running?'

'Stand out of the sunlight, will you!' exclaimed Hillary. 'How can I see and secure her with your shadow cast across the stone?'

'Where is she?'

'I tell you she is making direct for me. I knew the luck would come if I waited. Curse you! Get on one side, will you?'

'Don't swear,' said Langford, standing at the other end of the granite slab, and resting his hands on it. 'The money-spinner is a tickle (touchy) beast, and may take offence at a godless word. I see her, she has turned. You've scared her with your oaths, and now she is running towards me.'

'She's going to fetch some of your luck and bring it to my pocket; she's on the turn again.'

'No, she is not. She is making for me, not you.'

'But she is on my stone. She has brought the luck to me.'

'She may be on your stone now, but she is leaving it for my hand, as fast as her red legs can carry her.'

'You're luring her away from me, are you?' cried Hillary, blazing as red as any money-spinner.

'Luring! She's running her natural course as sure as a fox runs before the wind.'

'Stand out of the sun! It is the ugly shade you cast that chills her. She goes where she may be warmest!'

'Out of thine own mouth thou speakest thy condemnation,' scoffed Langford. 'Of course she goes to the warmest corner, and which is warmest, my pocket or thine?—the full or the empty?'

'The spinner is on my stone, and I will have her!' cried Hillary.

'Your stone!—yes, yours because you got it and Chimsworthy away from me.'

'The spinner is by your hand!' roared Nanspian, and with an oath he threw himself across the stone and swept the surface with his hands.

Langford uttered an exclamation of anger. 'You have crushed—you have killed her! There is an end of luck to you, you long-tailed Cornish ourang-outang!'

Hillary Nanspian staggered back. His face became dark with rage. He opened lips, but was inarticulate for a moment; then he roared, 'You say that, do you, you ——, that let yourself be led and tongue-lashed by your housekeeper.'

'Our friendship is at an end,' said Langford, turning livid, and his dark bushy brows met across his forehead. 'Never shall you set foot in Langford now.'

'Never! It will come to my Larry, and I'll drink your burying ale there yet.'

'Larry shall never have it.'

'You can't keep him out,' exclaimed Hillary.

'Do not be so sure of that,' said Taverner.

'I am sure. I have seen the parchments.'

'I know them better than you,' laughed Langford. Then he went to the stile to leave the field.

'I'll have the law of you,' shouted Hillary; 'you are trespassing on my land.'

'I trespassing!' mocked Langford; 'this is a stile leading to Swaddledown.'

'There is no right of way here. This is a private stile leading only to the Look-out Stone. I will have the law of you, I swear.'

Thus it was that the friendship of twenty-two years was broken, and the brothers-in-law became declared and deadly enemies. The friendship was broken irremediably by an insect almost microscopic,—a little scarlet spider no larger than a mustard-seed, invested by popular superstition with the power of spinning money in the pocket of him who secures it.

III

Wellon's Cairn

Whilst Hillary Nanspian and Taverner Langford were falling out over a minute red spider, Hillary junior, or Larry as he was called by his intimates, was talking to Honor Luxmore in a nook of the rubble of Wellon's Cairn.

Wellon's Cairn is a great barrow, or tumulus, on Broadbury, not far from Langworthy. Its original name has been lost. Since a certain Wellon was hung in chains on a gallows set up on this mound for the murder of three women, it has borne his name.

The barrow was piled up of stones and black peat earth, and was covered with gorse, so that the old British warrior who lay beneath may indeed be said to have made his bed in glory. The gorse brake not only blazed as fire, but streamed forth perfume like a censer. Only on the summit was a bare space, where the gallows had stood, and Wellon had dropped piecemeal, and been trodden by the sheep into the black soil.

On the south-west side, facing the sun, was a hollow. Treasure-seekers had dug into the mound. Tradition said that herein lay a hero in harness of gold. The panoply that wrapped him round was indeed of gold, but it was the gold of the ever-blooming gorse. Having found nothing but a few flint flakes and broken sherds, the seekers had abandoned the cairn, without filling up the cavity. This had fallen in, and was lined with moss and short grass, and fringed about with blushing heath and blazing gorse.

In this bright and fragrant hollow, secluded from the world, and sheltered from the wind that wafted down on her the honey breath of the furze, and exposed to the warmth of the declining sun, sat Honor Luxmore; and near her, not seated, but leaning against the side of the excavation, stood Hillary junior talking to her.

Hillary was like his father, well built, fair-haired, and flushed with life. His eyes were blue, quick and honest, sparkling with fun; and his bearing was that of the heir of Chimsworthy and Langford. There was unmistakable self-reliance in his face, making up, in measure, for lack of superior intelligence.

Honor Luxmore demands a fuller account than young Hillary.

Some way down the lane from Wellon's Cairn stood a cottage. This cottage was constructed on the bank or hedge above the roadway, so that the door was reached by a flight of steps, partly cut in the rock, partly constructed of stone. A handrail assisted ascent and descent. The cottage seemed to have taken refuge up the side of the bank to escape from the water in the lane. Actually the roadway was cut through shale to some depth, leaving the cottage on the true surface of the land. The road had no doubt in part been artificially cut, but certainly it had been also scooped in part by the water, which, issuing from the joints of the shale, converted it into a watercourse. The sides of the road were rich with moss and fern, and the moss and fern were spangled with drops that oozed out of the rock. Below the steps was a spring, in a hole scooped in the side of the loose, shaley rock.

The cottage itself was of cob, whitewashed, with a thatched roof, brown and soft as the fur of a mole. The windows were small and low. In this cottage lived Oliver Luxmore, a man poor in everything but children, and of these he possessed more than he knew how to provide for. The cottage was like a hive. Flaxen-haired boys and girls of all ages might be seen pouring out on their way to school, or swarming home in the evening. They were all pretty children, with dazzling blue eyes and clear complexions and fair hair, from the youngest, a little maid of three, upwards; and what was better than beauty, they were patterns of neatness and cleanliness. According to the proverb, cleanliness comes to goodliness, but these little Luxmores were both cleanly and goodly. The goodliness they drew from their parents, but the cleanliness was due to Honor, the eldest daughter of Oliver Luxmore, who stood to her brothers and sisters in the place of mother, for the wife of Luxmore had died three years ago, just after the birth of the youngest.

The father was a carrier, and drove a van on Fridays to Tavistock, and on Saturdays to Okehampton, the market-days at these respective places. On the other week-days he worked for the farmers, doing odd jobs, and so earning money for the sustenance of his many children.

Oliver Luxmore was a quiet, dreamy, unenergetic man, who was hampered by a belief that he was the right heir to a good property, which would certainly be his if only he were able to find the necessary registers, but what these registers were, whether of marriage or birth, he was uncertain. At the extreme limits of the parish, in a pretty situation, lay a good house of Queen Anne's reign, with fine trees, and traces of gardens, and a fishpond, Coombe Park, which had belonged to the Luxmoores or Luxmores. But this property had been sold, and Oliver maintained that if he had had but one hundred pounds wherewith to find the registers, Coombe Park could not have been sold, and he would be a squire there, with a good fortune. He had visited a lawyer in Okehampton, and another at Tavistock, to ask them to take up his case on speculation, but Oliver's ideas were so hazy as to his pedigree, never resolving themselves into definite statements of fact, that both one and the other declined to touch his claim unless they were given some certain ground on which to work.

Then he went to the Rector of Bratton, and with his help extracted all the entries of births, marriages, and deaths of the Luxmores—pages of them, showing that from the beginning of the sixteenth century the name had abounded there, and belonged to or was assumed by persons of all ranks and conditions. Then Oliver took this list to the Okehampton lawyer.

'Look here,' said he, 'my eldest daughter is called Honor, and in 1662 John Luxmore, gentleman, and Temperance, his wife, had a daughter baptised called Honor. That's proof, is it not?'

'Why was your daughter christened by this name?'

'Well, you see my wife was Honor, and so we called our first girl after her.'

This may be taken as a specimen that will suffice of Oliver's evidences, and as a justification of the solicitors declining to take up his claim.

'It is one hundred pounds that is wanted to do it,' said Oliver Luxmore. 'If I had that to spend on the registers, it would come right enough. I always heard my father say that if we had our rights we shouldn't be in the cottage in Water Lane.'

Oliver spent money and wasted time over his ineffectual attempts to prove his descent and establish his rights, but he had not the slightest idea what to search for and how to search. He did not even know his grandfather's Christian-name, but believed it began with a J, for he had an old shirt that was marked in the tail with J. L., and was so strong and sound that he wore it still. J. might stand for John, or James, or Joseph, or Jeremiah. But then he was not *quite* sure the shirt had belonged to his grandfather, but he had heard his mother say she believed it had.

On days when he might have been earning money he would wander away to Coombe Park, prowl round the estate estimating its value, or go into the house to drink cyder with the yeoman who now owned and occupied it, tell him that his claim might yet be established, and to assure him that he would deal honourably and liberally with him when he turned him out. The yeoman and his wife regarded him as something of a nuisance, but nevertheless treated him with respect. There was no knowing, they said, but that he might prove in the end to be the heir, and then where would they be? Oliver would have liked to see the title-deeds, but of these he was not allowed a glimpse, though he could not have read them had he seen them, or made his claim the clearer if he had been able to read them.

We have said that Oliver Luxmore worked for the farmers on the days of the week on which he was not carrying between Bratton and Tavistock and Okehampton; but Thursdays and Mondays were broken days. On Thursdays he went about soliciting order and on Mondays he went about distributing parcels. Thus he had only two clear days for jobbing. The work of a carrier is desultory, and unfits him for manual labour and for persevering work. He gets into idle, gossiping ways. When he picks up a parcel or a passenger he has to spend a quarter of an hour discussing what has to be done with the parcel, and has to settle the passenger comfortably among the parcels, without the passenger impinging on the parcels, or the parcels incommoding the passenger.

Oliver was an obliging, amiable man. In the front of the van was a seat, the top of which could be raised on hinges, and in which he deposited watches that went to be cleaned, books of the Reading Club that travelled between subscribers, medicine bottles and boxes of pills, ribbons, brooches, and other delicate goods. The lid of this box was sat on and kept secure by Oliver. He was devoid of humour. To every commission, to every joke, to every reprimand, he had but one answer, 'Certainly, certainly, very true.'

'Oliver,' said Nanspian one day, 'I can suggest to you a means of increasing your income. Put a sitting of eggs under you when you go to market, and sell the young chickens when you get there.'

'Certainly, certainly, sir, very true,' was his civil reply, without a muscle of his face moving.

'Oh, Mr. Luxmore!' exclaimed Mrs. Robbins, the rectoress, 'this is the same book you brought me last month from the parsonage at Maristowe. I have had it and returned it, and now you bring it me again. Mind it goes back on Friday; and you shall not be paid for your trouble, as I cannot be expected to read the same book over twice.'

'Certainly, certainly, ma'am, very true.'

'Oh, Mr. Luxmore,' said Mrs. Veale, 'you are to mind and match me the silk, cut on the cross, and if the shade be out, I won't take it, you must return it, and pay for it from your own pocket.'

'Certainly, certainly, ma'am.'

'The Vivid,' as Mr. Luxmore's van was called, belied its name. There was no vividity (pass the word) about it. It went slowly up hill, because the horse had so much to draw. It went slower down hill, because it had to back against such a prodigious weight, descending by natural velocity.

There was not a mile—not half a mile—of level road between Bratton Clovelly and the market-towns.

The carrier's horse was a rough creature, brown, with a long tail, thick mane, and coarse hair about the fetlocks, of the colour of tow. It lived in a precarious manner; the children cut grass in the hedges for it, and it was sometimes turned out on Broadbury, with hobbles on its feet. It ate the refuse of Luxmore's vegetable garden, the turnip-tops, the potato parings, the maggot-nibbled outer cabbage leaves, and the decayed apples from his trees. Once, when the horse had knocked his nose, and Luxmore had put a linseed poultice over it, in a bit of sacking tied round the head with four stout tapes, when his back was turned the horse, curled his tongue out of his mouth, detached the poultice, and ate it, linseed, sacking, and tapes, to the last grain and thread. There was nothing but stones that horse would not eat. He bit away great pieces from his manger. He took a bite out of Luxmore's trousers, he gnawed the bark off the cherry-tree by his gate, he gobbled up nettles, thistles, furze, as though his appetite were as vitiated as an East Indian's.

Oliver Luxmore had to put up with a good many bad debts; his business did not bring him in much money; he was never able to lay by a penny: how could he with so many mouths to feed at home? Honor would have been unable to make both ends meet unless she had been a manager. The family would have been better off if Charles, the eldest son, two years the senior of Honor, had fulfilled his duty to his own. But Charles, having reached the full wage-earning age, had enlisted, and was away on foreign service. His father and sister did not even know where he was, for he had not troubled to write since his departure. Charles had always been a wild and headstrong boy who needed a firm hand over him to direct him right. But Oliver Luxmore's hand was weak, and the mother, a shrewd, painstaking woman of decided character, had made the boy obstinate and sulky, by exerting over him the authority which should have been exercised by his father.

After the death of his wife, Oliver remained as weak as during her life, very good-natured, and so pliant as to bend to the wills of his children, even to that of his youngest, Temperance, aged three. The family would indisputably have run wild, and his affairs gone to ruin, had not Honor assumed her mother's place, and ruled the little house with energy and decision. Her rule was firm but loving, and few of the children ventured to disobey her, not even the thirteen-year-old Joseph, or her next sister, Kate, aged seventeen; no, not even her father, Oliver; indeed, he was the least difficult to manage of all. There were nine children in all. Charles, Honor, Kate, Joseph, have already been mentioned, so has little Temperance, the baby. Between Joseph and Temperance came Pattie, that is Patience, Willie, Martha, and Charity. The children were all pretty and well-conducted. Charles was no longer a child. He was away. He therefore is not reckoned among those who were pretty and well-conducted.

Honor was tall; her bearing very erect; her well-knit, vigorous frame, the glance of her clear hazel eyes, her firm mouth, all combined to inspire respect and insure submission. The respectability of her father, the honesty of her brothers and sisters were due to Honor, and to Honor alone. But for her presence in the house everything would have gone wrong. Kate was too lively and careless to manage it, the others too young, her father helpless. Had she not been there to keep home orderly, and the children neat, Oliver would have drifted to the tavern to bury his troubles in the ale-can, and the little ones would have sunk into squalor and strife, and struggled out of childhood into misery, beggary, and vice.

The children had inherited from their father blue eyes and very fair hair; they had lovely complexions, and clear, bright colour; some of them had certainly derived from him also an inertness of character which left them and their futures at the mercy of the persons and the chances that should surround or fall in their way. This was not the case with Kate, who had character of her own, though very diverse from that of her eldest sister. Kate promised to be the beauty of the family. Her blue eyes twinkled with mirth and mischief, like summer seas. She had a roguish dimple in her cheeks, and an expression of consciousness of her good looks on her face.

Honor was different in appearance as in character, from the rest. She hardly seemed to belong to the family. She had hair the colour of barley-sugar and haze-brown eyes. She looked every one whom she addressed straight in the face, and was absolutely void of vanity; she asked no admiration like Kate. She was contemptuously indifferent to her looks, and yet she was never untidy. All the rest were better dressed than herself. She never gave herself new clothes; she had an old store of her mother's to draw from for her own clothing; but though her gown was antiquated and often patched, it was never ragged, never had tape and thread ends hanging from it. She had inherited her grandmother's scarlet cloak, and was the last person in that neighbourhood to wear such a garment. This she only wore on Sundays, but she wore it on every Sunday, summer as well as winter, when she went to church. She also wore red stockings, and as she was taller than her mother, and her mother's gowns could not be lengthened, a good deal of red stocking showed. She wore these stockings simply because they were her mother's and had to be worn out, and because Kate objected to them for her own feet. Perhaps it was the shortness of the skirts that gave to Honor a look of length of red limb below the scarlet cloak a little grotesque, that occasioned the boys of Bratton to nickname her 'the Red Spider.'

The mischievous Kate teased her by asserting that she got her flame from her hair; but Honor's hair was not red, it was not even chestnut brown, it was golden brown, like beech-leaves in autumn—a very rare, but a most beautiful colour. It was all one to Honor what hair she had, all one to her that the boys styled her. No girl could be jealous of her; she had no eyes for the lads, her whole heart, her every thought was centred in home. As the chapter-house of a cathedral is built in a circle and leans on one central pillar, and as the fall of that pillar would insure the ruin of the house, so was it with the cottage of the Luxmores—on her it rested. This she knew, and the little self-consciousness she possessed was the consciousness that on her all leaned for support, and to her owed their uprightness.

'What a lot of socks and stockings you have got on the furze bushes about you,' said Hillary.

'Yes—like to have. There are so many little feet at home that tread holes.'

'You must be glad that they are two-footed, not four-footed animals, those brothers and sisters of yours.'

'I am, or I could not darn their stockings, much less knit them.'

Hillary thought a moment; then he said, looking at a pair of very much darned red stockings hung over a branch of heather, 'You know they call you the Red Spider, and they say true. The Red Spider brings luck wherever she goes. I am sure you are the money-spinner in your house.'

'I!' exclaimed the girl, who coloured slightly, and looked up; 'I—I spin, but never money.'

'Well, you bring luck.'

'I keep out ill-luck,' she answered with confidence; 'I can do no more, but that is something, and that takes me all my time. I have hardly leisure to sleep.'

'Why have you brought all these stockings out on the Down? Are you going to convert Wellon's Cairn into a second-hand mercer's shop?'

'Larry, in spite of proverb to the contrary, I am forced to do two things at a time. I have Diamond to watch as well as stockings to darn. The poor beast is not well, and I have brought him from the stable. The little ones are at school, except of course Temperance, and Kate is with her cutting grass in the lane for Diamond.'

'What would you do if you lost Diamond?' asked young Hillary.

'O Larry, don't even suggest such an evil. If you whistle you call up wind, and if you whisper the name of the devil he looks in at the door. We got into debt buying Diamond, and it took us three years to work our way out. Now we are clear, and it would be too dreadful to get into debt again. You know, Larry, what the mothers do with children who have the thrush. They pass them under a bramble that grows with a loop into the ground. Like enough the little creatures lose the thrush, but they carry away scratches. Debt, to my thinking, is like treatment: you get rid of one evil by sticking yourself full of thorns. So take my advice, and never get into debt.'

'I'm not like to,' laughed the young man, 'with Chimsworthy behind me and Langford before me.'

'Never reckon on what you've not got,' said Honor. 'That's like buying the hogshead before the apple hive set, or killing a pig without having the pickle-tub. Langford is not yours, any more than Coombe Park is ours.'

'Langford must come to us Nanspians some day, you know, Honor. Not that I reckon on it. God forbid. May Uncle Taverner live for ever. But it gives a chap confidence to know that a large estate will come to him in the end.'

'Don't reckon on that,' said Honor.

'It can't fail. It stands so in the deeds.'

'But Mr. Langford might marry'.

Hillary would have burst into a hearty laugh at the idea, had not Honor laid her hand on his arm to arrest him, and raised the forefinger of the other to impose silence.

Sitting up on its hind legs, in a begging posture, at the mouth of the excavation, was a *white hare*. It looked at the young people for a moment, doubtingly, inquiringly. Then Hillary stirred, and with a flash it was gone.

Hillary exclaimed, 'O Honor! is it not the picture of Mrs. Veale?'

IV

THE WHITE HARE

'I HAVE SEEN THE WHITE hare before, several times,' said Honor Luxmore.

'You have? Do you know what folks say?'

'They say that it is unlucky to see a white hare; but I think nothing of that.'

'I do not mean that,' said Hillary laughing. 'But they say that when a witch goes on her errands she takes this shape. Perhaps, Honor,' he went on with roguery in his twinkling eyes, 'Mrs. Veale is off over the Down in quest of her master. He has gone to the Look-out Stone to have a talk to my father.'

'Nonsense, Larry. I put no credit in those tales of witches; besides, I never heard that Mrs. Veale was one—not properly.'

'She is white with pink eyes, and so is the hare,' argued Hillary, 'and spiteful she is, certainly. I hope, if that were her, she won't be bringing mischief to you or to me. We shall see. If that were her, Uncle Taverner will be coming home directly. Folks say that he is afraid of her tongue, and that is the only thing in heaven or hell he is afraid of.'

Honor uttered an exclamation of surprise and alarm. A black ungainly figure stood before them, black against the glowing western sky. She recovered herself at once and rose respectfully. Hillary turned and recognised his uncle.

'Well, Uncle Taverner!' he exclaimed, 'you have come on us suddenly. We were just talking about you.'

'Ah!' answered Langford, leaning on his stick and glowering at him, 'leave me out of your talk and your calculations altogether. I dare say you have been reckoning on my shoes, and how well they would fit your young feet. No, no! no feet of yours shall ever be thrust into them.' Then seeing that Hillary was disconcerted, he laughed a harsh, bitter laugh. 'Your father and I have parted for ever. We have quarrelled; I will not speak to him more. To you I speak now for the last time also. As Nanspian has split with Langford, Chimsworthy and Langford will not splice. Remember that. Go to work, young man, go to work instead of standing idling here. Your father is in my debt, and you must help him to earn the money to pay it off.' Then he turned to Honor, and said, 'Why are you here, instead of watching your horse? Diamond is down in the gravel-pit, on his side, dead, or dying.'

Honor sprang up with a cry.

'The white hare,' said Hillary, 'has brought the ill-luck—to both of us at once.'

Neither of the young people gave another thought to Taverner. Honor was in distress about the horse, and Hillary was desirous of assisting her. He accompanied her to the spot, a hole dug in the surface of the moor for rubble wherewith to mend the road. Diamond had either made his way into it by the cart road, or had fallen over the edge. He lay on his side panting.

'Poor fellow,' said Hillary gravely, 'Diamond is done for.'

'Oh, I ought not to have let him from my sight,' cried Honor, stung with self-reproach.

'You could do nothing for him,' said the young man. 'He is not dying from your neglect. Look here, Honor, do you see that hoof-print? He walked in, he did not fall over the edge. Every beast when it feels death approach tries to hide its as though it were ashamed—as though death were a crime. It is so, Honor.'

'O Larry! What can I do? What can I do for poor Diamond?'

'You can do nothing but pat him and let him go out of the world with a word of love.'

'I will do that. I will indeed!' Then she caressed the old horse, and stroked its cheek and nose, and spoke to it tenderly. Diamond raised his head, snuffed, rubbed his head against his young mistress, then laid it down again on the stones and died.

Honor's tears flowed, but she was not one to make a demonstration of distress. She said: 'I must go home, Larry, and get supper ready for the children. I can do nothing here now.'

'I am very sorry for you,' said Hillary, showing more emotion than she; 'I am indeed, Honor. I know what a terrible loss this will be to your father, and he is too proud a man to go round with a brief. Put your hand to mine, Honor; we shall always be good friends, and I will do what I can for you; but it cannot be much now that Uncle Taverner is across with us, and about to exact his money. I will tell you what. I will get my father to lend you our horse Derby for a while, till we can scheme what is to be done. I wish I'd got a quarter of an acre of land of my own, and I would sell it and give you the money wherewith to buy another horse. I would, in truth and sincerity, Honor.'

'I am sure of that,' answered the girl; 'I know I can always trust to your good-will and kind offices. Good-bye! I must go.'

Then Hillary went slowly homewards. The sun had gone down in the west, and the sky was full of after glory. A few level bars, steps of vivid fire, were drawn against the sky, and there was, as it were, a pavement of sapphire strewn with the down from a flamingo. The moor stood with every furze-bush on its margin and two small cairns on the edge blotted black against the blaze. As Hillary descended from the moor he got into the Chimsworthy Lane, shadowed by a plantation of Scottish pines his father had made twenty years ago, and which stood up high enough to intercept the light.

'Poor Honor!' mused Hillary. 'Whatever will she and her father and all those little uns do without the horse? A carrier without a horse is a helpless animal. I don't like to ask my father too much for the

Luxmores, and seem hot about them, or he will be thinking I am in love with Honor, which I am not. Some chaps think a young fellow cannot speak to a girl, or even look at her, without being in love with her. I like Honor well enough, as a friend, but no more.'

The road was very rough, he could not descend fast because of the loose stones. In rainy weather the way was a watercourse, and the water broke up the shale rock that formed the floor and scattered it in angular fragments over the road.

'What a ridiculous notion, that I should be in love with a carrier's daughter! I, a Nanspian of Chimsworthy, and heir——' he stopped. 'No—that part is not to be, though how Uncle Taverner will do us out of Langford is more than I can imagine. That he should marry and have a family is clean too ridiculous! Confound that stone! It nigh turned and broke my ankle. If Honor's father had Coombe Park it would be another matter. Then, possibly, I might think of her in a different way; but—a cottage girl!—a carrier's daughter! Luxmore is not a bad name. But then they have the name and nothing else. I'll cut myself a stick, or I shall be down on my nose. I should not care for Honor to see me to-morrow with a broken nose. These pines may be a shelter, but they cast a very black shadow, and the rabbits breed in the plantation like midges in a duck-pond.'

He cut himself a stick and went on. 'If Honor were here, I should be forced to lend her a hand, and then if father or any one were to meet us, there'd be laughter and jokes. I'm mighty glad Honor is not here.'

Presently he got beyond the pines.

The hedges were high, the way still dark.

'Good heavens!' he exclaimed, 'the white hare again!'

As he cried out, a white animal ran up the lane, passed him and disappeared.

'Confound it,' said Hillary. 'I wish I had not seen that. Why—what have we here?'

He ran forward. In the lane, across it, where the stile to the Look-out Stone allowed a streak of western light to stream across the road, lay Hillary Nanspian senior, insensible, on his face, with the broken cyder jug in his hand.

'Father! what ails you? Speak!' cried Hillary junior. He tried to lift the old man; he could raise but not carry him. The anger aroused by his contention with Langford had brought on a fit.

V

'TIMEO DANAOS ET DONA FERRENTES'

HONOR LUXMORE SAT NEAR THE window, weaving a hamper out of willow twigs. Her sister Kate was similarly engaged. By the fire sat Oliver, smoking and watching the smouldering peat on the hearth. The sisters earned money by making baskets. Down in the bottoms, in the marshy land, grew willow-bushes; and they were allowed by the farmers to cut as much as they needed free of charge. Towards Christmas, indeed from the 1st of October, there was a demand for 'maunds,' in which to send away game as presents. Honor, Kate, and even some of the younger children could plait withies into hampers, which their father took into Launceston and Tavistock on market-days and sold. Little figures make up long sums, and so the small proceeds of the basket-weaving formed no inconsiderable profit in the year, out of which Honor was able to clothe her sister Kate and one of the other children.

Silence had lasted some time in the room; Oliver leaned forward with his elbows on his knees, dreamily watching the fire. At last he said, 'Whatever I am to do for a horse I cannot tell. I've sold the carcass to Squire Impey to feed the hounds with for a half-sovereign, and the skin for another ten shillings. That is all I got for Diamond. I suppose I shall have to give up carrying and go on the land. To think of that,

I that should be in Coombe Park riding about in a gilded coach with four cream horses and long tails and a powdered coachman on the box—that I should become a day labourer for lack of a horse!'

'Never mind about Coombe Park, father. It is of no use looking down a well for a lost shilling. Young Mr. Larry Nanspian will lend you a horse for while.'

'What will that avail?' asked Oliver. 'It is like sucking eggs when you've got the consumption. It puts off the dying a few days, but it don't cure.'

'The last horse was paid for. You are not in debt.'

'Ah! but then I had not so many little ones growing up. I could be trusted to pay. But now they consume every penny I earn.'

'They cost more as they grow up, but they also earn something, I've a mind to do this, father. You know I've been asked by several gentlefolk to go to their houses and reseat their cane chairs, but I've never liked to go because of the distance, and because I wouldn't leave the house and the children. But now Kate is old enough to take my place and do such little matters as are needed here during the day, I will go about and do the chairs.'

Oliver Luxmore laughed. 'You'll never buy a horse with cane bottoms. No, that won't do. I'll give up carrying and go work on the roads. You don't know what grand new macadamised roads are being laid out; they are carrying them round slopes, where before they went straight up. They are filling in bottoms, and slicing into hills. Thousands upon thousands of pounds are being spent, and there are gangs of men engaged upon them.'

'No, father, you are too old for that work. Besides, those who go on to the road-making are the rough and riotous young fellows who want high wages, and who spend their money in drink. No, such society is not for you.'

'I don't see that,' said the father. 'As you say, the wages are very high; I am not so old that I cannot work.'

'You are unaccustomed to the kind of work.'

'I should get into the way of it, and I am no drunkard to waste my money.'

'But you are a Luxmore.'

Oliver held up his head. That last was an unanswerable argument. He considered for awhile, and then he said, 'I cannot borrow the money of Mr. Nanspian, he is ill. It is, of course, useless my asking Mr. Langford, he is not a lending, but a taking man.'

'If we worked out the first debt, we can work out the second,' said Honor. 'I know that you can get nothing from Chimsworthy, and I do not suppose you can get any thing from Langford, nevertheless you might try. Mr. Langford knows you to be an industrious and a conscientious man. He has but to look in your face, father, to be sure that you would rather be cheated than cheat any one. Try Mr. Taverner Langford to-morrow.'

'It is no good,' sighed Oliver. 'Only wear out shoe leather for nothing. You go if you think anything of the chance. Folks say, walk with Hope, or you are walking backwards.'

'I—I go to Mr. Langford!'

'No need for that, when I have come to you,' answered a voice at the open window.

Honor started, looked up, and saw Taverner Langford there, looking at her, and then at Oliver.

'Won't you step in and take a chair, sir?' asked Honor, rising and moving towards the door.

'No, I am well where I am,' answered Taverner, leaning his elbows on the bottom of the window and peering in. He wore a broad-brimmed hat, that shadowed the upper part of his face, but out of this shadow shone his eyes with phosphoric light.

'Father,' exclaimed Honor, 'here is Mr. Langford.'

Oliver had risen and stood with his pipe in one hand leaning against one jamb of the chimney, looking wonderingly at the visitor. Langford had ascended the steps from the lane, and thus had appeared suddenly before the Luxmores.

From the window no one that passed was visible unless he were seated on the top of a load of hay carted along the lane from the harvest field.

Oliver Luxmore went to the window, and, like his daughter, asked, 'Will you step inside, sir?'

'No, thank you,' answered Langford, 'I can talk very comfortably standing where I am. I know you to be a sensible man, Luxmore, and to have your eyes about you, and your ears open. There is no man goes about the country so much as you. They say that in a town the barber knows all the news, and in the country the carrier. Now I'll tell you what I want, Luxmore, and perhaps you'll do me the favour to help me to what I want. I'm short of hands, and I want a trusty fellow who can act as cattle driver for me. I won't have a boy. Boys over-drive and hurt the cattle. I must have a man. Do you know of one who will suit?'

Oliver shook his head. 'I don't know that I do, and I don't know that I don't:'

'You are talking riddles, Luxmore. What do you mean?'

'Well, sir,' answered the carrier with sigh, 'my meaning is this. Poor Diamond is dead, and I am thinking of giving up the carrying trade.'

'Giving up the "Vivid"! You are not in your senses, man.'

'Ah, Sir, how am I to buy a new horse? The price is up and money is scarce—leastways with me. Horses ain't to be bought on promises no more than they are to be reared on wind.'

'Want a horse, do you? Of course the "Vivid" won't go by herself except down hill, and that is what every one and every thing can do unassisted. It is the getting up hill that costs a strain. Ah, Luxmore, I could show you two men, one going up and the other down, going down as fast as the laden van on Rexhill, without a horse to back against it. You've only to look to Chimsworthy to see that. I need not say in which direction to turn your eyes to see the contrary.'

He pushed up his hat and looked at the carrier, then at Honor. He did not deign to cast a passing glance at Kate.

'Then, sir,' said Oliver, 'if the worst came to the worst—I mean, sir, begging your pardon, and no offence intended, if I could not get another horse, and where it is to come from the Lord Almighty only knows—I'd have to work for my living some other way, and I might be glad to take service with you. I was even thinking on going to the roads that be making, but Honor won't hear of that, so I reckon it can't be.'

'No,' answered Taverner, with his eyes resting on Honor, 'no, she is quite right. Your proper place is at home with the family. The men on the roads are a wild lot.'

'So she said,' the carrier put in humbly, 'and of course Honor knows.'

'Now look you here, Luxmore,' said Taverner, 'I'm not a man to squander and give away, as every one in Bratton knows, but I'm not as hard as they are pleased to say, and where a worthy man is in need, and no great risk is seen by myself, and I'm not out of pocket, I don't mind helping him. I do not say but what I'll let you have my grey for keep. She's not an infant. There's not much gambol about her, but there is a deal of work. You shall have her for awhile; and pay me ten shillings a week, as hire. That is a favourable offer, is it not?'

The carrier stood silent with astonishment. Honor's cheeks flushed with pleasure and surprise, so did those of Kate.

'Your grey!' exclaimed Luxmore. 'I know her well. She's worth five-and-twenty pounds.'

'She may be. I do not know. I will not consider that. I do not want her just now, and shall be glad to lend her for her keep and a trifle. You are an honest man. Your family is like mine—come down in the world.'

'Ah!' exclaimed the carrier, raising his head proudly, 'I reckon Coombe Park is where I should be, and all I want wherewith to get it is a hundred pounds and a register.'

'That may be,' said Taverner; 'there were Luxmores in Bratton as long as there have been Langfords, and that goes back hundreds of years. I do not want to see you fall to the ground. I am ready to lend you a helping hand. You may fetch away the grey when you like. You will have to sign an acknowledgment and promise to return her in good and sound condition. Always safest to have a contract properly executed and signed, then there can be no starting up of a misunderstanding afterwards.'

'I am to have your grey!' Oliver Luxmore could not believe in his good fortune, and this good fortune coming to him from such an unexpected quarter. 'There now! Honor said I was to go up to Langford and see you. She thought you might help, and 'twas no use in the world asking at Chimsworthy.'

'Honor said that!' exclaimed Taverner and at the girl and nodded approvingly.

Then Luxmore, who had been sitting in his shirt-sleeves, took his coat and put it on, went to the nail and unhooked his hat.

'I don't mind if I go and look at the grey,' he said. He had sufficient prudence not to accept till he had seen.

Whilst Oliver Luxmore was assuming his coat, Langford, leaning on his arms in the window, watched the active fingers of Honor, engaged in weaving a basket. Her feet were thrust forward, with the red stockings encasing them.

'Ah!' said Taverner, half aloud, half to himself. 'I know a red spider that brings luck. Well for him who secures her.'

Just then voices were audible, bright and clear, coming from the lane; and in a few minutes up the steps trooped the younger children of the carrier, returning from school. Each, even the boy of thirteen, went at once to Honor, stood before her, and showed face and hands and clothes.

'Please, Honor,' said one little girl, 'I've got a tear in my pinafore. I couldn't help it. There was a nail in the desk.'

'Well, Pattie, bring me my workbox.'

How clean, orderly, happy the children were! Each before going to school was examined to insure that it was scrupulously neat; and each on returning was submitted to examination again, to show that it had kept its clothes tidy whilst at school, and its face and hands clean.

Regardless of the presence and observations of Langford, Honor mended Pattie's pinafore. She was accustomed to do at once what she observed must be done. She never put off what had to be done to a future time. Perhaps this was one of the secrets of her getting through so much work.

When each child had thus reported itself to Honor, she dismissed it with a kiss, and sent it to salute the father.

'You will find, each of you, a piece of bread-and-butter and a mug of milk in the back kitchen,' she said. Then the children filed out of the room to where their simple meal was laid out for them.

'Busy, systematic, thrifty,' said Taverner Langford, looking approvingly at Honor. 'The three feet that stay Honour.' Whether he made this remark in reference to her name the girl could not make out; she looked up suddenly at him, but his face was inscrutable, as he stood with his back to the light in the window, with his broad-brimmed hat drawn over his eyes.

Her father was ready to depart with Langford. As the latter turned to go, he nodded to the girl in an approving and friendly way, and then turning to her father, as he prepared to descend the steps, said, 'What a maid that daughter of yours is! Everything in your house is clean, everything in place, even the children. The sphere is not big enough for her, she has talents for managing a farm.'

'Ah!' groaned Luxmore, 'if we had our rights, and Coombe Park came to us——' The sisters heard no more. Their father had reached the foot of the steps.

When both he and Langford had disappeared, Kate burst out laughing.

'O Honor!' she said, 'that screw, Mr. Langford! how his voice creaked. I thought all the time he was speaking of a screw driven into father, creak, creak, creak!'

'For shame, Kate! Mr. Taverner Langford has done us a great kindness. He must not be ridiculed."

'I do not believe in his kindness,' answered the lively Kate. 'The grey has got the glanders, or is spavined, that is why he wants to lend her. Unless father is very keen, Mr. Langford, will overreach him.' Then she threw aside the basket she had been weaving. 'There Honor, that is done, and my fingers are sore. I will do no more. No—not even to buy the grey with my earnings. I am sure that grey is coming to bring us ill-luck. I turned my thumb in all the time that Mr. Langford was here, I thought he had the evil eye, and—Honor—his wicked eye was on you.'

VI

The Progress of Strife

So it fell out that two worthy men, landowners, brothers in-law, in the parish of Bratton Clovelly, each a churchwarden, each a pillar of religion, Jakim and Booz, one of the Temple, the other of the Tabernacle, were at variance. About what? About nothing, a little red spider, so minute that many a man could not see it without his spectacles.

The money-spinner had provoked the calling of names, the flying forth of fury, the rush of blood to the head of Hillary Nanspian, and a fit. It was leading to a good deal more, it was about to involve others beside the principals.

But the money-spinner was really only the red speck at the meeting-point of rivalries, and brooding discontents and growing grievances. Nanspian had long chafed at the superiority assumed by Langford, had been angry at his own ill-success, and envious of the prosperity of his brother-in-law. And Langford had fretted over the thriftlessness of Nanspian, and the prospect of his own gains being dissipated by his nephew.

Hillary was a boastful and violent man. Taverner was suspicious and morose. But Nanspian was good-natured at bottom: his anger, if boisterous, soon blew away. Langford's temper was bitter; he was not malevolent, but he harboured his wrongs, and made a sort of duty of revenging them.

The love of saving had become so much a part of Taverner's soul, that it caused him real agony of mind to think that all he had laid by might be wasted by young Hillary, who, brought up in his father's improvident ways, was sure to turn out a like wastrel. Moreover, he did not like young Larry. He bore him that curious aversion which old men sometimes manifest for the young. Taverner had been an ungainly youth, without ease of manner or social warmth. He had never made himself friends of either sex; always solitary, he had been driven in on himself. Now that he was in the decline of life he resented the presence in others of those qualities he had never himself possessed. The buoyant spirits, the self-confidence, the good humour, the pleasant looks, the swinging walk of young Larry were all annoyances to Langford, who would have taken a liking to the lad had he been shy and uncouth.

Formerly, scarcely a day had passed without the brothers-in-law meeting. Sometimes they encountered accidentally on Broadbury, or in the lanes, at other times they met by appointment at the Look-out-Stone. They discussed together the weather, the crops, the cattle, the markets. Hillary was a shrewd man, and had seen more of the world than Taverner, who had, however, read more books than the other. Langford had respect for the worldly experience of his brother and Nanspian venerated the book learning in the other. The Chimsworthy brother could see various ways in which money might be made, and had even made suggestions by which he of Langford had reaped a pecuniary profit, but he was too lazy a man to undertake new ventures himself, too lazy even to properly cultivate in the old way the land on which he lived.

Hillary was conscious that he was falling in the estimation of his brother-in-law. He was chafed by the sense of his indebtedness to him. He saw no way of escape from the debt he owed save by Taverner's death, and he began to have a lurking hope of release in that way. He was not stimulated to activity. 'What is the advantage of making a labour of life,' he asked—not of his brother-in-law—'when a man has a comfortable property, and another in reversion?'

The great day of all, on which the kindly relations of the brothers-in-law were brought forward and paraded before the parish, was on the feast day of Coryndon's Charity. Then Hillary Nanspian arrived arm-in-arm with Taverner Langford, Hillary in his badger-skin waistcoat with red lappets, Taverner in dark homespun, with black cravat and high collar. As they walked down the village every man touched his hat and every woman curtsied. When they came to a puddle, and puddles are common in roads of Bratton Clovelly, then Hillary Nanspian would say, 'Take care, Taverner, lest you splash your polished boots and dark breeches.' Thereupon the brothers-in-law unlinked, walked round the puddle, and hooked together on the further side. At the dinner—which was attended by the Rector, who sat at the head and carved, the way-warden and the overseer, the landlord of the 'Ring of Bells,' where the dinner was held, and several of the principal farmers, ex-feoffees, or feoffees in prospective—speeches were made. Hillary, with a glass of rum-and-water and a spoon in it, stood up and spoke of his fellow-churchwarden and feoffee and brother-in-law in such a rich and warm speech, that, under the united influence of hot strong rum, and weak maudlin Christianity, and sound general good-fellowship, and goose and suet pudding, the tears rose into the eyes of the hearers, and their moral feelings were as elevated as if they had heard a sermon of Mr. Romaine.

After that, Taverner proposed the health of his co-feoffee and churchwarden in a nervous, hesitating speech, during which he shuffled with his feet on the floor, and his hands on the table, and became hot and moist, and almost cried—not with tender emotion, but with the sense of humiliation at his own inability to speak with fluency. But, of course, all present thought this agitation was due to the great affection he bore to his brother-in-law.

When Parson Robbins, the Rector, heard of the quarrel, he was like one thunderstruck. He could not believe it. 'Whatever shall I do? I shall have to take a side. Mercy on us, what times we live in, when I am forced to take a side!'

As to the farmers generally, they chuckled. Now at last there was a chance of one of them getting into Coryndon's Charity and getting a lease of the poor's lands.

Hillary Nanspian recovered from his fit, but the breach between the brothers-in-law was not healed. When he again appeared at market he was greatly changed. The apoplectic stroke, the blood-letting, the call in of the money owed to Langford, had combined to alter him. He was not as florid, as upright, as imperious as before. His face was mottled, the badger-skin waistcoat no longer fitted him as a glove, it fell into wrinkles, and the hair began to look as though the moth had got into it. A slight stoop appeared in his gait. He became querulous and touchy. Hitherto, when offended, he had discharged a big, mouth-filling oath, as a mortar throws a shell; now he fumed, and swore, and grumbled. There was no appeasing him. He was like the mitrailleuse that was to be, but was not then. Hitherto he had sat on his settle, smoking, and eating his bread and had allowed the fowls to come in and pick up the crumbs at his feet. Now he threw sticks at them and drove them out of the kitchen.

Encounters between the brothers-in-law were unavoidable, but when they met they pretended not to see each other. They made circuits to avoid meeting. When they passed in the lane, they looked over opposite hedges.

The quarrel might, perhaps, have been patched up, had it not been for the tongue of Mrs Veale. Taverner Langford disliked this pasty-faced, bleached woman greatly, but he was afraid of dismissing her, because he doubted whether it would be possible for him to provide himself with as good a manager in his house and about the cattle. Though he disliked her, he was greatly influenced by her, and she found that her best mode of ingratiating herself with him was by setting him against others. She had a venomous dislike for the Nanspians. 'If anything were to happen to the master, those Nanspians would take all, and where should I be?' she reasoned. She thought her best chance of remaining at Langford and of insuring that something was left to her by the master in consideration for her faithful services was to make him suspect and dislike all who surrounded him. He listened to her, and though he discounted all she said, yet the repetition of her hints, and suggestions, and retailed stories, told on him more than he allowed himself to believe. Through her he heard of the boasts of his brother-in-law, and his attention was called to fresh instances of mismanagement at Chimsworthy. At one time Mrs. Veale had audaciously hoped to become mistress of the place. Langford was a lone shy man, how could he resist the ambuscades and snares of a designing woman? But Mrs. Veale in time learned that her ambition in this direction was doomed to disappointment and that efforts made to secure the master would effect her own expulsion. She therefore changed her tactics, dared to lecture and give him the rough of her tongue. Langford endured this, because it showed him she had no designs on him, and convinced him that she was severe and faithful. And she made herself indispensable to him in becoming the medium of communication between himself and those with whom he was offended. He had sufficient of the gentleman in him to shrink from reprimanding his servants and haggling with a dealer; he was miserly, but too much of a gentleman to show it openly. He made Mrs. Veale cut down expenses, watch against waste, and economise in small matters.

How is it that women are able to lay hold of and lead men by their noses as easily as they take up and turn about a teapot by its handle? Is it that their hands are fashioned for the purpose, and men's noses are fitted by Nature for their hands? Although the nose of Taverner Langford was Roman, and expressive of character and individuality, Mrs. Veale held him by it; and he followed with the docility of a colt caught and led by the forelock.

It was a cause of great disappointment to Hillary that Taverner was in a position to give him annoyance, whereas he was unable to retaliate. Langford had called in the money he had advanced to his brother-in-law; it must be repaid within three months. Langford had threatened the father and son with disinheritance. On the other side, he was powerless to punish Langford. The consciousness of this was a distress to Nanspian, and occasioned the irritability of temper we have mentioned. Unable to endure the humiliation of being hurt without being able to return the blow, he went into the office of the lawyer Physick, at Okehampton.

'Mr. Physick,' said he, 'I want to be thundering disagreeable.'

'By all means, Mr. Nanspian. Very right and proper.'

'I'm going to be very offensive.'

'To be sure. You have occasion, no question.'

'I want a summons made out against Mrs. Veale, that is, the housekeeper of Taverner Langford.'

'The deuce you do!' exclaimed the lawyer, starting into an erect position on his seat. 'The housekeeper of your brother-in-law!'

'The same. I want to hit him through her.'

'Why, Lord bless me! What has come to pass? I thought you and Mr. Langford were on the best of terms.'

'Then, sir, you thought wrong. We are no longer friends; we do not speak.'

'What has occasioned this?'

Nanspian looked down. He was ashamed to mention the red spider; so he made no reply.

'Well! and what is the summons to be made out for?'

'For giving me a stroke of the apoplexy.'

'I do not understand'

'You must know,' said Hillary, lowering his voice, 'that I have a notion Mrs. Veale is a witch; and when Langford and I fell out she came meddling with her witchcraft. She came as a White Hare.'

'As a what?'

'As a White Hare,' answered Hillary, drawing forth a kerchief and blowing his nose, and in the act of blowing fixing the lawyer over the top of it with his eyes, and saying through it, 'My Larry saw her.'

Mr. Physick uttered a sigh of disappointment and said ironically 'This is not a case for me. You must consult the White Witch in Exeter.'

'Can you do nothing?'

'Certainly not. If that is all you have come about, you have come on a fool's errand.'

But this was not all. Nanspian wanted to raise the money for paying his brother-in-law. Mr. Physick was better able to accommodate him in this. 'There is another matter I want to know,' said Nanspian. 'Taverner Langford threatens to disinherit me and my Larry. Can he do it? I reckon not. You have the settlements. The threat is idle and vain as the wind, is it not?'

'Langford is settled property in tail male,' answered the solicitor. 'Should Mr. Langford die unmarried and without male issue, it will fall to you, and if you predecease, to your son.'

'There!' exclaimed Hillary, drawing a long breath, 'I knew as much; Larry and I are as sure of Langford as if we had our feet on it now. He cannot take it from us. We could, if we chose, raise money on it.'

'Not so fast, Mr. Nanspian. What aged man is your brother-in-law?'

'Oh, between fifty-eight and sixty.'

'He may marry.'

'Taverner marry!' exclaimed Hillary; he put his hands on his knees and laughed till he shook. 'Bless me! whom could Taverner marry but Mrs. Veale?—and he won't take her. He is not such a fool as to turn a servant under him into a mistress over him. But let him. I give him Mrs. Veale, and welcome. May I be at the wedding. Why, she will not see this side of forty, and there is no fear of a family.'

'He may take some one else.'

'She would not let him. She holds him under her thumb. Besides, there are none suitable about our neighbourhood. At Swaddledown are only children, Farmer Yelland's sister at Breazle is in a consumption, and at the rectory Miss Robbins is old. No, Mr. Physick, there is absolutely no one suitable for him.'

'Then he may take some one unsuitable.'

VII

Coryndon's Charity

The opinion gained ground in Bratton Clovelly that it was a pity two such good friends and worthy brothers-in-law should quarrel and be drawn on into acts of violence and vengeance, as seemed probable. As the Coryndon feoffee dinner drew on, expression was given to their opinion pretty freely, and the question was debated, What would happen at the dinner? Would the enemies refuse to meet each other? In that case, which would cede to the other? Perhaps, under the circumstance the dinner would not take place, and the profits, not being consumed, would be given to the widows. That might establish a dangerous precedent. Widows in future years might quote this, and resist the reintroduction of the dinner. Fortunately widows, though often violent and noisy, are not dangerous animals and may be browbeaten with impunity.

Nevertheless a general consensus of opinion existed among the overseers and way-wardens, acting, ex-, and prospective, that the dinner must not be allowed to fall through even for one year. Englishmen with their habitual caution, are very much afraid of establishing a precedent.

Hillary Nanspian was spoken to on the subject, and he opined that the dinner must be held. 'If Taverner Langford is ashamed to meet me, let him stay away. I shall pay him every penny I owed, and can look him in the face. We shall be merrier without him.'

Notice of the dinner was sent to Langford; he made no reply, but from his manner it was concluded that he would not attend.

The day of the Trust dinner arrived. Geese had been killed. Whiff! they could be smelt all down the village to leeward of the inn, and widows came out and sniffed up all they were likely to receive of Coryndon's Charity. Beef was being roasted. Hah! The eye that peeped into the kitchen saw it turning and browning before the great wood fire, and when the landlord's wife was not talking, the ear heard the frizzle of the fat and the drop, drop into the pan beneath.

What was that clinking? Men's hearts danced at the sound. A row of tumblers was placed on the dresser, and spoons set in them. In the dairy a maid was taking cream, golden as the buttercup, off the pans to be eaten—believe it, non-Devonians, if you can, gnash your teeth with envy and tear your hair—to be eaten with plum-pudding. See! yonder stands a glass vessel containing nutty white celery in it, the leaves at the top not unfolded, not green, but of the colour of pale butter. Hard by is a plate with squares of cheese on it, *hard* by indeed, for, oh—what a falling off is there!—the Devon cheese is like board.

About the door of the 'Ring of Bells' was assembled a knot of men in their Sunday best, with glossy, soaped faces. They were discussing the quarrel between the brothers-in-law when the Rector arrived. He was a bland man, with a face like a suet-pudding; he shook hands cordially with every one.

'We've been talking, parson, about the two who have got across. 'Tis a pity now, is it not?'

Parson Robbins looked from one to another, to gather the prevailing opinion, before he committed himself. Then, seeing one shake his head, and hearing another say, 'It's a bad job,' he ventured to say, 'Well, it may be so considered.' He was too cautious a man to say '*I* consider it so;' he could always edge out of an 'It may be so considered.' Parson Robbins was the most inoffensive of men. He never, in the pulpit, insisted on a duty lest he should offend a Churchman, nor on a doctrine lest he should shock a Dissenter. It was his highest ambition to stand well with all men, and he endeavoured to gain his point by disagreeing with nobody and insisting on nothing.

'I hear,' said Farmer Yelland, 'that the two never meet each other and never speak. They are waiting a chance of flying at each other's throats.'

'Ah!' observed the Rector 'so it has been reported in the parish.' He was too careful to say 'reported to *me*.'

'Why, pity on us!' said a little cattle-jobber with a squint; 'when folks who look straight before them fall across, how am I to keep straight with my eyes askew?'

Every one laughed at these words. Harry Piper, the speaker, was a general favourite because his jokes were level with their comprehension, and he did not scruple to make a butt of himself. The sexton, a solemn man, with such command over his features that not a muscle twitched when a fly walked on his nose, even he unbent, and creases formed about his mouth.

'Now look here,' said Piper, 'if we don't take the matter in hand these two churchwardens will be doing each other a mischief. Let us reconcile them. A better day than this for the purpose cannot be found.'

'Mr. Piper's sentiments are eminently Christian,' said the Rector, looking round; then qualifying his statement with 'that is, as far as I can judge without going further into the matter.'

'Will Master Nanspian be here?' asked one.

'I know that he will,' answered the cattle-jobber 'but not the other, unless he be fetched.'

'Well, let him be fetched.'

'That is,' said the Parson, 'if he will come.'

There was then, leaning against the inn door, a ragged fellow with a wooden leg, and a stump of an arm into which a hook was screwed—a fellow with a roguish eye, a bald head, and a black full beard. Tom Crout lived on any little odd jobs given him by the farmers to keep him off the parish. He had lost his leg and arm through the explosion of a gun when out poaching. Now he drove bullocks to pasture, cows to be milked, sheep to the common, and wired rabbits. This was the proper man to send after Taverner Langford.

'You may ride my pony,' said the cattle-jobber, 'and so be quicker on your way.'

'And,' said the guardian of the poor, 'you shall dine on the leavings and drink the heel-taps for your trouble.'

As he went on his way, Crout turned over in his mind how he was to induce Taverner Langford to come to the dinner. Crout was unable to comprehend how any man needed persuasion to draw him to goose, beef, and plum-pudding.

On his way he passed Hillary Nanspian, in his badger-skin waistcoat with red lappets, riding his strawberry mare. He was on his way to the 'Ring of Bells.'

'Whither away, Crout?' shouted Hillary.

'Out to Broadbury, after Farmer Burneby's sheep that have broken.'

Then he rode on.

When he reached the gate of Langford, he descended. At once the black Newfoundland house-dog became furious, and flew at him, and with true instinct snapped at the calf of flesh, not the leg of wood. Tom Crout yelled and swore, and made the best of his way to the door, where Taverner and Mrs. Veale appeared to call off the dog.

'It is a shame to keep dogs like that, vicious brutes ready to tear a Christian to tatters.'

'I didn't suppose you was a Christian, hearing your heathenish oaths,' said Mrs. Veale; 'and as to the tatters, they were there before the dog touched you.'

'The parson has sent me,' said Crout, 'and he would not send me if I were not a Christian. As for my tatters, if you will give me an old coat, I'll leave them behind. Please, Mr. Langford, the feoffees and guests are at the "Ring of Bells," and cannot begin without you. The beef is getting cold, and the goose is becoming burnt.'

'Let them fall to. The dinner is sure to be good.'

'How can they, master, without you or Mr. Nanspian?'

'Is he not there?'

'Not a speck of his fur waistcoat visible, not a glimmer of his blue eye to be seen. Ah, Mr. Langford, such a dinner! Such goose, with onion stuffing, and sage, and mint, and marjoram! I heard the butcher tell our landlord he'd never cut such a sirloin in all his life as that roasting for to-day; smells like a beanfield, and brown as a chestnut! As for the plum-pudding it is bursting with raisins!'

'That will suffice,' said Taverner, unmoved by the description. 'I do not intend to go.'

'Not intend to go! Very well, then, I shall have to go to Chimsworthy and bring Mr. Nanspian. I'll tell him you haven't the heart to meet folks. You prefer to hide your head here, as if you had committed something of which you are ashamed. Very well. When he hears that you durstn't show, he will go and swagger at the "Ring of Bells" without you.'

'I do not choose to meet him. He may be there after all.'

'Not a bit. When I left all were assembled and he was not. May I be struck dead if he was there! The parson said to the rest, "Whatever shall we do without Master Langford, my own churchwarden, so to speak—my right hand and the representative of the oldest and grandest family in the place? That is a come-down of greatness if he don't turn up at the feoffees' dinner." May I die on the doorstep if these were not his very words! Then he went on, "I did reckon on Master Langford to be here to keep me in countenance. Now here I lay down my knife and fork, and not a bite will I eat, nor a cut will I make into that bubbling, frizzling, savoury goose, unless Taverner Langford be here. So go along, Crout, and fetch him."

'Is that true?' asked Langford, flattered.

'May my remaining leg and arm wither if it be not! Then Farmer Burneby up and said, "He durstn't come; he's mortally afraid of meeting Hillary Nanspian."

'Did he say that?' asked Taverner, flushing.

'Strike me blind if he did not!'

'I'll come. Go on, I will follow.'

When Crout returned to the 'Ring of Bells,' he found Nanspian there, large and red. The cripple slipped up to Piper and whispered, 'He'll be here, leave a place opposite the other, and fall to at the beef.'

'The fly,' observed the parson to a couple of farmers—'the fly is the great enemy of the turnip. It attacks the seed-leaves when they appear.'

'That is true.'

'Now, what you want with turnips is a good shower after the seed has been sown, and warmth to precipitate the growth at the critical period. At least, so I have been informed.'

'It is so, parson.'

'In wet weather the fly does not appear, or the plant grows with sufficient rapidity to outstrip the ravages of the fly.'

'To be sure, you are quite right, sir.'

This fact of the turnip-fly was one of the few scraps of agricultural information Parson Robbins had picked up, and he retailed it at the club, and feoffee dinners.

Then the landlord appeared at the inn door, and announced, 'All ready, gentlemen! sorry you have been kept waiting!'

At the moment that Nanspian and the parson entered, Langford arrived and went after them, without seeing the former, down the passage to the long room. The passage was narrow, tortuous, and dark. 'Wait a bit, gentlemen,' said the host, 'one at a time through the door; his Reverence won't say grace till all are seated.'

'Here is a place, Master Langford,' said Piper, 'on the right hand of the parson, with your back to the window. Go round his chair to get at it.'

Taverner took the place indicated. Then the Rector rapped on the table, and all rose for grace.

As Langford rose he looked in front of him, and saw the face of Nanspian, who sat on the Rector's left. Hillary had not observed him before, he was looking at the goose. When he raised his eyes and met the stare of Taverner, his face became mottled, whereas that of his brother-in-law turned white. Neither spoke, but sank into his place, and during dinner looked neither to right, nor left, nor in front. Only once did Taverner slyly peep at Hillary, and in that glimpse he noted his altered appearance. Hillary was oldened, fallen away, changed altogether for the worse. Then he drew forth his blue cotton pocket-handkerchief and cleared his nose. Neither relished his dinner. The goose was burnt and flavourless, the beef raw and tough, the potatoes under-boiled, the apple-tart lacked cloves, the plum-pudding was over-spiced, the cheese was tough, and the celery gritty. So, at least, they seemed to these two, but to these two alone. When the spirits were produced all eyes were turned on Hillary Nanspian, but he neither rose nor spoke. Taverner Langford was also mute. 'Propose the health of the chairman,' whispered Piper into Hillary's ear.

'I am people's churchwarden,' answered he sullenly.

'Propose the health of the chairman,' said his right-hand neighbour to Langford.

'I am a Dissenter,' he replied.

Then the Rector stood up and gave the health of the King, which was drunk with all honours.

'Shall we adjourn to the fire?' asked he; 'each take his glass and pipe.'

Then up rose the Rector once again, and said, 'Ahem! Fill your glasses, gentlemen. Mr. Langford, I insist. No shirking this toast. You, Mr. Nanspian, need no persuasion. Ahem!'

Piper came round and poured spirits into Langford's glass, then hot water.

'Ahem!' said the Rector. 'I have been in your midst, I may say, as your spiritual pastor, set—set—ahem!—under you these forty years, and, I thank heaven, never has there been a single discord—ahem!—between me and my parishioners. If I have not always been able to agree with them—ahem!—I have taken care not to disagree with them! I mean—I mean, if they have had their opinions, I have not always seen my way to accepting them, because I have studiously avoided having any opinions at all. Now—ahem!—I see a slight jar between my nearest and dearest neighbours,' he looked at Langford and Nanspian. 'And I long to see it ended.' ('Hear, hear, hear!') 'I express the unanimous opinion of the entire parish. On this one point, after forty opinionless years, I venture— ahem!—to have an opinion, a decided opinion, an emphatic opinion'—(immense applause)—'I call upon you all, my Christian brethren, to unite with me in healing this unseemly quarrel—I mean this quarrel: the unseemliness is in the quarrel, not in the quarrellers.'

Langford drank his gin-and-water not knowing what he did, and his hand shook. Nanspian emptied his glass. Both looked at the door: there was no escape that way, the back of burly Farmer Brendon filled it. All eyes were on them.

'Come now,' said Piper, 'what is the sense of this quarrel? Are you women to behave in this unreasonable manner? You, both of you, look the worse for the squabble. What is it all about?'

'Upon my word, I do not know,' said Nanspian. 'I never did Langford a hurt in my life. Why did he insult me?'

'I insult him!' repeated Taverner. 'Heaven knows I bore him no ill-will, but when he dared to address me as—'

'I swear by—' burst in Hillary.

'Do not swear!' said Langford, hastily. 'Let your yea be yea.' The ice was broken between them. One had addressed the other. Now they looked each other full in the face. Hillary's eyes moistened. Taverner's mouth twitched.

'Why did you employ offensive language towards me?' asked Hillary.

'I!' exclaimed Taverner; 'no, it was you who addressed me in words I could not endure.'

The critical moment had arrived. In another moment they would clasp hands, and be reconciled for life. No one spoke, all watched the two men eagerly.

'Well, Taverner,' said Hillary, 'you know I am a hot man, and my words fly from my tongue before I have cooled them.'

'I dare say I may have said what I never meant. Most certainly what I did say was not to be taken seriously.'

'But,' put in Parson Robbins, 'what was said?'

'Judge all,' exclaimed Taverner. 'I was angry, and I called Hillary Nanspian a long-tailed Cornish ourang-outang.'

The moment the words were uttered, he was aware that he had made a mistake. The insult was repeated in the most public possible manner. If the words spoken in private had exasperated Hillary, how much more so now!

Nanspian no sooner heard the offensive words than he roared forth, 'And I—I said then, and I repeat now, that you are nose-led, tongue-lashed by your housekeeper, Mrs. Veale.' Then he dashed his scalding rum-and-water in the face of his brother-in-law.

VIII

A Malingerer

THE TIME TAKEN BY THE 'Vivid' over the journey to and from the market towns was something to be wondered at. A good man is merciful to his beast. Certainly Oliver Luxmore was a good man, and he showed it by his solicitude for the welfare of the grey. On Friday he drove to Tavistock market at a snail's pace, to spare the horse, because it had to make a journey on the morrow to Launceston or Okehampton. On Saturday he drove to market at a slug's pace, because the grey had done such hard work on the preceding day. The road, as has been said, was all up and down hill, and the hills are as steep as house roofs. Consequently the travellers by the 'Vivid' were expected to walk up the hills to ease the load, and to walk down the hills lest the weight of the 'Vivid' should carry the van over the grey. The fare one way was a shilling, the return journey could be made for sixpence. All goods, except what might be carried on the lap, were paid for extra. As the man said who was conveyed in a sedan-chair from which the bottom had fallen out, but for the honour of the thing, he might as well have walked. Passengers by the 'Vivid' started at half-past six in the morning, and reached the market town about half-past eleven. They took provisions with them, and ate two meals on the way. They also talked their very lungs out; but the recuperative power of their lungs was so great that they were fresh to talk all the way home. The van left the town at four and reached Bratton at or about nine.

A carrier must naturally be endowed with great patience. Oliver Luxmore was by nature thus qualified. He was easy-going, gentle, apathetic. Nothing excited him except the mention of Coombe Park. His business tended to make him more easy-going and patient than he was naturally. He allowed himself to be imposed upon, he resented nothing, he gave way before every man who had a rough, and every woman who had a sharp, tongue. He was cheerful and kindly. Every one liked him, and laughed at him.

One Saturday night, after his return from Okehampton, Oliver was taking his supper. The younger children were in bed, but Kate was up; she had been to market that day with her father. Kate was a very pretty girl, sharp eyed, sharp witted—with fair hair, a beautiful complexion, and eyes blue and sparkling—turquoises with the flash of the opal in them. She was seventeen. Her father rather spoiled her. He bought her ribbons and brooches when the money was needed for necessaries.

'I brought Larry Nanspian back part of the way with me,' said Oliver. 'His father drove him into town, but the old man stayed to drink, and Larry preferred to come on with me.'

'That was well of him,' said Honor, looking up with a smile.

'We talked of the grey,' continued the carrier. 'Larry was on the box with me. I put Kate inside, among the clucking, clacking old women. Larry asked me about the grey, and I told him how that we had got her. He shook his head, and he said, "Take care of yourself, Luxmore, lest in running out of the rain you get under the drip. I don't believe that Uncle Taverner's the man to do favours for nothing."'

'Did he say that?' asked Honor. 'He meant nothing by it—he was joking.'

'Of course he was joking. We joke a good deal together about one thing or another. He is grown a fine fellow. He came swinging up to me with his thumbs in his armholes and said, "Mr. Luxmore, Honor won't be able to withstand me in this waistcoat. She'll fall down and worship."'

'Did he say that?' asked Honor, and her brow flushed.

'Tush! you must not take his words as seriously meant. He had got a fine satin waistcoat to-day, figured with flowers. He pulled his coat open to show it me. I suppose he thought the satin waistcoat would draw you as a scarlet rag will attract rabbits.'

Honor turned the subject.

'What more did he say about Mr. Langford?'

'Oh, nothing particular. He told me he was sorry that his father could not spare us a horse, to keep us out of the clutches of his uncle Taverner. Then he laughed and said you had warned him not to run into debt, and yet had led the way yourself.'

'Run into debt, how?'

Oliver evaded an answer. 'In going up the hills, I and he walked together. He got impatient at last, and walked on by himself, and we never caught him up again.'

Honor did not look up from her work. She was mending some clothes of one of the children.

'He asked me a great deal about you,' said Kate. 'He said it was a shame that you should stick at home and never go to market, and see life.'

'How can I, with the house to look after? When you are a little more reliable, Kate, I may go. I cannot now.' Suddenly they heard a loud, deep voice at the door.

'Halloo! what a climb to the cock-loft.'

They looked startled to the door, and saw a man standing in it, with military trousers on his legs, and his hands in his pockets, watching them, with a laugh on his face.

'You have some supper! That's well. I'm cussed hungry. Walked from Tavistock. Why weren't you there to-day, father?'

'It is Charles!' exclaimed Luxmore, springing to his feet, and upsetting the table as he did so—that the cyder jug fell and was broken, and spilt its contents, and some plates went to pieces on the slate floor.

'Charlie, welcome home! Who would have expected to see you? Where have you been? What have you done? Have you served your time? Have you got your discharge? Lord, how glad I am to see you!'

Charles Luxmore, who entered the cottage, was a tall man; he looked ragged and wretched. His shoes were worn out, and his feet, stockingless, showed through the holes. His military trousers were sun-scorched, worn, badly patched, and in tatters about the ankles. His coat was split down the back, brown where exposed to the brunt of the weather. His whole appearance was such that one who met him in a lonely lane would be sensible of relief when he had passed him, and found himself unmolested.

'Halloo! there,' said he, drawing near to the fallen table, picking up the broken jug, and swearing, because the last drops of cyder were out of it. 'What are you staring at me for, as if I were a wild beast escaped from a caravan? Curse me, body and bones, don't you know me?'

'Charles!' exclaimed Honor, 'you home, and in this condition?'

'Dash it! is that you, Honor? How you have shot up. And this you, Kate? Thunder! what a pair of pretty girls you are. Where are the rest of the panpipes? Let me see them, and get my greeting over. Lug them out of bed that I may see them. Curse it, I forget how many of them there are.'

'Seven, beside our two selves,' said Honor. 'Nine in all.'

'Let me see them. Confound it! It must be got over.'

'The rest are in bed,' said Honor. 'They must not be disturbed out of their sleep.'

'Never mind. Where is the old woman?'

'I do not know whom you mean, Charles.'

'Mother. Where is she?'

'Dead, Charles.'

He was silent for a moment. Then he said, 'Fetch the little devils, I want to see them.'

'Charles, for shame!' exclaimed Honor, reddening and frowning, and her brown eyes flashed an angry light.

'Tut, tut! soldier's talk. You won't find my tongue wear kid gloves. I meant no harm.'

'You shall not speak of the children in such terms,' said Honor, firmly.

'Halloo! Do you think I will stand being hectored by you?'

'There, there,' threw in Oliver Luxmore, 'the boy meant nothing by it. He has got into a careless way of expressing himself. That is all.'

'That is all,' laughed Charles, 'and now I have a true soldier's thirst, and I am not a dog to lap up the spilt liquor off the floor. What is it, beer? Is there any brandy in the house?'

'You can have a drop of cyder,' said Honor, with frowning brows. 'Or, if that does not please you, water from the spring. The cyder is middling, but the water is good.'

'No water for me. Fetch me the cyder.'

'There is a hogshead in the cellar under the stairs in the back kitchen,' said Honor. 'Fill yourself a mug of it.'

'You can fetch it for me.'

'I can do so, but I will not,' answered Honor. 'Charles, I will not stir hand or foot for a man who will speak of his innocent little brothers and sisters as you have done.'

'Take care of yourself!' exclaimed Charles, looking at her threateningly.

She was not overawed by his look. Her cheeks glowed with inner agitation. 'I am not afraid of you,' she said, and reseated herself at her work.

'I will fetch the cyder,' offered the good-natured Kate, springing into the back kitchen.

'That is a good, dear girl,' said Charles; 'you and I will be friends, and stand out against that dragon.'

He took the mug. 'Pshaw! this is not sufficient. I am thirsty as desert sand. Fetch me a jugful.'

'There is not another jug in the house,' said Kate. 'I will fill the mug again.'

Just then at the kitchen door appeared a white figure.

'Whom have we here?' exclaimed Charles.

'Joe! what has brought you down? Go to bed again,' said Honor.

'Not a bit; come here. I am the eldest in the house. I take the command by virtue of seniority,' shouted Charles, and springing from the chair, he caught the little white figure, brought the child in, and seated him on his knee. 'I am your brother,' said Charles. 'Mind this. From henceforth you obey me, and don't heed what Honor says.'

Honor looked at her father. Would he allow this? Oliver made no remark.

'What is your name, young jack-a-napes?' asked Charles, 'and what brings you here?'

'I am Joseph, that is Joe,' answered the little boy. 'I heard your voice, and something said about soldiers, and I crawled downstairs to see who you were.'

'Let the child go to bed,' asked the father. 'He will catch a chill in his nightshirt.'

'Not he,' replied Charles. 'The kid wants to hear what I have to say, and you are all on pins, I know.'

'Well, that is true,' said Oliver Luxmore. 'I shall be glad to learn what brings you home. You have not served your full time. You have not bought yourself out. If you were on leave, you would be in uniform.'

'Oh, I'm out of the service,' answered Charles. 'Look here.' He held out his right hand. The forefinger was gone. 'I cut it off myself, because I was sick of serving his Majesty, tired of war and its hardships. I felt such an inextinguishable longing for home, that I cut off my trigger finger to obtain my discharge.'

'For shame, Charles, for shame!' exclaimed Honor.

'Oh, you are again rebuking me! You have missed your proper place. You should be an army chaplain. I've been in India, and I've fought the Afghans. Ah! I've been with General Pollock, and stormed and looted Cabul.'

'You have been in battle!' exclaimed little Joe.

'I have, and shot men, and run my bayonet into a dozen naked Afghans.' He laughed boisterously. 'It is like sticking a pig. That sack of Cabul was high fun. No quarter given. We blew up the great bazaar, crack! boom! high into the air, but not till we had cleared away all the loot we could. And, will you believe it? we marched away in triumph, carrying off the cedar doors of Somnath, as Samson with the gates of Gaza. Lord Ellenborough ordered it, and we did it. But they were not the original gates after all, but copies. Then, damn it, I thought—'

'Silence,' said Honor indignantly. 'With the child on your knee will you curse and swear?'

'An oath will do no harm, will it, Joe?' asked the soldier, addressing the little boy, who sat staring in his face with wonder and admiration. 'A good oath clears the heart as a cough relieves a choking throat, is it not so, Joe? or as a discharge of guns breaks a waterspout, eh?' The little boy looked from his brother to his sister. It was characteristic of the condition of affairs in the house that he did not look to his father.

'I don't know, brother Charles,' answered he. 'Honor would not allow it, she says it is wicked.'

'Oh, she!' mocked the soldier. 'I suppose you are under petticoat government still, or have been. Never mind, Joe. Now that I am come home you shall take orders from me, and not from her.'

'Joe,' said Honor sternly, 'go at once to bed.'

'He shall stay and hear the rest of the story. He shall hear how I lost my finger.'

The child hesitated.

Then Honor said gravely, 'Joe, you will do that which you know to be right.'

At once the little boy slipped from his brother's knee, ran to Honor, threw his arms round her neck, kissed her on both cheeks, and ran away, upstairs.

'So, so,' said Charles, 'open war between us! Well sister, you have begun early. We shall see who will obtain the victory.'

'I don't think Honor need fear a soldier who cuts off his finger to escape fighting,' said Kate.

'What, you also in arms against me?' exclaimed Charles, turning on the younger sister.

'You asked Joe if he were under petticoat government, and sneered at him for it; but you seem to be valiant only when fighting petticoats,' retorted Kate.

'I'm in a wasp's nest here,' laughed Charles.

'Never mind Kate,' said Oliver, 'she has a sharp tongue. Tell us further about your finger.'

'I lost more than my finger—I lost prize-money and a pension. As I told you, I was weary of the service, and wanted to get home. I thought I should do well with all the loot and prize-money, and if I were wounded also and incapacitated for service, I should have a pension as well; so I took off my finger with an axe, and tried to make believe I was hurt in action. But the surgeon would not allow it. I got into trouble and was discharged with the loss of my prize-money as a malingerer.'

'You are not ashamed to tell us this?' exclaimed Honor.

'It was a mistake,' said Charles.

'We are ashamed to sit and listen to you,' said Honor, with an indignant flash of her eyes, and with set brows. 'Come, Kate, let us to bed and leave him.'

'Good-night, malingerer,' said Kate.

IX
Charles Luxmore

The next day was Sunday. Charles lay in bed, and did not appear to breakfast. Oliver Luxmore, Kate, and the younger children were dressed for church. Honor remained at home alternately with Kate on Sunday mornings to take care of Tempie, the youngest, and to cook the dinner. This was Honor's morning at home.

Oliver Luxmore stood in doubt, one moment taking his Sunday hat, then putting it back in its card box, then again changing his mind.

Before they started, Charles swaggered into the kitchen, and asked for something to eat.

'Where are you all going to, you crabs, as gay as if fresh scalded?' asked Charles.

'This is Sunday,' answered his father, 'and I was thinking of taking them to church; but if you wish it, I will remain at home.'

'Suit yourself,' said Charles contemptuously, 'only don't ask me to go with you. I should hardly do you credit in these rags, and the parson would hardly do me good. In India there were four or five religions, and where there is such a choice one learns to shift without any.'

'What had I better do?' asked Oliver turning to Honor.

'Go to church with the children, father. I will remain with Charles.'

'I am to have your society, am I?' asked the soldier. 'An hour and a half of curry, piping hot! Well, I can endure it. I can give as well as take. Let me have a look at you, Kate. A tidy wench, who will soon be turning the heads of the boys, spinning them like teetotums. Let me see your tongue.' Kate put out her tongue, then he chucked her under the chin and made her bite her tongue. The tears came into her eyes.

'Charles you have hurt me. You have hurt me very much.'

'Glad to hear it,' he said contemptuously. 'I intended to do it. The tongue is too long, and too sharp, and demands dipping and blunting. I have chastised you for your impertinence last night.'

'I suppose I had better go,' said Oliver.

'Certainly, father,' answered Honor.

Then, still hesitating at every step from the cottage to the lane, Oliver went forth followed by seven children.

Charles drew a short black pipe from his pocket, stuffed it with tobacco, which he carried loose about him, and after lighting it at the fire on the hearth, seated himself in his father's chair, and began to smoke. Presently he drew the pipe out of his mouth, and looking askance at his sister, said, 'Am I to forage for myself this morning?'

Honor came quietly up to him, and standing before him, said, 'I spoke harshly to you, Charles, last night. I was angry, when you talked of the dear little ones offensively. But I dare say you meant no harm. It is a bad sign when the words come faster from lips than the thoughts form in the heart. You shall have your breakfast. I will lay it for you on the table. I am afraid, Charles, that your service in the army has taught you all the vices and none of the virtues of the soldier. A soldier is tidy and trim, and you are dirty and ragged. I am sorry for you; you are my brother, and I have always loved you.'

'Blazes and fury!' exclaimed Charles; 'this is a new fangled fashion of showing love. I have been from home five years, and this is the way in which I am welcomed home! I have come home with a ragged coat, and therefore I am served with cold comfort. If I had returned with gold guineas I should have been overwhelmed with affection.'

'Not so,' said Honor gravely. 'If you had returned with a sound character we would respect the rags; but what makes my heart ache is to see, not the tattered jacket, but the conscience all to pieces. How long is it since you landed?'

'Five or six months ago.'

'Where have you been since your return?'

'Where I could spend my money. I did bring something with me, and I lived on it whilst it lasted. It is not all gone yet. Look here.' He plunged his hand into his trousers pocket and jingled his coins carelessly in it.

'There!' said he, 'you will feel more respect for me, and your love wake up, when you see I have money still, not much, but still, some. Curse it, I was a fool not to buy you a ribbon or a kerchief, and then you would have received me with smiles instead of frowns.'

Honor looked him steadily in the face, out of her clear hazel eyes. 'No, Charles, I want no presents from you. Why did not you return to us at once?'

'Because I had no wish to be buried alive in Bratton Clovelly. Are you satisfied? Here I am at last.'

'Yes,' she repeated, 'here you are at last. What are you going to do now you are here?'

'I don't know,' answered her brother with a shrug. Then he folded his arms, threw out his legs, and leaned back in the chair. 'A fellow like me, who has seen the world, can always pick up a living.'

Honor sighed. What had he learned? For what was he fitted?

'Charles,' she said, 'this is your father's house, and here you were born. You have as true a right to shelter in it as I. You are heartily welcome, you may believe that. But look about you. We are not in Coombe Park. Including you we make up twelve in this cottage. What we live on is what your father earns by his carrying; but he is in debt, and we have no money to spare, we cannot afford to maintain idlers.'

'Take my money,' said Charles, emptying his pocket on the table.

'No,' answered Honor. 'For a week we will feed you for nothing. That money must be spent in dressing you respectably. By next week you will have found work.'

'Maybe,' said the soldier. 'It is not every sort of work that will suit me. Any one want a gamekeeper about here?'

'No, Charles, there is only Squire Impey in this parish; besides, without your forefinger, who would take you as a gamekeeper?'

'The devil take me, I forgot that.'

'Curses again,' said Honor. 'You must refrain your mouth before the children.'

'I have not gone to church,' said Charles sullenly, 'because I didn't want to be preached to; spare me a sermon at home.'

'Charles,' said Honor, 'I have hard work to make both ends meet, and to keep the children in order. You must not make my work harder—perhaps impossible. If you remain here, you will need my help to make you comfortable and to put your clothes in order. You will throw an additional burden on me, already heavily weighted. I do not grudge you that. But remember that extra work for an additional member means less time for earning money at basket-weaving. We must come to an understanding. I do not grudge you the time or the trouble, but I will only give them to you on condition that you do not interfere with my management of the children, and that you refrain your tongue from oaths and unseemly speech.'

Charles stood up, went to her, took her by both ears and kissed her. 'There, corporal, that is settled.'

Honor resented the impertinence of laying hold of her by both ears, but she swallowed her annoyance, and accepted the reconciliation.

'I have a good heart,' said Charles, 'but it has been rolled in the mud.'

'Give us the goodness, and wash off the soil,' answered Honor. Then she brought him some bread and milk. 'Charles,' she said, 'I will see if I cannot find some of father's clothes that will fit you. I cannot endure to see you in this condition.'

'Not suitable to the heir of Coombe Park, is it?' laughed Charles. 'Is the governor as mad on that now as of old?'

'Say nothing to him about Coombe Park, I pray you,' urged Honor. 'It takes the nerve out of his arms and the marrow from his bones. It may be that we have gentle blood in us, or it may not. I have heard tell that in old times servants in a house took the names of their masters.'

'I have always boasted I was a gentleman, till I came to believe it,' said the soldier. 'You'd have laughed to hear me talk of Coombe Park, and the deer there, and the coaches and horses, and father as Justice of Peace, and Deputy-Lieutenant, and all that sort of thing, and his wrath at my enlisting as a private.'

'I should not have laughed. I should have cried.'

'And, Honor, I reckon it is the gentle blood in my veins which has made a wastrel of me. I could never keep my money, I threw it away like a lord.'

Honor sighed. The myth of descent from the Luxmores of Coombe Park had marred her father's moral strength, and depraved her brother's character.

'There they come, the little devils!' shouted Charles, springing up and knocking the ashes out of his pipe, which he put away in his waistcoat pocket.

'Charles!' again remonstrated Honor, but in vain. Her elder brother was unaccustomed to control his tongue. There was a certain amount of good nature in him, inherited from his father, and this Honor thankfully recognised; but he was like his father run to seed. Luxmore would have become the same but for the strong sustaining character of his daughter.

Charley went to the door, and stood at the head of the steps. Along the lane came Oliver Luxmore with his children, Hillary junior and Kate bringing up the rear.

'Now then, you kids, big and little!' shouted Charles, 'see what I have got. A handful of halfpence. Scramble for them. Who gets most buys most sweeties.' Then he threw the coppers down among the children. The little ones held up their hands, jumped, tumbled over each other, quarrelled, tore and dirtied their Sunday clothes, whilst Charles stood above laughing and applauding. Oliver Luxmore said nothing.

'Come in, come in at once!' cried Honor, rushing to the door with angry face. 'Charles, is this the way you keep your promises?'

'I must give the children something, and amuse myself as well,' said the soldier.

Honor looked down the road and saw Kate with young Hillary Nanspian. They were laughing together.

'There now,' said Kate, as she reached the foot of the steps, 'Honor, see the young fellow who boasts he will make you fall down and worship his waistcoat.'

'It was a joke,' said Larry, turning red. He poked his hat up from his right, then from his left ear; he was overcome with shame.

Honor's colour slightly changed at the words of her sister, but she rapidly recovered herself.

'So,' continued the mischievous Kate, 'you have come round all this way to blaze your new waistcoat in the eyes of Honor, because she could not come to church to worship it?'

Young Nanspian looked up furtively at Honor, ashamed to say a word in self-exculpation.

'Talk of girls giving themselves airs over their fine clothes!' said Kate, 'men are as proud as peacocks when they put on spring plumage.'

'It serves you right, Mr. Larry,' said Honor, 'that Kate torments you. Vanity must be humbled.'

'I spoke in jest,' explained Hillary. 'All the parish knows that when I joke I do not mean what I say. When word comes to my lips, out it flies, good or bad. All the world knows that.'

'All the world knows that,' she repeated. 'It is bad to wear no drag on the tongue, but let it run down hill to a smash. Instead of boasting of this you should be ashamed of it.'

'I am not boasting,' he said, with a little irritation.

'Then I misunderstood you. When a man has a fault, let him master it, and not excuse himself with the miserable reason, that his fault is known to all the world.'

'Come, Honor, do not be cross with me,' he said, running up the steps, and holding out his hand.

'I am not cross with you,' she answered, but she did not give him her hand.

'How can I know that, if you will not shake hands?'

'Because all the world knows I tell no lies,' she answered coldly, and turned away.

X

On the Steps

For a week Charles Luxmore made a pretence of looking for work. Work of various kind was offered him, but none was sufficiently to his taste for him to accept it. He had still money in his pocket. He did not renew his offer of it to Honor. She had fitted him in a suit of his father's clothes, and he looked respectable. He was often in the 'Ring of Bells,' or at a public-house in a neighbouring parish. He was an amusing companion to the young men who met in the tavern to drink. He had plenty to say for himself, had seen a great deal of life, and had been to the other side of the world. Thus he associated with the least respectable, both old and young, the drunkards and the disorderly.

He was not afflicted with bashfulness, nor nice about truth, and over his ale he boasted of what he had seen and done in India. He said no more about his self-inflicted wound; and was loud in his declamation against the injustice of his officers, and the ingratitude of his country which cast him adrift, a maimed man, without compensation and pension. When he had drunk he was noisy and quarrelsome; and those who sat with him about the tavern table were cautious not to fall into dispute with him. There was a fire in his eye which led them to shirk a quarrel.

About a mile from the church in a new house lived a certain Squire Impey, a gentleman who had bought a property there, but who did not belong to those parts. No one knew exactly whence he came. He was a jovial man, who kept hounds, hunted and drank. Charles went to him, and he was the only man for whom he condescended to do some work, and from whom to take pay; but the work was occasional. Charles was an amusing man to talk to, and Impey liked to have a chat with him. Then he rambled away to Coombe Park, where he made himself so disagreeable by his insolence, that he was ordered off the premises. His father and brothers and sisters did not see much of him; he returned home occasionally to sleep, and when the mind took him to go to market, he went in the van with his father.

Much was said in the place of the conduct of Charles Luxmore—more, a great deal, than came to the ears of Honor. Oliver heard everything, for in the van the parish was discussed on the journey to market, and those who sat within did not consider whether the driver on the box heard what they said. Oliver never repeated these things to his eldest daughter, but Honor knew quite enough of the proceedings of Charles without this. She spoke to Charles himself, rebuked him, remonstrated with him, entreated him with tears in her eyes to be more steady; but she only made matters worse; she angered him the more because he knew that she was right. He scoffed at her anxiety about himself; he swore and burst into paroxysms of fury when she reprimanded him.

'Do not you suppose,' said he, 'that I am going to be brought under your thumb, like father and the rest.'

Possibly she might have been more successful had she gone to work more gently. But with her clear understanding she supposed that every one else could be governed by reason, and she appealed to his sense, not to his heart. He must see, she argued, to what end this disorderly life would lead if she put it before him nakedly. She supposed she could prove to him her sisterly affection in no truer way than by rebuke and advice.

Although Honor's heart was full of womanly tenderness there was something masculine in her character. There could not fail to be. Since her mother's death she had been the strength of the house; to her all had held. Circumstances had given her a hardness which was not natural to her.

Charles vowed after each fresh contest with Honor that he could not go near the cottage again. He would go elsewhere, out of range of her guns; but he did not keep his vow. It was forgotten on the morrow. Honor was not a scold. She had too good judgment to go on rebuking and grumbling, but she spoke her mind once, and acted with decision. She withstood Charles whenever his inconsiderate good nature or his disorderly conduct threatened to disturb the clocklike working of the house, to upset the confidence the children had in her, and to mar their simplicity. She encountered his violence with fearlessness. She never became angry, and returned words for words, but she held to her decision with toughness. Her father was afraid of Charles, and counselled his daughter to yield. Opposition, he argued, was unavailing, and would aggravate unpleasantnesses.

Honor suffered more than transpired. Her brother's disrepute rankled in her heart. She was a proud girl, and though she placed no store on her father's dreams of Coombe Park, she had a strong sense of family dignity, and she was cut to the quick when Charles's conduct became the talk of the neighbourhood. Never a talker, she grew more than ever reserved. When she went to or returned from church on Sunday, she shunned acquaintances; she would not linger for a gossip in the churchyard, or join company with a neighbour in the lane. She took a child by each hand, and with set face, and brows sternly contracted, looking neither right nor left, she went her way. Brightness had faded from her face. She was too proud to show the humiliation she felt at heart. 'Oh my,' said the urchins, 'bain't Red Spider mighty stuck up! Too proud to speak to nobody, now, seeming.'

Honor saw little of young Larry. Once or twice he made as though he would walk home with her from church, but she gave him no encouragement; he held little Charity's hand, and made Charity hold that of Martha, and kept Charity and Martha between her and the young man, breaking all familiar converse. She had not the heart to talk to him.

'You need not take on about Charles,' said her father one day. 'Every one knows that you are a good girl, and makes allowances for a soldier.'

'Disorderly ways,' answered Honor, 'are like infectious diseases. When one has an attack, it runs through the house.'

'Why do you not encourage folk to be friendly? You hold yourself aloof from all.'

Honor sighed.

'I cannot forget Charles, and the shame he is bringing on us. For me it matters little, but it matters much to the rest. The children will lose sense of fear at bad language, lies and bragging. Kate is a pretty girl, and some decent lad may take a fancy to her; but who would make a maid his wife who had such a brother?'

'Oh! as for that, young Larry Nanspian is after her. You should see how they go on together, tormenting and joking each other.'

Honor coloured and turned her face aside. She said nothing for a minute, then with composed voice and manner she went on.

'See the bad example set to Joe. He tries his wings to fly away from me, as is natural; boys resist being controlled by the apron. He sees his elder brother, he hears him, he copies him, and he will follow him down the road to destruction We must get Joe away into service unless we can make Charles go, which would be the better plan of the two.'

'Charles has been away for some years. We must not drive him out of the house now we have him home again.'

'Father, I wish you would be firm with him.'

'I—I!' he shook his head. 'I cannot be hard with the boy. Remember what he has gone through in India, in the wars. Look at his poor hand. Home is a place to which a child returns when no other house is open to it.'

Honor looked sadly at the carrier. No help was to be had from him.

'I suppose, father,' she said, 'that there are rights all round. If Charles comes home claiming the shelter of our roof and a place at our table, he is bound in some way. He has no right to dishonour the roof and disturb the table. I grudge him no pains to make him comfortable, but

I do expect he will not make it impossible for me to keep the home decent.'

'Of course, of course, Honor,' said the carrier, rubbing his palms slowly between his knees, and looking vacantly into the fire. 'That is reasonable.'

'And right,' said Honor. 'And, father, you should make a stand. Now, all the responsibility falls on me.'

'Oh, yes. I will make a stand; certainly, certainly,' said Luxmore. 'Now let us change the subject.'

'No,' answered the girl. 'I cannot, and I will not. Charles must be made to conduct himself properly. I will not allow the little ones to hear his profane talk, and see his devil-may-care ways. Mother committed them to me, and I will stand between them and evil. If it comes to a fight, we shall fight. All I wish is that the fight was not to be between brother and sister.' Her voice became hard, her brows contracted, her face became pale with intensity of feeling.

'There, there!' groaned Oliver Luxmore, 'don't make out matters worse than they are. A sheep looks as big as a cow in a fog. You see ghosts where I see thorn-trees. Be gentler with Charles, and not so peremptory. Men will not be ordered about by women. Charles is not a bad boy. There is meat on a trout as well as bones. All will come right in the end.'

Honor said no more. Her eyes filled; she stooped over her needlework to conceal them; her hand moved quickly, but the stitches were uneven.

'I will do something, I will indeed,' said Luxmore rising. He took his hat and went out, but returned quickly a few minutes later, agitated, and went through the room, saying hastily, 'Honor! he is coming, and—I think—drunk.'

Then he escaped into the back kitchen and out into the paddock in the rear where he kept his horse. That was all the help Honor was likely to get from him—to be forewarned.

Next moment two of the children flew up the steps frightened and heated.

'O, Honor! Charlie is tight!'

Honor stood up, folded her needlework, put it aside, and went to the door.

'Children,' she said, 'go behind into the field to father.' Then she went to the head of the steps and looked down.

She saw her brother coming on with a lurching walk, holding a stick, followed by a swarm of school-children, recently dismissed, who jeered, pelted him, and when he turned to threaten, dispersed to gather again and continue tormenting. Charles was not thoroughly drunk, but he was not sober. Honor's brow became blood-red for a moment, and her hand trembled on the rail; but the colour left her forehead again, and her hand was firm as she descended the steps.

At the sight of Honor Luxmore the children fell back, and ceased from their molestations.

'Halloo, Honor!' shouted Charles, staggering to the foot of the steps. 'A parcel of gadflies, all buzz and sting! I'll teach 'em to touch a soldier! Let me pass, Honor, and get away from the creatures.'

'No, Charles,' answered his sister, 'you do not pass.'

'Why not?'

'Because I will not let you—drunk.'

'I am not drunk, not at all. It is you who are in liquor. Let me pass.' He put his hand on the rail, and took a step up.

'You shall not pass!' she spoke coolly, resolutely.

'Curse you for a pig-headed fool,' said Charles, 'I'm not going to be stopped by such as you.'

'Such as I shall stop you,' answered Honor. 'Shame on you to dishonour the steps by which our mother went down to her burial! Verily, I saw her in my dreams, putting her hands over her face in her grave to hide the sight of her son.'

'Stand aside.'

'I will not budge!'

'I was a fool to come home,' muttered Charles, 'to be pickled in vinegar like walnuts. I wish I'd stayed away.'

'I wish you had, Charles, till you had learned to conduct yourself with decency.'

'I will not be preached to,' he growled; then becoming lachrymose, he said, 'I come home after having been away, a wanderer, for many years. I come home from bloody wars, covered with wounds, and find all against me. This is a heartless world. I did expect to find love at home, and pity from my sister.'

'I love and pity you,' said Honor, 'but I can only respect him who is respectable.'

'Let me pass!'

'I will not, Charles.'

Then he laid hold of her, and tried to pull her off the steps; but she had a firm grip of the rail, and she was strong.

The children in the lane, seeing the scuffle, drew near and watched with mischievous delight. Charles was not so tipsy that he did not know what he was about, not so far gone as to be easily shaken off. Honor was obliged to hold with both hands to the rail. He caught her round the waist, and slung her from side to side, whilst oaths poured from his lips. In the struggle her hair broke loose, and fell about her shoulders.

She set her teeth and her eyes glittered. Fire flamed in her cheeks. She was resolved at all costs not to let him go by. She had threatened that she would fight him, and now, before she had expected it, the fight was forced upon her.

Finding himself foiled, unable to dislodge her, and unable to pass her, Charles let go, went down the steps, and kicked and thrust at the support of the handrail, till he broke it down. Then, with a laugh of defiance, he sprang up the steps brandishing the post. But, when the rail gave way, Honor seized it, and ascending before him, facing him, stepping backward, she planted herself against the cottage door, with the rail athwart it, behind her, held with both hands, blocking the entrance.

Charles was forced to stay himself with the broken post he held, as he ascended the steps.

'Honor!' he shouted, 'get out of the way at once, I am dangerous when opposed.'

'Not to me,' she answered; 'I am not afraid of you, drunk or sober. You shall not cross this doorstep.'

He stood eyeing her, with the post half raised, threateningly. She met his unsteady gaze without flinching. Was there no one to see her there but the tipsy Charles and the frightened children? A pity if there was not. She was erect, dignified, with bosom expanded, as her bare arms were behind her. Her cheeks were brilliant with colour, her fallen hair, raining about her shoulders, blazed with the red evening sun on it, her large hazel eyes were also full of fire. Her bosom heaved as she breathed fast and hard. She wore a pale, faded print dress, and a white apron. Below, her red ankles and feet were planted firm as iron on the sacred doorstep of Home, that she protected.

As Charles stood irresolute, opposite her, the children in the lane, thinking he was about to strike her, began to scream.

In a moment Hillary Nanspian appeared, sprang up the steps, caught Charles by the shoulder, struck the post out of his hand, and dragging him down the steps, flung him his length in the road.

'Lie there, you drunken blackguard!' he said; 'you shall not stand up till you have begged your sister's pardon, and asked permission to sleep off your drink in the stable.'

XI
In the Linney

Next morning, when Charles Luxmore awoke, he found himself lying on the hay in the little 'linney,' or lean-to shed, of his father. The door was open and the sun streamed in, intense and glaring. In the doorway, on a bundle of straw, sat his sister Honor, knitting. The sun was shining in and through her golden hair, and the strong, fiery light shone through her hands, and nose, and lips, crimson—or seemed to do so. Charles watched her for some time out of his half-closed eyes, and confessed to himself that she was a fine, noble-looking girl, a girl for a brother to be proud of. Her profile was to the light, the nose straight, the lips sharp-cut, now expanded, then closed tight, as moved by her thoughts, and her hair shone like the morning clouds above the rising sun.

'What! sentinel, keeping guard?' shouted Charles, stretching his limbs and sitting up. 'In custody, am I? Eh?'

'I have brought you your breakfast, Charles,' answered Honor. 'There is a bowl of bread and milk at your elbow.'

He was hungry, so he took the bowl. His hair was ruffled, and full of strands of hay; he passed his hand over his face.

'I've had many a sleep in a barn before now,' he said; 'there are worse bedrooms, but there is one drawback. You can't smoke a pipe in one, or you run the chance of setting fire to bed and house. I did that once, and had a near scratch to escape before the flames roasted me. Best was, I managed to escape before any one was on the spot, so I was not taken up; suspicion fell on a labourer who had been dismissed a fortnight before.'

'And you said nothing?'

'Certainly not. Do you take me for a fool?'

Honor's lips contracted, so did her brow.

Charles put the spoon into the bread and milk, then, as he was setting it to his mouth, burst out laughing, and spilt the sop over his clothes.

'It was enough to make a fellow laugh,' he explained. 'To see last night how scared the kids were—Martha and Charity—and how they cut along when they saw me coming home.'

'This is not a cause for laughter. If you had a heart you would weep.'

'I thought I caught sight of father.'

'You did, but he also turned and left you. He could not face you as you were. You should be ashamed of yourself, Charles.'

'There, there!' he exclaimed impatiently, 'I will listen to no rebukes. I was not drunk, only a bit fresh.'

'Drunk or fresh matters little, you were not in a fit condition to come and what is more, I will not allow you to live in this cottage longer.'

'You will not?'

'No, I will not.'

'Who is to prevent me?'

'I will.'

'You!—and what if I force you out of the way, and go in and brave you?'

'You may go in, but I leave and take with me all the little ones. I have made up my mind what to do; I can work and earn enough to support the children, but I will not—no, I will not let them see you and hear you more.'

He looked at her. Her face was resolute. She was the girl to carry out her threat.

'I curse the day I came back to see your wry face,' he muttered, and rolled over on his side, away from her.

She made no reply. Her lips quivered. He did not see it, as he was no longer looking at the door.

'Home is home,' he said, 'and go where one will there are threads that draw one back to it.'

Honor was softened. 'I am glad, Charles, that you love home. If you love it, respect it.'

'Don't fancy that I came home out of love for you.'

Honor sighed.

'I came home to see how father fared about Coombe Park, and how mother was flourishing.'

'Well, Charles, I am glad you thought of father and mother. You must have a right heart, at ground. Mother is dead, but I know she shames over your bad conduct, and would rejoice were you to mend.'

'How do you know that? There is no postal communication with the other world, that I am aware of.'

'Never mind how I know it, but I do.'

'I was a fool to return. There is no kindness left in the world. If there were I should find a pinch at home, and pity from you.'

'Charles, if I have been harsh with you, it has been through your own fault. God, who reads all hearts, knows that I love you. But that, I love all the rest of my brothers and sisters, and now that mother is not here to see after them, whom have they got but myself to protect them? I defend them as a cat defends her kittens from a dog. Charles, I am sorry if I have been rough and unkind, and unsisterly to you, but indeed, indeed I cannot help myself. Mother laid the duty on me when she was dying. She caught my hand—so,' she grasped his wrist, and looking earnestly in his face, said, 'and laid it on me to be father and mother to the little ones. I bent over her and kissed her, and promised I would, and she died with her hand still holding my wrist. I feel her grip there to this day, whenever danger threatens the children. When you first came into the house, on your return, I felt her fingers close as tight on me as when she died. She is always with me, keeping me up to my duty. I cannot help myself, Charles; I must do what I know I ought; and I am sure it is wrong for me to allow you to remain with us longer. Consider, Charles, what the life is that you are now leading.'

'The life is all right,' said he moodily. 'I can pay my way. I have more brains than any of these clodhoppers round, and can always earn my livelihood.'

'Begin about it,' urged Honor.

'Time enough for that when the last copper is gone wherewith to stop a pipe and fill a can of ale.'

'O Charles! Charles!' exclaimed his sister, 'your own coppers are spent long ago. Now you are smoking the clothes off your little brothers' and sisters' backs, and drinking and squandering the little money I have for feeding them. For shame!' the blood rushed into her cheeks with sudden anger, as the injustice of his conduct presented itself before her vividly. 'Your father works that you may idle! It is a shame! It is a sin.'

'Hold your tongue!'

'I will not hold my tongue,' she answered hotly. 'You know how good, and gentle, and forbearing father is, how ready he is to give everything to his children, how unwilling to say to any one a harsh word, and you take advantage of his good nature; you, that should be building up the house, are tearing it down on the heads of all of us, father, Kate, Patience, Joe, Willy—do to little Temperance, all, all!'

'That is right, Honor, comb his head with a rake and the locks will lie smooth.'

Both Honor and Charles looked up. Hillary stood before them in the doorway. The girl had turned her face to her brother, and had not observed his approach. She was ill-pleased at his arrival. She wished no stranger to intermeddle with her family troubles.

'You here?' exclaimed Charles, starting to one knee. 'Mr. Larry Nanspian, I owe you something, and I shall repay it when the occasion comes. Not now, though I have a mind to it, because I have a headache. But I can order you off the premises. Get along, or I'll kick you.'

Larry gave a contemptuous shrug with his shoulders, and looked to Honor.

'Well, Honor, have you a good-morning for me?'

'I have ordered you off the premises,' shouted Charles.

'Shall I pitch him into the road again?' asked Larry of the girl.

Then Honor said, 'I did not ask your help yesterday, and I do not seek your interference now.'

Charles burst into a rude laugh. 'You have your answer, Mr. Larry,' he said; 'about face and away with you, and learn that there is one girl in the place whose head you have not turned.'

'If I am not wanted, of course I go,' said Hillary annoyed.

Then he walked away, whistling, with his hands in his pockets. 'There are more cherries on the tree than that on the topmost twig,' he said to himself in a tone of dissatisfaction. 'If Honor can't be pleasant others are not so particular.'

Larry Nanspian was a spoiled lad. The girls of Bratton made much of him. He was a fine young man, and he was heir to a good estate. The girls not only did not go out of their way to avoid him, but they threw themselves, unblushingly, ostentatiously in his path; and their efforts to catch him were supported by their mothers. The girls hung about the lanes after church hoping to have a word with him, and sighed and cast him languishing glances during Divine worship. Their mothers flattered him. This was enough to make the lad conceited. Only Honor kept away from him. She scarcely looked at him, and held him at a distance. The other girls accepted his most impudent sallies without offence; he did not venture a jest with Honor. Her refusal of the homage which he had come to regard as his due piqued him, and forced him to think of Honor more often than of any other girl in the place. He did not know his own mind about her, whether he liked or whether he disliked her, but he knew that he was chagrined at her indifference.

Sulky, he sauntered on to Broadbury, towards Wellon's Cairn. The moor was stretched around, unbroken by a hedge, or wall, or tree. Before him rose the Tumulus. 'Hah!' he said to himself, 'she was ready to talk to me here; we were to have been good friends, but that cursed White Hare brought us all ill-luck.'

As he spoke, to his surprise he saw something white emerge from the cutting in the side. He stood still, and in a moment Mrs. Veale leaped out of the hollow, went over the side, and disappeared down a dyke that ran in the direction of Langford.

The apparition and disappearance were so sudden, the sight of the woman so surprising, that Hillary was hardly sure he was in his senses, and not the prey to a hallucination. He was made very uncomfortable by what he had seen, and instead of going on towards the mound, he turned and walked away.

'This is wonderful,' he said. 'Whatever could take Mrs. Veale to Wellon's Cairn? If it were she—and I'd not take my oath on it—I'm too bewildered to guess her purpose.'

He halted and mused. 'I always said she was a witch, and now I believe it. She's been there after her devilries, to get some bones or dust of the gibbeted man, or a link of his chain, to work some further wickedness with. I'll see Honor again, I will, for all the airs she gives herself, and warn her not to sit on Wellon's mount. It's not safe.'

XII

Langford

Honor put on her hat and threw a kerchief over her shoulders, and took her little brother Willy by the hand.

'Whither are you going, Honor?' asked Kate.

'I am going to find a place for Charles, as he will not seek one for himself. I have turned him out of this house, and must secure him shelter elsewhere.'

'Who will have him?' asked Kate contemptuously. She was less forbearing with Charles than Honor. Honor did not answer immediately.

'Try Chimsworthy,' suggested Kate; 'Larry would put in a word for us.'

Honor slightly coloured. She put on her red cloak.

'I cannot, Kate. Larry and Charles have quarrelled.'

'Larry bears no grudges. I will answer for him.'

'I do not wish to ask a favour of the Nanspians.'

'Why not?'

Honor made no reply. She clasped the child's hand tightly and closed her lips. Then, without another word, she left the cottage. Kate shrugged her shoulders.

Honor went slowly up the lane to Broadbury; she did not speak to her little brother, her head was slightly bowed, she was deep in thought, and hectic spots of colour tinged her cheeks.

'What! Honor, in your scarlet!' exclaimed Larry. She looked up in surprise. He had come up to Broadbury the second time that day, drawn there irresistibly by desire to see Honor. He thought it probable, as the day was fine, that she would go there with her knitting.

'What has brought you to Broadbury in this array, Honor?' asked Hillary, standing before her, and intercepting her path.

'I am on my road to Langford,' answered the girl with composure.

'Take care, Honor, take care where you go. There is a witch there, Mrs. Veale; if you get in her bad books you will rue it. I have seen her to-day at Wellon's Cairn gathering the dead man's dust, out of which to mix some hell-potion.'

Honor shook her head.

'It is true,' said Hillary earnestly, 'she jumped and ran—and her ways were those of that White Hare we saw at the mound. Nothing will now persuade me that she was not that hare. Do not go on, Honor; leave Langford alone. No luck awaits you there.'

'Nonsense, Larry, you cannot have seen Mrs. Veale up there.'

'I tell you that I did. I saw something white hopping and running, and I am sure it was she in the hole scooped by the treasure-seekers.'

'What can she have wanted there?'

'What but the dust of old Wellon? And what good can she do with that? None—she needs it only for some devilry. Do not go near her, Honor; I have come here on purpose to warn you that the woman is dangerous.'

'I must go on,' said Honor. 'It is kind of you, Larry, but I have business which I must do at Langford. I have never harmed Mrs. Veale, and she will not want to hurt me. But now, Larry, let me say that I am sorry if I offended you this morning. I spoke rather rough, because I was afraid of a quarrel and a fight between you and Charles. Do not take it amiss. Now do not stay me, I must go forward.'

'I will let you go on one promise—that you will not cross Mrs. Veale!' He caught her hand.

'How can I give offence to her? She is nothing to me, nor I to her. You must really make way, Larry.'

He shook his head. 'I don't like it,' he said; but could not further stay her.

Langford lies under the brow of Broadbury, looking over the tossing sea-like expanse of hill and dale. It lies at a very considerable elevation, nearly a thousand feet above the sea, and to protect it from the weather is covered with slate, as though mail-clad. Few trees stand about it affording shelter. Honor walked through the yard to the door and thrice knocked. Very tardy was the reply. Mrs. Veale opened the door, and stood holding it with one hand, barring the entrance with her body and the other hand. She was in a light cotton dress, from which the colours had been washed. Her face, her eyes, her hair had the same bleached appearance. Her eyelashes were white, overhanging faded eyes, to which they gave a blinking uncertain look.

'What do you want?' asked the housekeeper, looking at her with surprise and with flickering eyes.

'I have come to see Mr. Langford,' answered Honor; 'is your master at home?'

'My *master,* oh yes!' with a sneer, 'my master is at home—my mistress not yet. Oh no! not yet.'

'I want to see him.'

'You do? Come, this is sharp, quick work. You follow one on another as April on March.'

Honor did not understand her. She thought the woman was out of her mind. She made no reply, but looking firmly at her, said, 'I will go into the kitchen and sit down till your master is disengaged. Is he in the house now?'

'You know he is, and you know who is with him.'

Honor drew her brother after her, and entered. She was too proud to give the woman words.

'What do you want? Where are you going?' asked the housekeeper, standing aside to let Honor pass; but casting at her a look so full of malevolence, that Honor turned down her thumb in her palm instinctively to counteract the evil eye. Honor took a kitchen chair and seated herself. 'I will wait here,' she said, 'till Mr. Langford can see me.'

Before the housekeeper could speak again men's voices were audible in the passage, and, to her astonishment, Honor recognised that of her father. She rose at once, and confronted him and Taverner Langford as they entered the kitchen.

'What—you here?' exclaimed Oliver Luxmore with undisguised astonishment. 'Why, Honor, what in the world has drawn you to Langford? I did not know that you and Mrs. Veale were friends.'

'I have come to speak to Mr. Langford,' was her reply, spoken quietly; 'but I am glad, father, that you are here, as I should prefer to speak before you. May we go into the parlour?'

She looked at Mrs. Veale as much as to say that she did not care to speak before witnesses.

'Mrs. Veale,' said Langford, with a sharp tone, 'I heard steps from the parlour door two minutes ago. I object to listeners at key-holes. Do you understand?'

He did not wait for an answer, but turned and led the way down the passage he and Luxmore had just emerged from.

Little Willy uttered a cry. 'Don't leave me with the old woman, please, please, Honor!'

'You shall come with me,' answered the girl, and she drew the child with her into the parlour.

'Here we are,' said Taverner, shutting the door. 'Take a seat, take a seat! The little boy can find a stool at the window.'

'Thank you, Mr. Langford, I will not detain you five minutes. I prefer to stand. I am glad my father is here. Doubtless he has come on the same matter as myself.'

The two men exchanged glances.

'I have come to ask you to try Charles,' she continued. 'Some little while ago you told father that you wanted a man to act as drover for you. I have not heard that you have met with such a servant. Try my brother Charles. He is doing no work now, and Satan sets snares in the way of the idle. If you will please to give him a chance, you will confer on us a great favour, and be doing a good work as well, for which the Lord will reward you.'

'That is what has brought you here?' asked the yeoman.

'Yes, sir.'

'Have you heard it said throughout the country that I am not a man to grant favours?'

'I do not heed what folks say. Besides, I know that this is not so. You have already acted very kindly to us. You lent father a very good horse.'

'Why have you not applied elsewhere? at Chimsworthy, for instance.'

'Because I do not wish to be beholden to the Nanspians, sir,' answered Honor.

'You do not approve of your sister keeping company with that Merry Andrew,' said Taverner approvingly.

'She does not keep company with him,' answered the girl gravely.

'At any rate she lets him dance after her, draws him on. Well, well! it is natural, perhaps. But don't advise her to be too eager. Young Larry is not so great a catch as some suppose, and as he and his father give out. Look at Chimsworthy—a wilderness of thistles, and rushes springing where grass grew to my recollection. There is no saying, some day you may be seated at Coombe Park, and then the Nanspians will be below you.'

'Coombe Park!' echoed Honor, looking at her father, then at old Langford. 'Surely, sir, you think nothing of that! Do not encourage father in that fancy; we never were and never will be at Coombe Park.'

'Honor!' exclaimed Oliver Luxmore, working his feet uneasily under the table, 'there you are wrong. The Luxmores have had it for many generations. You have only to look in the registers to see that.'

'Yes, father, some Luxmores have been there, but not our Luxmores as far as we know. I wish you would not trouble your head about Coombe Park. We shall never get it. I doubt if we have a thread of a right to it. If we have, I never saw it.'

'We shall see, we shall see,' said the carrier. 'Girls haven't got lawyers' minds, and don't follow evidence.'

'I have undertaken to go with your father to Lawyer Physick at Okehampton,' said Taverner Langford, 'and to help him to have his right examined.'

'Nothing can come of it but heart-breakings,' sighed Honor; 'father will slip certainties to seize shadows.'

'I have nothing to lose,' said Oliver, 'and much to gain!'

Honor knew it was in vain to attempt to disabuse him of his cherished delusion. She so far shared his views as to believe that the family had gentle blood in their veins, and were descended somehow, in some vague, undefined manner, from the Luxmores of Coombe Park, through, perhaps, some younger son of a junior branch, and she liked to suppose that the beauty and superiority of manner in her brothers and sisters were due to this, but she did not share in her father's expectations of recovering the property. Her understanding was too clear to harbour this.

'I will go back to what I asked of Mr. Langford,' she said, after a pause. 'Will you take my brother Charles into your service, sir? He wants a firm hand over him. He is not bad at heart, but he is infirm of purpose, easily led astray. If he were here with you, he would be far from the "Ring of Bells," and his work would sever him from idle companions.'

'So, you don't want him to be at Chimsworthy?'

'I do not desire to be under obligation there.'

'You have no objection to placing yourself under obligation to me?'

Honor did not like the tone. She did not understand his returning to the same point; she turned uneasily to her father, and asked him to put in a word for poor Charles.

'Mr. Langford is more likely to grant a boon to you than to me,' answered Oliver evasively.

'Sit down, Honor,' he said. 'You have remained standing the whole time you have been here.'

'I have been making a request,' she answered.

'The request is granted. Sit down.'

She was reluctant, yet unwilling to disoblige.

Oliver signed to her to take a place. She obeyed. She was uncomfortable. There was an indefinable something in the way in which the old yeoman looked at and addressed her, something equally indefinable in her father's manner, that combined to disturb her.

Mrs. Veale came in on some excuse, to ask her master a question, with her white eyelashes quivering. She cast a sidelong glance at Honor full of malice, as she entered. When she left the room she did not shut the door, and the girl saw her white face and flickering eyes turned towards her, watching her out of the darkness of the passage. She was for a moment spell-bound, but recovered herself when Taverner Langford, with an impatient exclamation, slammed the door.

'I shall be glad to be rid of the old prying cat,' he said.

'Is Mrs. Veale going to leave you?' asked Honor. Then she caught her father and Langford exchanging glances, and her brow became hot—she hardly knew wherefore.

'I am thinking of a change,' said the yeoman.

'I hope you are going to have as good a housekeeper,' said Honor; 'a better you cannot have.'

'Oh!' he laughed, 'a better, certainly, and—what is quite as certain—a prettier one. If I had not been sure of that; I would not have—' he checked himself and nodded to the carrier, who laughed.

Honor looked from one to the other inquiringly, then asked somewhat sternly, 'You would not have—what, Mr. Langford?'

'Humph! I would not have taken Charles.'

'What is the connection?' asked the girl.

'More things are connected than sleevelinks,' answered Langford. 'I would not have let your father have the horse if you were thriftless at home. I would not take Charles into service, unless I thought to find in him some of the qualities of the sister.'

'Put my qualities, such as they are, on one side,' said Honor roughly.

'That,' said Langford, looking across at Luxmore, 'that is not to be thought of.'

Then the carrier laughed nervously, and with a side glance at his daughter.

Honor coloured. She was offended, but unable to say at what. She put her hand on her little brother's head and stroked it nervously.

Then the yeoman began to talk to the carrier about his estate, the quality of the land, his cows and horses, his woods, his pastures, the money he was able to put away every year, and contrasted his style of farming with that of the Nanspians at Chimsworthy. As he spoke he fixed his eyes on Honor, to see if his wealth impressed her. But her face expressed no concern. It was clouded; she was thinking, not listening.

All at once the insinuations of Mrs. Veale rushed into her mind. She saw her meaning. She connected that with the looks of the two men. Blood rushed to her face. She sprang to her feet. The room swam before her eyes.

'I must go,' she said. 'I am wanted at home.'

XIII
The Revel

If to Sally in our alley and the apprentice who loved her, 'Of all the days within the week there was no day but one day,' so to all the maids and all the lads in country villages, in olden times there was no day in all the year that might compare with the day of the village Revel.

The Revel is now a thing of the past, or lingers on, a limp and faded semblance of the robust festival that fifty years ago was looked forward to through half the year, and looked back on through the other half, and formed the topic of conversation for the entire twelve months.

On Revel day horse-races were run, got up by the village taverner, for a plated mug or a punch ladle; wrestling matches were played for a champion belt, booths were set up in streets of canvas and board for the sale of brooches, ribbons, toys, sweetstuff, and saffron-cakes. There were merry-go-rounds, peep-shows, menageries, and waxworks. The cheap-jack was never wanting, the focus of merriment.

In and about 1849 the commons were enclosed on which the races had been run, and the tents pitched, and gipsies had encamped. Magistrates, squires, parsons, and police conspired against Revels, routed them out of the field, and supplied their places with other attractions—cottage-garden shows, harvest thanksgivings, and school teas.

Possibly there were objectionable features in those old Revels which made their abolition advisable, but the writer remembers none of these. He saw them through the eyes of a child, and recalls the childish delight they afforded.

The day was clear and sunny. People streamed into Bratton Clovelly from the country round, many on foot, others in gigs and carts, all in gayest apparel. Honor had dressed the children neatly, had assumed her scarlet cloak, and stood at the cottage door turning the key ready to depart with the little eager company, when the tramp of a horse's hoof was heard, and Larry Nanspian drew up before the house. He was driving his dappled cob in the shafts of a two-wheeled tax-cart.

'What, Larry!' exclaimed Kate, 'mounted on high to display the flowery waistcoat? Lost your legs that you cannot walk a mile?'

'Not bit, sharp-tongue,' answered the young man, good-naturedly. 'I have come round for Honor and you and the little ones.'

'We have feet, sixteen among us.'

'But the tiny feet will be tired with trotting all day. You will have fairings moreover to bring home.'

'Thank you for the kind thought, Larry,' said Honor, softened by his consideration and by the pleasant smile that attended his words. 'Kate and I will walk, but we accept your offer for the children.'

'I cannot take them without you,' said the young man. 'I hold the whip with one hand and the reins with the other. I have not a third wherewith to control a load of wriggling worms.'

'Jump in, Honor,' said Kate, 'sit between me and the driver, to keep the peace.'

The eldest sister packed the children in behind and before, then, without more ado, ascended the seat by Larry, and was followed by Kate, with elastic spring.

'Heigho!' exclaimed the young man, 'I reckon no showman at the Revel has half so fine wares as myself to exhibit.'

'What, the waistcoat?' asked Kate, leaning forward to look in his face.

'No, not the waistcoat,' answered he; 'cutlery, keen and bright.'

'Your wit must have gone through much sharpening.'

'I do not allude to my wit. I mean the pretty wares beside me.'

'But, driver, the wares are not and never will be yours.'

As they drew near Bratton they heard a shout from behind, and turning saw Taverner Langford driving in, with Mrs. Veale beside him, at a rattling pace. Larry drew aside to let them pass; as they went by Taverner looked keenly at Honor, and Mrs. Veale cast her a spiteful glance, then turned to her master and whispered something.

'Upon my word!' exclaimed Larry, 'I've a mind to play a lark. Say nothing, girls, but don't be surprised if we give Uncle Langford a hare-hunt.'

He drew rein and went slow through the street of the 'church town.' The street and the open space before the church gate were full of people. It was, moreover, enlivened with booths. Larry was well content to appear in state at the fair, driving instead of walking like a common labourer, and driving with two such pretty girls as Honor and Kate at his side. He contrasted his company with that of his uncle. 'I wonder my uncle don't get rid of that Mrs. Veale. No wonder he has turned sour with her face always before him.' He shouted to those who stood in the road to clear the way; he cracked his whip, and when some paid no attention brought the lash across their shoulders. Then they started aside, whether angry or good-humoured mattered nothing to the thoughtless lad.

He drew up before the 'Ring of Bells,' cast the reins to the ostler, jumped out, and helped the sisters to descend, then lifted the children down with a cheerful word to each.

The little party strolled through the fair, Honor holding Charity by her left and Temperance by her right hand; but the crowd was too great for the youngest to see any thing. Honor stooped and took the little girl on her right arm, but immediately Larry lifted the child from her to his shoulder.

'See!' whispered Joe, holding a coin under Kate's eyes, 'Larry Nanspian gived me this.'

'And I have something too from him,' said Pattie.

'And so have I,' whispered Willy.

Honor pretended not to hear, but she was touched, and looked with kindly eyes at the young man. He had his faults, his foolish vanity; but there was good in him, or he would not trouble himself about the little ones. She had not been able to give the children more than a penny each for fairing. The village was thronged. The noise was great. The cheap-jack shouted in a voice made hoarse by professional exercise. The ringers had got to the bells in the church tower. At a stall was a man with a gun, a target, and a tray of nuts, calling 'Only a halfpenny a shot!' There was Charles there trying the gun, and his failures to hit the bull's-eye elicited shouts of laughter, which became more boisterous as he lost his temper. The barrel was purposely bent to prevent a level shot reaching the mark. A boy paraded gaudy paper-mills on sticks that whirled in the wind—only one penny each. A barrel organ ground forth, 'The flaxen-headed Plowboy,' and a miserable blinking monkey on it held out a tin for coppers. Honor was so fully engrossed in the children, watching that they did not stray, get knocked over or crushed, that she had not attention to give to the sights of the fair; but Kate was all excitement and delight. Larry kept near the sisters, but could not say much to them: the noise was deafening and little Temperance exacting.

Presently the party drew up before a table behind which stood a man selling rat poison. A stick was attached to the table, and to this stick was affixed a board, above the heads of the people, on which was a pictorial representation of rats and mice expiring in attitudes of mortal agony. The man vended also small hones. He took a knife, drew the edge of the blade over his thumb to show that it was blunt, then swept it once, twice, thrice, this way, that way, on the bit of stone, and see! he plucked a hair from his beard, and cut, and the blade severed it. Fourpence for a small stone, sixpence, a shilling, according to sizes. The coins were tossed on the table, and the hones carried away.

'What is it, ma'am—a hone?' asked the dealer.

'No, the poison.'

A white arm was thrust between those who lined the table. Hillary turned, and saw Mrs. Veale.

'Keep it locked up, ma'am. There's enough in that packet to poison a regiment.'

Whether a regiment of soldiers or of rats he did not explain.

At the crockery stall Larry halted, and passed Temperance over to Honor. Now his reason for driving in the spring-cart became apparent. He had been commissioned to purchase a supply of pots, and mugs, and dishes, and plates, for home use. Honor also made purchases at this stall, and the young man carried them for her to his cart, as well as his own supply. Then she lingered at a drapery stall, and bought some strong material for frocks for the youngest sisters. Whilst she was thus engaged, Larry went to a stall of sweetstuff, presided over by a man in white apron, with copper scales, and bought some twisted red and white barbers' poles of peppermint. Immediately the atmosphere about the little party was impregnated with the fragrance of peppermint.

A few steps beyond was a menagerie. A painted canvas before the enclosure of vans represented Noah's ark, with the animals ascending a plank, and entering it by a door in the side. In another compartment was a picture of a boa-constrictor catching a negro, and opening his jaws to swallow him. Over this picture was inscribed, 'Twine, gentle evergreen,' and the serpent was painted emerald. In another compartment, again, was a polar scene, with icebergs and white bears, seals and whales.

'Oh, we must see the wild beasts!' exclaimed Kate.

A consultation ensued. Larry wished to treat the whole party, but to this Honor would not agree. Finally, it was decided that Kate, Joe, and Pattie should enter, and that Honor should remain without with the children. Accordingly the three went in with Larry, and presently returned disappointed and laughing. The menagerie had resolved itself into a few moulting parrots, a torpid snake in a blanket, two unsavoury monkeys, and an ass painted with stripes to pass as a zebra.

Adjoining the menagerie was another exhibition, even more pretentious. Three men appeared before it on a platform, one with a trumpet, another with cymbals, the third with a drum. Then forth leaped clown, harlequin, and columbine, and danced, cut jokes, and went head over heels. The clown balanced a knife on his nose; then bang! toot, toot! clash! bang, bang, bang! from the three instruments, working the children into the wildest speculation. Honor had spent the money laid aside for amusement, and could not afford to take her party in, and she would accept no further favours from Larry.

Just then up came Charles.

'Halloo, mates! you all here!' he shouted, elbowing his way to them. 'That is prime. I will treat you; I've a yellow boy,' he spun a half-sovereign in the air and caught it between both palms. 'Come along, kids. I'm going to treat half a dozen young chaps as well. Shall I stand for you, Larry?' he asked contemptuously, 'or have the thistles and rushes sold so well you can afford to treat yourself?'

Larry frowned. 'I see my father yonder signing to me,' he said. 'I must go to him.'

Then Hillary worked his way to the rear, offended at the insolence of Charles, red in the face, and vowing he would not do another kindness to the family.

Old Nanspian was in the long-room of the 'Ring of Bells,' at the window. He had caught sight of his son, whose flowered satin waistcoat was conspicuous, and was beckoning to him with his clay pipe; he wanted to know whether he had bought the crookery—*vulgo* 'cloam'—as desired, and what he had paid for it.

'Come on, you fellows!' called Charles to some of his companions. 'How many are you? Six, and myself, and the two girls, that makes nine sixpences, and the little uns at half-price makes five threepences. Temperance is a baby and don't count. That is all, five-and-nine shovel out the change, old girl, four-and-three.'

He threw down the gold coin on the table, where a gorgeous woman in red and blue and spangles, wearing a gilt foil crown and huge earrings, was taking money and giving greasy admission tickets. The circus was small. The seats were one row deep, deal planks laid on trestles. Only at one end were reserved places covered with red baize for the nobility, gentry, and clergy, who, as a bill informed the public, greedily patronised the show. On this occasion these benches were conspicuously empty. The performers appeared in faded fleshings, very soiled at the elbows and knees the paint on the faces was laid on coarsely; the sawdust in the ring was damp and smelt sour.

The clown cut his jests with the conductor, carried off his cap, and received a crack of the whip. He leaped high in the air, turned a somersault, and ran round the arena on hands and feet, peering between his legs.

A dappled horse was led out, and the columbine mounted and galloped round the ring. Every now and then the hoofs struck the enclosing boards, and the children shrank against Honor and Kate in terror. Then a spray of sawdust was showered over the lads, who roared with laughter, thinking it a joke.

A second horse was led out to be ridden by the harlequin, but the clown insisted on mounting it, and was kicked off. Then the harlequin ran across the area, whilst the horse was in full career, and leaped upon its back, held the columbine's hand, and round and round they went together. All was wretchedly poor. The jokes of the clown were as threadbare as the silks, and as dull as the spangles on the equestrians. Poverty and squalor peered through the tawdry show. But an audience of country folk is uncritical and easily pleased. The jests were relished, the costumes admired, and the somersaults applauded. All at once a commotion ensued. The queen in red and blue, who had sold the tickets of admission, appeared in a state of loud and hot excitement, calling for the manager and gesticulating vehemently. The performance was interrupted. The horses of harlequin and columbine were restrained, and were walked leisurely round the arena, whilst the lady in gauze (very crumpled) seated herself on the flat saddle and looked at the spectators, who curiously scrutinised her features and compared opinions as to her beauty. Presently the clown ran to the scene of commotion. The queen was in very unregal excitement, shaking her head, with her pendant earrings flapping, very loud and vulgar in voice; some of the audience crowded about the speakers.

Then Honor was aware that faces and fingers were pointed towards the bench which she and her party occupied, and in another moment the manager, the crowned lady-manageress, the clown, now joined by the harlequin, who had given his horse to a boy, and a throng of inquisitive spectators, came down—some across the arena, others stumbling over the deal benches—towards the little party.

'That's he!' shouted the lady in crimson and blue, shaking her black curls, puffing with anger, and indicating with a fat and dirty hand. 'That's the blackguard who has cheated us.' She pointed at Charles.

The columbine drew rein and stood her horse before the group, looking down on it. She had holes in her stockings, and the cherry silk of her bodice was frayed. Kate saw that.

'Look here, you rascal! What do you mean by trying to cheat us poor artists, with horses and babies to feed, and all our wardrobe to keep in trim, eh? What do you mean by it?'

Then the clown in broad cockney, 'What do you mean by it, eh? Some one run for the constable, will you? Though we be travelling showmen we're true-born Britons, and the law is made to protect all alike.'

'What is the matter?' asked Honor rising, with the frightened Temperance in her arms clinging to her neck and screaming, and Charity and Martha holding her skirts, wrapping themselves in her red cloak and sobbing.

'Ah, you may well ask what is the matter!' exclaimed the queen. 'If that young chap belongs to you in any way, more's the pity.'

'It is an indictable offence,' put in the manager. 'It is cheating honest folk; that is what it is.'

Charles burst out laughing.

'I've a right to pay you in your own coin, eh?' he said contemptuously, thrusting his hands into his pockets, and planting a foot on the barrier.

'What do you mean by our own coin?' asked the angry manageress, planting her arms akimbo.

'Giving false for false,' mocked Charles.

'It is insulting of us he is!' exclaimed the columbine, from her vantage post. 'And he calls himself a gentleman.'

'Pray what right have you to invite the public to such a spectacle as this?' asked Charles. 'You have only a couple of screws for horses, and an old girl of forty for columbine, a harlequin with the lumbago and a clown without wit—and you don't call this cheating?'

'Turn him out!' cried the lady in crumpled muslin, 'it's but twenty-three I am.'

'What is this all about?' asked Honor, vainly endeavouring to gather the cause of the quarrel and compose the frightened children at the same time. The bystanders, indignant at the disparagement of the performance, hissed. All those on the farther side of the arena, losing their awe of the sawdust, came over it, crowding round the gauzy columbine and her horse, asking what the row was about, and getting no answer.

The columbine was obliged to use her whip lightly to keep them off. Boys were picking spangles off the saddle cloth, and pulling hairs out of the mane of the horse.

'How many was it? Fourteen persons let in?' asked the manager.

'And I gave him back change, four-and-three,' added the manageress.

'You shall have your cursed change,' said Charles. 'Get along with you all. Go on with your wretched performance. Here are four shillings, the boys shall scramble for the pence when I find them.' He held out some silver.

'No, I won't take it. You shall pay for all the tickets,' said the woman. 'You ain't a-going to defraud us nohows if I can help it. Let's see, how many was you? Four-and-three from ten makes five-and-nine'

'I can't do it,' said Charles, becoming sulky. 'If you were the fool to accept a brass token you must pay for the lesson, and be sharper next time. I have no more money.'

'Cheat! cheat! Passing bad money!' the bystanders groaned, hissed, hooted. Charles waxed angry and blazed red. He cursed those who made such a noise, he swore he would not pay a halfpenny, he had no money. They might search his pockets. They might squeeze him. They would get nothing out of him. They might keep the brass token, and welcome, he had nothing else to give them. He turned his pockets out to show they were empty.

The whole assembly, performers in tights, muslin, velvets, ochre and whitening, the spectators—country lads with their lasses, farmers and their wives—were crushed in a dense mass about the scene of altercation. Many of the lads disliked Charles for his swagger and superiority, and were glad to vent their envy in groans and hisses. The elder men thought it incumbent on them to see that justice was done; they called out that the money must be paid.

Charles, becoming heated, cast his words about, regardless whom he hurt. The manager stared, the queen screamed, the clown swore, and columbine, who held a hoop, tried to throw it over the head of the offender, and pull him down over the barrier. By a sudden movement the young man wrenched the whip from the hand of the manager, and raising it over his head threatened to clear a way with the lash. The people started back. Then into the space Honor advanced.

'What has he done? I am his sister. Show me the piece of money.'

'Look at that—and turn yeller,' exclaimed the manager's wife. 'Darn it now, if I ain't a-gone and broke one o' them pearl drops in my ear. Look at the coin,' she put the token into the girl's hand. 'What do yer say to that?' Then she whisked her head of curls about as if to overtake her ear and see the wreck of pearl-drop—silvered glass which had been crushed in the press. 'And this also, young man, comes of yer wickedness. What am I to do with one pendant? Can't wear it in my nose like an Injun. Now then, young woman in scarlet, what do yer call that?'

Honor turned the coin over in her palm.

'This is a brass tradesman's token,' she said; 'it is not money. We stand in your debt five-and-ninepence. I have nothing by me. You must trust me; you shall be paid.'

'No, no we won't trust none of you,' said the angry woman. 'We ain't a-going to let you out without the money. Pay or to prison you walk. Someone run for the constable, and I'll give him a ticket gratis for this evening's entertainment.'

Then many voices were raised to deprecate her wrath 'This is Honor.' 'Trust Honor as you'd trust granite.' 'Honor in name and Honor in truth.' 'Honor never wronged a fly.' 'Red spider is a lucky insect.' 'Why don't the red spider spin money now?'

'Leave her alone, she's good as gold. She can't help if the brother is a rascal.'

But though many voices were raised in her favour, no hands were thrust into pockets to produce the requisite money.

Honor looked about. She was hot, and her brow moist; her lips quivered; a streak of sun was on her scarlet cloak and sent a red reflection over her face.

'We will not be beholden to you, madam,' she said, with as much composure as she could muster. Then she unloosed her cloak from her neck and from the encircling arms of Temperance. 'There,' she said, 'take this; the cloth is good. It is worth more money than what we owe you. Keep it till I come or send to redeem it.'

She put the scarlet cloak into the woman's hands, then turned, gathered the children about her, and looking at those who stood in front, said with dignity, 'I will trouble you to make way. We will interrupt the performance no longer.'

Then, gravely, with set lips and erect head, she went out, drawing her little party after her, Kate following, flushed and crying, and Charles, with a swagger and a laugh and jest to those he passed, behind Kate.

When they came outside, however, Charles slunk away. The six young men whom Charles had treated remained. They had worked their way along the benches to dissociate themselves from the party of the Luxmores, and put on a look as if they had paid for their own seats. 'We needn't go, for sure,' whispered one to another. 'We be paid for now out of Miss Honor's red cloak.'

XIV
The Lamb-Killer

Honor could not recover herself at once. Her heart beat fast and her breathing was quick. Her hands that clasped the children twitched convulsively. She looked round at Charles before he slipped away, and their eyes met. His expression rapidly changed, his colour went, his eyes fell before those of his sister. He drew his cap over his face, and elbowed his way through the crowd out of sight.

Honor felt keenly what had occurred; she was the sister of a rogue; the honourable name of Luxmore was tarnished. How would her father bear this? This, the family honour, was the one thing on which he prided himself. And what about Charles? Would not he be forced to leave the place she had found for him? Would Taverner Langford keep in his employ a man who cheated?

But Honor took a more serious view of the occurrence than the general public. Popular opinion was not as censorious as her conscience. Those whom Charles had attempted to defraud were strangers—vagrants belonging to no parish, and without the pale, fair game for a sharp man to overreach. If the public virtue had protested loudly in the show, it was not in the interests of fair dealing, but as an opportunity of annoying a braggart.

Honor, wounded and ashamed, shrank from contact with her acquaintances, and with Kate worked her way out of the throng, away from the fair, and home, without seeing more of Larry.

Kate took Charles's misconduct to heart in a different way from Honor; she was angry, disappointed because her pleasure was spoiled, and fretted. But the children, as they trotted homewards, were not weary of talking of the wonders they had seen and the enjoyment they had had.

In the evening Hillary drove up with his spring-cart, and called the girls out to take their fairings from his trap, some crocks, a roll of drapery, and some other small matters. Hillary was cheerful and full of fun. He repeated the jokes of the cheap-jack, and told of the neighbours that had been taken in. He mentioned whom he had met, and what he had seen. He allowed the dappled horse to stand in the road, with the reins on the ground, whilst, with one foot planted on the steps, he lingered chatting with the girls before their door. He was so bright and amusing that Kate forgot her vexation and laughed. Even the grave Honor was unable to forbear a smile. Of the disturbance in the circus caused by Charles he said nothing, and Honor felt grateful for his tact. He remained talking for half an hour. He carried the girls' parcels into the cottage for them, and insisted on a kiss from the tiny ones. It almost seemed as if he were tarrying for something—an opportunity which did not offer but this did not occur to the girls. They felt his kindness in halting to cheer them. Their father was not yet returned from the fair. They were not likely to see Charles again that day.

'By the way, Honor,' said Larry, 'you have some lambs, have you not?'

'Yes, five.'

'Can you fasten them and the ewes in at night?'

'No—we have no place. But why? They will not take hurt at this time of the year.'

'Don't reckon on that,' said the young man; 'I've heard tell there is a lamb-killer about. Farmer Hegadon lost three, and one went from Swaddledown last night. Have you not heard? Watches must be set. None can tell whose dog has taken to lamb-killing till it is seen in the act.'

'A bad business for us if we lose our lambs,' said Honor. 'We reckon on selling them and the ewes in the fall, to meet our debt to Mr. Langford for the horse.'

'Then forewarned is forearmed. Lock them up.'

'It can't be done, Larry. You can't pocket your watch when you're without a pocket.'

'In that case I hope the lamb-killer will look elsewhere. That is all. Good-night. But before I go mind this. If you have trouble about your lambs, call on me. I'll watch for you now you have not Charles at your command. We're neighbours and must be neighbourly.'

'Thank you heartily, Larry. I will do so.'

Then the lad went away, whistling in his cart, but as he went he turned and waved his hand to the sisters.

The children were tired and put to bed. Kate was weary and soon left. Honor had to sit up for her father, whose van was in request that day to convey people and their purchases from the fair to their distant homes. After Oliver had come in and had his supper, Honor put away the plates, brushed up the crumbs, set the chairs straight, and went to bed. Kate and the children were sound asleep. Honor's brain was excited, and she kept awake. She was unobserved now, and could let her tears flow. She had borne up bravely all day; the relaxation was necessary for her now. Before her family and the world Honor was reserved and restrained. She was forced to assume a coldness that was not natural to her heart. There was not one person in the house who could be relied on. Her father was devoid of moral backbone. He remembered the commissions of his customers, but his memory failed respecting his duties to his children and the obligations of home. Kate had too sharp a tongue and a humour too capricious to exercise authority. She set the children by the ears. As for the little ones, they were too young to be supposed to think. So Honor had to consider for her father and the other seven inmates of the cottage, also of late for Charles—to have a head to think for nine creatures who did not think for themselves. There was not one of the nine who stood firm, who was not shiftless. There are few occupations more trying to the temper than the setting up of nine-pins on a skittle-floor. Honor did not become querulous, as is the manner of most women who have more duties to discharge than their strength allows. She was over-taxed, but she sheltered herself under an assumption of coldness. Some thought her proud, others unfeeling. Kate could not fathom her. Oliver took all she did as a matter of course. He neither spared her nor applauded her. Perhaps no one in the parish was so blind to her excellence as her father. Kate was his favourite daughter.

Honor dried her tears on the pillow. What would the end be? Kate was at her side fast asleep. Honor leaned on her elbow and looked at her sleeping sister. The moon was shining. A muslin blind was drawn across the window, but a patch of light was on the whitewashed wall, and was brilliant enough to irradiate the whole chamber. Kate's light silky hair was ruffled about her head. She lay with one arm out, and the hand under her head; her delicate arm was bare. Honor looked long at her; her lips quivered, she stooped over Kate and kissed her, and her lips quivered no more. 'How pretty she is,' she said to her own heart; 'no wonder he went away whistling "Kathleen Mavourneen."'

All at once Honor started, as though electrified. She heard the sheep in the paddock making an unwonted noise, and recalled what Larry had said. In a moment she was out of bed, and had drawn aside the window-blind. The sheep and lambs were running wildly about. Some leaped at the hedge, trying to scramble up and over; others huddled against the gate leading to the lane. Honor opened the casement and put forth her head. Then she saw a dark shadow sweep across the field, before which the clustered sheep scattered.

Honor slipped on a few garments, descended the stair, opened the kitchen door, and went forth armed with a stick. The lamb-killer was in the paddock, chasing down one of the flock that he had managed to separate from the rest. Honor called, but her voice was unheeded or unheard, owing to the bleating of the frightened sheep. She ran through the dewy grass, but her pace was as nothing to that of the dog. The frightened lamb fled from side to side, and up and down, till its powers were exhausted; and then it stood piteously bleating, paralysed with terror, and the dog was at its throat and had torn it before Honor could reach the spot.

When she approached the dog leaped the hedge and disappeared through a gap in the bushes at the top. The girl went about the field pacifying the sheep, calling them, and counting them. They came about her skirts, pressing one on another, bleating, entreating protection, interfering with her movements. Two of the lambs were gone. One she had seen killed; a second was missing. She searched and found it; it had been overrun and had got jammed between two rails. In its efforts to escape, it had become injured. Its life was spent with exhaustion and fear, but it was not quite dead. It still panted. She disengaged the little creature, and carried it in her arms into the house, followed by the agitated ewes, whom she could hardly drive back from the garden gate.

Honor did not expect the dog to return that night, but she sat up watching for a couple of hours, and then returned to her bedroom, though not to sleep.

Here was a fresh trouble come upon the family. The loss of two lambs, in their state of poverty, was a serious loss, and she could not be sure that this was the end. The dog might return another night and kill more, and that was a crushing loss to poor people.

Next morning, when Kate and the children heard the news, their distress was great. Many tears were shed over the dead lambs. Kate was loud in her indignation against those who let their dogs rove at night. She was sure it was done on purpose, out of malice. It was impossible to suppose that the owner of a lamb-killer was ignorant of the proclivities of his dog. If they could only find out whose dog it was they would make him pay for the mischief.

'I suppose, father, you will sit up to-night and watch for the brute.'

'I—I!' answered the carrier. 'What will that avail? I never shot anything in my life but one sparrow, and that I blew to pieces. I rested my gun-barrel on the shiver (bar) of a gate, and waited till a sparrow came to some crumbs I had scattered. Then I fired, and a splash of blood and some feathers were all that remained of the sparrow. No, I am no shot. The noise close to my ear unnerves me. Besides, I am short-sighted. No; if the dog takes the lambs, let him, I cannot prevent it.'

'But you must sit up, father.'

'What can I do? If I saw the dog I should not know whose 'twas. Honor saw it, she can say whose it was.'

'I do not know. It struck me as like Mr. Langford's Rover, but I cannot be sure; the ash-trees were between the moon and the meadow, and flickered.'

'Oh! if it be Rover we are all right.'

'How so, father?'

'Langford will pay if his dog has done the damage.'

'He must be made to pay,' said Kate. 'He won't do it if he can scrape out.'

'I cannot be sure it was Rover,' said Honor. 'I saw a dark beast, but the ash flickered in the wind, and the flakes of moonlight ran over the grass like lambs, and the shadows like black dogs. I was not near enough to make sure. Unless we can swear to Rover, we must be content to lose.'

'Mr. Langford will not dispute about a lamb or two,' said Oliver, rubbing his ear.

'Then he will be different in this to what he is in everything else,' said Kate.

'He won't be hard on us,' said her father. Honor was accustomed to see him take his troubles easily, but he was unwontedly, perplexingly indifferent now, and the loss was grave and might be graver.

'I will watch with you to-night, Honor,' said Kate. 'And what is more, I will swear to Rover, if I see the end of his tail. Then we can charge the lambs at a pound a-piece to old Langford.'

'As for that,' said the father, with a side-glance at his eldest daughter, 'Mr. Langford—don't call him old Langford any more, Kate, it's not respectful—Mr. Langford won't press for the horse. It lies with you whether we have him for nothing or have to return him.'

He spoke looking at Honor, but he had addressed Kate just before. The latter did not heed his words. Honor had been crossing the room with a bowl in her hands. She stood still and looked at him. A question as to his meaning rose to her lips, but she did not allow it to pass over them. She saw that a knowing smile lurked at her father's mouth-corners, and that he was rubbing his hands nervously. The subject was not one to be prosecuted in the presence of her brothers and sisters. She considered a moment, then went into the back kitchen with the bowl. She would make her father explain himself when they were together alone.

Dark and shapeless thoughts passed through her mind, like the shadows of the ash foliage in the moonlight. She was full of undefined apprehension of coming trouble. But Honor had no time to give way to her fears. There was no leisure for an explanation. The dead lambs had to be skinned and their meat disposed of.

Honor was busily engaged the whole morning. She was forced to concentrate her mind on her task, but unable to escape the apprehension which clouded her. It did not escape her that her father's manner changed, as soon as the children were despatched to school and Kate had gone forth. He became perceptibly nervous. He was shy of being in the room with Honor, and started when she spoke to him. He pretended to look for means of fastening up the flock for the night, but he went about it listlessly. His playful humour had evaporated; he seemed to expect to be taken to task for his words, and to dread the explanation. His troubled face cleared when he saw Hillary Nanspian appear at the top of the hedge that divided the Chimsworthy property from the carrier's paddock. The young man swung himself up by a bough, and stood on the hedge parting some hazel-bushes.

'What is this I hear? The lamb-killer been to you last night?'

'Yes, Larry, and I am trying to find how we may pen the sheep in out of reach. I've only the linney, and that is full.'

'Are you going to sit up?'

'No, Larry, I am not a shot, and like a beetle at night.'

'I'll do it. Where are Kate and Honor? I promised them I would do it, and I keep my word. Little Joe tells me Honor thinks the dog was Rover. What a game if I shoot Uncle Taverner's dog! I hope I may have that luck. Expect me. I will bring my gun to-night.'

XV

A Bolt from the Blue

HONOR'S KITCHEN WORK WAS DONE. She came to her father after Larry Nanspian had departed, and said, 'Now, father, I want to know your meaning, when you said that it lay with me whether you should keep the horse or not?'

Then she seated herself near the door, with a gown of little Pattie's she was turning.

'It was so to speak rigmarole,' answered Oliver colouring, and pretending to plait a lash for his whip.

She shook her head. 'You did not speak the words without purpose.'

'We lead a hard life,' said Oliver evasively. 'That you can't deny and keep an honest tongue.'

'I do not attempt to deny it,' she said, threading a needle at the light that streamed in through the open door. The carrier looked at her appealingly. Behind her, seen through the door, was a bank of bushes and pink foxgloves, 'flopadocks' is the local name. He looked at the sunlit picture with dreamy eyes.

'I shouldn't wonder,' he said, 'if there was a hundred flowers on that there tallest flopadock.'

'I should not either,' said Honor without looking off her work. Then ensued another pause.

Presently the carrier sighed and said, 'It be main difficult to make both ends meet. The children are growing up. Their appetites increase. Their clothes get more expensive. The carrying business don't prosper as it ought. Kate, I reckon, will have to go into service, we can't keep her at home; but I don't like the notion—she a Luxmore of Coombe Park.'

'We are not Luxmores of Coombe Park, but Luxmores out of it,' said Honor.

'Coombe Park should be ours by right, and it rests with you whether we get our rights.'

'How so? This is the second hint you have given that much depends on me. What have I to do with the recovery of Coombe Park? How does the debt for the horse rest with me?'

'It is a hard matter to be kept out of our rights,' said Oliver. 'A beautiful property, a fine house and a fish pond—only a hundred pounds wanted to search the registers to get it.'

'No hundred pounds will come to us,' said Honor. 'The clouds drop thunderbolts, not nuggets. So as well make up our minds to be where we are.'

'No, I can't do that,' said the carrier, plaiting vigorously. 'You haven't got a bit of green silk, have you, to finish the lash with?'

'Whether from wishing or from working, no hundred pounds will come,' continued the girl.

'And see what a rain of troubles has come on us,' said the carrier. 'First comes your poor mother's death, then the horse, now the lambs, and on top of all poor Charles.'

'More the reason why we should put aside all thought of a hundred pounds.'

'Providence never deserts the deserving,' said Luxmore. 'I'm sure I've done my duty in that state o' life in which I am. It is darkest before dawn.'

'I see no daylight breaking.'

'Larry Nanspian makes great count of Kate,' mused Luxmore, and then abruptly, 'confound it! I've plaited the lash wrong, and must unravel it again.'

'What will come of Larry's liking for Kate? Will that bring us a hundred pounds and Coombe Park?' asked Honor bluntly.

'I can't quite say that. But I reckon it would be a rare thing to have her settled at Chimsworthy.'

'No,' said Honor, 'not unless Larry alters. Chimsworthy grows weeds. The old man is more given to boasting than to work. Larry cares more to be flattered than to mind the plough.'

'I won't have a Luxmore of mine marry out of her station. We must hold up our heads.

'Of course we must,' said Honor. 'What am I doing all day, thinking of all night, but how we may keep our heads upright?'

'What a mercy it would be not to be always fretting over ha'pence! If you and Kate were well married, what satisfaction it would be to me and what a comfort all round.'

'Do not reckon on me,' said Honor; 'I shall not marry, I have the children to care for. You do not want to drive me out of the house, do y', father?'

'No, certainly not. But I should like to see you and Kate well married, Kate to Larry Nanspian and Chimsworthy, and you—well, you equally well placed. Then you might combine to help me to my own. Consider this, Honor! If we had Coombe Park, all our troubles would clear like clouds before a setting sun. Charles would no longer be a trouble to us. He shows his gentle blood by dislike for work. If he were not forced to labour he would make a proper gentleman. Why then, Honor, what a satisfaction to you to have been the saving, the making of your brother!'

'*Then* won't stand on the feet of *If*,' said Honor.

'It depends on you.'

'How on me?' she rested her hands on her lap, and looked steadily at her father. He unravelled his lash with nervous hands. Honor saw that they shook. Then without turning his eyes from his plaiting, he said timidly, 'I only thought how well it would be for us if you were at Langford!'

'How can I be at Langford? Mrs. Veale is the housekeeper, and I do not wish for her place.'

'Oh no, not her place—not her place by any means,' said her father.

'What other place then?' she was resolved to force him to speak out, though she guessed his meaning.

He did not answer her immediately. He looked at the 'flopadocks' through the front door, then he looked to see if there was a way of escape open by the back.

'I—I thought—that is to say—I hoped—you might fancy to become Mrs. Langford.'

Honor rose proudly from her seat, and placed needlework in the chair. She stood in the doorway, with the illumined hedge behind her. If Oliver had looked her face he could not have seen it; he would have seen only the dark head set on a long and upright neck, with a haze of golden brown about it. But he did not look up; he drew a long breath. The worst was over. He had spoken, and Honor knew all.

In the morning the carrier had flattered himself it would be easy to tell Honor, but when he prepared to come to the point he found it difficult. He knew that the proposal would offend his daughter, that it would not appear to her in the light in which he saw it. He was afraid of her as an inferior nature fears one that is greater, purer than itself. Now he felt like a schoolboy who has been caught cribbing, and expects the cane.

'You see, Honor,' said he in an apologetic tone, 'Taverner Langford is a rich man, and of very good family. It would be no disgrace to him to marry you, and you cannot reckon to look higher. I don't know but that his family and ours date back to Adam. He has kept his acres, and we have lost ours. However, with your help, I hope we may recover Coombe Park and our proper position. What a fine thing, Honor, to be able to restore a fallen family, and to be the means of saving a brother! Taverner Langford is proud, and would like to see his wife's relations among the landed sentry. He would help us with a hundred pounds. Indeed, he has almost promised the money. As to the horse, we need not concern ourselves about that, and the lambs need trouble you no more. There is a special blessing pronounced on the peace-makers, Honor, and that would be yours if you married Taverner, and Kate took Hillary, for then Langford must make up his quarrel with the Nanspians.'

Honor reseated herself, and put her work back on her lap. Oliver had not the courage to look at her face, or he would have seen that she was with difficulty controlling the strong emotion that nigh choked her. He sat with averted eyes, and maundered on upon the advantages of the connection.

'So,' exclaimed Honor at length, 'Taverner Langford has asked for me to be his wife! But, father, he asked before he knew of that affair yesterday. That alters the look. He will back out when he hears of Charles's conduct.'

'Not at all. I saw him yesterday evening, and he laughed at the story. He took it as a practical joke played on the circus folk—and what harm? Everyone likes his jokes, and the Revel is the time for playing them.'

'He has not dismissed Charles?'

'Certainly not.'

'I would have done so, had he been my servant.'

Then she leaned her head on her hand and gazed before her, full of gloomy thought. Her father watched her, when he saw she was not looking at him.

'The advantage for Charles would be so great,' he said.

'Yes,' she exclaimed, with a tone of impatience. 'But there are some sacrifices it is not fair to expect of a sister.'

'Consider that, instead of being a servant in the house, Charles would regard himself as at home at Langford. He is not a bad fellow, his blood is against his doing menial work. When he mounts to his proper place you will see he will be a credit to us all. You don't take razors to cut cabbages. I, also, will no longer be forced to earn my livelihood by carrying. If your mind be healthy, Honor, you will see how unbecoming it is for a Luxmore to be a common carrier. Lord bless me! When I am at Coombe Park, you at Langford, and Kate at Chimsworthy, what a power we shall be in the place. Why, I may even become a feoffee of Coryndon's Charity! Langford is rich. He has a good estate. He has spent nothing on himself for many years. There must be a lot of money laid by somewhere. He cannot have saved less than three hundred pounds a year, and I should not stare to hear he had put by five. Say this has been going on for twenty years. That amounts to ten thousand pounds at the lowest reckoning. Ten thousand pounds! Think of that, Honor. Then remember that old Hillary Nanspian is in debt to Taverner Langford and pressed to raise the money, as the debt has been called up. You must persuade Taverner to let the money lie where it is, and so you will bring peace to Chimsworthy.'

Honor shook her head.

'It cannot be, father,' she said, in a low tone.

'I feared you would raise difficulties,' he said, in an altered, disappointed voice. 'Of course he is too old for you. That is what you girls think most about.'

She shook her head.

'Perhaps you have fancied someone else,' he went on 'well, we can't have plum bake every day. It is true enough that Taverner Langford is not a yellow gosling; but then he has ten thousand pounds, and they say that a young man's slave is an old man's darling. He won't live for ever, and then you know—'

Honor's cheeks flushed; she raised her head, passed her hand over her brow, and looking at her father with dim eyes, said, 'That is not it—no, that is not it.' Then with an access of energy, 'I will tell you the real truth. I cannot marry whom I do not love, and I cannot love whom I do not respect. Mr. Langford is a hard man. He has been hard on his kinsman, Mr. Nanspian, and though the old man had a stroke, Mr. Langford never went near him, never sent to ask how he was, and remained his enemy. About what? I've heard tell about a little red spider. Mr. Langford may be rich, but he loves his money more than his flesh and blood, and such an one I cannot respect.'

The carrier forced a laugh. 'Is not this pot falling foul of kettle?' he asked. 'Who is hard if you are not? Have you shown gentleness to Charles, who is your very brother? Whereas Nanspian is but a brother-in-law.'

'I have not been hard with Charles. I must protect the children from him. He is my brother, and I love him. But I love the others also. I will do all I can for him, but I will not have the others spoiled for his amusement.'

'We don't all see ourselves as others see us,' said Oliver sulkily. Honor was stung by his injustice, but she made no reply. She took up her sewing again, but she could not see to make stitches. She laid her work again on her lap, and mused, looking out of the door at the fox-gloves, and the honeysuckle and wild rose in the hedge. The scent of the honeysuckle was wafted into the room.

'Why should Mr. Langford want me as his wife?' she asked dreamily; 'surely Mrs. Veale will suit him better. She is near his age, and accustomed to his ways. Besides,' she paused, then resumed, 'there have been queer tales about him and her.'

'Pshaw, Honor! a pack of lies.'

'I have no doubt of that,' she said; 'still—I cannot see why he wants me.'

'Honor, my child,' said her father slowly and with his face turned from her; 'he and Nanspian of Chimsworthy don't hit it off together, and the property is so left that if he hasn't children it will pass to his sister's son, young Larry. The old man can't bear to think of that, and on their reckoning on his dead shoes, and he'd draw a trump from his pack against those Nanspians.'

Honor flamed crimson and her eyes flashed. 'And so—so this is it! I am to help to widen the split! I am to stand between Larry and his rights! Father, dear father, how can you urge me? How can you hope this? No, never, never will I consent. Let him look elsewhere. There are plenty of maidens in Bratton less nice than me. No, never, never will I have him.'

Oliver Luxmore stood up, troubled and ashamed.

'You put everything upside down,' he said; 'I thought you would be a peace-maker.'

'You yourself tell me that I am chosen out of spite to make the strife hotter. Now you have told me the why, the matter is made worse. Such an offer is an outrage. Never, father, no, never, never,' she stamped, so strong, so intense was her disgust. 'I will hear no more. I grieve that you have spoken, father. I grieve more that you have thought such a thing possible. I grieve most of all that you have wished it.'

'Turn the offer over in your mind, Honor,' he said, sauntering to the door, from which she had withdrawn. She was leaning against the wall between the door and the window, with her hands over her face. 'Milk runs through the fingers when first you dip 'em, but by turning and turning you turn out butter. So, I dare be bound, the whole thing will look different if you turn it over.'

'I will put it away from me, out of my thought,' she said hotly. She was hurt and angry.

'If you refuse him we shall have to buy a horse.'

'Well, we must buy. I will work the flesh from my fingers till I earn it, and get out of obligation. But I never, never, never will consent to be Taverner Langford's wife, not for your sake, father, nor for that of Charles.'

'Well,' said the carrier; 'some folks don't know what is good for 'em. I reckon there's a hundred bells on that there flopadock, I'll go and count 'em.'

XVI
Keeping Watch

In the evening Hillary the younger arrived, according to promise, with his gun. Oliver Luxmore feebly protested against troubling him. 'It is very good of you, Larry, but I don't think I ought to accept it.'

'It is pleasure, not trouble;' answered Larry.

'If the dog does not come to-night, I will keep guard on the morrow,' said the carrier. 'I may not be able to shoot the dog, but I can scare him away with a bang.'

'I hope to kill him,' said Hillary. 'Have you not heard that a guinea is offered for his carcass? Several farmers have clubbed and offered the reward.'

'Have your lambs suffered, Larry?'

'Ours are all right; driven under cover.'

The young man supped with the Luxmores. He was full of mirth. Kate did not spare her tongue; she attacked and he retaliated, but all good-humouredly. 'They make a pair, do they not?' whispered Oliver to his eldest daughter. 'Better spar before marriage and kiss after, than kiss first and squabble later.'

'Larry,' said Honor, 'I will keep the fire up with a mote (tree-stump). You may be cold during the night, and like to run in and warm yourself.'

'Ay, Honor,' said her father. 'Have a cider posset on the hob to furnish inner comfort.'

'Let no one sit up for me; I shall want nothing,' answered Hillary, 'unless one of you girls will give me an hour of your company to break the back of the watch.'

'Your zeal is oozing out at your elbows,' said Kate. 'Honor or I, or even little Joe, could manage to drive away the dog.'

'But not shoot it,' retorted Hillary. 'Lock your door, and leave me without. I shall be content if I earn the guinea.'

'I will remain below,' said Honor quietly. 'We must not let all the burden rest on you. And if you are kind enough, Larry, to look after our lambs, we are bound to look after you.'

'If one of you remains astir, let it be Honor,' said the young man. 'Kate and I would quarrel, and the uproar would keep the dog away.'

'I do not offer to sit up to-night,' said the carrier, 'as my turn comes on the morrow, and I have had heavy work to-day that has tired me.'

Then he rose, held out his hand to Larry, kissed his daughters, and went upstairs to his room. Kate followed him speedily. Larry took up his gun and went out, and walked round the field. Then he came to the kitchen and said, 'All is quiet, not a sign to be seen of the enemy. I hope he will not disappoint me. You must have your red cloak again.'

'My red cloak?' repeated Honor.

'Ay, your red cloak that you parted with to the woman at the circus. I heard about it. If I shoot the dog, half the prize money goes to you.'

'Not so, Larry. It is, or will be, all your own.'

'But you first saw the dog, you share the watch, you keep up the fire, and brew me a posset. How was it with David's soldiers? What was his decision? They that tarried with the stuff should share with those that went to war. You have Scripture against you, Honor, and will have to take ten-and-six.'

'Don't reckon and divide before the dog is shot.'

'If he comes this way he shall sup off lead, never doubt. Then you shall have your red cloak again.'

Honor sighed. 'No, Larry, I shall never see it more. The fair is over, the circus gone, whither I know no more than what has become of yesterday.'

'Charles behaved very badly. Of course I did not mention it before, but we are alone together now, and I may say it.'

'He did not act rightly—he meant it as a joke.'

'I can't forgive him for robbing you of your pretty red cloak. Here, Honor, take it. I have it.'

Then he pulled out a closely folded bundle and extended it to her. The girl was surprised and pleased. This was considerate and kind of Larry. She had noticed him carrying this bundle, but had given no thought as to what it was. Her eyes filled.

'Oh Larry! God bless you for your kindness.'

'I was tempted to hang it round my neck till I gave it back; I should have looked quite military in it.'

'It was my mother's cloak,' she answered quickly. 'You might have worn it and it would have done you good. My mother will bless you out of paradise for your consideration. Oh my dear, dear mother! she was so wise, and thoughtful, and good.' Honor spread the cloak over the young man's head. 'There,' she said, 'take that as if she had touched you. You have lost your mother.'

'Yes, but I do not remember her.'

'Oh! it is a bad thing for you to be without your mother, Larry.' She paused, then held out her hand to him, and her honest eyes met his glowing with gratitude, swimming with feeling.

'All right,' he said. 'No thanks. We are neighbours and good friends. If I help you to-day you will stand by me to-morrow. That is so, is it not, dear Honor?'

He threw his gun over his shoulder and went out into the meadow. He was glad to escape the pressure of her hand; the look of her eyes had made his heart beat with unwonted emotion. She had never given him such a look before. She was not as cold as he supposed. He was aware that he had acted well in the matter of the cloak. He had gone to the manageress of the circus directly he heard what had taken place, and had made an offer for the garment. The woman, seeing his eagerness to secure it, refused to surrender it under a sum more than its value. He had bought it with the sacrifice of the rest of his pocket-money. That was one reason why he hoped to kill the dog. He would replenish his empty purse. In this matter he had acted as his heart dictated, but he was quite aware that he had done a fine thing. Honor paid him his due, and that raised Honor in his estimation. 'She has heart,' he said, 'though she don't often show it. A girl must have heart to do as she did for that worthless brother.'

Whilst Larry stood without waiting for the dog, Honor was within, sitting by the fire, a prey to distressing thoughts. She was not thinking of Larry or of Charles; she was thinking of what had passed between her and her father.

She occupied a low stool on the hearth, rested her head in her lap, folded her hands round her knees. The red glow of the smouldering fire made her head like copper, and gave to her faded red stockings a brilliancy they lacked by day.

She had dimly suspected that something was plotted against her on the occasion of her visit to Langford, when she had found her father with Langford. What she had dreaded had come to pass. Her father had consented to sell her so as to extricate himself from a petty debt, but, above all, that he might be given means of prosecuting his imaginary claims. Coombe Park was a curse to them. It had blighted Charles, it had spoiled her father's energies, it was doomed to make a breach between her and her father. She had never herself thought of Coombe Park; she had treated its acquisition as an impossible dream, only not to be put aside as absurd because harboured by her father. She was conscious now of a slight stirring of reproach in her heart against him but she battled against it and beat it down. Strong in her sense of filial respect, she would not allow herself to entertain a thought that her father was unjust. She apologised to herself for his conduct. She explained his motives. He had supposed that the prospect of being mistress of a large house, over wide acres, would fill her ambition. He meant well, but men do not understand the cravings of the hearts of women. But, explain away his conduct as she would, she was unable to dissipate the sense of wrong inflicted, to salve the wound caused by his apparent eagerness to get rid of her out of the house. The back door was opened softly.

'Honor! still awake?'

'Yes, Larry.'

'Will you give me a drop of hot cider? I am chilled. Have you a potato sack I can cast over my shoulders? The dew falls heavily.'

'No sign of the dog yet?'

'None at all. The sheep are browsing at ease. It is dull work standing at a gate watching them. I wish the dog would come.'

'Let us change places, Larry. You come by the fire and I will watch at the gate. The moment that I see him I will give warning.'

'And scare him away! No, Honor, I want the prize money.'

'Then I will come out and keep you company. Here are two potato sacks, one for your shoulders, the other for mine. If we talk in a low tone we shall not warn off the dog.'

'That is well, Honor. So we shall make the hours spin. The moon is shining brightly. There have been clouds, and then the dew did not fall as cold and chill. I have been hearkening to the owls, what a screeching and a hooting they make, and there is one in the apple-tree snoring like my father.'

'Have you been standing all the while, Larry?'

'Yes, Honor, leaning against the gate. If there had been anything to sit on I should have seated myself. My fingers are numb. I must thaw them at your coals.'

He went to the fire and held his hands in the glow. 'Honor!' he said, 'you have been crying. I see the glitter of the tears on your cheeks.'

'Yes, I have been crying—not much.'

'What made you cry?'

'Girl's troubles,' she answered.

'Girl's troubles? What are they?'

'Little matters to those they do not concern. Here is a low stool on which the children sit by the hearth. I will take it out and set it under the hedge. We can sit on it and talk together awaiting the dog.'

'What is the time, Honor? Is the clock right? Eleven! I will wait till after midnight and then go. He will not come to-night if he does not come before that. He will have gone hunting elsewhere. Perhaps he remembers that you scared him last night.' Honor carried out a low bench, and placed it near the gate under the hedge where a thorn tree overhung.

'We shall do well here,' said Hillary. 'The dog will not see us, and we shall know he is in the field by the fright of the sheep.'

He seated himself on the bench and Honor did the same at a distance from him—as far away as the bench permitted. She had thrown the potato sack over her head, and wore it as a hood; it covered her shoulders as well, and shaded her face. The dew was falling heavily, the meadow in the moon was white with it, as though frosted, and through the white sprinkled grass went dark tracks, as furrows, where the sheep had trodden and dispersed the sparkling drops.

'Do you hear the owls?' asked Larry. 'I've heard there are three which are seen every night fleeting over Wellon's Cairn, and that they are the souls of the three women Wellon killed. I've never been there at night, have you, Honor?'

'No, I do not go about at night.'

'I should not like to be on Broadbury after dark, not near the old gibbet hill, anyhow. Listen to the old fellow snoring in the apple-tree. I thought owls slept by day and waked by night, but this fellow is dead asleep, judging by the noise he makes.'

After silence of a few moments, during which they listened to the owls, 'I wonder, Honor,' said the young man, 'that you liked to sit on the mound where Wellon was hung. It's a queer, whisht (uncanny) place.'

'I only sit there by day, and that only now and then when I can get out a bit. I have not been there for some time.'

Then ensued another pause.

'I wish you would tell me one thing,' said the girl, 'yet it is what I have no right to ask. Do you owe Mr. Langford a great deal of money?'

'Oh yes,' answered Hillary carelessly, 'a great deal. He has called it in, and we shall have to pay in a month or two.'

'Can you do so out of your savings?'

'We have no savings. We shall go to Mr. Physick—father and I—and get a mortgage made on the property. It is easily done. I am of age. Father couldn't have done it, by himself, but I can join and let him.'

He held up his head. He was proud of the consequence gained by consenting to a mortgage.

'The first thing you have to do with the property is to burden it,' said Honor.

Hillary screwed up his mouth.

'You may put it so if you like.' Instead of looking round at him admiring his consequence, she reproached him.

'That is something to be ashamed of, I think,' she said.

'Not at all. If I did not, Uncle Taverner could come down on us and have a sale of our cattle and waggons and what not. But, maybe, that would suit your ideas better?'

'No,' said Honor gravely, 'not at all. No doubt you are right; but you are old enough not to have let it come to this. Your service on the farm ought to have been worth fifty pounds a year for the last four years. I doubt if it has been worth as many shillings.'

He clicked his tongue in the side of his mouth, and threw out his right leg impatiently.

'Mr. Langford has saved thousands of pounds. He puts by several hundreds every year, and his land is no better than yours.'

'Uncle Taverner is a screw.'

Then, jauntily, 'We Nanspians are open-handed, we can't screw.'

'But you can save, Larry.'

'If Uncle Taverner puts away hundreds, I wonder where he puts them away?'

'That, of course, I cannot say.'

'I wonder if Mrs. Veale knows?' Then he chuckled, and said, 'Honor, some of the chaps be talking of giving him a hare-hunt. We think he ought to be shamed out of letting that woman tongue-lash him as she does.'

'Larry!' exclaimed Honor, turning sharply on him and clutching his arm, 'for God's sake do not be mixed up in such an affair. He is your uncle, and you may be very unjust.' He shrugged his shoulders.

'I'm not over sweet on Uncle Taverner,' he said. 'It is mean of him calling in that money, and he deserves to be touched tip on the raw.'

'Larry, you warned me against Mrs. Veale. Now I warn you to have no hand in this save to hold it back. It must not be; and for you to share in it will be scandalous.'

'How the owls are hooting! To-whoo! Whoo! I wonder what sort of voice the old white owl has. He goes about noiseless, like a bit of cotton grass blown by the wind.'

Then Honor went back to what she was speaking of before. 'It goes to my heart to see good land neglected. Your nettle-seeds sow our land, and thistle-heads blow over our hedge. Now that your father is not what he was, you should grasp the plough-handle firmly. Larry, you know the knack of the plough. Throw your weight on the handles. If you do not, what happens?'

'The plough throws you.'

'Yes, flings you up and falls over. It is so with the farm. Throw your whole weight on it, through your arms, or it will throw you.'

'That old snorer is waking,' said Hillary.

'You love pleasure, and do not care for work,' pursued Honor. 'You are good and are everyone's friend and your own enemy. You shut your eyes to your proper interest and open your purse to the parish. The bee and the wasp both build combs, both fly over the same flowers and enjoy the same summer, but one gathers honey and the other emptiness. Larry, do not be offended with me if I speak the truth. The girls flirt with you and flatter you, and the elder folk call you a Merry Andrew, and say you have no mischief in you, and it is a pity you have not brains. That is not true. You have brains, but you do not use them. Larry, you have no sister and no mother to speak openly to you. Let me speak to you as if I were your sister, and take it well, as it is meant.'

So she talked to him. Her voice was soft and low, her tone tremulous. She was afraid to hurt him, and yet desirous to let him know his duty.

She was stirred to the depth of her heart by the events of the day.

Larry was unaccustomed to rebuke. He knew that she spoke the truth, but it wounded his vanity, as well as flattered it, to be taken to task by her. It wounded him, because it showed him he was no hero in her eyes; it flattered him, because he saw that she took a strong interest in his welfare. He tried to vindicate himself. She listened patiently; his excuses were lame. She beat them aside with a few direct words. 'Do not be offended with me,' she pleaded, turning her face to him, and then the moonlight fell over her noble features; the potato sack had slipped back. 'I think of you, dear Larry, as a brother, as a kind brother who has done many a good turn to us, and I feel for you as an elder sister.'

'But, Honor, you are younger than I am by eighteen months.'

'I am older in experience, Larry; in that I am very, very old. You are not angry with me?'

'No, Honor, but I am not as bad as you make out.'

'Bad! Oh Larry, I never, never thought, I never said you were bad. Far otherwise. I know that your heart is rich and deep and good. It is like the soil of your best meadows. But then, Larry, the best soil will grow the strongest weeds. Sometimes when I look through the gates of Chimsworthy I long to be within, with a hook reaping down and rooting up. And now I am peering through the gates of your honest eyes, and the same longing comes over me.'

He could see by the earnest expression of her face, by the twinkle of tears on her lashes, that she spoke out of the fullness of her heart. She was not praising him, she was rebuking him, yet he was not angry. He looked intently at her pure, beautiful face. She could not bear his gaze, he saw her weakness. He put his finger to her eyelashes. 'The dew is falling heavily, and has dropped some diamonds here,' he said.

She stood up.

'Hark!' she said, and turned her head. 'The cuckoo clock in the kitchen is calling midnight. We need remain here no longer.'

'I should like to remain till day,' said Larry.

'What, to be scolded?'

'To be told the truth, dear Honor.'

'Do not forget what I have said. I spoke because I care for you. The sheep will not be disturbed to-night. Will you have some posset and go home?'

'Your father will keep guard to-morrow night, but the night after that I will be here again. Oh Honor, you will sit up with me, will you not?' He took her hand. 'How much better I had been, how the Chimsworthy coomb would have flowed with honey, had God given me such a sister as you.'

'Well, begin to weed yourself and Chimsworthy,' she said with a smile.

'Will you not give me a word of praise as well as of blame?'

'When you deserve it.'

She pressed his hand, then withdrew it, entered the cottage, and fastened the door.

Hillary walked away with his gun over his shoulder, musing as he had not mused before.

XVII
MRS VEALE

CHARLES LUXMORE HAD LEFT THE Revel shortly after the departure of his sisters. He returned to Langford covered with shame and full of anger. He was not ashamed of his rascality. He thought himself justified in playing a trick on tricksters. But he was ashamed at being conquered by his sister, and he was unable to disguise to himself that he cut an ignoble figure beside her. At the circus there had been a general recognition of her worth, and as general a disparagement of himself. Why had she interfered? He had courted a 'row' in which he might have held his own against the equestrians, sure of support from the young Brattonians. That would have been sport, better than tumbling in the saw-dust and skipping through hoops. If he could only have excited a fight, the occasion would have been forgotten in the results; he would have come out in flaming colours as a gallant fellow. Now, because Honor had interfered and put him in the wrong, he had been dismissed as a rogue.

He knew well enough the red cloak Honor had given away. He knew that it had belonged to her mother, and that Honor prized it highly, and that it was very necessary to her.

Let him excuse himself as he would, a sense of degradation oppressed him which he was unable to shake off.

The behaviour of his comrades had changed towards him, and this galled him. After leaving the circus he had essayed swagger, but it had not availed. His companions withdrew from him as if ashamed to be seen in his society. The popular feeling was roused in behalf of Honor, who was universally esteemed, rather than offended at the fraud played on the equestrians. It was well known that he, Charles, had not behaved towards her with consideration, that he had increased the burden she bore so bravely. This last act was the climax of his wrong-doing. Charles's inordinate vanity had been hurt, and he was angry with everyone but himself.

He returned to the farm-house, where he had been taken in, cursing the stupidity of the villagers, the meddlesomeness of his sisters, the cowardice of his companions, and his own generosity.

He was without money now, and with no prospect of getting any till his wage was paid.

He turned out his pockets; there was nothing in them, not even the brass token. He was too proud to borrow of his boon companions; he questioned whether, if he asked, they would lend him any. He doubted if the innkeeper would let him drink upon trust. How intolerable for him to be without money! To have to lounge his evenings away in the settle before the fire at Langford, or loafing about the lanes. 'I know well enough,' he muttered, 'Why the louts keep away from me. 'Tis because they know I'm cleaned out. It's not along of that cursed token, not a bit. If I'd my pockets full they'd be round me again as thick as flies on a cow's nose.'

He had only been a few days in the service of Taverner Langford. He had entered the service rather surlily, only because forced to do so, as Honor refused to allow him to sleep and have meals at home. 'It'll keep me in meat for a bit, and I'll look about me,' he said; 'but it is not the sort o' place for a gentleman Luxmore.'

He had not asked leave to take a holiday on the occasion of the Revel. He had taken it as a matter of course. The Revel was a holiday, of course; so is Sunday. 'I don't ask old Langford whether I'm to keep the Sabbath by doing nothing: I do nothing. I don't ask him if I'm to enjoy myself Revel day: I enjoy myself. These are understood things.'

He curled his lip contemptuously 'What a shabby wage I get, or am to get!' he muttered. 'No pay, no work; short pay, short work. That stands to reason—like buttering parsnips.'

He sauntered into the Langford kitchen and threw himself into the settle, with his hat on, and his legs outstretched and his hands in his pockets. Disappointment, humiliation, impecuniosity combined to chafe his temper, and give him a dejected, hang-dog appearance.

Mrs. Veale passed and repassed without speaking. She observed him without allowing him to perceive that she observed him. Indeed, he hardly noticed her, and he was startled by her voice when she said, as he bent over the fire, 'Charles Luxmore, what do y' think of the Revel now? I've a-been there, and to my reckoning it were grand, but, Lord! you've been over the world, and seen so many fine things that our poor Revel is nought in your eyes, I reckon.'

'Bah! poor stuff, indeed. You should see Bombay, or the bazaar at Candahar! Bratton Clovelly! Bah! Punjab, Cawbul, Delhi, Peshawur, Ghuznee, Hyderabad!' The utterance of these names, which he knew would convey no idea whatever to the mind of Mrs. Veale, afforded him relief. It morally elevated him. It showed him that he knew more of the world than Mrs. Veale. 'You don't happen to know Dost Mahommed?'

'Oh, dear, no!'

'Nor ever heard tell of him?'

'No, Mr. Luxmore.'

'He's an Ameer.'

'Is he now?'

'I've fought him. Leastways his son, Akbar Khan.'

'You wasn't hard on him, I hope?'

'No, I wasn't that. I merely carried off the doors of his mosque.'

'Did that hurt him much?'

'His feelings, Mrs. Veale, awful.'

'Lord bless me!' exclaimed the woman, looking at him over her shoulder as she stirred a pot on the fire, with her queer blinking eyes studying his expression but expressing nothing themselves.

'I do wonder you be home from the Revel so early. A soldier like you, and a fine young chap, ought to have stayed and enjoyed yourself. The best of the fun, I've heard tell, is in the evening.'

'How can I stay at the Revel when I haven't a copper to spend there?' asked Charles surlily.

'I don't like to see a grand young fellow like you sitting at home like an old man with the rheumatics. We will be friends, Charles. I will give you a crown to buy your good will.' She took the money from her pocket and handed it to him.

'I thank you,' he said grandly—she had called him a grand young man—'but I can't go to the Revel now.' Nevertheless he pocketed the crown. 'I've seen enough of it, and got sick of it. Wretched stalls where nothing is for sale worth buying, wretched shows where nothing is seen worth seeing. I came away because the Revel wearied me.'

'You'll find it dull here,' said the housekeeper. 'We poor ignorant creatures think the Revel and all in it mighty fine things, because we know no better and haven't seen the world. It seems to me, Mr. Luxmore, you're in the wrong place, as the elephant said to the stickleback that had got into the ark.'

'I should just about think I was,' said Charles, kicking out with both his heels. Mrs. Veale was a plain, not to say unpleasant woman, much older than himself; he would not have given her a thought had she not called him 'Mr. Luxmore,' and so recognised that he was a superior being to the Dicks and Toms on the farm.

'Peshawur! Jelalabad! Cawbul! that's how they come,' said Charles. Mrs. Veale stood with her hand on the handle of the pan, an iron spoon uplifted in the other, waiting to drink in further information. 'Through the Khyber Pass,' he added, drawing his brows together and screwing up his mouth.

'No doubt about it,' said Mrs. Veale. 'It must be so, if you sez it. And Solomon in all his glory was not arrayed like one of these.' She stirred the pot; then, thinking she had not made herself intelligible, she explained, 'I mean that Solomon, though the wisest of men, didn't know that, I reckon.'

'How could he,' asked Charles, 'never having been there?'

'I do wonder now, if you'll excuse the remark,' said the housekeeper, 'that you didn't bring the silver belt here and hang it up over the mantel-shelf.'

'Silver belt? What silver belt?'

'Oh! you know. The champion wrestler's belt that is to be tried for this afternoon. I suppose you didn't go in for it because you thought it wouldn't be fair on the young chaps here to take from them everything.'

'I did not consider it worth my while trying for it,' said Charles, with a kick at the hearth with his toes—not an irritated kick, but a flattered, self-satisfied, pleased kick. 'Of course I could have had it if I had tried.'

'Of course you might, you who've been a soldier in the wars, and fought them blood-thirsty Afghans. Lord! I reckon they was like Goliaths of Gath, the weight of whose spear was as a weaver's beam.'

Charles jerked his head knowingly.

'Afghanistan was a hard nut to crack.'

'Ah!' acquiesced Mrs. Veale. 'So said old Goodie as she mumbled pebbles.' Then she stood up and looked at him. 'I know a fine man when I see him,' she said, 'able to hold himself like the best gentleman, and walking with his head in the air as if the country belonged to him.'

'Ah!' said Charles, taking off his hat and sitting erect, 'if all men had their rights Coombe Park would be ours.'

'Don't I know that?' asked the housekeeper. 'Every one knows that. Nobody can look at you without seeing you're a gentleman born. And I say it is a shame and a sin that you should be kicked out of your proper nest, and it the habitation of strangers, cuckoos who never built it, but have turned out the rightful owners. I reckon it made me turn scarlet as your sister's cloak to see her come crawling here t'other day on bended knees to ask the master to take you in. She's no lady, not got a drop of blue blood in her veins, or she'd not ha' done that. I'll tell you what it is, Mr. Charles. All the gentle blood has run one way and all the vulgar blood the other, as in our barton field the sweet water comes out at the well, and the riddam (ferruginous red water) at the alders.' She spoke with such acrimony, and with a look so spiteful, that Charles asked, 'What has Honor done to offend you?'

'Oh nothing, nothing at all! I don't stoop to take offence at her.' Then, observing that the young man resented this disparagement of his sister, she added hastily, 'There, enough of her. She's good enough to wash and comb the little uns and patch their clothes. We will talk about yourself, as the fox said to the goose, when she axed him if duck weren't more tasty. Why have you come from the Revel? There be some better reason than an empty pocket.'

'I have been insulted.'

'Of course you have,' said Mrs. Veale, 'and I know the reason. The young men here can't abide you. For why? Because you're too much of a gentleman, you're too high for 'em. As the churchyard cross said to the cross on the spire, "Us can't talk wi'out shouting." Do you know what the poacher as was convicted said to the justice o' peace? "I'm not in a position, your worship, to punch your head, but I can spit on your shadow."'

'Without any boasting, I may admit that I and these young clodhopping louts ain't of the same sort,' said Charles proudly.

'That's just what the urchin hedgehog said to the little rabbits when he curled up in their nest.'

'Ah!' laughed Charles, 'but the urchin had quills and could turn the rabbits out, and I have not.'

'You've been in the army, and that gives a man bearing, and you've been half over the world and that gives knowledge; and nature have favoured you with good looks. The lads are jealous of you.'

'They do not appreciate me, certainly,' said Charles, swelling with self-importance.

'This is a wicked world,' said Mrs. Veale. Then she produced a bottle of gin and a glass, and put them at Charles's elbow. 'Take a drop of comfort,' she said persuasively, 'though for such as you it should be old crusted port and not the Plymouth liquor, as folks say is distilled from turnips.'

Young Luxmore needed no pressing; he helped himself.

'I reckon,' pursued Mrs. Veale, 'you were done out of Coombe Park by those who didn't scruple to swear it away. Money and law together will turn the best rights topsy- turvy.'

'No doubt about that, ma'am,' said Charles. 'I've heard my father say, many a time, that with a hundred pounds he could win Coombe Park back.'

'Then why do you not lay out the hundred pounds?'

'Because I haven't got 'em,' answered Charles.

'Oh! they're to be got,' said the housekeeper, 'as the gipsy said to his wife when she told 'n she was partial to chickens.'

'It seems to me,' said the young man, 'that it is a hard world for them that is straight. The crooked ones have the best of it.'

'Not at all,' answered the housekeeper, 'The crooked ones can't go through a straight hole. It is they who can bend about like the ferret as gets on best, straight or crooked as suits the occasion.'

Charles stood up, drank off his glass, and paced the room. The housekeeper filled his glass again. The young man observed her actions and returned to his seat. As he flung himself into the settle again he said, 'I don't know what the devil makes you take such an interest in my affairs.'

Mrs. Veale looked hard at him, and answered, 'A woman can't be indifferent to a good-looking man.' Charles tossed off his glass to hide his confusion. So this bleached creature had fallen in love with him!—a woman his senior by some fifteen years. He was flattered, but felt that the situation was unpleasant.

'This is a bad world,' he said, 'and I wish I had the remaking of it. The good luck goes to the undeserving.'

'That is only true because those who have wits want readiness. A screw will go in and hold where a nail would split. Coombe Park is yours by right; it has been taken from you by wrong. I should get it back again were I you, and not be too nice about the means.' Charles sighed and shook his head.

'What a life you would lead as young squire,' said Mrs. Veale. 'The maidens now run after Larry Nanspian, because he is heir to Chimsworthy, and don't give much attention to you, because you've nothing in present and nothing in prospect. But if you were at Coombe Park they'd come round you thick as damsels in Shushan to be seen of Ahasuerus, and Larry Nanspian would be nowhere in their thoughts.'

She laughed scornfully. 'And the fellows that turn up their noses at you now, because you eat Langford's bread crusts and earn nine pence, how they would cringe to you and call you sir, and run errands for you, and be thankful for a nod or a word! Then the farmers who now call you a good-for-naught would pipe another note, and be proud to shake hands. And Parson Robbins would wait with his white gown on, and not venture to say, "When the wicked man," till he saw you in the Coombe Park pew. And the landlord's door at the "Ring of Bells" would be ever open to you, and his best seat by the fire would be yours. And I—poor I—would be proud to think I'd poured out a glass of Plymouth spirit to the young squire, and that he'd listened to my foolish words.'

Charles tossed his head, and threw up and turned over the crown in his trousers pocket. Then, unsolicited, he poured himself out another glass and tossed it off. That would be a grand day when he was squire and all Bratton was at his feet.

Mrs. Veale stood erect before him with flickering eyes. 'Do y' know the stone steps beside the door?' she asked.

'Yes.'

'What be they put there for?'

'They are stepping-stones to help to mount into the saddle.'

'What stones be they?'

'I'm sure I can't say.'

'Right; no more does he know or care who uses them. Well, I'm naught, but I can help you into the saddle of Coombe Park.'

XVIII
Treasure Trove

Charles Luxmore was not able to sleep much that night. It was not that his conscience troubled him. He gave hardly a thought to the affair at the circus. His imagination was excited; that delusive faculty, which, according to Paley, is the parent of so much error and evil. The idea of Coombe Park recurred incessantly to his mind and kept him awake. But it was not the acquisition of wealth and position that made the prospect so alluring; it was the hope of crowing over all those who had despised him, of exciting the envy of those who now looked down on him.

The 'Ring of Bells' was on the Coombe estate. How he could swagger there as the landlord's overlord! The Nanspians, Taverner Langford, had but a few hundred acres, and the Coombe Park property was nigh on two thousand.

Squire Impey and he would be the two great men of the place, and as the squire at Culm Court was a hunting man, he, Charles Luxmore, would be hand in glove with him.

It would be worth much to ride in scarlet after the hounds, with his top boots and a black velvet cap, and the hand holding a whip curled on the thigh so, and to jog past old Langford, and cast him a ''Do,

Taverner, this morning? Middling, eh?' and to crack the whip at Hillary Nanspian and shout, 'Out o' the way, you cub, or I'll ride you down.' He sat up in bed and flapped his arms, holding the blanket as reins, and clicked with his tongue, and imagined himself galloping over the field after the hounds at full cry. Right along Broadbury, over the fences of Langford, across Taverner's land, tearing, breaking through the hedges of Chimsworthy, tally-ho! With a kick, Charles sent the bed-clothes flying on the floor.

'By George!' he said. 'We shall have a meet in front of Coombe Park, and Honor and Kate shall serve out cherry-brandy to the huntsmen.' Then he scrambled about the floor collecting his bed-clothes and rearranging them. 'I'll go to Coombe Park to-morrow, and look where the kennels are to be. I'll give an eye also to the pond. I don't believe it has been properly cleaned out and fit for trout since the place left our hands. I'm afraid Honor will never rise to her situation—always keep a maid-of-all-work mind. Confound these bed-clothes, I've got them all askew.'

So possessed was Charles with the idea that it did not forsake him when morning came. It clung to him all the day. 'There's only a hundred pounds wanted,' he said, 'for us to establish our claim.'

Then he paused in the work on which he was engaged. 'How am I to reach a hundred pounds on nine pence a day, I'd like to know? Nine pence a day is four-and-six a week, and that makes eleven guineas or thereabouts per annum. I must have something to spend on clothing and amusement. Say I put away seven guineas in the year, why it would take me thirteen to fourteen years to earn a hundred pounds—going straight as a nail, not as a screw, nor as a ferret.'

In the evening Charles wandered away to Coombe Park. The owner, a yeoman named Pengelly, who, however, owned only the home farm, not the entire property, had been accustomed to the visits of Oliver Luxmore, which had been regarded as a sort of necessary nuisance. He was by no means disposed to have his place haunted by the young man also, of whose conduct he had received a bad report from all sides. He therefore treated Charles with scant courtesy, and when young Luxmore tried bluster and brag, he ordered him off the premises.

Charles returned to Langford foaming with rage. Mrs. Veale awaited him.

'The master is not home,' she said; 'where have you been?'

'Been to see my proper home,' he answered, 'and been threatened with the constable if I did not clear away. What do you mean by giving me all sorts of ideas and expectations, and subjecting me to insult, eh? answer me that.'

'Don't you fly out in flaming fury, Mr. Charles.'

'I'm like to when treated as I have been. So would you. So will you, if what I hear is like to come about. There's talk of a hare hunt.'

'A what?'

'A hare hunt.'

'Where?' Mrs. Veale stood before him growing deadlier white every moment, and quivering in all her members and in every fibre of her pale dress, in every hair of her blinking eyelids.

'Why here—at Langford.'

She caught his arm and shook him. 'You will not suffer it! You will stay it!'

'Should they try it on, trust me,' said Charles mockingly. 'Specially if Larry Nanspian be in it. I've a grudge against him that must be paid off.'

Mrs. Veale passed her hand over her brow. 'To think they should dare! should dare!' she muttered. 'But you'll not suffer it. A hare hunt! what do they take me for?'

Charles Luxmore uttered a short ironical laugh. 'Dear blood![1] ' she muttered, and her sharp fingers nipped and played on his arm as though she were fingering a flute. 'You'll revenge me if they do! Trust me! when I'm deadly wronged I can hurt, and hurt I will, and when one does me good I repay it—to a hundred pounds.'

She laughed bitterly. There was something painful in her laugh. It was devoid of mirth, and provoked no laughter. Although she said many odd things, invented quaint similes, or used those which were traditional, they hardly ever awoke smile, her tone was so cheerless, husky and unpleasant.

'So Farmer Pengelly insulted you! Ha! it would be a most laughable conceit to prove that he had no title, and had thrown away his thousands.'

'On Coombe Park?'

'On what else? What did he say to you?'

'Never mind what he said. What he said hurt me. He called me a vagabond and empty pocket, and said I might go back to the devil.'

'And when you have established your right, and shown that he bought without a proper title, then you'd stand on the doorsteps, stick in hand, and say, Pengelly! who has the empty pocket? Who is the vagabond without house? Go back to the devil. What be you to stye in a gentleman's mansion? Whom God Almighty made an ass bides an ass. And cats as ain't got manners must keep off Turkey Carpets.'

Then, still holding his arm, she said, 'Come here! I've never shown you over this house; not that Langford is fit to compare with Coombe Park. Yet this were a gentleman's house once. But what were the Langfords as compared with the Luxmores? You'll see a Luxmore monument at the very altar-steps o' the chancel in Bratton Church, but that of a Langford is half-way down the nave, which shows how different they were estimated.' After a short silence Charles felt a spasmodic quiver pass over her, like the thrill of a peacock when spreading its tail. 'They would have a hare hunt, would they, and put me to a public shame?'

'No, no, Mrs. Veale,' said Charles caressingly, 'I'll put a stop to that; and if they venture I'll break the necks of those that have to do with it.'

'Come with me;' said the woman hoarsely, 'I'll show you all. Here,' she flung open the sitting-room door, 'here is the parlour where your sister went down on her knees to the master. If he'd ha' axed her to lick his boots she'd ha' done it—no proper pride in her—and all for nine pence a day.'

Charles became very red in the face.

'This is the desk at which the master writes and does his accounts. In it, I reckon, be his books. I've never seed them, and I doubt if I could make much out of 'em if I did. Them things don't agree wi' my faculties, as the cherub said of the armchair.'

'Does old Langford always sit in this room?'

'Oh yes! too proud to sit in the kitchen wi' such as me—not even in winter. Then I must make his fire here every day, and have the worry of keeping it in. There is one thing don't suit him now he is cut wi' the Nanspians. Formerly he got all his fuel from their wood. There are no plantations on Langford, and the old trees are cut down. When he got his fuel at Chimsworthy he hadn't to pay, and now he must get a rick of firing elsewhere.' She pointed to an old-fashioned cupboard in the wall. 'There he keeps his sugar and his tea and his currants. He keeps all under key, lest I or the maidens should steal them. Now you look at me and I'll show you something.' She opened an empty place under the cupboard and knocked upwards thrice with her fist, and the glass doors of the repository of the groceries flew open. She laughed huskily. 'There! if I strike I shoot up the bolt, and the lock won't hold the doors together. When I press them together and shut back, down falls the bolt.'

'That is ingenious, Mrs. Veale—stay, don't shut yet. I have a sweet tooth, and see some raisins in the bag there.'

'Now leave them alone. I've something better to show you. Men reckon themselves clever, but women beat them in cleverness. Go to the fire-place. Kneel at it and put your hand up on the left side, thrust in your arm full length and turn the hand round.'

'I shall dirty myself. I shall get a black hand.'

'Of course you will. That is how I found it out. Don't be afraid of a little soot. There is a sort of oven at the side. This room were not always a parlour, I reckon; there were a large open fire-place in it, and when the grate was put in it left the space behind not at all, or only half, filled in—leastways, the road to the oven door was not blocked. Have you found it?'

'Yes,' answered Charles. 'I have my hand in something.'

'And something in your hand, eh?'

'Yes, a box, a largish box.'

He drew forth a tin case, very heavy, with a handle at the top. It was locked with a letter padlock.

'Into that box the master puts all his savings. I reckon there be hundreds of pounds stowed away there, may be thousands. The master himself don't know how much. He's too afeared of being seen or heard counting it. When he has money he takes out the box, opens it, and puts in the gold, only gold and paper, no silver. Banks break. He will have none of them, but this old cloam oven he thinks is secure. He may be mistaken.'

'How did you find this out?'

'By his black hand. Whenever he had sold bullock or sheep, and I knew he had received money, so sure was he to come in here with a white hand and come out with one that was black, that is how I found it. I know more. I know the word that will open the box.'

'How did you find that out?'

'The master was himself afraid of forgetting it, and I chanced to see in the first leaf of his Bible here in pencil the reference Gen. XXXVI. 23. One day I chanced to look out the passage, and it was this: The children of Shobal were these: Alvan, and Manahath and Ebal, Shepho, and Onam. I thought a man must have a bad conscience to find comfort in such a passage as that. And what do y' think? I found the same reference in his pocket-book. Then I knew it must mean something I didn't see the end of. And one day I were full o' light, like a lantern. I saw it all. Do y' see, this new padlock makes only four letter words, and in that verse there are two words of four letters, and I found as how the master changed about. One year he took Ebal and next year Onam. It be the turn o' Ebal now.'

Charles felt the weight of the case and turned the padlock towards him.

'Lord!' exclaimed Mrs. Veale, 'what if the master have got his thousand or two there! It's nothing to what might be yours if you had Coombe Park.'

Suddenly both started. Langford's voice was heard outside. Charles hastily replaced the case where he had found it, and slipped out of the room with Mrs. Veale, who held him and drew him after her, her nervous fingers playing on his arm-bone as on a pipe.

'Come here,' she whispered, 'let me wash your hand. It is black. Here, at the sink.' She chuckled as she soaped his hand and wrist. 'And here the master have washed his, and thought I did not consider it.'

Then she quivered through her whole body and her eyes blinked. She put up her shaking finger and whispered 'Ebal!'

1. A Devonshire expression, meaning 'Dear fellow.'

XIX

A Dead Dog

The second night of watch proved unavailing, for the best of good reasons, that the watch was not kept. Oliver Luxmore sat up, but, finding the night chilly outside the house, attempted to keep watch with a pipe of tobacco and a jug and glass of cider posset within. The consequence was that he went to sleep over the fire. During that same night another of the lambs was worried. Mischief had also been done at Swaddledown, as the family heard during the day. There a ewe had been killed, overrun, thrown into a grip (dyke by hedge) whence it could not rise, and where it had been torn, and had died.

'We must not ask your father to watch again,' said Hillary, with the corners of his mouth twitching. 'We believe what he says now when he tells us he is very short-sighted. I will come to-night and the night after, if need be, till I earn my guinea. The rascal has been here twice and has escaped. He shall not succeed the third time. I will take a nap by day and be lively as an owl at night.'

The maids at Chimsworthy joked the lad about his visits to the cottage: he did not go there after the dog, but after Kate. A guinea! What was a guinea to the heir of Chimsworthy? A young man cares more for girls' hearts than for money. He did not contradict them, he turned aside their banter with banter. But the lively conversation of Kate had lost its charm for him. He exchanged jests with her, but took less pleasure than heretofore in doing so. That night and the next he spent at his post watching for the lamb-killer. Honor gave him her company. He was surprised at himself for becoming serious, still more that the conversation and society of the grave Honor should afford him so much pleasure. In her company everything assumed a new aspect, was seen through coloured glass.

Honor herself was changed during these still night watches. A softness, inbred in her, but to which she was unable to yield during the day, manifested itself in her manner, her speech, her appearance, a bloom as that on the plum. Her inner heart unfolded like a night-flower, and poured forth fragrance. Thoughts that had long dwelt and worked in her mind, but to which she had never given words, found expression at last. Her real mind, her great, pure, deep soul, had been as a fountain sealed to her father and sister Kate; they could not have understood her thoughts; she knew this without acknowledging it other than by instinctive silence. But now she had beside her a companion, sympathetic, intelligent; and the night that veiled their faces and the working of their emotions allowed them to speak with frankness. Banter died away on Hillary's lips, he respected her and her thoughts too highly to treat either lightly. Though he could not fully understand her he could not withhold his reverence. He saw the nobility of her character, her self-devotion made beautiful by its unconsciousness, her directness of purpose, her thoroughness, and her clear simplicity running through her life like a sparkling river. Her nature was the reverse of his own. He treated life as a holiday, and its duties as annoyances; she looked to the duties as constituting life, and to pleasures as accidents. He became dissatisfied with himself without feeling resentment towards Honor for inspiring the feeling. With all his frivolity and self-conceit there was good stuff in Hillary. It was evidence of this that he now appreciated Honor. At night, under the dark heavens strewn with stars, or with the moon rising as a globe of gold over Dartmoor, these two young people sat on the bench, with potato-sacks over their shoulders sheltering them from the dew, or at the hearth suffused by the glow of the peat embers, and talked with muffled voices as if in church.

The second, the third night, during which Hillary watched, passed uneventfully. Each night, or morning rather, as Hillary left, the pressure of his hand clasping that of Honor became warmer. After he was gone, the girl sat musing for some minutes, listening to his dying steps as he passed along the lane homewards. Then she sighed, shook her head, as though to shake off some dream that stole over her, and went to bed.

Hillary's determined watching was not, however, destined to remain fruitless. Early on the fourth night, after he had been at his post an hour, the bleating and scampering of the sheep showed that their enemy was at hand.

In another moment both saw a dark animal dash across the field in pursuit. Hillary fired and the creature fell over.

'Bring a lantern, Honor,' he shouted. 'Let us see whose dog it is.'

She ran indoors. Her father and Kate had been roused by the report.

When she returned with the lantern to the field, 'You were right, Honor,' said Hillary, 'this is Uncle Taverner's Rover. Poor fellow, we were friends once, when I was allowed at Langford. Now he and his master have fallen to bad ways. I have put the seal on my misdoing and Uncle Taverner will never forgive me for having shot his dog.'

'Well, perhaps you will recover your wits now,' said Kate.

'Wits! why?'

'Wits—you have been dull enough lately. Perhaps as the dog went sheep-killing, your wits went wool-gathering. They have been dead, or not at home.'

'Go home, Larry,' said Honor; 'and take our best thanks to warm you.'

Hillary however, seemed ill-disposed to go. He hung about the kitchen pretending that his fingers wanted warming, or considering what was to be done with the carcass of the dog. What he really desired was a further chat with Honor. But Kate would not allow him to be alone with her sister though unsuspicious of the state of his feelings, and indifferent to them herself. She was like a mosquito that buzzes about a sleeping man, threatening him, rousing him, settling, and stabbing, and escaping before his hand can chastise. The more she plied him with her jokes, the more dispirited he became, and incapable of repartee.

'Well,' said he at length, 'I suppose it is time for all to go to bed. You have all seen enough of the dead dog.'

'And we of the live lion,' said Kate.

He went hesitatingly to the door, then came back, tied the dog's hind feet together, and slung the body over his back on his gun. Then he went back to the door.

Kate said something to Honor, gave Larry a nod, and went away to bed.

Honor accompanied him to the door, to fasten it after him.

'I wish Rover had not come for a couple of hours,' he said, as he held out his hand.

'You have won your guinea, and must be content,' she answered with a smile.

'Do you suppose I care for the guinea, except that I may share it with you?' he asked. 'I'll tell you what we will do with it, break it in half, and each keep a half.'

'Then it will be of no good to either,' answered Honor. 'You told me yourself that the money was a consideration to you, as you were empty-pocketed.'

'I forgot all about the guinea after the first night in the pleasure of being with you. I would give the guinea to be allowed to come here again to-morrow night. Confound old Rover for being in such a hurry for his dose of lead.'

'What is that about lead?' called Kate from the steps of the stairs. 'I think, Larry, the lead has got into your brains, and into your feet.'

Honor shook her head, and tried to withdraw her hand from that of the young man; but he would not release it. 'No, Larry, no, that cannot be.'

'May I not come again?'

'No, Larry, on no account,' she said gravely.

'But, Honor, if I come down the lane, and you hear the owls call very loud under the bank, you will open the door and slip out. You will bring the potato-sacks, and let us have a talk again on the bench with them over our shoulders?'

'No, I will not—indeed I will not. I pray you, if you have any thought for me, do not try this. Good-night, Larry—you are a brother to me.'

She wrenched her hand from his, and shut the door. He heard her bolt it. Then he went down the steps and walked away, ill pleased. But after he had gone some distance, he turned, and saw the cottage door open, and Honor standing in it, her dark figure against the fire glow. Had she relented and changed her mind? He came back. Then the door was shut and barred again. He was offended, and, to disguise his confusion, whistled a merry air, and whistled it so loud as that Honor might hear it and understand that her refusal gave him no concern.

Hillary had not reached the end of the lane before he stumbled against Charles.

'Hallo!' exclaimed the latter. 'What are you doing here at this time o' night? Got your gun, eh? And game too, eh? Poaching on Langford. A common poacher. I'll report you. Not hare hunting yet? Take care how you do that. I'll break your neck if you come near Langford after that game.'

'What you have been doing is clear enough,' said Hillary, stepping aside. 'You have been at the "Ring of Bells," drinking.'

'What if I have? No harm in that, if I have money to pay my score. Nothing against that, have you?'

'Nothing at all; but I doubt your having the money. A week ago you were reduced to a brass token.'

'You think yourself cock of the walk, do you,' said Charles insolently, 'because you are heir to Chimsworthy? What is Chimsworthy to Coombe Park? Come! I bet now you've naught but coppers in your pocket. Hands in and see which can make the most show.'

As he spoke, he thrust forth his palm, and Hillary heard the chink of money, and the sound of coins falling on the stones.

'If you had money at the fair-time,' said Hillary coldly, 'all I can say is that you behaved infamously.'

'I had no money then.'

'How you have got it since, I do not know,' said Hillary.

'That is no concern of yours, Master Larry,' answered Charles roughly. 'You will live to see me Squire at Coombe Park; and when I'm there, curse me if I don't offer you the place of game-keeper to keep off rogues. An old poacher is the best keeper.'

'You cur!' exclaimed Hillary, blazing up. 'This is my game.' He swung the dead dog about, and struck Charles on the cheek with the carcass so violently as to knock him into the hedge. 'This is my game. Your master's dog, which has been worrying and killing your father's lambs whilst you have been boozing in a tavern.'

'By George!' swore Charles, with difficulty picking himself up. 'I'll break your cursed neck, I will.'

But Larry had gone on his way by the time Charles had regained equilibrium.

'This is the second time he's struck me down,' said Charles, and next moment a great stone passed Larry, then another struck the dead dog on his back with sufficient force to have stunned him had it struck his head.

He turned and shouted angrily, 'You tipsy blackguard, heave another, and I'll shoot. The gun is loaded.'

'And, by George! I'll break your neck!' yelled Charles after him.

XX

A Five-pound Note

No sooner had Hillary got the guinea for shooting the sheep-killer than he went to the cottage and offered half to Honor Luxmore. She refused it, and would by no persuasion be induced to accept it.

'No, Larry, no—a thousand times no. You redeemed my cloak, and will not let me pay you for that. I will not touch a farthing of this well-earned prize.'

Then Larry went to Tavistock and expended part of the money in the purchase of a handsome silk kerchief, white with sprigs of lilac, and slips of moss-rose on it. He returned in the carrier's van instead of waiting for his father, who remained to drink with other farmers. This entailed the walking up of the hills. When he got out for this object, he left his parcel on the seat. On his return he found the women within sniggering.

'Don't y' be offended at us now,' said one. 'But it is just so. Your parcel came open of herself wi' the jolting of the 'Vivid' and us couldn't help seeing what was inside. Us can't be expected to sit wi' our eyes shut. 'Taint in reason nor in nature. I must say this—'tis a pretty kerchief and Kate Luxmore will look like a real leddy in it o' Sunday, to be sure.'

Then the rest of the women laughed.

Hillary coloured, and was annoyed. The parcel had not come open of itself. The women's inquisitive fingers had opened it, and their curious eyes had examined the contents. They had rushed to the conclusion that the kerchief was intended for Kate—Larry was much about with the maiden, they were always teasing each other, laughing together, and Hillary had been several evenings to the carrier's cottage guarding the lambs and sheep.

The young man did not disabuse them of their error. He was vexed that they should suppose him caught by the rattle Kate, instead of by the reliable Honor; it showed him that they supposed him less sensible than he was. But he thought with satisfaction of the surprise of the gossips on Sunday, when they saw the kerchief about the neck of the elder sister, instead of that of Kate.

In this expectation, however, he was disappointed. Next day, he went to the cottage at an hour when he was sure to find Honor there alone, and, with radiant face and sparkling eyes, unfolded the paper, and offered his present to the girl.

Honor was more startled than pleased—at least, it seemed so—and at first absolutely declined the kerchief. 'No, Larry, I thank you for your kind thought, but I must not accept it. I am sorry that you have spent your money—the kerchief is very pretty; but I cannot wear it.'

'How wrong-headed and haughty you are, Honor! Why will you not take it?' The blood made his face dark, he was offended and angry. He had never made a girl a present before, and this, his first, was rejected. 'It gave me a vast deal of pleasure buying it. I turned over a score, and couldn't well choose which would look best on your shoulders. You have given me good advice; and here is my return, as an assurance that I will observe it.'

'I am not wrong-headed and haughty, Larry,' answered Honor gently. 'But see! in spite of what I said, in spite of my better judgment, rather than wound you I will take the handkerchief. Indeed, indeed, dear Larry, I am not unthankful and ungracious, though I may seem so. And now I will only take it as a pledge that you have laid my words to heart.

Let it mean that, and that only. But, Larry, the women in the van saw it. I cannot wear it just now, certainly not on Sunday next. You know yourself what conclusions they would draw, and we must not deceive them into taking us to be what we are not, and never can be, to each other.'

'Why not, Honor?'

Instead of answering, she said with a smile, 'My brother, Larry, this I will undertake. When I see that you have become a man of deeds and not of words, then I will throw the kerchief round my neck and wear it at church. It shall be a token to you of my approval. Will that content you?'

He tried his utmost to obtain a further concession. She was resolute. She did not wish to be ungracious, but she was determined to give him no encouragement. She had thought out her position, and resolved on her course. She knew that her way was chalked for her. She must be mother to all her little sisters and brothers, till they were grown up and had dispersed. There was no saying what her father might do were she away. He might marry again, and a stepmother would ill-treat or neglect the little ones. If she were to marry, it could be on one understanding only, that she brought the family with her to the husband's house—and to that no man would consent. It would be unfair to burden a young man thus. Her father, moreover was not a man to be left. What Charles had become, without a firm hand over him, that might Oliver Luxmore also become, even if he did not marry. His dispositions were not bad, but his character was infirm. No! it was impossible for her to contemplate marriage. Kate might, but not she. The line of duty lay clear before her as a white road in summer heat, and she had not even the wish to desert it. It was right for her to nip Larry's growing liking for herself, at once and in the bud.

After Larry had gone, she folded and put away his present among her few valuables. She valued it, as the first warm breath of spring is valued. She said nothing to Kate or the others about it. Her heart was lighter, and she sang over her work. The little offering was a token that through the troubled sky the sun was about to shine.

A day or two after, Charles lounged in, and seated himself by the fire. She was pleased to see him. He was at honest work with Mr. Langford, earning an honest wage. She said as much. Charles laughed contemptuously 'Nine pence,' he said, 'nine pence a day. What is nine pence?'

'It is more than you had as a soldier.'

'But as a soldier I had the uniform and the position. Now I am a day-labourer—I a Luxmore, the young squire with nine pence and lodging and meat.'

'Well, Charles, it is a beginning.'

'Beginning at nine pence. As Mrs. Veale says, "One can't stand upon coppers and keep out of the dirt." What is the meat and drink? The cider cuts one's throat as it goes down, and the food is insufficient and indigestible. If I had not a friend to forage for me, I should be badly off.'

'If you keep this place a twelve month you will get a better situation next year.'

'Keep at Langford a twelve month!' exclaimed Charles 'Not if I know it. It won't do. Never mind why. I say it won't do.'

Then he began working his heel in a hole of the floor where the slate was broken.

'You know Mrs. Veale?' he asked, without looking at his sister.

'Yes, Charles. That is, I have seen her, and have even spoken to her, but—know her—that is more than I profess. She is not a person I am like to know.'

'You had better not,' said Charles. 'She don't love you. When I mention your name her face turns green. She'd ill-wish you if she could.'

'I have never done her an injury,' said Honor.

'That may be. Hate is like love, it pitches at random, as Mrs. Veale says. You may laugh, Honor, but that same woman is in love with me.'

'Nonsense!' Honor did not laugh, she was too shocked to laugh.

'What is there nonsensical in that? I tell you she is. She cooks me better food than for the rest of the men, and she favours me in many ways.'

'She cannot be such a fool.'

'There is no folly in fancying me,' said Charles sharply. 'I have good looks, have seen the world, and compare with the louts here as wheat with rye. Many a woman has lost her heart to a younger man than herself.'

'Charles, you must be plain and rough with her if this be so—though I can scarce believe it.'

'No one forces you to believe it. But don't you think I'm going to make Mrs. Veale your sister in-law. I'm too wide-awake for that. She is ugly, and—she's a bad un. Yes,' musingly, 'she is a bad un.'

Then he worked his heel more vigorously in the hole. 'Take care what you are about, Charles, you are breaking the slate, and making what was bad, worse.'

'I wish I had Mrs. Veale's heart under that there stone,' said Charles viciously. 'I'd grind my heel into it till I'd worked through it. You don't know how uncomfortable she makes me.'

'Well, keep her at arm's length.'

'I can't do it. She won't let me. She runs after me as a cat after a milk-maid.'

'Surely, Charles, you can just put a stop to that.'

'I suppose I must.'

He continued, in spite of remonstrance, grinding through the broken slate into the earth. His face was hot and red. He put his elbow up, and wiped his brow on his sleeve.

'It is cursed warm here,' he said at last.

'Then keep away from the fire. I'm glad you have come to see me, Charles; I always wish you well.'

'Oh, for the matter of that I only came here to be out of the way of Mrs. Veale.'

Then Honor laughed. 'Really, Charles, this is childish.'

'It is not kind of you to laugh,' said he sulkily. 'You do not know what it is to have your head turned, and to feel yourself pulled about and drawn along against your will. It is like "oranges and lemons," as we played at school, when you are on the weakest side.'

'Whither can Mrs Veale draw you? Not to the altar rails, surely.'

'Oh no! not to the altar rails. Mrs. Veale is a bad un.'

His manner puzzled Honor. She was convinced he was not telling her everything.

'What is it, Charles?' she said; 'you may give me your confidence. Tell me all that troubles you. What is behind? I know you are keeping back something from me. If I can advise and help you, I will do so. I am your nearest sister.' Then she put her arms round his neck and kissed him.

'Don't do that,' said he roughly 'I hate scenes, sisterly affection and motherly counsel, and all that sort of batter-pudding without egg and sugar. I reckon I am out-grown that long ago. I have been a soldier and know the world. If you think to pin me to your apron, as you have pinned father, you are mightily mistaken. No; I will tell you no more, only this—don't be surprised if I leave Langford. Nine pence a day is not enough to hold me.'

'Oh Charles, I entreat you to stay. You have regular work there and regular pay. As for Mrs. Veale—'

'Curse Mrs. Veale!' interrupted Charles, and with a stamp of his iron-shod heel he broke the corners of the slate slab. Then he stood up.

'Look here, Honor. I mustn't forget a message. Old Langford wants to see my father mighty particular, and he is to come up to the house to have a talk with him. He told me so himself, and indeed sent me here. Father is to come up this evening, as he is not at home now. You will remember to send him, Honor?'

'Yes,' she answered, bending her face over her work, 'yes, I shall not forget, Charles.'

Her brother had not the faintest suspicion that his master was a suitor for Honor's hand. Mrs. Veale knew it, but she did not tell him. She had reasons for not doing so.

'Nine pence per diem!' muttered the young man, standing in the doorway. 'That makes four pence for ale, and four pence for baccy, and a penny for clothing. Taint reasonable. I won't stand it. I reckon I'll be off.'

Then, after a moment of irresolution, he came back into the middle of the room, and, taking Honor's head between his hands, said in an altered tone, as he kissed her, 'After all, you are a good girl. Don't be angry if I spoke sharp. I'm that ruffled I don't know what I say, or what I do. You mayn't be a proper Luxmore in spirit—that is, not like father and me—but you are hard-working, and so I forgive you in a Christian spirit. As Mrs. Veale says, even the Chosen People must have Gibeonites to hew wood and draw water for them. After I am gone, look under the china dog on the mantel-shelf.'

Then he went hastily away.

Honor shuddered. His breath smelt of brandy.

Half an hour later, Oliver Luxmore came in. Then Honor told him that Charles had been to the house with a message for him from Mr. Langford. Oliver rubbed his head and looked forlorn. He knew as well as his daughter what this meant.

'I suppose,' said he, in a timid, questioning tone, 'I suppose, Honor, you have not thought better of what we was discussing together. No doubt Mr. Langford is impatient for his answer.'

'No doubt,' answered the girl.

'You haven't reconsidered your difficulty in the matter? It seems to me—but then I am nobody, though your father—it seems to me that if there be no prior attachment, as folks call it—and you assure me there is none—there can't be great hardship in taking him. Riches and lands are not bad things; and, Honor, it is worth considering that in this world we never can have everything we desire. Providence always mixes the portions we are given to sup.'

'Yes, father, that is true. I am content with that put to my lips. It is sweet, for I have your love, and the love of all my brothers and sisters. Charles has been here, and he kissed me as he never kissed me before. That makes nine lumps of sugar in my cup. If there be a little bitterness, what then?'

'Well, Honor, you must decide. We cannot drive you, and you count our wishes as nought.'

He was seated, rubbing his hands, then his hair, and turning his head from side to side in a feeble, forlorn, irresolute manner. Honor was sorry for his disappointment, but not inclined to yield.

'Father dear, consider. If I did take Mr. Langford he could not receive you and all the darlings into Langford house as well—and I will not be parted from you. Who takes me takes all the hive. I am the queen-bee.'

'I will ask,' said the carrier, breathing freer. 'I can ask. He can but refuse; besides, it will look better, putting the refusal on his hands. It may be that he will not object. There be a lot o' rooms, for sure, at Langford he makes no use of; and I dare say he might accommodate us. There be one, I know, full o' apples, and another of onions, and I dare say he keeps wool in a third.'

Honor, who was standing by the fire, started, and said hastily, with shaking voice, 'You misunderstand me, father. On no account will I take him. No—on no conditions whatever.' Her hand was on the mantelshelf, and as it shook with her emotion she touched and knocked over a china dog spotted red, a rude chimney ornament. A piece of folded paper fell at her feet. She stooped and picked it up. It was a five-pound note.

She looked at it at first without perceiving what it was, as her mind was occupied. But presently she saw what it was that she held, and then she looked at it with perplexity, and after a moment with uneasiness, and changed colour.

'Father!' she said, 'here is a five-pound note of the Exeter and Plymouth Bank, left by Charles. What does it mean? How can he have got it? Before he parted from me, he said something about looking under the china dog, but I gave no heed to his words; his breath smelt of spirits, and I thought he spoke away from his meaning. His manner was odd. Father! wherever can Charles have got the money? Oh father! I hope all is right.'

She put her hand to her heart; a qualm of fear came over her.

'Right! Of course it is right,' said the carrier. 'Five pounds! Why that will come in handy. It will go towards the cost of the horse if you persist. As for these lambs, he ought to pay me for them, but I don't like to press it, as I hear he won't allow it was his dog killed them, and he swears Hillary shot Rover out of spite, and lays the lamb-killing on the dog unjustly. Well, Honor, I suppose you must have your own way; but it is hard on Charles and me, who work as slaves—we who by rights should be squires.'

XXI
REFUSED!

THE CARRIER WALKED SLOWLY AND reluctantly to Langford. He was uncomfortable with the answer he had to take to Taverner Langford. Oliver was a kindly man, ready to oblige anyone, shrinking from nothing so sensitively as from a rough word and an angry mood. 'It would have saved a lot of trouble,' said he to himself, 'if Honor had given way. I shouldn't have been so out of countenance now—and it does seem an ungrateful thing after the loan of the horse.'

He found Langford in his parlour at his desk. The old man spun round on his seat.

'Ha, ha!' said he, 'come at my call, father-in-law. Well—when is the wedding to be?'

The carrier stood stupidly looking at him, rubbing his hands together and shifting from foot to foot. 'The wedding!'

'Yes, man, the wedding; when is it to be?'

'The wedding!' repeated Oliver, looking through the window for help. 'I'm sure I don't know.'

'You must find that out. I'm impatient to be married. Ha, ha! what faces the Nanspians will pull, father and son, when they see me lead from church a blooming, blushing bride.'

'Well, now,' said the carrier, wiping the perspiration from his brow, 'I'm sorry to have to say it, but Honor don't see it in the proper light.'

'What—refuses me?'

'Not exactly refuses, but begs off.'

'Begs off,' repeated Taverner incredulously He could hardly have been more disconcerted if he had heard that all his cattle were dying and his stacks blazing. 'Begs off!' he again exclaimed; 'then how about my horse?'

The carrier scratched his head and sighed.

'Do you suppose that I gave you the horse?' said Taverner. 'You can hardly have been such a fool as that. I am not one to give a cow here, and a sheep there, and a horse to a third, just because there are so many needy persons wanting them. You must return me the horse and pay me ten shillings a week for the hire during the time you have had him, unless Honor becomes my wife.'

'I will pay you for the horse,' said Luxmore faintly.

'Whence will you get the money? Do you think I am a fool?' asked Langford angrily. His pride was hurt. His eyes flashed and his skin became of a livid complexion. He, the wealthiest man in Bratton Clovelly; he, the representative of the most respectable family there—one as old as the parish itself; he, the parson's churchwarden, and the elder of the Methodist chapel—he had been refused by a poverty-stricken carrier's daughter. The insult was unendurable. He stood up to leave the room, but when he had his hand on the latch he turned and came back. In the first access of wrath he had resolved to crush the carrier. He could do it. He had but to take back his horse, and the Vivid was reduced to a stationary condition. Luxmore might offer to buy the horse, but he could not do it. He knew how poor he was. Moreover, he could cut his business away from him at any moment by setting up the cripple as carrier.

But he thought better of it. Of what avail to him if Luxmore were ruined? He desired to revenge himself on the Nanspians. The carrier was too small game to be hunted down, he was set on the humiliation of much bigger men than he. His envy and hatred of the Nanspians had by no means abated, and the killing of his dog Rover by young

Hillary had excited it to frenzy. That his dog was a sheep-killer would not excuse Larry's act. He did not allow that Rover was the culprit. His nephew had shot the dog out of malice, and had feigned as an excuse that he had caught the dog pursuing lambs.

The wealthy yeoman might certainly, without difficulty, have found another girl less hard to please than Honor. All girls would not have thought with her. His money would have weighed with them. He could not understand his refusal. 'What is the matter with the girl?' he said surlily. 'I thought her too wise to be in love. She has not set her heart on any boyish jackanapes, has she?'

'Honor? Oh no! Honor has no sweetheart,' said the father. 'It certainly is not that, Mr. Langford.'

'Then what is it? What possible objection can she make? I'm not a beardless boy and a rosy-faced beauty, that is true.'

'No, Mr. Langford, I am sure she has not a word against your age and personal appearance. Indeed, a young girl generally prefers as a husband one to whom she can look up, who is her superior in every way.'

'I am that. What is it, then?'

'Well, Mr. Langford,' said the carrier, drawing the back of his hand across his lips, 'I think it is about this. She don't like to desert me and the children. She promised her mother to stand by us, and Honor is so conscientious that what she has promised she will stick to.'

'Oh,' said Taverner, somewhat mollified to find that neither his age nor lack of beauty was objected to, 'that is it, is it?'

'Yes, sir,' answered the carrier sheepishly; 'you see there are six little uns; then comes Kate, and then Charles, and then I. That makes nine of us Honor has to care for. And,' he said more eagerly, heaving a sigh of relief, 'you see, she didn't think it quite a fair thing to saddle you with us all, with Pattie and Joe, Willie, Martha, Charity, Temperance, Kate, Charles, and myself. It does make a lot when you come to consider.'

It did certainly, as Taverner admitted. He had no intention whatever of incumbering himself with Honor's relations, if he did marry her. He took a turn up and down the room, with his heavy dark brows knit and his thin lips screwed together. Oliver watched his face, and thought that it was a very ugly and ill-tempered face.

'It does Honor some credit having such delicacy of feeling,' suggested he. 'I very much doubt how you could accommodate us all in this house.'

'I do not see how I could possibly do it,' said Taverner sharply.

'And Honor couldn't think to tear herself away from us. I suppose you wouldn't consider the possibility of coming to us?'

'No, I would not.'

Taverner Langford was perplexed. He entirely accepted Oliver's explanation. It was quite reasonable that Honor should refuse him out of a high sense of duty; it was not conceivable that she should decline alliance with him on any other grounds. Now, although Taverner had not hitherto found time or courage to marry, he was by no means insensible to female beauty. He had long observed the stately, upright daughter of the carrier, with her beautiful abundant auburn hair and clear brown eyes. He had observed her more than she supposed, and he had seen how hard-working, self-devoted she was, how economical, how clean in her own person and in her house. Such a woman as that would be more agreeable in the house than Mrs. Veale. He would have to pay her no wage for one thing, her pleasant face and voice would be a relief after the sour visage and grating tones of the housekeeper. He knew perfectly that Mrs. Veale had had designs on him from the moment she had entered his house. She had flattered, slaved; she had assumed an amount of authority in the house hardly consistent with her position. Langford had not resisted her encroachments; he allowed her to cherish hopes of securing him in the end, as a means of insuring her fidelity to his interests. He chuckled to himself at the thought of the rage and disappointment that would consume her when he announced that he was about to be married.

He was a suspicious man, and he mistrusted every woman, but he mistrusted Honor less than any woman or man he knew. He had observed no other with half the attention he had devoted to her, and he had never seen in her the smallest tokens of frivolity and indifference to duty. If she was so scrupulous in the discharge of her obligations to father and sisters, how dependable she would be in her own house, when working and saving for husband and children of her own.

She was no idler, she was no talker, and Taverner hated idleness and gossip. Of what other girl in Bratton Clovelly could as much be said? No, he would trust his house and happiness to no other than Honor Luxmore.

Taverner dearly loved money, but he loved mastery better. A wife with a fortune of her own would have felt some independence, but a wife who brought him nothing would not be disposed to assert herself. She would look up to him as the exclusive author of her happiness, and never venture to contradict him, never have a will of her own.

'If that be her only objection, it may be circumvented, said Langford, 'if not got over. I thought, perhaps, she declined my hand from some other cause.'

'What other cause could there be?' asked Oliver.

'To be sure there is no other that should govern a rational creature. but few women are rational. I have done something for you already, for you have my horse. I have done a good deal for Charles also; I pay him nine pence a day and give him his food. It is quite possible that I may do a vast deal for the rest of you. But of course that depends. I'm not likely to take you up and make much of you unless you are connected with me by marriage.You can judge for yourself. Should I be likely to leave you all unprovided for if Honor were Mrs. Langford? Of course I would not allow it to be said that my wife's relations were in need.'

These words of Taverner Langford made Oliver's pulse beat fast.

'And then,' continued the yeoman, 'who can say but that I might give you a hand to help you into Coombe Park.'

Luxmore's eye kindled, and his cheeks became dappled with fiery spots. Here was a prospect but it was like the prospect of the Promised Land to Moses on Pisgah if Honor proved unyielding.

'You are the girl's father,' said Langford. 'Hoity-toity! I have no patience with a man who allows his daughter to give herself airs. He knows what is best for her, and must decide. Make her give way.'

Oliver would have laughed aloud at the idea of his forcing his daughter's will into compliance with his own, had not the case been so serious.

'Look here, Mr. Langford,' he said. 'I'll do what I can. I'll tell Honor the liberal offer you have made; and I trust she'll see it aright and be thankful.' He stood up. 'Before I go,' he said, producing the five-pound note, 'I'd just like to reduce my debt to you for the horse, if you please.'

'How much?' asked Taverner.

'Five pounds,' answered the carrier. 'If I kept it by me I should spend it, so I thought best to bring it straight to you. You'll give me a slip o' paper as a receipt.'

Langford took out his pocket-book, folded the note, and put it in the pocket of the book; then made a pencil entry. 'I always,' said he, 'enter every note I receive with its number. Comes useful at times for reference. To be sure, you shall have a receipt.'

XXII
The Haysel

Hillary became impatient. He made no way with Honor; if any change in his position had taken place, he had gone back. In spite of her entreaty, he went to the cottage down the lane hooting like an owl, but she did not answer the call. Then he plucked up courage and went in on the chance of getting a word with her alone, but he went in vain. Oliver Luxmore was glad to see him, chatted with him, and offered him a place at their supper board, or a drink of cider. He defended himself against the sallies of Kate. He spoke now and then to Honor, and was answered in friendly tone; but that was all. If by chance he met her during the day in the lane or on the down, and she could not escape him, she would not stay to talk, she pleaded work. Hillary was disappointed, and, what was more, offended. His vanity was hurt, and vanity in a young man is his most sensitive fibre. No other girl in the parish would treat his advances as did Honor. The other girls laid themselves out to catch him, Honor shrank from him. He knew that she liked him, he was angry because she did not love him.

Hillary's nature, though sound, was marred by his bringing-up. He had been spoiled by flattery and indulgence. His father's boasting, the great expectations held out to him, the consciousness of vigour, health, and good looks, combined to make Larry consider himself the very finest young fellow, not in Bratton only, but in all England. Self-conceit is like mercury, when it touches gold it renders it dull, and a strong fire is needed to expel the alloy and restore the gold to its proper brilliancy.

Mortified in his self-consequence, stung by Honor's indifference, after a few attempts and failures Hillary changed his tactics. He resolved to show Honor, if she did not meet him, he could turn elsewhere. Unfortunately, Kate was at hand to serve his purpose. Kate did not particularly care for Larry. She had a fancy for Samuel Voaden, the farmer's son at Swaddledown; but of this Honor neither knew nor suspected anything. Kate was pleased to see Hillary whenever he came, as she was glad to have a butt for her jokes, and with feminine ingenuity used him to throw dust in the eyes of her father, sister, and companions to obscure their perception of her attachment for Sam Voaden.

At first Hillary was in a bad temper, disinclined for conversation, and unable to retaliate upon Kate; but by degrees his old cheerfulness returned, and he received and replied to her banter with what readiness he possessed.

One day he came into the cottage with a hay-fork over his shoulder. 'You maidens,' he said, 'come along to the hayfield. We want help badly. Bring the little ones and let them romp and eat cake. Whilst the sun shines we must make hay.'

Honor, without a word, rose and folded her work.

'If you can toss hay as you can toss chaff,' said the young man addressing Kate, 'you will be useful indeed.'

'Larry, it is reported that your uncle Langford will not save hay till it has been rained on well. "If it be too good," he argues, "the cows will eat too much of it." Your wit is ricked like Langford's hay; it is weak and washed out. A little goes a long way with those who taste it.'

A happy and merry party in the hayfield, women and girls tossing the hay into cocks, and the men with the waggon collecting it and carrying it home. The air was fragrant with the scent. In a corner under a hedge were a barrel of cider, and blue and white mugs, and a basketful of saffron-cake. Whoever was thirsty went to the cider cask, whoever was hungry helped himself to the plum loaf. The field rang with laughter, and occasional screams, as a man twisted a cord of hay, cast the loop round a girl's neck, drew her head towards him and kissed her face.

That is called 'the making of sweet hay.'

Honor worked steadily. No one ventured to make 'sweet hay' with her, and Kate was too much on the alert, though one or two young men slyly crept towards her with twisted bands. The little ones were building themselves nests of hay, and burying one another, and jumping over haycocks, and chasing each other with bands, to catch and kiss, in imitation of their elders. Hillary turned in his work and looked at Honor and Kate, hoping that the former would commend his diligence and that the latter would give him occasion for a joke. But Honor was too much engrossed in her raking, and had too little idea of necessary work being lauded as a virtue; and the latter was looking at Samuel Voaden who had come over from Swaddledown to help his neighbour—the haysel at home being over.

When the half-laden waggon drew up near where Honor was raking, Hillary said to her in a low tone, 'I have been working ever since the dew was off the grass.'

'I suppose so, Larry.'

'I have been working very hard.'

'Of course you have, Larry.'

'And I am very hot.'

'I do not doubt it.'

'How cool you are, Honor!'

'I—cool!' she looked at him with surprise. 'On the contrary I am very warm.' She had no perception that he pleaded for praise.

'Larry,' said Kate, 'you were right to press us into service It will rain tomorrow.'

'How do you know that?'

'Because you are working to-day.'

Quick as thought, he threw some hay strands round her head, and kissed both her rosy cheeks.

Kate drew herself away, angry at his impudence, especially angry at his kissing her before Samuel Voaden. She threw down her pitchfork ('heable' in the local dialect), and folding her arms, said with a frown and a pout, 'Do the rest yourself. I will work for you no more.'

'Oh Kate, do not take offence. I went naturally where was the sweetest hay.'

In her anger she looked prettier than when in good humour. She glanced round out of the corners of her eyes, and saw to her satisfaction that Samuel was on the further side of the waggon, unconscious of what had taken place. Hillary was humble, he made ample apology, and offered lavish flattery. Kate maintained, or affected to maintain, her anger for some time, and forced Larry to redouble his efforts to regain her favour. Her fair hair, fine as silk just wound from a cocoon, was ruffled over her brow, and her brow was pearled with heat-drops. She was a slender girl, with a long neck and the prettiest shoulders in the world. She wore a light gown, frilled about the throat and bosom and sleeves, tucked up at the side, showing a blue petticoat and white stockings. She picked up the 'heable' with a sigh, and then stood leaning on it, with the sleeves fallen back, exposing her delicate arms as far as the rosy elbows.

It was not possible for Kate to remain long angry with Larry, he was so good-natured, so full of fuss, so coaxing; he paid such pretty compliments, his eyes were so roguish, his face so handsome—besides, Samuel was on the other side of the waggon, seeing, hearing nothing.

The dimples formed in her cheeks, the contraction of lips and brows gave way, the angry sparkle disappeared from her blue eyes, and then her clear, laugh announced that she was pacified. Hillary, knowing he had conquered, audacious in his pride of conquest, put his arm round her waist, stooped, and kissed the bare arm nearest him that rested on the pitchfork, then he sprang aside as she attempted to box his ears.

Honor was hard by and had seen both kisses, and had heard every word that had passed. She continued her work as though unconscious. For a moment, a pang of jealousy contracted her bosom, but she hastily mastered it. She knew that she could not, must not regard Hillary in any other light than as a brother, and yet she was unable to see her sister supplanting her in his affections without some natural qualms. But

Honor was unselfish, and she hid her suffering. Kate as little suspected the state of her sister's heart as Honor suspected Kate's liking for Sam Voaden. And now, all at once, an idea shot through Honor's mind which crimsoned her face. How she had misread Hillary's manner when they were together watching for the lamb-killer. She had fancied then that his heart was drawing towards her, and the thought had filled her with unutterable happiness. Now she saw his demeanour in another aspect. He really loved Kate, and his affection for her was only a reflection of his love for the younger sister. He had sought to gain her esteem, to forward his suit with Kate. When this thought occurred to Honor, she hid her face, humbled and distressed at having been deluded by self-conceit. She made it clear to herself now that Hillary had thought only of Kate. Her sister had said nothing to her about Hillary—but was that wonderful, as he had not declared himself? A transient gleam had lightened her soul. It was over. Work was Honor's lot in life, perhaps sorrow, not love.

'The last load is carried, and in good order. Where is the dance to be?' asked Samuel Voaden, coming into sight as the waggon moved on.

'In the barn,' answered Hillary.

'Kate,' said Hillary, 'give me the first dance.'

'And me the second,' pleaded Samuel.

When Combe wrote and Rowlandson illustrated the 'Tour of Doctor Syntax,' a dance was the necessary complement of a harvest whether of corn or hay—especially of the latter, as then the barn was empty. The Reverend Doctor Syntax thought it not derogatory to his office to play the fiddle on such occasions. Moreover, half a century ago, the village fiddler was invited into any cottage, when, at the sound of his instrument, lads and maidens would assemble, dance for a couple of hours and disperse before darkness settled in. The denunciation of dancing as a deadly sin by the Methodists has caused it to fall into desuetude. Morality has not been bettered thereby. The young people who formerly met by daylight on the cottage floor, now meet, after chapel, in the dark, in hedge corners.

Hillary and Samuel had engaged Kate. Neither had thought of Honor, though she stood by, raking the fragrant hay.

'Up, up!' shouted both young men. 'Kate, you must ride on the last load.'

The waggon moved away, with Kate mounted on the sweet contents, and with the young men running at the side. Honor remained alone, looking after them, resting on her rake, and, in spite of her efforts, the tears filled her eyes.

But she did not give way to her emotion.

Honor called the children, when the last load left the field, and led them home. She was hot and tired, and her heart ached, but she was content with herself. She had conquered the rising movement of jealousy, and was ready to accept Hillary as her sister's acknowledged lover.

Kate followed her. An hour later the dance in the barn would begin. The lads and maidens went home to smarten up, and wash off the dust and stain of labour, and the barn had to be decorated with green branches, and the candles lit.

Kate went upstairs at once to dress. Honor remained below to hear the children's prayers, and get the youngest ready for bed. Then she went up to the room she shared with Kate, carrying little Temperance in her arms.

'Oh Honor, bundle them all in. What a time you have been! We shall be late; and I have promised to open the dance with Larry.'

'I am not going, Kate.'

'Not going! Of course you are going.'

'No, I am not. Father is not home, and will want his supper. Besides, I cannot leave the house with all the little ones in it unprotected.'

'There are no ogres hereabouts that eat children,' said Kate hastily. 'We can manage. This is nonsense; you must come.'

'I do not care to, Kate. Sit down in that chair, and I will dress your hair. It is tossed like a haycock.'

Kate seated herself, and Honor combed and brushed her sister's hair. Then she put a blue ribbon through it; and took the kerchief from her box, and drew it over Kate's shoulders, and pinned it in place.

'Oh Honor! What a lovely silk kerchief! Where did you get this? How long have you had it? Why have you not shown it me before?'

'It is for you, dearest Kate; I am glad you like it.'

Kate stood up, looked at herself in the glass, and then threw her arms round her sister and kissed her.

'You are a darling,' exclaimed Kate. 'Always thinking of others, never giving yourself anything: Let me remain at home—do you go instead of me.'

Honor shook her head. She was pleased to see Kate's delight, but there was an under-current of sadness in her soul. She was adorning her sister for Hillary.

Kate did not press Honor to go instead of her, though she was sufficiently good-hearted to have taken her sister's place without becoming ill-tempered, had Honor accepted the offer.

'Do I look very nice?' asked Kate, with the irresistible dimples coming into her cheeks. 'I wonder what Larry will say when he sees me with this blue ribbon, and this pretty kerchief.'

'And I,' said Honor slowly, not without effort, 'I also wonder.'

XXIII
A Brawl

WHEN KATE CAME TO THE barn, she found it decorated with green boughs. There were no windows, only the great barn door, consequently the sides were dark; but here four lanterns had been hung, diffusing a dull yellow light. The threshing-floor was in the middle, planked; on either side the barn was slated, so that the dancing was to be in the middle. Forms were placed on the slate flooring for those who rested or looked on. On a table sat the fiddler with a jug of cider near him.

The season of the year was that of Barnaby bright, when, as the old saw says, there is all day and no night. The sun did not set till past eight, and then left the north-west full of silver light. The hedgerows, as Kate passed between them, streamed forth the fragrance from the honeysuckle which was wreathed about them in masses of flower, apricot-yellow, and pink. Where the incense of the eglantine ceased to fill the air it was burdened with the sweetness of white clover that flowered thickly over the broad green patches of grass by the road-side.

Hillary was awaiting Kate to open the dance with her. He had gone to the gate to meet her; he recognised his kerchief at once; he was surprised and hurt. Why was Honor not there? Kate came with her little brother Joe holding her hand. Joe had begged permission to attend the dance. Why had Honor made over Larry's present to her sister? It was a slight, an intentional slight. Larry bit his lips and frowned; his heart beat fast with angry emotion. He approached Kate with an ungracious air, and led her to the dance without a pleasant word.

Kate was unquestionably the prettiest girl present. She held her fair head erect, in consciousness of superiority. Her hair was abundant, full of natural wave and curl, and the sky-blue ribbon in it seemed to hold it together, and to be the only restraining power that prevented it breaking loose and enveloping her from head to foot in the most beautiful gloss silk. Her complexion was that of the wild rose, heightened by her rapid walk and by excitement; her eyes were blue as the forget-me-not.

The evening sun shone in at the barn door, as yellow, but purer and brighter than the lantern light. Had there been a painter present he would have seized the occasion to paint the pretty scene—the old barn with oaken timbers, its great double doors open, from under a penthouse roof leaning forward to cover the laden wains as they were being unpacked of their corn-sheaves; the depths of the barn dark as night, illumined feebly by the pendent lanterns: and the midst, the threshing-floor, crowded with dancers, who flickered in the saffron glow of the setting sun.

Kate noticed that Hillary, whilst he danced with her, observed the kerchief intently.

'Is it not pretty?' she asked innocently. 'Honor gave it me. She had kept it for me in her box ever since the Revel, and not told me that she had it; nor did I see her buy it then. Honor is so good, so kind.'

Hillary said nothing in reply, but his humour was not improved. His mind wandered from his partner.

'When is Honor coming?' he asked abruptly.

'She is not coming at all.'

'Why not?'

'Father is not home, and will want his supper when he does return.'

'Honor must do all the drudging whilst others dance,' he said peevishly.

'I offered to stay and let her come, but she would not hear of it.'

Hillary danced badly; he lost step. He excused himself; but Kate was dissatisfied with her partner, he was dull, and she was displeased to see that Sam Voaden was dancing and laughing and enjoying himself with someone else.

'You are a clumsy partner,' she said, 'and dance like old Diamond when backing against a load going down hill.'

'Honor gave you that kerchief? What did she say when she gave it you?'

'Nothing.'

He said no more, and led her to a bench in the side of the barn.

'What! tired Larry? I am not.'

'I am,' he answered sulkily.

Directly, Sam Voaden came to her, and was received with smiles.

'Larry Nanspian came left leg foremost out of bed this morning,' she said. 'He is as out of tune as Piper's fiddle.'

Kate was in great request that evening. The lads pressed about her, proud to circle round the floor with the graceful pretty girl; but she gave the preference to Samuel Voaden. Hillary asked her to dance with him in 'The Triumph,' but she told him sharply she would reserve her hand for him in the Dumps, and he did not ask her again.

The girls present looked at Kate with envy. They were unable to dispute her beauty; but her charm of manner and lively wit made her even more acceptable to the lads than her good looks. She was perfectly conscious of the envy and admiration she excited, and as much gratified with one as with the other.

Samuel Voaden was infatuated. He pressed his attentions, and Kate received them with pleasure. As she danced past Larry she cast him glances of contemptuous pity.

Hillary was angry with Honor, angry with Kate, angry with himself. The spoiled prince was cast aside by two girls—a common carrier's daughters. He was as irritated against Kate now as he was previously against Honor. When he heard Kate laugh, he winced, suspecting that she was joking about him. His eyes followed the kerchief, and his heart grew bitter within him. He made no attempt to be amusing. He had nothing to say to any one. He let the dances go on without seeking partners. He stood lounging against the barn door, with a sprig of honeysuckle in his mouth, and his hands behind his back.

The sun was set, a cool grey light suffused the meadow, the stackyard, the barn, the groups who stood about, and the dancers within.

A dog ventured in at the door, and he kicked it out.

The dog snarled and barked, and he nearly quarrelled with young Voaden because the latter objected to his dog being kicked.

Then, all at once, his mood changed. It occurred to him that very probably Honor stayed away just for the purpose of showing him she did not care for him. If that were so, he would let her know that he was not to be put out of heart by her slights. He would not afford her the gratification of hearing through her sister that he was dispirited and unhappy. Then he dashed into the midst of the girls, snatched a partner, and thenceforth danced and laughed and was uproariously merry.

At ten o'clock the dancing was over. Country folk kept early hours then; the cider barrel was run out, the basket of cakes emptied, and the tallow lights in the lanterns burnt down to a flicker in a flood of melted grease.

The young men prepared to escort their partners home.

Hillary saw that Samuel was going with Kate. He was exasperated to the last degree. He did not care particularly for Kate, but he did care that it should not be talked of in the village that Sam Voaden had plucked her away from under his very nose. Gossip gave her to him as a sweetheart, and gossip would make merry over his discomfiture. Besides, he wanted an excuse for going to the cottage and having an explanation with Honor about the kerchief.

As Voaden's dog passed in front of him at a call from his master, Larry kicked it.

'Leave my dog alone, will you!' shouted Samuel. 'That is the second time you have kicked Punch. The dog don't hurt you, why should you hurt him?'

'I shall kick the brute if I choose,' said Hillary. 'It has no right here in the barn.'

'What harm has Punch done? And now, what is against his leaving?'

'You had no right to bring the dog here. It has been in the plantation after young game.'

'Punch is wrong whether in the barn or out of it. The guinea you got for shooting Rover has given you a set against dogs seemingly,' said young Voaden.

'The dog took your lambs at Swaddledown, and you were too much a lie-a-bed to stop it,' sneered Hillary.

'Some folk,' answered Samuel, 'have everything in such first-rate order at home they can spare time to help their neighbours.'

'No more!' exclaimed Kate; 'you shall not quarrel.'

Hillary looked round. Near him were two women who had been in the van when he returned from Tavistock with the kerchief. They, no doubt, recognised it over Kate's shoulders. They made sure it was his love-token to her, and, wearing it, she was about to affront him in their eyes. His wounded vanity made him blind to what he said or did.

'Here, Kate,' he said, thrusting himself forward, 'I am going to take you home. You cannot go with Samuel. His cursed Punch is an ill-conditioned brute, and will kill your chickens.'

'Nonsense,' laughed Kate, 'our chickens are all under cover.'

'I'll fight you,' said Hillary, turning to Samuel. 'Kate was engaged to me for the Tank,[1] and you carried her off without asking leave. I will not be insulted by you on my father's land, and under my own roof. If you are a man you will fight me.'

'Nonsense, Larry,' answered Samuel good-humouredly, 'I'll not quarrel with you. It takes two to make a quarrel, as it takes two to kiss.'

'You are afraid, that is why.'

'I am not afraid of you, Larry,' said Samuel. 'You are as touchy this evening as if whipped with nettles.'

'Come with me, Kate,' exclaimed Hillary. 'You have known me longer than Voaden. If he chooses to take you, he must fight me first.'

'I will not fight you, Larry,' answered the young Swaddledown farmer; 'but I don't object to a fling with you, if you will wrestle.'

'Very well; throw off your coat.'

The young men removed their jackets, waistcoats, and the handkerchiefs from their throats. They were both fine fellows—well-built and strong. Those who had been dancing surrounded them in a ring, men and maids.

'Cornish fashion, not Devon,' said Samuel.

'Ay, ay!' shouted the bystanders, 'Cornish wrestle now.'

'Right—Cornish,' answered Hillary.

The difference between Devon and Cornish wrestling consists in this, that in a Devon wrestle kicking is admissible; but then, as a protection to their shins, the antagonists have their legs wreathed with haybands (*vulgo* skillibegs). As the legs were on this occasion unprotected, Devon wrestling was inadmissible. Both fashions were in vogue near the Tamar, and every young man would wrestle one way or the other as decided beforehand.

The opponents fixed each other with their eyes, and stood breathless, and every voice was hushed. Instantaneously, as moved by one impulse, they sprang at each other, and were writhing, tossing, coiling in each other's embrace. Neither could make the other budge from his ground, or throw him, exerting his utmost strength and skill. The haymakers stood silent, looking on appreciatively—the girls a little frightened, the men relishingly, relishing it more than the dance. Not one of the lads at that moment had a thought to cast at his partner. Their hands twitched, their feet moved, they bent, threw themselves back, swung aside, responsive to the movements of the wrestlers.

The antagonists gasped, snorted, as with set teeth and closed lips they drew long inspirations through their nostrils. Their sweat poured in streams from their brows.

Simultaneously, moved by one impulse, they let go their hold, and stood quivering and wiping their brows, with labouring breasts; then, with a shout, closed again.

'Ho!' a general exclamation. In the first grapple Hillary had slipped, and gone down on one knee. Immediately Samuel let go.

'There!' said he, holding out his hand. 'We have had enough. Strike palms, old boy.'

'No,' gasped Hillary, blazing with anger and shame. 'I was not flung. I slipped on the dock-leaf there. I will not allow myself beaten. Come on again.'

'I will not do so,' answered Samuel. 'If you have not had enough, I have.'

'You shall go on. You are a coward to sneak out now when an accident gave you advantage.'

'Very well, then,' said Samuel; 'but you have lost your temper, and I'll have no more than this round with you.'

The young men were very equally matched. They grappled once more, twisted, doubled, gasped; the ground was torn up under their feet. As the feet twirled and flew, it was hard to say how many were on the ground at once, and whose they were.

Samuel suddenly caught his antagonist over the arms, and pushed them to his side.

'He'll have Larry down! he will, by George!' shouted several. 'Well done, Samuel. Go it, Samuel Voaden!'

'Ha!' shouted Sam, starting back. 'Who goes against rules? You kicked.'

'You lie! I did not.'

'You did! you did, Larry,' shouted three or four of the spectators. It was true in his excitement Larry had forgotten that he and his opponent were without skillibegs and wrestling in Cornish fashion, and he had kicked; but in good faith he had denied doing it, for he was unconscious of his actions, so blinded and bemuzzed was he with anger, disappointment, and shame.

'I'll not wrestle any more,' said Samuel, 'if you don't wrestle fair. No—I won't at all. You are in a white fury. So—if it's unfair in you to kick, it is unfair in me to take advantage of your temper.'

'It is not done. One or other must go down.'

Then Kate pushed forward. 'Neither of you shall attend me home,' she said; 'I am going with little Joe only.'

Whether this would have ended the affray is doubtful. Another interruption was more successful. Suddenly a loud blast of a horn, then a yelping as of dogs, then another blast—and through the yard before the barn, breaking the ring, sweeping between the combatants, passed a strange figure—a man wearing a black bull's hide, with long brown paper ears on his head; the hide was fastened about his waist, and the tail trailed behind. He was followed by a dozen boys barking, baying, yelping, and after them hobbled Tom Crout blowing a horn.

'It's no good,' said the lame fellow, halting in the broken ring; 'I can't follow the hare, Mr. Larry Nanspian; the hunt is waiting for you. On wi' a green coat, and mount your piebald, and take my horn. I wish I could follow; but it's un-possible. Whew! you hare! Heigh! Piper, stay, will you, and start fair.'

'I'll have nothing to do with it,' said Hillary, still panting.

'That is right, Larry,' said Kate in his ear, 'you oughtn't. Honor said as much, and that she hoped you would keep out of it.'

'Did she?' said Hillary angrily; 'then I'll go in for it.'

'Larry, old chap,' exclaimed Voaden, patting him on the shoulder, 'I wasn't the better man, nor was you. You slipped on the dock-leaf, and that don't reckon as a fall. We'll have another bout some other day, if you wish it. Now let us have the lark of the hare hunt.'

Hillary considered a moment, and wiped his face. He had fallen in the general estimation. He had been sulky, he had provoked Sam, and the wrestle had not turned to his credit. Here was a chance offered of taking the lead once more. If he did not act the huntsman, Sam would.

'All right, Crout,' said he, 'give me the horn; I'll have my horse round directly, and the green coat on.'

'Do not, do not, Larry,' entreated Kate.

'Tell Honor I'm not pinned to her apron,' answered the young man, and ran into the house.

1. An old country dance.

XXIV

THE HAND OF GLORY

THE READER MAY HAVE BEEN puzzled by the hints made by Larry to Honor, and by Charles to Mrs. Veale, of a threatened hare hunt, and he may have wondered why such a threat should have disturbed Honor and angered the housekeeper. There are plenty of hares on Broadbury Moor; there have been hare hunts there as long as men could remember; frequently, all through the winter. An ordinary hare hunt would not have stirred much feeling in women's bosoms. The menaced hare hunt was something very different. A stag and a hare hunt are the rude means employed by a village community for maintaining either its standard of morals or expressing its disapprobation of petticoat rule. The stag hunt is by no means an institution of the past, it flourishes to the present day; and where the magistrates have interfered, this interference has stimulated it to larger proportions The hare hunt, now extinct, was intended to ridicule the man who submitted to a rough woman's tongue.

The stag hunt takes place either on the wedding night of a man who has married a girl of light character, or when a wife is suspected of having played her husband false. The hare hunt more properly satirised the relations between Taverner Langford and Mrs. Veale. In not a few cases, especially with a stag hunt, there is gross injustice done. It cannot be otherwise: the Vehm-Gericht is self-constituted, sits in the tavern, and passes its sentence without summons and hearing of the accused. There is no defence and no appeal from the court. The infliction of the sentence confers an indelible stain, and generally drives those who have been thus branded out of the neighbourhood. Petty spite and private grudges are sometimes so revenged; and a marriage in a well-conducted family, which has held itself above the rest in a parish, is made an occasion for one of these outrages, whereby the envy of the unsuccessful and disreputable finds a vent.

There probably would have been no hare hunt near Langford had not the quarrel between Langford and Nanspian agitated the whole parish, and given occasion for a frolic which would not have been adventured had the brothers-in-law been combined.

'Well, Mr. Charles,' said Mrs. Veale, 'what have you done with the five-pound note I let you have? Is it all spent?'

'I gave it to my father and sister,' answered Charles. 'I've occasioned them some expense, and I thought I'd make it up to them whilst I could.'

'That was mighty liberal of you,' sneered Mrs. Veale.

'I am liberal, pretty free-handed with my money. It comes of my blood.'

'Ah!' said the housekeeper, 'and I reckon now you'll be wanting more.'

'I could do with more,' replied young Luxmore, 'but I will not trouble you.'

'Oh! it's no trouble,' said Mrs. Veale, 'I know very well that lending to you is safe as putting into the Bank of England. You must have your own some day, and when you're squire you won't see me want.'

'Rely on me, I will deal most generously with you. I shall not forget your kindness, Mrs. Veale.'

'But,' said the woman slyly, eyeing him, 'I can't find you as much as you require. You can't spin more out of me than my own weight, as the silkworm said. I've put aside my little savings. But as you see, the master don't pay freely. He gives you only nine pence, and me——' she shrugged her shoulders.

'If I were in your place,' she went on, after a pause, 'I should be tempted to borrow a hundred or so, and go to Physick the lawyer with it, and say, help me to Coombe Park, and when I've that, I'll give you a hundred more.'

'Who'd lend me the money? You have not so much.'

'No, I have not so much.'

'What other person would trust me?'

'The money might be had.'

'Others don't see my prospects as you do.'

'I'd be inclined to borrow wi'out asking,' said the housekeeper cautiously. She was as one feeling her way; she kept her eyes on Charles as she talked. Charles started. He knew her meaning.

'How dare you suggest such a thing!' he said in a low tone, looking at her uneasily. 'Curse you! Don't wink at me with your white lashes that way, you make me uneasy.'

'I only suggested it,' said Mrs. Veale, turning her head aside. 'I reckon no harm would be done. The master don't know how much he has in his box. We had it out t'other day between us, and counted. There be over a thousand pounds there. Do y' think he counts it every week? Not he. Who'd know! The money would be put back, and wi' interest, six, seven, ten per cent, if you liked, when you'd got Coombe Park.'

'Have done,' said Luxmore with nervous irritation; 'I'm no thief, and never could become one.'

'Who asked you to be one? Not I. I said as how you might become his banker for a hundred pounds. The bank gives but three per cent, and you would give nine. Who'd be the loser? Not master. He'd gain nine pounds without knowing it—and wouldn't he crow!'

Charles Luxmore caught his hat and stood up. 'Where be you going to?' asked Mrs. Veale.

'I cannot stand this,' he said in an agitated voice. 'You torment me. You put notions into me that won't let me sleep, that make me miserable. I shall go.'

'Whither? To the "Ring o' Bells." There be no one there to-night, all be away to Chimsworthy at the Haysel. You sit down again, and I will give you some cherry cordial.'

He obeyed sulkily.

'You can't go to dance at Chimsworthy, because you be here at Langford, and there's no dancing and merry here. But wait till you're at Coombe Park, and then you'll have junketings and harvest and dances when you will. That'll be a rare life.'

He said nothing, but thrust his hands into his pockets, and looked moodily before him.

'Shall I tell you now who'll find you the money?'

He did not speak.

'Wellon will.'

'What?' he looked up in surprise.

'Ay! old Wellon as was gibbeted, he will.'

Charles laughed contemptuously. 'You are talking folly. I always thought you mad.'

'Did you ever hear of the Hand of Glory?'

'No, never.'

'I wonder what became of Wellon's hand—the hand that throttled Mary Rundle, and stuck the knife into the heart of Jane, and brought down their aunt wi' a blow of the fist. That hand was a mighty hand.'

'Wellon was hung in chains, and fell to dust.'

'But not the hand. Such a hand as that was too precious. Did you never hear it was cut off, and the body swung for years without it?'

'No, I did not.'

'It was so.'

'What good was it to anyone?'

'It was worth pounds and pounds.'

'As a curiosity?'

'No, as a Hand of Glory. It were washed in mother's milk to a child base-born, and smoked in the reek of gallows-wood, and then laid with tamarisk from the sea, and vervain, and rue, and bog-bean.'

'Well, what then?'

'Why, then, sure it's a Hand of Glory.' She paused, then struck her hand across her forehead, 'And grass off the graves of them as it killed—I forgot to say that was added.'

'What can such a hand do?'

'Everything. If I had it here and set it up on the mantelshelf, and set a light to the fingers, all would flame blue, and then every soul in the house would sleep except us two, and we might ransack the whole place and none would stir or hinder or see. And if we let the hand flame on, they would lie asleep till we were far away beyond their reach.'

'If you had this Hand of Glory, I wouldn't help you to use it,' said Charles, writhing on his seat.

'That is not all,' Mrs. Veale went on, standing by a little tea-table with her hand on it, the other against her side. 'That hand has wonderful powers of itself. It is as a thing alive, though dead and dry as leather. If you say certain words it begins to run about on its fingers like a rat. Maybe you're sitting over the fire of nights, and hear something stirring, and see a brown thing scuttling over the floor and you think it is a rat. It is not. It is the dead man's hand. Perhaps you hear a scratching on the wall, and look round, and see a great black spider—a monstrous spider going about, running over and over the wainscot, and touching and twitching at the bell wires. It is not a spider, it is the murderer's hand. It hasn't eyes, it goes by the feel, till it comes to gold, and then, at the touch the dark skin becomes light and shines as the tail of a glow-worm, and it picks and gathers by its own light. I reckon, if that hand o' Wellon's were in the oven behind the parlour-grate it would make such a light that you'd see what was on every guinea, whether the man and horse or the spade, and you could read every note as well as if you had the daylight. Then the ring-finger and the little finger close over what money the hand has been bidden fetch, and it runs away on the thumb and other two—and then, if you will, it's spider-like with a bag behind.'

'I don't believe a word of it,' said Charles, but his words were more confident than his tone.

'You see,' Mrs. Veale went on, 'there is this about it, you tell the hand to go and fetch the money, but you don't say whither it is to go, and you don't know. You get the money and can swear you have robbed no one. I reckon, mostly the money is found by the hand in old cairns and ruins. I've been told there's a table of gold in Broadbury Castle that only comes to the top on Midsummer night of an hour, and then sinks again.

Folks far away see a great light on Broadbury, and say we be swaling (burning gorse) up here; but it no such thing; it is the gold table coming up, and shining, like fire, and the clouds above reflecting its light.'

'Pity the hand don't break off bits of the gold table,' said Charles sarcastically; but his face was mottled with fear; Mrs. Veale's stories frightened him.

'Yes, 'tis a pity,' she said. 'Maybe it will some day.'

'Pray what do you say to the hand to make it run your errands?'

'Ah!' she continued, without answering his question. 'There be other things the Hand of Glory can do. It will go if you send it to some person—bolts and locks will not keep it out, and it will catch the end of the bedclothes, and scramble up, and pass itself over the eyes of the sleeper, and make him sleep like a dead man, and it will dive under the clothes and lay its fingers on the heart; then there will come aches and spasms there, or it will creep down the thighs and pinch and pat, and that brings rheumatic pains. I've heard of one hand thus sent as went down under the bedclothes to the bottom of the sleeper's foot, and there it closed up all the fingers but one, and with that it bored and bored, working itself about like a gimlet, and then gangrene set in, and the man touched thus was dead in three days.'

'It is a mighty fortunate thing you've not the hand of old Wellon,' growled Charles.

'I have got it,' answered Mrs. Veale.

Charles looked at her with staring eyes.

'You shall see it,' she said.

'I do not want to. I will not!' he exclaimed shuddering.

'Wellon's hand will fetch you a hundred pounds, and we will not ask whence it comes,' said Mrs. Veale.

'I will not have it, I will not touch it!' He spoke in a hoarse, horrified whisper.

'You shall come with me, and I will show you where I keep it, and perhaps you will find the hand closed; and when I say, Hand of Glory! open! Hand of Glory! give up! then you will see the fingers unclose, and the glittering gold coins will be in the brown palm.'

'I will not touch them.'

'No harm in your looking at them. Come with me.'

She stood before him with her firm mouth set, and her blinking eyes on him. He tried to resist. He settled himself more comfortably into his seat. But his efforts to oppose her will were in vain. He uttered a curse, drew his hands out of his pocket, put his hat on his head.

'Go on,' he said surlily; 'but I tell y' I won't go without the lantern. Where is it?'

'In Wellon's Cairn.'

'I will not go,' said Charles, drawing back, and all colour leaving his cheek.

'Then I'll send the hand after you. Come.'

'I'll take the lantern.'

'As you like, but hide the light till we get to the hill. There it don't matter if folks see a flame dancing about the mound. They will keep their distance—Come on, after me.'

XXV

The Hare Hunt

Directly Mrs. Veale, followed by Charles, came outside the house the former turned and said, with a chuckle, 'You want a lantern, do y', a summer night such as this?'

The sky was full of twilight, every thorn tree and holly bush was visible on the hedges, every pebble in the yard.

'I'm not going to Wellon's Cairn without,' said Luxmore sulkily. 'I don't want to go at all; and I won't go there without light.'

'Very well. I will wait at the gate for you.'

He went into the stable, where was a horn-sided tin lantern, and took it down from its crook, then went back into the kitchen and lighted the candle at the fire.

'I've a mind not to go,' he muttered. 'What does the woman want with me, pulling me, driving me, this way and that? If I'd been told I was to be subjected to this sort of persecution, I wouldn't have come here. It's not to be endured for nine pence. Nine pence! It would be bad at eighteen pence. I wish I was in Afghanistan. Cawbul Ghuznee, Candahar don't astonish her. She ain't open-mouthed at them, but sets my hair on end with her Hand of Glory, and talks of how money is to be got. I know what she is after; she wants me to run away with her and the cash box. I won't do it—not with her, for certain; not with the cash box if I can help it. I don't believe a word about a Hand of Glory. I'm curious to know how she'll get out of it, now she's promised to show it me.'

He started, and swore.

'Gorr!' he said; 'it's only a rat behind the wainscot; I thought it was the hand creeping after me. I suppose I must go. For certain, Mrs. Veale is a bad un. But, what is that? The shadow of my own hand on the wall, naught else.'

He threw over him a cloak he wore in wet weather, and hid the lantern under it.

'For sure,' he said, 'folks would think it queer if they saw me going out such a summer night as this with a lantern; but I won't go to Wellon's Cairn without, that is certain.'

'Well,' said Mrs. Veale; 'so you have come at last!'

'Yes, I have come. Where is the master? I've not seen him about.'

'He never said nothing to no one, and went off to Holsworthy to-day.'

'When will he be back?'

'Not to-morrow; there's a fair there; the day after, perhaps.'

A heavy black cloud hung in the sky, stretching apparently above Broadbury. Below it the silvery light flowed from behind the horizon. To the east, although it was night, the range of Dartmoor was visible, bathed in the soft reflection from the north-western sky. The tumulus upon which Wellon had been executed was not far out on the heath. Mrs. Veale led the way with firm tread; Charles followed with growing reluctance. A great white owl whisked by. The glow-worms were shining mysteriously under tufts of grass. As they pushed through the heather they disturbed large moths. A rabbit dashed past.

'Hush!' whispered Charles. 'I'm sure I heard a horn.'

'Ah!' answered Mrs. Veale, 'Squire Arscott rides the downs at night, they say, and has this hundred years.'

'I don't care to go any further,' said the young man.

'You shall come on. I am going to show you the Hand of Glory.'

He was powerless to resist. As his father had fallen under the authority of Honor, so the strong over-mastering will of this woman domineered Charles, and made him do what she would. He felt his subjection, his powerlessness. He saw the precipice to which she was leading him, and knew that he could not escape.

'I wish I had never come to Langford,' he muttered to himself. 'It's Honor's doing. If I go wrong she is to blame. She sent me here, and all for nine pence.' Then, stepping forward beside the housekeeper, 'I say, Mrs. Veale, how do you manage to stow anything away in a mound?'

'Easy, if the mound be not solid,' she replied. 'There is a sort of stone coffin in the middle, made of pieces of granite set on end, and others laid on top. When the treasure-seekers dug into the hill, they came as far as one of the stones, and they stove it in, but found nothing, or, if they found aught, they carried, it away. Then, I reckon, they put the stone back, or the earth fell down and covered all up, and the heather bushes grew over it all. But I looked one day about there for a place where I could hide things. I thought as the master had his secret place I'd have mine too; and I knew no place could be safer than where old Wellon hung, as folk don't like to come too near it—leastways in the dark. Well, then, I found a little hole, as might have been made by a rabbit, and I cleared it out; and there I found the gap and the stone coffin. I crept in, it were not over big, but wi' a light I could see about. I thought at first I'd come on Wellon's bones, but no bones were there, nothing at all but a rabbit nest, and some white snail shells. After that I made up the entrance again, just as it was, and no one would know it was there. But I can find it; there is a bunch of heath by it, and some rushes, and how rushes came to grow there beats me.'

'So you keep Wellon's hand in there, do you?'

'Yes, I do.'

'How did you manage to get it?'

'I will not tell you.'

'I do not believe you have it; I don't believe but what you told me a parcel of lies about the Hand of Glory. I've been to Afghanistan, and Cawbul, and the Bombay Presidency, and never heard of such a thing.

It is not in reason. If a dead hand can move, why has not my finger that was cut off in battle come back to me?'

'Shall I send the hand after it?'

The suggestion made Charles uneasy. He looked about him, as afraid to see the black hand running on the grass, leaping the tufts of furze, carrying his dead finger, to drop it at his feet.

'What are you muttering?' asked he sharply.

'I'm only repeating, Hand of Glory! Hand of Light! Fetch, fetch! Run and bring——'

'I'll strike you down if you go on with your devilry, you hag,' said Charles angrily.

'We are at the place.'

They entered the cutting made by the treasure-seekers, the gap in which Honor had often sat in the sun, unconscious of the stone kistvaen been hidden behind her, indifferent to the terrors of the haunted hill, whilst the sun blazed on it.

'The night is much darker than it was,' said Charles uneasily, as he looked, about him.

It was as he said. The black mass of cloud had spread and covered the sky, cutting off the light except from the horizon.

'I don't like the looks of the cloud,' said Charles. 'There will be rain before long, and there's thunder aloft for certain.'

'What is that to you? Are you afraid of a shower? You have your cloak. Bring out the lantern. It matters not who sees the light now. If anyone does see it, he'll say it's a corpse-candle on its travels.'

'What is a corpse-candle?'

'Don't you know?' She gave a short, dry laugh. 'It's a light that travels by night along a road, and comes to the door of the house out of which a corpse will be brought in a day or two.'

'Does no one carry the candle?'

'It travels by itself.' Then she said, 'Give me the light.'

'I will not let it out of my hand,' answered Charles, looking about him timorously. 'I don't think anyone will see the light, down in this hole.'

'Hold the lantern where I show you—there.'

He did as required. It gave a poor, sickly light, but sufficient to show where the woman wanted to work. She began to scratch away the earth with her hands, and Charles, watching her, thought she worked as a rabbit or hare might with its front paws. Presently she said:

'There is the hole, look in.'

He saw a dark opening, but had no desire to peer into it. Indeed, he drew back.

'How can I see if you take away the lantern?' asked Mrs. Veale. 'Put your arm in and you will find the hand.'

He drew still further away. 'I will not. I have seen enough. I know of this hiding-place. That suffices. I will go home.'

The horror came over him lest she should force him to put his hand into the stone coffin, and that there, in the blackness and mystery of the interior, the dead hand of the murderer would make a leap and clasp his.

'I have had enough of this,' he said, and a shiver ran through him, 'I will go home. Curse me! I'm not going to be mixed up with all this devilry and witchery if I can help it.'

'Perhaps the hand is gone,' said Mrs. Veale.

'Oh! I hope so.'

'I sent it after your finger.'

'Indeed; may it be long on its travels.' He was reassured. It was not pleasant to think of so close proximity to the murderer's embalmed, still active hand. He suspected that Mrs. Veale was attempting to wriggle out of her undertaking. 'Indeed—I thought I was to see the hand, and now the hand is not here.'

'I cannot say. Anyhow, the money is here.'

'What money?'

'That for which you asked.'

'I asked for none.'

'You desired a hundred pounds for the purpose of getting back Coombe Park. Put in your hand and take it.'

'I will not.'

His courage was returning, as he thought he saw evasion of her promise in the woman.

'For the matter of that, if this Hand of Glory can fetch money, it might as well fetch more than that.'

'How much?'

'A hundred is not over much. Two hundred—a thousand.'

'Say a thousand.'

'So I do.'

'Put in your hand. It is there.'

'Hark!'

'Put in your hand.'

'I will not.'

'Then you fool! you coward! I must take it for you!' she hissed in her husky voice. She stooped, and thrust both her hands and arms deep into the kistvaen.

'Hush!' whispered Charles, as he laid his hand on her shoulder, and covered the light with a flap of his mantle. She remained still for a minute with her arms buried in the grave. There was certainly a sound, a tramp of many feet, and the fall of horses' hoofs, heard, then not heard, as they went over road or turf.

'There,' whispered Mrs. Veale, and drew a box from the hole and placed it on Charles's lap. As she did so, the mantle-flap fell from the lantern, and the light shone over the box. Charles at once recognised Taverner Langford's cash box, with the letter padlock.

'Ebal,' whispered Mrs. Veale. 'A thousand pounds are yours.'

At that instant, loud and startling, close to the cairn sounded the blast of a horn, instantly responded to by the baying and yelping of dogs, by shouts, and screams, and cheers, and a tramp of rushing feet, and a crack of whips.

The suddenness of the uproar, its unexpectedness, its weirdness, coming on Charles's overwrought nerves, at the same moment that he saw himself unwillingly involved in a robbery, completely overcame him; he uttered a cry of horror, sprang to his feet, upset the money box, and leaped out of the cutting, swinging the lantern, with his wide mantle flapping about him. His foot tripped and he fell; he picked himself up and bounded into the road against a horse with rider, who was in the act of blowing a horn.

Charles was too frightened and bewildered to remember anything about the hare hunt. He did not know where he was, what he was doing, against whom he had flung himself. The horse plunged, bounded aside, and cast his rider from his back. Charles stood with one hand to his head looking vacantly at the road and the prostrate figure in it. In another moment Mrs. Veale was at his elbow. 'What have you done?' she gasped. 'You fool! what have you done?'

Charles had sufficiently recovered himself to understand what had taken place

'It is the hare hunt,' he said. 'Do you hear them? The dogs! This is—my God! it is Larry Nanspian. He is dead. I said I would break his neck, and I have done it. But I did not mean it. I did not intend to frighten the horse. I—I——' and he burst into tears.

'You are a fool,' said Mrs. Veale angrily. 'What do you mean staying here?' She took the horn from the prostrate Larry and blew it. 'Don't let them turn and find you here by his dead body. If you will not go, I must, though I had no hand in killing him.' She snatched the lantern from his hand and extinguished it. 'That ever I had to do with such an one as you! Be off as you value your neck; do not stay. Be off! If you threatened Larry and have fulfilled your threat, who will believe that this was accident?'

Charles, who had been overcome by weakness for a moment, was nerved again by fear.

'Take his head,' said Mrs. Veale, 'lay him on the turf, among the dark gorse, where he mayn't be seen all at once, and that will give you more time to get off.'

'I cannot take his head,' said Charles trembling.

'Then take his heels. Do as I bid,' ordered the housekeeper. She bent and raised Larry.

'Sure enough,' she said, 'his neck is broken. He'll never speak another word.'

Charles let go his hold of the feet. 'I will not touch him,' he said. 'I will not stay. I wish I'd never come to Langford. It was all Honor's fault forcing me. I must go.'

'Yes, go,' said Mrs. Veale, 'and go along Broadbury, where you will meet no man, and no footmarks will be left by which you may be traced.' Mrs. Veale, unassisted, dragged the senseless body out of the rough road over the turf.

'Is he dead? is he really dead?' asked Charles.

'Go!' said Mrs. Veale, 'or I shall have the chance of your hand to make into a better Hand of Glory than that of Wellon.'

XXVI
Bitter Medicine

The hare and hounds ran some distance before they perceived that they were not pursued by the huntsman and that the horn had ceased to cheer them on. Then little Piper, the cattle-jobber, clothed in the black ox-hide, stopped panting, turned, and said, 'Where be the hunter to? I don't hear his horse nor his horn.' The dogs halted. They were boys and young men with blackened faces. Piper's face was also covered with soot. His appearance was diabolical, with the long ears on his head; his white eyes peering about from under them, a bladder under his chin, and the black hide enveloping him. According to the traditional usage on such occasions, the hunt ends with the stag or hare, one or the other, being fagged out, and thrown at the door of the house whose inmates' conduct has occasioned the stag or hare hunt. Then the hunter stands astride over the animal, if a stag, and with a knife slits the bladder that is distended with bullock's blood, and which is thus poured out before the offender's door. If, however, the hunt be that of a hare the pretence is—or was—made of knocking it on the head. It may seem incredible to our readers that such savage proceedings should still survive in our midst, yet it is so, and they will not be readily abolished.[1]

Not suspecting anything, the hare and the pack turned and ran back along the road they had traversed, yelping, shouting, hooting, blowing through their half-closed hands, leaping, some lads riding on the backs of others, one in a white female ragged gown running about and before the hare, flapping the arms and hooting like an owl.

Would Taverner Langford come forth, worked to fury by the insult? Several were armed with sticks in the event of an affray with him and his men. Would he hide behind a hedge and fire at them out of his trumpet-mouthed blunderbuss that hung over the kitchen mantel piece in Langford? If he did that, they had legs and could run beyond range. They did not know that he was away at Holsworthy. The road to that town lay over the back of Broadbury and passed not another house in the parish.

The wild chase swept over the moor, past Wellon's Cairn, past Langford, then turned and went back again.

'I'll tell you what it be,' said Piper, halting and confronting his pursuers. 'Larry Nanspian have thought better of it, and gone home. T'es his uncle, you know, we'm making game of, and p'raps he's 'shamed to go on in it.'

'He should have thought of that before,' said one of the dogs. 'Us ain't a going to have our hunt spoiled for the lack of a hunter.'

'Why didn't he say so in proper time?' argued a second.

'Heigh! there's his horse!' shouted a third, and ran over a moor towards the piebald, which, having recovered from its alarm, was quietly browsing on the sweet, fine moor grass.

'Sure eneaf it be,' said Piper; 'then Larry can't be far off.'

Another shout.

'He's been thrown. He is lying here by the roadside.'

Then there was a rush of the pack to the spot indicated, and in a moment the insensible lad was in the arms of Piper, surrounded by an eager throng.

'Get along, you fellows,' shouted the hare, 'you'll give him no breathing room.'

'Ah! and where'll he think himself, I wonder, when he opens his eyes and sees he is in the hands of one with black face and long ears, and tail and hairy body? I reckon he won't suppose he's in Abraham's bosom.'

'What'll he take you for either, in your black faces?' retorted Piper. 'Not angels of light, surely.' Then old Crout hobbled up. He had followed far in the rear, as best he could with his lame leg and stick.

'What be the matter, now?' he asked. 'What, Larry Nanspian throwed? Some o' you lads run for a gate. Us mun' carry 'n home on that. There may be bones abroke, mussy knows.'

'I reckon we can't take 'n into Langford,' suggested Sam Voaden.

'Likely, eh?' sneered Piper. 'You, Sam, get a gate for the lad. He must be carried home at once, and send for a doctor.'

He was obeyed; and in a few minutes a procession was formed, conveying Larry from the moor.

'He groaned as we lifted 'n,' said Sam Voaden. 'So he's got life in him yet.'

'His hand ain't cold, what I may call dead cold,' said another.

'You go for'ard, Piper,' said Tom Crout, 'that he mayn't see you and be frightened if he do open his eyes.'

Then the cattle-jobber walked first, holding the long cow's tail over his arm, lest those who followed should tread on it and be tripped up. Sam Voaden and three other young men raised the gate on their shoulders, and walked easily under it. Behind came the hounds, careful not to present their blackened faces to the opening eyes of their unconscious friend, and, lastly, Tom Crout mounted on the piebald. One of the boys had found the horn, and unable to resist the temptation to try his breath on it, blew a faint blast.

'Shut up, will you?' shouted Piper turning. 'Who is that braying? You'll be making Larry fancy he hears the last trump, and he'll jump off the gate and hurt himself again.'

Larry Nanspian had not broken his neck nor fractured his skull. He was much bruised, strained, and his right arm and collar-bone were broken. His insensibility proceeded from concussion of the brain; but even this was not serious, for he gradually recovered his consciousness as he was being carried homewards. Too dazed at first to know where he was, what had happened, and how he came to be out and lying on a gate, he did not speak or stir. Indeed, he felt unwilling to make an effort, a sense of exhaustion overmastered him, and every movement caused him pain. He lay with his face to the night sky, watching the dark cloud, listening to the voices of his bearers, and picking with the fingers of his left hand at a mossy gate bar under him. At first he did not hear what words were passing about him, he was aware only of voices speaking: the first connected sentence he was able to follow was this

''Twould be a bad job if Larry were killed.'

'Bad job for him, yes,' was the reply.

'What do y' mean by that?' asked Sam Voaden. He recognised Sam's voice at once, and he felt the movement of Sam's shoulder tilting the fore end of the gate as he turned his head to ask the question.

'O, I mean naught but what everyone says. A bad job for any chap to die; but I don't reckon the loss would be great to Chimsworthy. Some chance, then, of the farm going to proper hands. Larry ain't much, and never will be, but for larks and big talk. I say that Chimsworthy is a disgrace to the parish; and what is more there is sure to be a smash there unless there comes an alteration. Alteration there would never be under Larry.'

'I've heard tell that the old man has borrowed a sight of money from Taverner Langford, and now he's bound to pay it off; and can't do it.'

'Not like to, the way he's gone on; sowing brag brings brambles.'

'You, see,' said Voaden, 'they always reckoned on getting Langford, some day, when the old fellow died.'

'And what a mighty big fool Larry is to aggravate his uncle. Instead of keeping good terms with the old gentleman he goes out o' his road to offend him.'

'I say it's regular un-decent his being out to-night hunting the hare before his own uncle's door.'

'I say so, too. It weren't my place to say naught, but I thought it, and so did every proper chap.'

'It is an ill bird that fouls its own nest.'

'Does his father know what he's been after?'

'No, of course not; old Nanspian would ha' taken' a stick to his back, if he'd heard he was in for such things.'

'I know that however bad an uncle might use me, I'd never have nothing to do with a hare hunt that concerned him—no, nor an aunt neither.'

'Larry was always a sort of a giddy chap.'

'He's a bit o' a fool, or he wouldn't have come into this.'

'Maybe this will shake what little sense he has out of his head.'

'I'll tell y' what. If Larry had been in the army—he'd have turned out as great a blackguard as Charles Luxmore.'

'The girls have spoiled Larry, they make so much of him.'

'Make much of him! They like to make sport of him, but there's not one of them cares a farthing for him, not if they've any sense. They know fast enough what Chimsworthy and idleness are coming to. Why, there was Kate Luxmore. Everyone thought she and Larry were keeping company and would make a pair; but this evening, you saw, directly she had a chance of Sam, she shook him off, and quite right too.'

'Never mind me and Kate,' said Sam, turning his head again.

'But us do mind, and us think as Kate be a sensible maiden, and us thought her a fool before to take up wi' Larry Nanspian.'

This conversation was not pleasant for the young man laid on the gate to hear, and it took from him the desire to speak and allow his bearers to know he was awake, and had heard their criticism on his character and conduct. The judgment passed on him was not altogether just, but there was sufficient justice in it to humble him. Yes, he had acted most improperly in allowing himself to be drawn into taking part in the hare hunt. No—he was not, he could never have become such a blackguard as Charles Luxmore.

'Halt!' commanded Piper, and the convoy stood still.

'We can't go like this to Chimsworthy,' said the little cattle-jobber; 'it'll give the old man another stroke. Let us stop at the Luxmores' cottage, and wash our faces, and put off these things, and send on word that we're coming; the old fellow mustn't be dropt down on wi' bad news too sudden.'

'Right! Honor shall be sent on to break the news.'

Honor! Larry felt the blood mount to his brow. She had herself dissuaded him from having anything to do with this wretched affair, which had ended so disastrously to himself, and when Kate advised him to keep away from it because Honor disapproved, he had sent her an insolent defiance. Now he was to be laid before her door, bruised and broken, because he had disobeyed her warning. He tried to lift himself to protest—but sank back. No—he thought—it serves me right.

The party descended the rough lane from Broadbury, and had to move more slowly and with greater precaution. The bearers had to look to their steps and talk less. Larry's thoughts turned to Honor. Now he had found out how true were her words. What she had said to him gently was said now roughly, woundingly. She had but spoken to him the wholesome truth which was patent to everyone but himself, but she had spoken it so as to inflict no pain. She had tried to humble him, but with so pitiful a hand that he could have kissed the hand, and asked it to continue its work. But he had not taken her advice, he had not learned her lesson, and he was now called to suffer the consequences. Those nights spent beside Honor under the clear night sky—how happy they had been.

How her influence had fallen over him like dew, and he had felt that it was well with him to his heart's core. How utterly different she was from the other girls of Bratton. They flattered him. She rebuked him. They pressed their attentions on him. She shrank from his notice. He could recall all she had said. Her words stood out from his recollection like the stars in the night heavens—but he had not directed his course by them.

Now, as the young men carried him down the lane, he knew every tree he passed, and that he was nearing Honor, step by step. He desired to see her, yet feared her reproachful eye.

1. The author once tore down with his own hands the following bill affixed to a wall at four cross roads:

'Notice!—On Thursday night the Red Hunter's pack of stag-hounds will meet at … Inn, and will run to ground a famous stag. Gentlemen are requested to attend.'

The police were communicated with, but were unable to interfere as no breach of the peace was committed.

XXVII
After Sweetness

Oliver Luxmore had returned home before Kate came from the dance, and had eaten his supper and gone to bed. Her father had been a cause of distress to Honor of late. He said, indeed, no more about Taverner's suit, but he could not forget it, and he was continually grumbling over the difficulties of his position, his poverty, the hardships of his having to be a carrier when he ought to be a gentleman, and might be a squire if certain persons would put out a little finger to help him to his rights.

His careless good humour had given place to peevish discontent. By nature he was kind and considerate, but his disappointment had, at least temporarily, embittered his mood. He threw out oblique reproaches which hurt Honor, for she felt that they were aimed at her. He complained that times were altered, children were without filial affection, they begrudged their parents the repose that was their due in the evening of their days. He was getting on in years, and was forced to slave for the support of a family, when his family—at least the elder of them—ought to be maintaining him. He wished that the Thrustle were as deep as the Tamar, and he would throw himself in and so end his sorrows. His children—his ungrateful children—must not be surprised if some day he did not return. There was no saying; on occasions, when a waterspout broke, the Thrustle was so full of water that a man might drown himself in it.

In vain did Honor attempt to turn his thoughts into pleasanter channels. He found a morbid pleasure in being absorbed in the contemplation of his sores. He became churlish towards Honor and refused to be cheered. She had fine speeches on her tongue, but he was a man who preferred deeds to words. A girl of words and not of deeds was like a garden full of weeds. When the weeds began to grow, like the heavens thick with snow, when the snow began to fall—and so on—and so on—he had forgotten the rest of the jingle.

Now for the first time, dimly, was Honor conscious of a moral resemblance between her father and Charles. What Charles had become, her father might become. The elements of character were in germ in him that had developed in the son. As likenesses in a family come out at unexpected moments, that had never before been noticed, so was it with the psychical features of these two. Honor saw Charles in her father, and the sight distressed her.

Oliver Luxmore did not venture to say out openly what he desired, but his hints, his insinuations, his grumblings, were significant; they pierced as barbed steel, they bruised as blows. Till recently, Oliver had recognised his daughter's moral superiority, and had submitted. Now his eye was jaundiced. He thought her steadfastness of purpose to be doggedness, her resistance to his wishes to be the result of self-will, and his respect for her faded.

Although Honor made no complaint, no defence, she suffered acutely. She had surrendered Larry because her duty tied her to the home that needed her. Was it necessary for her to make a further sacrifice—a supreme sacrifice for the sake of her father? She had no faith in the verbal promises of Taverner Langford to stand by and assist her brothers and sisters, but it was in her power to exact from him a written undertaking which he would be unable to shake off. Suppose she were to marry Langford then? Then—the dark cloud would lift and roll away. There would be no more struggle to make both ends meet, no more patching and darning of old clothes, no more limiting of the amount of bread dealt out to each child. Her father's temper would mend. He would recover his kindly humour, and play with the little ones, and joke with the neighbours and be affectionate towards her. There would be no more need for him to travel with a waggon in all weathers to market, but he would spend his last years in comfort, cared for by his children, instead of exhausting himself for them.

However bright such a prospect might appear, Honor could not reconcile herself to it. Her feminine instincts revolted against the price she must pay to obtain it.

That evening Oliver Luxmore ate his supper in sulky silence, and went to bed without wishing Honor a goodnight. When Kate arrived, she found her sister in tears.

'Honor!' exclaimed the eager, lively girl, 'what is the matter? You have been crying—because you could not go to the dance.'

'No, dear Kate, not at all.'

'Honor! what is the meaning of this? Marianne Spry tells me she saw the silk kerchief you gave me before to-day.'

'Well, why not?'

'But, Honor, I do not understand. Mrs. Spry says that Larry bought it—bought it at Tavistock after he had killed the dog that worried our lambs—after he had got the guinea, and she believes he bought it with that money.'

'Well, Kate!' Honor stooped over her needlework.

'Well, Honor!'—Kate paused and looked hard at her. 'How is it that Larry bought it, and you had it in your chest? That is what I want to know.'

'Larry gave it me.'

'Oh—oh! He gave it you!'

'Yes, I sat up with him when he was watching for the lamb-killer; he is grateful for that trifling trouble I took.'

'But, Honor! Marianne Spry said that she and others chaffed Larry in the van about the kerchief he had bought for me—and it was *not* for me.'

Honor said nothing; she worked very diligently with her fingers by the poor light of the tallow candle on the table. Kate stooped to get sight of her face, and saw that her cheek was red.

'Honor, dear! The kerchief was not for me. Why did you make me wear it?'

'Because, Kate—because you are the right person to wear his present.'

'I—why I?' asked Kate impetuously.

Honor looked up, looked steadfastly into her sister's eyes.

'Because Larry loves you, and you love him.'

'I can answer for myself that I do not,' said Kate vehemently. 'And I don't fancy he is much in love with me. No, Honor, he was in a queer mood this evening, and what made him queer was that you were not in the barn, and had decked me out in the kerchief he gave you to wear. I could not make it out at the time, but now I see it all.'

Then Kate laughed gaily. 'I don't suppose you care very much for him; he's a Merry Andrew and a scatterbrain, but I do believe he has a liking for you, Honor, and I believe there is no one in the world could make a fine good man of Larry but you.' Then the impulsive girl threw her arms round her sister. 'There!' she exclaimed, 'I'm glad you don't care for Larry, because he is not worthy of you—no, there's not a lad that is—except, maybe, Samuel Voaden, and him I won't spare even to you.'

'Oh Kate!'

So the sisters sat on, and the generous, warm-hearted Kate told all her secret to her sister.

When girls talk of the affairs of the heart, time flies with them. Their father and brothers and sisters were asleep, and they sat on late. Kate was happy to confide in her sister.

All at once Kate started, and held her finger to her ear.

'I hear something. Oh Honor, what is it? I hope these hare hunters be not coming this way.'

She had not told Honor Larry's message.

'I hear feet,' answered the elder. 'Do not go to the door, Kate. It is very late.'

The tramp of feet ceased, the two girls with beating hearts heard steps ascend to their door, then a rap at it. Honor went at once to open. Kate hung back. She suspected the hare hunters, but was afraid of the black faces, and she could not understand the halt and summons.

'Don't y' be frightened, Honor,' said a voice through the door, 'us want y' out here a bit, if you don't mind.' Honor unbolted, and the black-faced, white-eyed, long-eared, skin-clothed Piper stood before her, holding the black cow tail in his hand.

'Don't y' be scared. I'm only the hare. I won't touch a hair of your head.'

'What do you want, Mr. Piper?' asked Honor without trepidation.

'Well, it is this. There's been an accident, and Master Larry Nanspian hev fallen on his head off his horse and hurted himself bad.'

Honor began to tremble, and caught the door with one hand and the door-post with the other.

'Now do y' take it easy. He ain't dead, only hurt. Us don't want to go right on end carrying him into Chimsworthy, all of us dressed as we are. First place, it might frighten Master Nanspian; second place, he mightn't like the larks Larry has been on. So us thought if you would let us clean our faces, and take off our skins and other things, and cut the green coat off the back of Larry, here; and then, you'd be so good as run on to Chimsworthy and prepare the old gentleman, you'd be—well, you'd be yourself—I couldn't put it better.'

Honor had recovered her composure.

'I will do what you wish,' she said, and her voice was firm, though low.

'You see,' Piper went on, 'it's a bit ockered like; I reckon the old man wouldn't be satisfied that Larry were mixed up in a hare hunt that made game of Taverner Langford, his own wife's brother; and I don't say that Larry acted right in being in it. Howsomever, he has been, and is now the worse for it. Will you please to bring the candle and let us see how bad he be.'

Honor took the tin candlestick with the tallow dip, and descended the steps, holding it.

The four bearers set the gate upon the ground, and Honor held the candle aloft, that the light might fall on Larry. But a soft wind was blowing, and it drove the flame on one side, making the long wick glow and then carrying it away in sparks.

'Mr. Piper, go into the cottage and ask my sister Kate to give you my scissors. I will remove the coat. Go all of you, either to the well a few steps down the lane, or into our kitchen, and wait. Kate will give you towel and soap. Leave me with Larry. I must deal very gently with him, and I had rather you were none of you by.'

'You're right,' said Piper. 'Us had better have white faces and get clear of horses and other gear before he sees us.'

'We must be quick,' said Sam Voaden. 'Larry must be got home as fast as may be.'

Then they ran, some to the well in the bank, some—Sam, of course—into the cottage, and left Honor for a moment or two beside the prostrate man, kneeling, holding the guttering candle with one hand, and screening the flame from the wind with the other.

Then Larry opened his eyes, and looked long and earnestly into her face. He said nothing. He did not stir a finger; but his eyes spoke.

'Larry!' she breathed. Her heart spoke in her voice, 'Larry, are you much hurt?'

He slightly moved his head.

'Much, Larry? where?'

'In my pride, Honor,' he answered.

She looked at him with surprise: at first hardly comprehending his meaning.

Then Kate came down the steps with the scissors.

'Oh Honor! How dreadful! I told him not to go! I told him you disapproved! And now he is punished. Oh Honor! is he badly injured? He is not killed?'

'No, Kate, he is not killed. How far hurt I cannot tell. Larry! you must let me move you. I may hurt you a little.'

'You cannot hurt me,' he said. 'I have hurt myself.'

'Oh Honor!' exclaimed Kate. 'If he can speak he is not so bad. Shall I help?'

'No, Kate,' answered Honor, 'go back to the cottage and give the young men what they want to clean their faces; those at the well also. I can manage Larry by myself.'

She stooped over him.

'Larry! you must let me raise you a little bit. Tell me truly, are any bones broken?'

'I do not know, Honor. I feel as if I could not move. I am full of pain, full in all my limbs, but most full in my heart.'

She began to cut up the seams of the sleeves.

'I cannot move my right arm,' he said. 'I suppose there is some breakage there.'

'Yes,' she said gravely, 'I can feel a bone is broken.'

'If that be all it does not matter,' he said more cheerfully, 'but I want to say to you, Honor, something whilst no one is by.'

'What is it?'

'I have done very wrong in many ways. I have been a fool, and I shall never be anything else unless you—'

'Never mind that now,' she, hastily interrupted him. 'We must think only at present of your aching joints and broken bones.'

Then Oliver Luxmore's voice was heard calling, and asking what was the matter. Who were in the house? He had been roused from his sleep and was alarmed. Kate ran up the stairs to pacify him, and when he knew the circumstances he hastily dressed.

An altercation broke out at the well. There was not room for all to get at the water. One came running up with streaming face to Honor. 'Am I clean?' he asked. 'How is Larry? Not so bad hurt after all, is he?' Then he went up the steps into the cottage to consult his fellows as to the condition of his face, and to wipe it.

Honor removed the coat in pieces.

'Thank you,' said Larry. 'The candle is out.'

'Yes, the wind has made it out.' (extinguished it).

'My left hand is sound. Come on that side.'

She did as he asked.

'And this,' he said, 'is the side where my heart is. Honor, I'm very sorry I did not follow your advice. I am sorry now for many things. I want you to forgive me.'

'I have nothing to forgive.'

'Lean over me. I want to whisper. I don't want the fellows to hear.'

She stooped with her face near his. Then he raised his uninjured arm, put it round her neck, and kissed her.

'Honor! dear Honor! I love no one! no one in the world but you! And I love you more than words can say.'

Did she kiss him? She did not know herself. A light, then a darkness, were before her eyes. What time passed then? A second or a century? She did not know. A sudden widening of the world to infinity, a loss of all limitations—time, space—an unconsciousness of distinction, joy, pain, day, night, a loss of identity—was it she herself, or another?

Then a wakening as from a trance, with tingling veins, and dazed eyes, and whirling brain, and fluttering heart, and voice uncontrolled, as from the cottage door, down the steps, and from the well, up the lane came simultaneously the rabble of boys and men.

'Well, how is he?' 'Have you got the coat off?' 'Can he speak?' 'Any bones broke?'

Honor could not answer the questions; she heard them, but had no voice wherewith to speak.

'Raise the gate again,' said Piper. 'Sam, are you ready? Why are you behind? We must get on.'

'Honor,' said Larry in a low voice, 'walk by the side of me. Hold my hand.'

'He is better,' said one of the young men; 'he can speak. He knows Honor.'

'Yes, he is better,' she said, 'but he has his right arm broken, and he is much shaken and bruised. Let me walk beside him, I can stay the gate and ease him as you carry him over the ruts and stones.' So she walked at his side with her hand in his. In a few minutes the party had arrived at the granite gates of Chimsworthy.

'Stay here,' ordered Piper. 'Now, Honor Luxmore, will you go on up the avenue and tell the old gentleman. Us'll come after with Master Larry in ten minutes.'

'I will go,' said Honor, disengaging her hand.

'How are you now?' asked Piper, coming up to the young man.

'Better,' he said, 'better than ever before.'

XXVIII

A First Step

FOR THE NEXT TWO DAYS and nights Larry was in great pain. His arm and collar-bone had been set, but strains are more painful than breakages, and the young fellow in his fall had managed to bruise and sprain his muscles as well as fracture his bones. He could not sleep; he could not move in bed; every turn, even the slightest, caused him agony. The doctor enjoined perfect rest. Through the two long sleepless nights his mind was active, and the train of thought that had begun as he was being carried from Broadbury continued to move in his brain. What different nights were these to those spent by him on the bench with Honor! He considered what she had said to him, and he knew that what she had said was right. How careless of his best interests he had been! How regardless of his duties! How neglectful of his proper self-respect! Of course she was right. His father never had properly managed the farm, and since his stroke he had paid it less attention than before. He, the son and heir, ought to have devoted himself to the work of the farm, and made that his main object, not to amuse himself.

His father came up to his room several times a day to inquire how he was.

'There's Physick coming here,' said the old man, 'and I want you to use your hand when he comes.'

'I have only my left.'

'Well, the left must do. If you can't sign your name, you can make a cross and that will suffice.'

'What do you want me to sign, father?'

'The mortgage. Physick will find the money, and then we shall pay off Taverner Langford, and have done.'

Larry sighed. He remembered what Honor had said. He was helping to burden, not to relieve, the property.

'Can't it be helped, father? I'd rather not, if the money could be raised any other way.'

'But that is impossible without a sale.'

'Why did Uncle Taverner lend the money?'

'We were behind in a score of things.'

'Is it all gone, father?'

'Gone! of course it is. Now I'm wanting more, and I must raise double what Taverner lends me, half to pay him off, and half to meet present demands.'

'How is this?'

'Bad times. Things will come round some day.'

'How long have they been bad?'

'Ever since your mother died. That was a bad day for us.' The old man sat rubbing his chin. 'The next bad day was when I quarrelled with Taverner, or rather, when Taverner quarrelled with me. 'Tis a pity. I made up his orchard with my new grafts; and a more beautiful lot of apple-trees are not to be seen—and he for to cut them. Shameful.'

'What was the quarrel about, father?'

'I've told you afore. A red spider. Taverner tried to sloke (draw) her away, when she was running straight as a line into my pocket. But I reckon he can't keep you forever out of Langford. He may live for ten or twelve years out of wicked spite, but he is not immortal, and Langford will come to you in the end. Then you can clear off the mortgages—I reckon I shall be gone then.'

'Don't say that, father.'

'I know I shall. When Taverner sloked that spider away he carried off my health, and I were took with the stroke immediately. I've not been myself since.' He continued rubbing his chin. 'And now comes this mortgage, and you laid up in bed as you never was before. It all comes o' sloking away the spider.'

'Father,' said Larry earnestly but timorously, 'I wish you would let me bring another here.'

'Another what?'

'Red spider.'

'What do you mean?'

'Honor Luxmore.'

The old man looked puzzled, then gradually an idea of his son's meaning crept into his head.

'I thought,' said he slowly, 'I thought it was t'other maid.'

'No, dear father, I love Honor. Let me bring her here, let her be my wife, and I'm sure she will bring luck to this house.'

Hillary senior continued rubbing his chin. 'Her mayn't have money,' he mused, 'but her's good up and down the backbone; as a money-spinner is all redness and naught else, so is Honor all goodness and not a speck of black in her.'

'It is so indeed, father.'

'I'm better pleased than if it were Kate.'

'I never really thought of Kate.'

'Well, you was sly about it then. All folks said that Kate had stolen your fancy. Well now, Honor mayn't be a money-bringer, I reckon she's got nothing—Oliver be poor as rushy land—but she may spin it. There's no saying.'

'Say yes, father.'

'Her's a red spider that Taverner won't try to sloke away,' chuckled old Nanspian. Then he continued musing. He was an altered man of late, not ready with his thoughts, quick of motion, lively of tongue as before. He took time to come to a decision, and drifted in his ideas from one matter to another. 'Things haven't gone quite right since Blandina died, they haven't—though I don't allow that to others. I've had five years of wool heamed (laid) up. I said I'd not sell with wool so low, and it has been sorry down ever since, and now it's risen a penny and I tried to sell—the worm is in it and the staple is spoiled, and it won't fetch any price. Then there be the maidens. They've let the thunder get into the milk and turn it sour, and wasted the Lord knows how much butter, because they were lazy and wouldn't leave their beds in time at five o'clock, and make before the sun is hot. If you'd a good wife, her'd mend all that. And Honor! well, no one has other than a good word for her. I'm main pleased wi' your choice, Larry. Yes, I be.'

'Oh, father! Thank you! thank you!'

'It's not for me to go into the maidens' room and rake them out of bed at half-past three in the mornings. I put it to you, Larry. Folks would say it was ondecent. And if I don't, the butter ain't made, the thunder gets in the pans, and I lose many pounds. I reckon Honor Luxmore would do that. I've been racking my brains as you rack cider, how to get over the difficulty, and it was all dark before me, but now I see daylight at last. Honor will rake the maids out o' their beds, and I needn't interfere. You'll be quick about it, won't you, Larry, before the blazing hot summer weather sets in, with thunder in the air, and spoils the milk.'

He passed his hand through his grey hair. 'I had a bell put up in their bedroom, and a wire brought along to mine, and a handle nigh my bed, that I might ring them up in the mornings early. It cost me nigh on thirty shillings did that bell. The hanger had to come all the way from Tavistock, and it took him two days to put up, and there were a lot of cranks to it. Well, it was just so much money thrown away. What do y' think the maidens contrived? Why, they stuffed an old worsted stocking into the bell and tied it round the clapper; I might pull the rope as if I were pealing a triple bob major, and not a sound came out of the bell, because of the stocking. Well, I wouldn't go into the maidens' room and see what was the matter, and so I sent to Tavistock for the bell-hanger out again, and he charged me three shillings for himself, and half a crown for his man, and ten shillings for the hire of a trap, and all he did was to remove the stocking. Next night the maidens tied up the clapper with the fellow stocking. If Honor were here she'd put all that to rights, wouldn't she?'

'I'm sure of it, father.'

'You be sharp and get well,' continued the old man, 'then we'll have it all over, and save pounds of butter.' He stood up. 'I mustn't shake hands wi' you, Larry, but I'm main pleased. Honor's good through and through as a money-spinner is scarlet.'

Larry was fain to smile, in spite of his pain. This was like his father. The old man went on vehemently, hotly for some new fancy, and in a few weeks tired of it, and did nothing more about it.

Next day Physick the lawyer came, and brought the mortgage and the money. The signatures were appended, a cross for Larry, and the money received.

'Now,' said the old man, 'I'd like you, Mr. Physick, to go over to Langford and pay the sum I owe to my brother-in-law. I can't go myself. He's spoken that insolent to me, and that too before the whole of Coryndon's Charity, that I can never set foot over his drexil (threshold) again. So I'd wish you to go for me, and bring me my note of hand back all square.'

'I will go as well,' said Larry, who was up, able to walk about, but without his jacket, because of his bandaged bones and arm strapped back.

'You!' exclaimed his father. 'Why should you go?'

'I wish it,' answered the lad. 'I'll tell you the reason after.'

'You'd better not go out yet.'

'Why not? Mr. Physick will drive me there and back in his gig. I shall not be shaken. The gig has springs.'

'I reckon there's a certain cottage the rogue will want to get out at on the way. Don't let him, Mr. Physick, or he won't be home for hours.'

Although the gig had springs Larry suffered in it, and was glad to descend with Mr. Physick at Langford.

Taverner Langford had returned home but an hour before; he had been to the fair at Holsworthy, and thence had gone into Bideford about a contract for young bullocks. He had just finished his dinner of bread and cheese, washed down with water, when Mrs. Veale opened the parlour door, and without a word showed in Mr. Physick and Larry.

Langford greeted the lawyer with a nod. 'Please to take a chair.' He stared at Hillary with surprise, and said nothing to him.

'We've come to pay you the loan you called in,' said Physick.

'Right,' answered Taverner, 'I was expecting the money, though why?—grapes of thorns and figs of thistles is against nature as well as Scripture.' Then he eyed his nephew furtively. He saw that he was looking pale and worn, that his arm was bandaged, and he was without a jacket. He saw that the lad moved stiffly when he walked. 'You may sit down,' he said gruffly. Larry took the back of an armchair with his left hand and drew it to him, then slowly let himself down into it. All his movements, and the twitching of the muscles in his face, showed he was in pain. His uncle watched him and saw this, but he asked no questions.

When the money had been counted, and the release handed over, and Physick had indulged in some desultory talk, and disparagement of water, which he saw that Taverner was drinking, he rose to leave. Langford was not in a conversationable mood, his dark brows were knit.

Then Larry stood up, and came towards the table, against which he stayed himself with his hand.

'I beg your pardon, Uncle Taverner,' he said in a voice somewhat tremulous, whilst colour came into and spotted his brow. 'I came here, though I thought you would not care to see me.'

'I don't mind when I see your back,' interrupted Langford surlily, 'your father insulted me grossly.'

'I have come, Uncle Taverner—'

'Ah! I suppose your father has sent you. He wants to patch up the quarrel; you may go back and tell him it is too late. I won't make it up. It is of no use. I have nothing to lose by estrangement. You and he are the losers, and that to a heavy amount, as you shall learn some day.'

'I have not come with any message from my father.'

'You've come for yourself, have you? You think that Langford would be a fine farm for the growth of wild oats? You shan't try it.'

'I came here of my own accord,' said the young man. 'My father knows nothing of my purpose. I have come to tell you that I am very sorry for what I did—what I did, I dare say you have not heard, as you have been away. You shall hear from me.'

'What have you done? Some foolery, I warrant.'

'Yes, uncle, something worse than foolery. The night you were away, and when we did not know but you were at Langford, there was a hare hunt before your doors.'

'What!' almost screamed the old man.

Physick was unable to restrain a laugh.

'There was a hare hunt, and I was in it. I took a principal part. I was thrown from my horse, and picked up unconscious, and the thing came to an end, it went no further. I have been badly hurt. I might have been killed.'

'And pray how came that about?' asked the old man quivering with anger. 'A light from heaven—struck you to the ground, like Saul when breathing out threatenings and slaughters against the Elect? And now you're a converted character, eh? and so think I'll take you back into favour, and let you have Langford?'

'No, uncle. I do not know quite what it was threw me down. Don't think me mad if I say it—but it seemed to me to be old Wellon rising from the cairn and rushing down on me, to strike me to the earth.'

Langford looked at him with amazement.

'I tell you just what happened. I was riding in the hunt—more shame to me—and I had the horn to my lips, and was just by the Gibbet Hill, when my piebald stood bolt still, and shivered with fear, and all at once there came a yellow light out of the barrow, and a great black figure with flapping clothes about it, and I remember no more.'

Langford was like the rest of his class, full of belief in the supernatural. Larry spoke with such earnestness of tone, his face so fully expressed his conviction, that the old man was awed.

'I have broken my right arm and collar-bone. I have suffered a great deal. I have not slept for three nights, and this is the first day I have been out of my bedroom. Uncle Taverner, I made up my mind the very first night that I would come to you directly I was able, and tell you that I am ashamed of myself. When the fellows were carrying me away on a gate, and I woke up—then I knew I had done wrong. I was warned beforehand twice to have nothing to do with the hunt. I heard those who were carrying me say how bad I behaved in taking part in the game against my own uncle. There—uncle! I'm very sorry, and I hope I'll never be such a fool and so wicked again.'

Taverner's lips quivered, whether from suppressed rage, or from a rising better emotion, neither Physick nor Larry knew, for they left the room, whilst the old man stared after them with his dark brows contracted over his keen, twinkling eyes, and he sat motionless, and without speaking.

Larry was some little while getting into the gig. Mrs. Veale stood on the doorsteps watching him. All at once they heard a cry from the inside of the house—a cry, whether of terror, or rage, or pain, could not be told.

'What is it?' asked Physick. 'What's the matter?'

'It's master,' said Mrs. Veale; 'something has disagreed with him, I reckon.'

XXIX
A Blow

Honor felt like one who has looked into the lightning. A glimpse of surpassing light, a vision into a heaven of fire, was succeeded by darkness and numbness of mind.

She was unable for some while to recover her mental and moral balance. The joy that had wrapped her soul as in flame had left a pain of fire. What had she done? What would come of this? Must she go on or could she step back? The moment when Larry's lips had met her cheek, and his words of love had rushed in at her ear and boiled through her veins, had been one in which her self-control had deserted her.

She thought over and over what had taken place. She felt his grasp of her hand, his arm about her neck, the pressure of his lips. What must follow on this? She had not withdrawn herself from him at his touch. She could not have done so. The power of resistance had left her. But now, as her clear mind arranged duties and weighed them against passion, she was doubtful what to do. It was strange for her to feel need of advice, to be forced to ask another what to do, yet now she felt that she could not judge for herself; but she also knew of no one who could advise her. There was nothing for her but to wait. Her simple faith raised her soul to God, and she prayed for a right judgment. She would leave the future in His hands: events must decide her course for her. Of one thing she was clear in her view; her duty to her father and brothers and sisters—she must not desert them. Whether she must wholly surrender her happiness for them, or whether she could combine her duty with her inclination, she could not tell; that Larry and the future must decide.

She waited in patience. She knew that he would come to her as soon as he could. She heard daily from Chimsworthy how he was. Little Joe ran up and inquired.

She saw him drive by with Mr. Physick. Whither was he going? To Okehampton? It was not the shortest road. As he passed the cottage his face was turned towards it, and she saw his eyes looking for her, but the gig was not arrested. She was in the house, and had but a glimpse of him through the open door. Whether he had seen her or not she could not tell.

Presently he returned. He must have been to Langford. She stood in the doorway, and their eyes met. He did not stay the horse; he could not. He sat beside the lawyer, who was driving, and the broken right arm was near the reins. Physick was between him and Honor; but Larry turned his head and looked at her as the trap went by. How pale and thin he seemed! What marks of suffering were on his face! The tears of pity came into Honor's eyes.

'He will come and see me soon,' she said to herself. 'May I have my strength to do what is right.' Then she seated herself at her work.

Kate was in the house, lively as a finch. Honor was always reserved; she was now more silent than usual. Kate's humour was unusually lively. Her tongue moved as nimbly as her feet and fingers, her conversation sparkled, and her tones danced like her eyes. When she was not talking she was singing. She made her jokes and laughed over them herself, as Honor was in no laughing mood.

Oddly enough, Sam Voaden was daily in the lane. He came round by the cottage from Swaddledown to ask at Chimsworthy after Larry; he made two miles out of a journey that need not have been three-quarters across the fields. When Sam went by he whistled very loud, and then Kate found that the pitcher was empty and needed replenishing at the well; on such occasions, moreover, the pitcher took a long time filling. Kate made no secret of her heart's affairs to her sister. It was in her nature to talk, and a girl in love likes nothing better, when not with her lover, than to talk about him.

Honor put away her needlework and got the supper-table ready, and whilst she was putting the cold pasty on the table her father walked in. He was going next day to Tavistock, and had been round for commissions.

He was out of spirits, did not say much, wiped his face with his sleeve, and complained of the weather—it was sultry, he was tired. Some of his customers had been exacting and had worried him. 'The pasty is heavy; it goes against me,' he grumbled. 'All well for young appetites.'

'Shall I do you a bit of bacon, father?' asked Honor.

'Rich that,' he said discontentedly. 'I'm fanciful in my eating. I can't help it; I'm too poor to have what would suit me. It is in my constitution. Those who have the constitutions of gentlefolk want the food of gentlefolk.' He took a little piece of pasty, but pushed it away. 'It makes my throat rise; look at that great hunch of suet in it, like a horse-tooth (quartz spar) in granite. I can't eat anything; you may clear away.'

Actually Oliver Luxmore had eaten supper at one of the farms; that was why he had now no appetite; but he made occasion of his having no relish for his food to grumble and make Honor uncomfortable.

'The fog was a hunting this morning, so we've had a fine day for going nowhere; and it's gone a fishing this evening, to let me understand it will rain to-morrow when I go into Tavistock. It is always so. Rain on market days to spoil my custom and run away with profits.'

In explanation of his words, it is necessary to say that, when the white fog mounts the hills it is said to go hunting, when it lies along the rivers it is said to be fishing, and these conditions of fog are weather indications.

'I don't know what you call that,' said Oliver, pointing with his fork to a piece of meat in the pasty. 'It looks to me as if it were a goat caterpillar got in. I suppose you found it crawling across the lane from one of the willow trees, and, because we're poor and can't afford meat; stuck it in.'

'Father, it is wholesome; it is nothing but a bit of pig-crackling. You know we were given a piece of young pork by Mrs. Voaden, the other day.'

Then Oliver sprang to his feet, and Honor started back in surprise.

Without a word of salutation, with white face, and glaring eyes, with hand extended and shaking, Taverner Langford came in at the door.

'There! there!' he said, in a voice raised almost to a scream. 'This is what comes of doing a favour. Now I am punished.'

'What is the matter, Mr. Langford?' asked the carrier deferentially.

'What is the matter? Everything is the matter,' he cried. He turned to Honor: 'It is your doing, yours, yours.'

'What have I done?' she asked, with composure.

'You asked me to take him in; the scoundrel, the rogue.'

'You cannot mean my brother Charles,' said Honor with dignity; 'or you would not speak thus under our roof to his father and sisters.'

'Oh no, of course not, you don't like to hear it; but that is what he is.'

'What has Charles done?' asked Oliver in alarm.

'Robbed me!' shrieked Taverner, with his whole body quivering, and with vehement action of his hands. 'Robbed me, and run away with my money.'

He gasped for breath, his eyes glared, the sweat ran off his brow. He was without his hat, he had run bareheaded from Langford, and his, grizzled hair was disordered.

'He has robbed me of nigh on a thousand pounds, and he has gone away with the money. He took occasion of my being from home; he has taken all—all—all I had laid by. I thought no one knew where was my bank. He must have watched me; he found out; he has taken the box and all its contents.'

'Charles could not, would not, do such a thing,' said Honor, with heaving bosom; she was more angry at the charge than alarmed.

'Could not! would not! Where is he now?'

'I do not know. We have not seen him for several days.'

'He has not been seen at Langford either. As soon as I was off to Holsworthy he bolted. He knew he would have three days clear, perhaps more, for getting away with the money.'

'It is impossible,' said Honor. 'Charles may be idle, but he is not wicked.'

'He has robbed me,' repeated Taverner vehemently. 'Do you want proof? The five-pound note.'

Honor shuddered; she had forgotten that.

'Do you remember, Luxmore, you paid me a note of the Exeter and Plymouth Bank? Do you remember that I took the number?'

Oliver looked helplessly about the room, from Langford to Honor and Kate.

'I ask you whence you got that note? Come, answer me that? You, Luxmore, who gave you that note?'

'Charles,' moaned the carrier, and covered his face with his hands, as he threw himself into a chair.

'I thought as much. Let me tell you that that note had been abstracted from my box. I had the list of all the notes in it, but I did not go over them till I found that I had been robbed. Here is the note. I did not restore it to the box. I kept it in my pocket-book. I can swear—I have my entries to prove it—that it had been stolen from me. When I found Charles was gone, I thought it must have been he who had robbed me. When I saw the number of the note agreed with one I had put into the box a month ago, then I knew it must be he. You brought me the note, and he is your son.'

Kate burst into tears and wrung her hands.

Honor saw the faces of the children frightened, inclined for tears; she sent them all upstairs to their bedrooms.

Oliver sat at the table with his forehead in his hands and his fingers in his hair.

None spoke. Langford looked at the carrier, then at Honor. Kate threw herself into the chair by the window and wept aloud. Honor stood in the middle of the room, with her head bent; she was deadly pale, she dared not raise her eyes.

'What will you do?' she asked in a low tone.

'Do!' exclaimed Taverner; 'oh, that is soon answered. I send at once to Tavistock, Launceston, and Okehampton, and communicate with the proper authorities and have him arrested. There are magistrates, and constables, and laws, and prisons in England, for the detention and chastisement of thieves and burglars.'

Oliver moaned. 'I cannot bear the disgrace. I shall drown myself.'

'What will that avail?' sneered Langford. 'Will it save my thousand pounds? Will it save Charles from transportation? It is a pity that there is no more hanging for robbery, or Wellon's mound would be handy, and the old gibbet beam in my barn would serve once more.'

The words were cruel. Honor's teeth clenched and her hands closed convulsively.

Then Oliver Luxmore withdrew his hands from his face, dragged himself towards Langford, and threw himself on the ground at his feet.

'Have pity on him, on me, on us all. The shame will kill us, brand us. It will kill me, it will stain my name, my children, for ever.'

'Get up,' said Langford roughly. 'I'm not to be moved by men's tears.'

But Oliver was deaf; his great absorbing agony momentarily gave dignity to his feeble pitiful character, to him even crouching on the slate floor.

'Spare us the dishonour,' he pleaded. 'I cannot bear it; this one thing I cannot. Luxmore —thief—convict!' He passed his hand over his brow and raised his eyes; they were blank. 'Luxmore, of Coombe Park—Luxmore! Take care!' his voice became shrill. 'Dishonour I cannot bear. Take care lest you drive me desperate. Rather let us all die, I, Honor, Kate, and the little ones, and end the name, than that it should live on stained.' He tried to rise, but his knees shook and gave way under him.

'You may sell all I have. Take the van, everything. We cannot find you a thousand pounds. We will all work as slaves—only—spare us the dishonour! spare us this!'

Kate came up and cast herself at her father's side and raised her streaming eyes.

'Well,' said Taverner, turning to Honor, 'do you alone not join? Are you too proud?'

'Mr. Langford,' she answered, with emotion, 'you are too hard. I pray to God, who is merciful.'

'You are proud! You are proud!' he said scowling. 'You, Oliver Luxmore! you, Kate! do not kneel to me. Go, turn to her. The fate of Charles, the honour of your name, your happiness, that of your children, rest with her—with her.'

He looked at her.

She did not speak; she understood his meaning. A pang as of a sword went through her soul. She raised her clenched hands and put them to her mouth, and pressed the knuckles against her teeth. In the agony of that moment she was near screaming.

'There!' said Langford, pointing to her. 'Look how haughty she is. But she must bend. Entreat her, or command her, as you will. With her the issue lies. I will wait till to-morrow at ten, and take no steps for the capture of Charles. If before that hour I have yes, it is well. I pay a thousand pounds for that yes. I shall be content. If not, then——' he did not finish the sentence; he went out at the door.

Then only did Honor give way. She saw as it were a cloud of blue smoke rising round her. She held out her hands, grasping, but catching nothing, and fell on the floor insensible.

XXX
YES!

HONOR COULD NOT REST IN her bed that night. Oliver Luxmore in the adjoining room groaned and sighed, he was sleepless. Kate, who shared her bed, was awake and tossed from side to side. Poor Kate knew that the disgrace would separate her from Sam. She was too generous to urge her sister to make the costly sacrifice. Oliver felt that words would be unavailing, the matter must be left to Honor; his best advocate was in her own conscience. The resolution one way or the other must be come to by Honor unresisted, unswayed. She lay still in her bed, but Kate knew she did not sleep. She lay with her hands clasped as in prayer on her heaving bosom. Her eyes were on the little latticed window, and on a moth dancing dreamily up and down the panes, a large black moth that made the little diamonds of glass click at the stroke of its wings. Her hair over her brow was curled with the heat of her brain, the light short hair that would not be brushed back and lie with the copper-gold strands. Great drops rolled off her forehead upon the pillow. Afterwards, Kate felt that the cover was wet, and thought it was with Honor's tears, but she was not crying. Her eyes were dry and burning, but the moisture poured off her brow. Her feet were like ice. She might have been dead, she lay so still. Kate hardly heard her breathe.

She held her breath and listened once, as she feared Honor was in a swoon. She did not speak to her sister. An indefinable consciousness that Honor must not be disturbed, must be left alone, restrained her. Once she stole her hand under the bedclothes round her sister, and laid it on her heart. Then she knew for certain what a raging storm was awake in that still, hardly breathing form.

That touch, unattended by word, was more than Honor could bear. She said nothing, but stole from bed, and put on some of her clothes. Kate watched her through her half-closed lids, and dared not speak or otherwise interfere. Honor went softly, barefooted down the stairs, that creaked beneath her tread. Her father heard the step. He knew whose it was. He also would not interfere. It was best for all—for Kate, for Charles, for himself, for Joe, and Pattie, and Willie, and Martha, and Charity, and little Temperance—that Honor should be wholly undisturbed.

The girl unfastened the back door, took up the little bench, cast a potato-sack over her head, and went forth, shutting the door gently behind her.

She carried the seat under the hedge in the paddock, where she had watched with Larry, and placed herself on it, then rested her elbow on her knee, and her head in her hand. Her feet were bare, dipped in the dewy grass; a seeded dandelion, stirred by them, shed its ripe down over them. She thrust the sack from her head. She could not endure the weight and the heat, and laid it across her shoulders; from them it slipped, unheeded. Her arms were bare from the elbow. The cold night wind stroked the arm that stayed up her scorched brain. She had prayed that God would guide her, and the guidance had led into a way of sorrows. 'It is expedient that one man should die for the people,' those words of the High Priest recurred to Honor, and she thought how that He to whom they referred had accepted the decision. She would have died—died! O how willingly, how eagerly!—for the dear ones under the thatched roof; she would have leaped into fire, not for all, but for any one of them, for little Temperance, for dear Charity, for Martha, for Willie, for darling Pattie, for good, true Joe, for Kate, for her father of course—yes, even for Charles—but this that was demanded of her was worse than a brief spasm of pain in fire; it was a lifelong martyrdom, a sacrifice infinitely more dreadful than of life. The thrushes were singing. There was no night in the midst of June, and the birds did without sleep, or slept in the glare of midday. The only night was within the girl's soul. There was no singing or piping there, but the groaning of a crushed spirit.

She started. She was touched. She put out her hand and sighed. The horse that Langford had let them have was in the paddock; it had become much attached to Honor, and the beast had come over to her, unperceived, and was resting his head on her shoulder and rubbing it against her ear and cheek. She stroked the nose of the beast with her left hand without altering her position, mechanically, and without much diversion of her thoughts. When poor Diamond was dying in the gravel pit, Honor had sat by him and caressed him; now Diamond's successor had come to comfort Honor, as best he could, when her girlhood was dying in anguish, passing into a womanhood of sorrow.

Chink! chink! chink! a finch was perched on the top most twig of an alder that swayed under its light weight in the wind, repeating its monotonous cry, chink! chink! chink!

The cold about Honor's feet became stronger, the dew looked whiter, as if it were passing into frost, the breath of the horse was as steam. High, far aloft, in the dusky sky some large bird was winging its way from sea to sea, from the Atlantic boisterous barren coast about Bude, to the summer, luxuriant bays of the Channel. What bird it was Honor could not tell. She would not have seen it but that the winking of its wings as they caught the light from the north attracted her attention. Strange as it may seem, though engrossed in her own sorrows, she watched the flap of the wings till they passed beyond range of vision.

Not a cloud was in the sky. The stars were but dimly seen in the silvery haze of summer twilight. One glow-worm in the edge opposite her shone brighter than any star, for it shone out of darkness deeper than the depths of heaven.

One long leaf near Honor was as if it had been varnished, wet with dew, and as the dew gathered on it, it stooped and the moisture ran to the lanceate end, bowing it further, and forming a clear drop; then the drop fell, and the leaf with a dancing rebound recovered its first position. Honor's eye rested on the leaf; as the dew formed on it, and bent it down, so were tears forming on her soul and bowing it. The leaf shook off the drop; would her spirit ever recover?

What wondrous sounds are heard at night! How mysterious, how undiscoverable in origin! It seemed to Honor less still in the meadow, under the thorn hedge, than in the cottage. Insect life was stirring all about; the spiders were spinning, moths flitting, leaves rustling, birds piping, the wind playing among the thorns; the field mice were running, and the night birds watching for them on wing.

All was cool, all but Honor's head. Whatever sounds were heard were pleasant, whatever movement was soothing. Through all the intricate life that stirred there ran a breath of peace—only not over the heaving soul of Honor.

Poor Larry! Honor's thoughts were less of herself than of others. She was sure to the ground of her heart that he loved her. She knew, without riddling out the why and how, that she could have made him happy and good at once. There was sterling gold in him; the fire would purge away the dross. As in the cocoon there is an outer shell of worthless web which must be torn away before the golden thread is discovered, so was it with him; the outer husk of vanity and idleness and inconsiderateness was coming away, and now all that was needed was a tender hand to find and take hold of the end of the thread and spin off the precious fibre. Another hand, rough and heedless, might break and confuse and ruin it.

But, though she knew she could have made Larry's life right and orderly, yet she would not undertake to do so unless she saw the other lives committed to her trust cared for and safe.

Above all, high as the highest star, in her pure soul shone the duty imposed on her by her mother. If she could not combine her duty to the dear ones under the brown thatch with the charge of Larry's destiny, she would not undertake the latter.

And now, most horrible gall to her womanly mind, came the knowledge that she—she whom Larry loved and looked up to—she, she who loved the careless lad, even she must step in between him and his uncle's property, that she was chosen by old Langford as the weapon of his revenge on the Nanspians.

The Langford estate must descend to Larry should his uncle die childless, and she——

Her breath came in a gasp. She tore up the cold dock-leaves and pressed them to her brow to cool the burning there, to take the sting out of her nettled brain.

There was no rest for Honor anywhere, in the meadow or in her bed—no rest for her evermore.

She rose and went back to the house, but when she reached the door, true to her regular habits, remembered that she had left the sack and the bench in the field, and went back, fetched them, and put each in its proper place. Nothing was ever left littering about by Honor. If she had been dying and had seen a chip on the floor, she would have striven to rise and remove it.

In the morning the carrier and his two eldest daughters looked haggard and pale. The children seemed aware of trouble. Joe was attentive and helped to quiet and amuse the youngest, and watched his father, but especially Honor, to read what was menaced in their faces. He had not been at home when Langford came, and his sister Pattie could give him but the vaguest idea of what had occurred. All she knew was that it was a trouble connected with Charles, who had run away. The carrier had to be ready early to start for Tavistock market. Honor and Kate prepared breakfast for him and the children, without a word passing between them on what was uppermost in their minds. As they were eating, the Ashbury post-boy passed down the lane and called at the steps.

The carrier went out.

'A letter for you.'

Oliver took and paid for it, then brought it in and opened it slowly with shaking fingers. He, Honor, Kate, knew that it must have reference to their trouble. It was in the handwriting of Charles; it bore the Plymouth postmark. The carrier spread it on his plate; he did not read it aloud because Joe and the other children were present; but Honor and Kate stood behind him and read over his shoulder without uttering a word.

This was the letter:

'Dear Father,—I take my pen in hand, hopping this finds you as it leafs me, with a bad running at the noaz, and a shockin corf, gripes orful in my innerds, and bakes all over me. I dersay you've eard what I gone and done; don't judge me harshly, I couldn't do otherwise, and I'm not so bad to blame as you may suppoge. I didn't intend delibberat to do 't, but I did it off-hand so to speke. Wot's dun can't be undun. It's no use crying over spilt milk. Wot can't be kured must be undured. That's wot Mrs. Veale would say, and her's a bad un. I ketched a cold with getting wet running away, but I shall be all rite soon, please God when I'm away on the i seez. I'm goin t' Ameri'kay, which is the place to which the flour of the British aristokracy go when its ockerd or embarassing at ome. As it is ockerd and embarassing to me, I'm orf, and I hope with the Almighty's aid to do well in the new whirid, wheer I intend to found a new Coom Park, to which I shall invite you all to come, when I can drive you about in a carridge and pare. I want to know how it is with Larry, whether he be alive or dead. I came away in such aste I couldn't stay to know, but I'm very desiring to know. Don't rite to me by my proper name, there may be disagreeables in my wereabout being knone, so direct to Mr. Charles, poast resteny, Plymouth.—From your loving sun,

'Charles Luxmore,
'of Coom Park, Esquire.

'P.S.—Doan't say nothink to nobody of were I be, wot ever you do, and kiss the kids for me. Poast anser at Tavistock or Lanson.'

Oliver Luxmore refolded the letter, and put it away in his pocket without a word. Neither Honor nor Kate spoke or looked at each other. It was too clear to all that Charles was guilty. The last doubt of his guilt disappeared.

Oliver went about the horse and van. Honor did not fail to observe the change effected in him by one night. He seemed older by ten years—to have tumbled down the decline of life, and been shaken by the fall. His clothes did not appear to fit him, his walk was unsteady, his hand shook, his eye wandered, his hair had a greyer tinge, and was lank and moist. Joe ran to help in the harnessing of the horse. His father was trying to force on the collar without turning it. He put on the saddle wrong, and fastened the wrong buckles. The boy corrected his father's errors. Then the man brought the van into the lane, and stood with his hand to his forehead.

'I've forgotten 'em all,' he said. 'Whatever were the commissions I don't know.' The whip was shaking in his hand as a withy by a water brook. 'I shouldn't wonder if I never came back,' he said, then looked up the steps at Honor. It was the first time he had met her eye since Taverner Langford had left the house. 'I shan't know what is to be till I come home,' he muttered. 'The cuckoo-clock has just called seven, and it is three hours to ten. I think my heart will die within me at Tavistock. I shan't be home till night. However I shall bear it and remember my commissions I do not know. Joe shall come with me. I can't think. I can't drive. I can do nothing.'

Then Honor came down the steps with her scarlet cloak about her shoulders, and her red stockings on her feet, slowly, looking deadly pale, and with dark rings about her eyes.

'Where are you going?' asked the carrier, 'not coming with me to Tavistock?'

She shook her head.

'Are you—are you going to—to Langford?' he asked. 'To say what?'—he held his breath.

'Yes!'

XXXI
The New Mistress

'Hallo! where be you off to, Red Spider?' asked Farmer Nanspian, who was on Broadbury, when he saw Honor Luxmore in her scarlet coming over the down. 'Stay, stay!' he said, and put his hand to her chin to raise her face:

'You never come Chimsworthy road—leastways, you haven't yet.—Where be you going to now?'

'To Langford, sir.'

'To Langford, eh?' his face clouded. 'I didn't think you was on good terms with Mr. Langford. Take care—take care! I won't have he sloke away this Red Spider from Chimsworthy.' Then he nodded, smiled, and went on. He little knew, he had no suspicion, that what he hinted at was really menaced.

Honor went on to the old, lonely house, and asked to speak to Mr. Langford. She was shown into his parlour. Taverner was about the farm. She had some minutes to wait, and nerve herself for the interview, before he arrived.

'Well,' said he when he came in, 'you are in good time. You have brought me the answer.'

'Yes,' she replied, looking down.

'Do I take that Yes as a reply to this question or to that I made yesterday?'

'To both.'

'There's not another woman in all England to whom I'd have behaved as I have to you.'

'I hope not, sir!'

'I mean,' said Langford, knitting his brows and reddening, 'I mean, I would not have foregone a thousand pounds for any other. I would not have spared the man who had robbed me for any other woman's sake.'

'I have come here,' she said, 'myself, instead of sending a message, because I wished to speak with you, in private.'

'There is no one here to overhear you. I have stopped up the keyhole; Mrs. Veale listened, she can catch nothing now.'

'Mr. Langford, I was told by my father that you had promised to do something for my brother and sisters.'

'Oh, do not be afraid—I will do something for them.'

'I want you to grant me one request, the only one I will ever make of you. Promise me some small yearly sum assured to thy father, I do not ask for much. When I am in the house, I can manage, but it is hard work for me to do so. When I am gone, Kate will find it hard, and she may not remain long there; she is a pretty girl, and has her admirers, she is sure to marry soon—then what will become of my father and the little ones? I do not ask you to take them in here. That would not be reasonable—except so far as they can work for you, and be of use to you. Joe will be a valuable servant, and Pattie is growing up to be neat and active and thoughtful.'

'How many more?' asked Langford.

'That is all,' replied Honor quietly. 'If I ask you to do anything for these two it is only because they will be worth more than you will pay them. But I ask for my father. It will be a loss to him, my leaving the house. He will not be happy. Kate is very good, but she does not understand thrift, and she is light-hearted. Promise me a small sum every year for my father and the little ones to relieve them from the pinch of poverty, and to give them ease and happiness.'

'How many have you?'

'There are Joe, and Pattie, Willie, Martha, Charity, and Temperance. If I might bring Temperance with me I should be very thankful; she is but three, and will miss me.'

'In the Proverbs of Solomon we are told that the horse-leech hath three daughters, which cry Give, give, give! Here are more, some seven, all wanting to suck blood. If I marry you, I don't marry the family.'

Honor was silent, for a moment, recovering herself; his rudeness hurt her, angered her.

'I make a request. I will ask nothing more.'

She looked up at him, and rested her eyes on his face. He had been observing her; how pale she was—how worn; and it annoyed him: it seemed to him that it had cost her much to resolve to take him, and this was not flattering to his pride.

'I cannot grant it,' he said. 'It is not reasonable. I am not going to be eaten out of house and home by a parcel of ravenous schoolchildren. I want you, I do not want all your tail of brothers and sisters, and, worst of all, your helpless father. I know very well what will happen. I shall be thrown to them like an old horse to Squire Impey's pack—to have my flesh torn off and my bones even crunched up. I cut this away in the beginning; I will not have it.'

'I ask only for a small sum of money for my father. The van barely sustains him. The family is so large. I will not bring any of the children here, except little Temperance, who is very, very dear to my heart.'

'No, I will have none of them.'

'I may not have Temperance?'

'No, I said, none of them. Give an inch, and an ell is taken. Put in the little finger and the fist follows.'

'Then you will grant me an allowance for my father?'

He laughed. 'A thousand pounds is what you have cost me. When that thousand pounds is made up, or repaid, then we will talk about an allowance. Not till then—no, no! I may pay too dear for my bargain. A thousand pounds is ample.'

'That is your last word?'

'My last.'

Then Honor, looking steadily at him, said: 'Mr. Langford, it is true that you lose money by me; but I lose what is infinitely more precious by you. I lose my whole life's happiness. When my mother was dying, I promised her to be a mother to her darlings. Now I am put in this terrible position, that, to save them from a great disgrace and an indelible stain, I must leave them. I have spent the whole night thinking out what was right for me to do. If I remain with them, it is with a shame over our whole family. If I go, I save them from that, but they lose my care. One way or other there is something gone. It cannot be other. I have made my choice. I will come to you; but I have strings from my heart to little Temperance, and Charity, and Martha, and Willie, and Pattie, and Joe, and Kate, and father. If they are unhappy, uncomfortable, I shall suffer in my soul. If ill comes to them, I shall be in pain. If the little ones grow up neglected, untidy, untruthful, my heart and my head will ache night and day. If my father is uncared for, the distress of knowing it will be on me ever. I shall be drawn by a hundred nerves to my own dear ones, and not be able to do anything for them. You cannot understand me. You must believe me when I say that the loss to me is ten thousand times greater than the loss of a thousand pounds to you. My happiness is in the well-being and well-bringing up of my brothers and sisters. You take all that away from me. Did you ever hear the tale of the widower who married again, and his new wife neglected the children by the dead wife?—One night the father came to the nursery door, and saw the dead woman rocking and soothing the babes. She had come from her grave. The crying had drawn her. She could not sleep because they called her. I do not know that I can bear it, to be separated from my brothers and sisters—I cannot say. If they suffered or were neglected I fancy nothing could withhold me from going to them.'

Taverner remained silent: her eyes seemed to burn their way into him. She shifted her position from one foot to the other, and went on, in an earnest tone, with a vibration in it from the strength of her emotion: 'I am bound to tell you all. If you are to be my husband, you must know everything. I cannot love you. What love I have that is not taken up by Temperance, and Charity, and Martha, and Willie, and Pattie, and Joe, and Kate, and father, and—' still looking frankly, earnestly at him, 'yes, and by Charles, I have given elsewhere. I cannot help it. It has been taken from me in a whirlwind of fire, as Elijah was caught up into heaven; it is gone from me; I cannot call it down again. If you insist on knowing to whom I gave it, I will tell you, but not now, not yet—afterwards. To show you, Mr. Langford, how I love my home, I had made up my mind to give him up, to throw away all that beautiful happiness, to forget it as one forgets a dream, because I would not be parted from my dear ones. I was resolved to give him up whom I love for them, and now I am required to give them up for you whom I love not.' She breathed heavily, her labouring heart beat. She drew the red cloak about her, lest the heaving bosom and bounding heart should be noticed. Langford saw the long drops run down her brow, but there were no tears in her eyes.

'You will never love me?' he asked.

'I cannot say; it depends how you treat my dear ones.'

She took a long breath.

'There is one reason why my consent costs me more when given to you than to another: but I cannot tell you that now. I will tell you later.'

She meant that by marrying him she was widening the breach between the uncle and nephew—that she was marrying the former for the express purpose of depriving the latter of his inheritance. She could not tell Langford this now.

'I will do my duty by you to the best of my lights. But I shall have one duty tying me here, and seven drawing me to the little cottage in the lane, and I feel—I feel that I shall be torn to pieces.'

Taverner Langford stood up and paced the room with his arms folded behind his back. His head was bowed and his cheeks pale. The girl said no more. She again shifted her feet, and rested both hands, under her cloak, on the table. Langford looked round at her; her head was bent, her yellow-brown hair was tied in a knot behind. As her head was stooping, the back of her neck showed above the red cloak, it was as though she bent before the executioner's axe. He turned away.

'Sit down,' he said. 'Why have you been standing? You look ill. What has ailed you?'

'In body nothing,' she answered.

'Who is it?' he asked surlily, looking out of the window, and passing his own fingers over his face.

She slightly raised her head and eyes questioningly.

'I mean,' he said, without turning to see her, but understanding by her silence that she asked an explanation—'I allude to what you were saying just now. Who is it whom you fancy?'

'If you insist, I will tell. If you have any pity you will spare me. In time—before the day, you shall know.'

He passed his hand over his face again.

'This is a pleasant prospect,' he said, but did not explain whether he alluded to the landscape or to his marriage. He said no more to force further confidence from her.

'Come,' said he roughly, and he turned suddenly round, 'you shall see the house. You shall be shown what I have in it, all the rooms and the furniture, also the cowsheds, and the dairy—everything. You shall see what will be yours. You would get no other man with so much as I have.'

'Not to-day, Mr. Langford. Let me go home. I should see nothing to-day. My eyes are full, and my heart fuller.'

'Then go,' he said, and reseated himself at the table.

She moved towards the door. He had his chin on his hand, and was looking at the grate. She hesitated, holding the handle.

'Ha!' exclaimed Langford, starting up. 'Did you hear that? a-fluttering down the passage? That was Mrs. Veale, trying to listen, but could hear nothing; trying to peep, but could see nothing, because I have covered every chink. Come here! come here, Mrs. Veale!'

As she did not respond, he rang the bell violently, and the pale woman came.

'Come here, Mrs. Veale! show the future mistress out of the house! Not by the kitchen, woman! Unbar the great door. Show her out, and curtsey to her, and at the same time take your own discharge.'

'"When one comes in the other goes out," as the man said of the woman in the weather-house,' remarked Mrs. Veale with a sneer. She curtsied profoundly. 'There's been calm heretofore. Now comes storm.'

XXXII
THE CHINA DOG

NO SOONER WAS THE SCARLET cloak gone than Mrs. Veale leaned back against the wall in the passage and laughed. Langford had never heard her laugh before, and the noise she made now was unpleasant. Her face was grey, her pale eyes glimmered in the dark passage.

'Will you be quiet?' said Taverner angrily. 'Get along with you into the kitchen and don't stand gulping here like water out of a narrow-necked bottle.'

'So!—that be the wife you've chosen, master! It is ill screwing a big foot into a small shoe; best suit your shoe to the size of your foot.'

'You have received notice to leave. A month from today.'

'This is breaking the looking-glass because you don't like your face,' said the housekeeper. '"Come help me on with the plough," said the ox to the gadfly. "With the greatest of pleasure," answered the fly, and stung the ox.'

'Gadfly!' shouted Taverner. 'Sheathe your sting, please, or don't practise on me.'

'You marry!' scoffed Mrs. Veale. '"I'm partial to honey," said the fox, and upset the hive. "You must learn how to take it," answered the swarm, and surrounded him.'

'I'll turn you out at once,' said Langford angrily.

'No, you will not,' answered the housekeeper; 'or you will have to pay my wage and get nothing for it. I've served you faithfully all these years, and this is my reward. I am turned away. What has been my pay whilst here? What! compared with my services? And now I am to make room for the sister of a thief. What will become of your earnings when she comes? If her brother picked a stranger, he will skin a relative. And the rest of them! "I am tilling for you," said the farmer to the rabbits; "come into my field and nibble the turnips." Love in an old man is like a spark in a stackyard. It burns up everything, even common sense.'

He thrust her down the passage. She kept her white face towards him, and went along sliding her hands against the wall, against which she leaned her back.

'I did suppose you had more sense than this. I knew you were bit, but not that you were poisoned. I thought that you would be too wise to go on with your courting when you found that you had been robbed by Charles. Who that is not a fool will give the run of his house to the man who has plundered him? Can you keep him out when you have married his sister? What of the young ones? They will grow up like their brother. Roguery is like measles, it runs through a house. Have not I been faithful? Have I taken a thread out of your clothes, or a nail from your shoe? Have I relations to pester you for help? Mine might have begged, but would not have stolen; yours will have their hands in all your pockets. Now you are everything in the house, and we are all your slaves. All is yours, your voice rules, your will governs. Will it be so when you bring a mistress home—and that Honor Luxmore? Everyone knows her; she governs the house.' Mrs. Veale laughed again. 'That will be a fine sight to see Master Taverner Langford under the slipper. "I'm seen in the half but lost in the full," said the man in the moon.'

Langford thrust her through the kitchen door and shut it, then returned to his parlour, where he bolted himself in, and paced the room with his arms folded behind his back.

There was enough of truth in what Mrs. Veale had said to make him feel uncomfortable. It was true that now he was absolute in his house;

but would he reign as independently when married? Was not the ox inviting the gadfly to help to draw the plough? In going after the honey, like the fox, was he not inviting stings? Langford had suffered great loss from rabbits. They came out of Chimsworthy plantation and fell on his turnips, nibbled pieces out of hundreds, spoiling whole rows, which when touched rotted with the first frost. Therefore Mrs. Veale's allusion to them went home. Yes!—there were a swarm of human rabbits threatening, the children from the cottage. They would all prey on him. He was inviting them to do so. 'I till for you,' said the farmer. Confound Mrs. Veale! Why was she so full of saws and likenesses that cut like knives? And Charles!—of course he would return when he knew that he would not be prosecuted. How could he be prosecuted when the brother-in-law of the man he had robbed? When he returned, how could he be kept away, how prevented from further rascality? A thousand pounds gone! and he was not to punish the man who had taken the money. This was inviting him to come and rob him again. He did not think much of what Honor had said of an attachment to some unknown person. Taverner had never loved, and knew nothing of love as a passion. He regarded it as an ephemeral fancy. Every girl thought herself in love, got over it, and bore no scars. It would be so with Honor. Presently he rang for his breakfast. Mrs. Veale came in. She saw he was disconcerted, but she said nothing, till the tray was on the table, and she was leaving; then, holding the handle of the door, she said, 'It is a pity.'

'What is a pity?'

'The hare hunt.'

'What of that?' he asked angrily.

'That it was not put off a month, then changed to a stag hunt,' she replied, and went through the door quickly, lest he should knock her down.

Mrs. Veale went to her kitchen, and seated herself by the fire. She was paler than usual, and her eyelids blinked nervously. There was work to be done that morning, but she neglected it.

Her scheme had failed. She had endeavoured to force Charles Luxmore on to steal of his master, thinking that this must inevitably break the connection with the Luxmores. Taverner, she thought, could not possibly pursue his intentions when he knew he had been robbed by Charles. She was disappointed. What next to attempt she knew not. She was determined to prevent the marriage if she could. She had not originally intended to steal the cash-box, nor, indeed, to rob it of any of its contents, but she had been forced to take it, as Charles would not. Now she was given her dismissal, and if she left, she would take the money with her. But she had no desire to leave without further punishment of her ungrateful master.

She had spent fifteen years in his service. She had plotted and worked and had not gained any of her ends. She had at first resolved on making him marry her. When she found it impossible to achieve this, she determined to make herself so useful to him, so indispensable, that he would in his old age fall under her power, and then, he would leave her by his will well off. She was now to be driven out into the cold, after all her labour, disappointments, to make room for a young girl. This should not be. If she must go, she would mar the sport behind her back. If Taverner Langford would not take her, he should take none other. If she was not to be mistress in the house, no young chit of a girl should be.

She stood up and took down from the chimney-piece a china dog blotched red, and turning it over, removed from the inside a packet of yellow paper.

She was so engrossed in her thoughts that she did not see that someone had entered the kitchen by the open backdoor.

'I declare! They'd make a pair!'

Mrs. Veale started, a shiver ran through her from head to foot. She turned, still quivering, and looked at the speaker. Kate Luxmore had entered, and stood near the table.

'Well, now,' said Kate, 'this is curious. We've got a dog just like that, with long curly ears, and turns his dear old head to the left, and you've one with the same ears, and same colour, turns his head to the right. We'd a pair once, but Joe broke the fellow. I reckon you'd a pair once, but your fellow is broke. 'Tis a pity they two dogs should be widowers and lonely.'

Mrs. Veale stared at her; Kate had never been there before. What had brought her there now? Were all the Luxmores coming to make that their home, even before the marriage?

'And what have you got there?' pursued Kate, full of liveliness. 'Why, that is one of the yellow paper rat-poison packets the man sold at the fair. I know it. 'Tis a queer thing you keeping the poison in the body of the dog. But I suppose you are right; no one would think to go there for it.'

'What do you want here?' asked Mrs. Veale, hastily replacing the packet and the dog on the mantel-shelf. 'Why have you come? We've had enough of you Luxmores already. Your brother Charles has played us a pretty tune, and now your sister's like to lead a dance.'

'I have come for Honor. Is she here?'

'She—no! She's been gone some time. Ain't she home? Perhaps she's walking over the land, and counting the acres that may be hers, and prizing the fleeces of the sheep.'

'She is wanted. As for Charles, there's naught proved against him, and till there is, I won't believe it. I've just had a talk with someone and he tells me another tale altogether. So there—not another word against poor Charles. He wasn't ever sweet on you, I can tell you. 'Tis a pity, too, about those dogs. They're both water-spaniels—what intelligent eyes they have, and what lovely long curly ears! They ought to be a pair some day.'

'I tell you,' said Mrs. Veale, 'your sister is not here.'

'Our dog,' went on Kate unabashed, 'don't belong to father. He is Honor's own. She had the pair, till Joe knocked one of them over. Her mother gave it her. 'Tis curious now that her dog should turn his blessed nose one way, and this dog should turn his nose the other way. It looks as if they were made for each other, which is more than is the case with some that want to be pairing. A mantel-shelf don't look as well with a spaniel in the middle as it do with one at each end. That is, I suppose, why your master is looking out for a wife. Well! I think he'd have matched better with you than with someone else whom I won't name. A house with one in it is like a mantel-shelf with one odd dog on it. Does this chimney ornament belong to you or to the house?'

'Never mind, go your ways. Don't you think ever to pair them two dogs, nor your sister and the master. There is a third to be considered. If one be broken, there is no pairing. Do y' know what the ash said to the axe?

> Whether coupled or counter is wisht (unlucky) for me,
> My wood makes the haft for to fell my tree.'

XXXIII
Among the Gorse

'Where be you going to, Larry?' asked his father. 'I've just seen the Red Spider running Langford way. Take care Uncle Taverner don't sloke that one away as he tried to sloke t'other.'

Hearing that Honor was gone over the moor to Langford, Hillary took that direction, and, as he had expected, encountered her as she was returning to her cottage, before she had left the down.

'You are going to give me a quarter of an hour,' said Larry. 'I dare say you may be busy, but I can't spare you till we've had it out with each other. I've but one arm now that I can use, but I'll bar the way with that, if you attempt to escape me.'

Honor looked at him hesitatingly. She was hardly prepared for the inevitable trial, then. She would have liked to defer it. But, on second thoughts, she considered that it was best to have it over. Sooner or later, an explanation must be made, so perhaps it would be as well for her that day to pass through all the fires. There on Broadbury, when the gorse is swaled (burnt), the cattle are driven through the flames. They plunge and resist, but a ring of men and dogs encloses them, armed with sharp stakes, and goad them forward, and at last, with desperation, lowing, kicking, leaping, angry and terrified, they plunge through the flames.

Honor thought of this familiar scene, and that she was herself being driven on. Sooner or later she must enter the fire, be scorched, and pass through; she would traverse it without further resistance at once.

'I am ready, Larry,' she said in a low voice.

'My dear, dear Honor, what ails you? You are looking ill, and deadly white! What is it, Honor?'

'We all have our troubles, Larry. You have a broken arm, and I have a breakage somewhere, but never mind where.'

'I do mind,' he said vehemently. 'What is amiss?'

'You told me, Larry, the night your arm was hurt, that—your pride had sustained a fall and was broken.'

'So it was.'

'So also is mine.'

'But what has hurt you? How is it? Explain to me all, Honor.'

She shook her head. 'It is not my affair only. I have others to consider beside myself, and you must forgive me if my lips are locked.'

He put his left arm round her, to draw her to him, and kiss her. 'I will keep the key of those lips,' he said, but she twisted herself from his grasp.

'You must not do that, Larry.'

'Why not? We understand each other. Though we did not speak, that night, our hearts told each other everything.'

'Larry, do you remember what I said to you when we were together in the paddock?'

'I remember every word.'

'I told you that I regarded you—as a brother.'

'I remember every word but that.'

'You have been a friend, a dear friend, ever since we were children. You were always thoughtful towards us, my sister and me, when you thought of nothing else. You were always kind, and as Charles was away, of late, I came to think of you as a brother.'

'But I, Honor, I never have and never will consent to regard you as a sister. I love you more dearly than brother ever loved sister. I never had one of my own, but I am quite sure I could not think of one in the way I think of you. I love you, Honor, with all my heart, and I respect you and look up to you as the only person who can make me lead a better life than I have led heretofore.'

Honor shook her head and sighed. It was her way to answer by nod or shake rather than by word.

'I have good news to tell you,' he went on; 'my father is delighted at the prospect, and he is nearly as impatient as I am to have your dear self in Chimsworthy.'

'I cannot go there,' said Honor in a tone that expressed the desolation of her heart.

'Why not?'

She hesitated.

'Why not, Honor? When I wish it, when my father is eager to receive you?'

'Dear Larry,' she said sadly, 'it can never, never be.'

'Come here,' he exclaimed impatiently, and drew her along with him. 'What is the meaning of this? I will understand.' Before them for nearly a mile lay a sheet of gold, a dense mass of unbroken gorse, in full blaze of flower, exhaling a nectareous fragrance in the sun, that filled the air. So dense were the flowers that no green spines could be seen, only various shades of orange and gold and pale yellow. Through it a path had been reaped, for rabbit-shooters, and along this Hillary drew her. The gorse reached to their waists. The fragrance was intoxicating.

'Look here, Honor,' said he, 'look at this furze. It is like my nature. It is said that there is not a month in the year in which it does not blossom. Sometimes there is only a golden speck here and there—when the snow is on the ground, not more than a few flowers, and then one stalk sets fire to another, as spring comes on, and the whole bush burns and is not consumed, like that in the desert, when God spoke to Moses from it. It has been so with me, Honor. I have always loved you. Sometimes the prickles have been too thick, and then there have been but few tokens of love; but never, never has the blood died away altogether. In my heart, Honor, love has always lived, and now it is all blazing, and shining, and full of sweetness.'

'Larry,' answered Honor slowly, 'look here;' she put her hand to a gorse bush and plucked a mass of golden bloom.

'Honor!' he exclaimed, 'what have you done?' She opened her hand, it was full of blood.

'I have grasped the glorious flower,' she said, 'and am covered with wounds, and pierced with thorns.'

'No—no, dear Honor,' he said, taking her hand, removing from it the prickles, and wiping the blood away with the kerchief that bound his broken arm. 'There shall be no thorns in our life together. The thorns will all go from me when I have you to prune me. I have been wild and rough, and I dare say I may have given you pain. I know that I have. I was angry with you and behaved badly; but I was angry only because I loved you.' Then his pleasant sweet smile broke over his pale face, and he said in an altered tone, 'You do not harbour anger, Honor; you forgive, when the offender is repentant.'

She raised her eyes to him, and looked long and steadily into his.

'I forgive you for any little wrong you may have done me, heartily and wholly. But, oh Larry! I must wrong you in a way in which I can expect to get no forgiveness from you.'

'That is quite impossible,' he said smiling.

'Larry, you cannot even dream what my meaning is. When you know—there will not be a flower on the furze bush, the last gold bud of love will fall off.'

'Never, never, Honor!'

'You do not know.'

He was perplexed. What could stand in the way of her ready acceptance of him, except his own former bad conduct?

'Honor,' he said, 'I have had some sleepless nights—these have not been altogether caused by my arm—and during the dark hours I have thought over all my past manner of life, and I have quite resolved to break with it. I will no longer be idle. I will no more boast. I will no more let the girls make a fool of me. I will work hard on the farm as any labourer—indeed, Honor, I will work harder and longer than they. If you mistrust me, prove me. I deserve this trial. My father would like you to be his daughter-in-law at once; but I know that I do not deserve you. In the old story, Jacob served fourteen years for Rachel, and I am not a Jacob—I will wait, though fourteen years is more than my patience will bear, still—dear Honor, dear heart!—I will wait. I will wait your own time, I will not say another word to you till you see that I am keeping my promise, and am becoming in some little way worthy of you. I know,' he said in a humble tone, 'that really I can never deserve you—but I shall be happy to try and gain your approval, and, if you do not wish me to say more of my love till I show you I am on the mend, so shall it be. I am content. Put on the kerchief when I am to speak again.'

He stopped, and looked at her. She was trembling, and her eyes cast down. Now, at last, the tears had come, and were flowing from her eyes. One, like a crystal, hung on her red cloak. Knowing that he awaited an answer, she raised her head with an effort, and looked despairingly right and left, but saw no help anywhere, only the flare of yellow blossom flickering through a veil of tears.

Oh, infinitely sweet, infinitely glorious was this sight and this outpouring of Larry's heart to her—but infinitely painful as well—piercing, wounding, drawing forth blood— like the gorse.

'Larry!' she said earnestly, 'no—no—not for one moment do I doubt your word. I believe everything you say. I could trust you perfectly. I know that with your promise would come fulfilment, but—it is not that.'

'What is it then?'

She *could* not tell him. The truth was too repugnant to her to think, much less to tell—and tell to *him*.

'I cannot tell you; my father, my brothers and sisters.'

'I have thought of that, you dear true soul,' he interrupted. 'I know that you will not wish to hurt them. But, Honor, there will be no desertion. I have only to cut a gap through the hedge of your paddock, and in three minutes, straight as an arrow, you can go from one house to the other. Round by the road is longer, but when you are at Chimsworthy we'll have a path between; then you can go to and fro as you like, and the little ones will be always on the run. You can have them all in with you when and as long as you like; and my father will be over-pleased if your father will come and keep him company on the Look-out stone. Since Uncle Taverner and he have quarrelled father has been dull, and felt the want of someone to talk to. So you see all will be just right. Everything comes as though it were fitted to be as we are going to make it.'

Again he paused, waiting for her answer. Whilst he had been speaking she had worked herself up to the necessary pitch of resolution to tell him something—not all, no all she could not tell.

'Larry! it cannot be. I am going to marry another.'

He stood still, motionless, not even breathing, gazing at her with stupid wonder. What she said was impossible. Then a puff of north-west wind came from the far ocean, rolling over the down, gathering the fragrance of the yellow sea, and condensing it; then poured it as a breaking wave over the heads of those two standing in the lane cut through the golden trees. And with the odour came a humming, a low thrilling music, as the wind passed through the myriad spines beneath the foam of flower, and set them vibrating as the tongues of Aeolian harps. The sweetness and the harmony were in the air, all around, only not in the hearts of those two young people, standing breast deep in the gorse-brake. The wind passed, and all was still once more. They stood opposite each other, speechless. Her hand, which he had let go, had fallen, and the blood dropped from it. How long they thus stood neither knew. He was looking at her; she had bent her head, and the sun on her hair was more glorious than on the gorse-flowers. He would have pierced to the depth of her soul and read it if he could, but he was baffled. There was an impenetrable veil over it, through which he could not see.

'You do not—you have not loved me,' he said with an effort. This was the meaning of her coldness, her reserve. Then he put out his left hand and touched her, touched her lightly on the bosom. That light touch was powerful as the rod of Moses on the rock in Horeb. Her self-control deserted her. She clasped her hands on her breast, and bowed, and burst into convulsive weeping, which was made worse by her efforts to arrest it and to speak.

Hillary said nothing. He was too dazed to ask for any explanation, too stupefied by the unexpected declaration that cut away for ever the ground of his happiness.

She waved her hand. 'Leave me alone. Go, Larry, go! I can tell you nothing more! Let me alone! Oh, leave me alone, Larry!'

He could not refuse to obey, her distress was so great, her entreaty so urgent. Silent, filled with despair, with his eyes on the ground, he went along the straight-cut path towards the road, and nearly ran against Kate.

'Oh! you here!' exclaimed the lively girl, 'then Honor is not far distant. Where is she? What, yonder! and I have been to Langford to look for her. What is the matter? Oh, fiddlesticks! you have been making yourselves and each other miserable. There is no occasion for that till all is desperate, and it is not so yet. Come along, Larry, back to Honor. I must see her; I want to tell her something, and you may as well be by. You are almost one of the family.'

She made him follow her. Honor had recovered her composure when left to herself, unwatched, and she was able to disguise her emotions from her sister.

'Oh Honor!' exclaimed Kate, 'I have something to tell you. I think you've been a fool, and too precipitate—I do indeed, and so does Sam Voaden. A little while ago I chanced to go down the lane after some water, when, curiously enough, Sam was coming along it, and we had a neighbourly word or two between us. I told Sam all about Charles and what Mr. Langford charged him with.'

'Kate—you never—!' gasped Honor in dismay.

'I did. Why not? Where's the hurt? Sam swore to me he'd tell no one.'

'What is this?' asked Hillary.

'Don't you know?' retorted Kate. 'What, has Honor not told you? Faith! there never was another girl like her for padlocking her tongue. I'm sure I could not keep from telling. Sam saw I was in trouble and asked the reason, and my breast was as full as my pitcher, so it overflowed. Well, Honor, Sam is not such a fool as some suppose. He has more sense than all we Luxmores put together—leastways, than we had last night. He says he don't believe a word of it, and that you was to blame for acting on it till you knew it was true.'

'It is true. I know it is true,' said Honor disconsolately. 'It is no use denying it.'

'But, as Sam said, why act on it till it is proved? Where is Charles? All you know is from Taverner Langford, and he is an interested party; he may be mistaken, or he may put things wrong way on wilfully.'

'No, Kate, no! You should not have spoken.'

'But I have spoken. If a pitcher is full, will it not run over the brim? I have been over-full, and have overflowed. That is nature, my nature, and I can't help it. No hurt is done. Sam will not talk about it to anyone; and what he says shows more sense than is to be found in all the nine heads that go under our cottage roof, wise as you consider yourself, Honor. Sam says nothing ought to be promised or done till Charles has been seen and you have heard what account he can give of himself.'

'His letter, Kate?'

'Well, what of his letter? He says nothing about stealing in it—stealing a thousand pounds. What he says may mean no more than his running away and leaving nine pence a day for nothing.'

'I am sorry you spoke,' said Honor.

'I am glad I spoke,' said Kate sharply. 'I tell you Sam's brain is bigger than all our nine. He saw the rights of the matter at once, and—look here!—he promised me that he would go and find Charles if he's gone no further than Plymouth.'

'You told him where he was!' exclaimed Honor aghast.

'Of course I did. I wasn't going to send him off searching to Lundy Isle or Patagonia. Well, Sam says that he'll go and find him on certain conditions?'

'On what conditions?

'Never mind, they don't concern you, they are private. And he wants to have a talk with Larry first; but Sam says he don't believe Charles took the money. He's too much of a Luxmore to act dishonourable, he said.' Honor was still unconvinced. 'Larry,' continued Kate, 'will you go at once to Swaddledown and see Sam?'

'Yes; but I understand nothing of what this is about. You must explain it to me.'

'No, Larry, go to Sam—he knows all.'

In after years, when the gorse was flowering full, Honor said to Larry, 'The honey scent always brings back to my memory one day.'

'Yes,' he replied; 'the furze is like love, thorns and flowers; but the flowers grow, and swell, and burst, and blaze, and swallow up the thorns, that none are seen.'

XXXIV
The Visitation

The amazement of Larry was equalled by his indignation when he heard from Sam Voaden the whole story of the charge against Charles, and of Honor consenting to save him at the cost of herself. He did not share Sam's confidence in the groundlessness of the charge; he thought Charles quite rascal enough to have robbed his master and bolted with the money. Nevertheless he thought that the best thing that could be done was for Sam to go after Charles, as he himself could not do so, on account of his arm and collar-bone: and he urged on Voaden to use his best endeavours, if he found Charles, which was doubtful, to persuade him to return the money through him, to Langford.

'When he finds that he is suspected he may do that, especially if you threaten to hand him over to the constables should he refuse.'

'I don't believe he ever took it,' said Sam. 'I know Charles better than you.'

Hillary was coming away from Swaddledown along the road or lane to Broadbury, when he met his uncle Taverner in his Sunday suit, a hat on his head, walking along lustily, with a stick in his hand.

Larry stood in the way.

'Uncle Taverner,' he said.

'Stand aside,' said Langford roughly.

'One word.'

'Not one! I have nothing to do with you or yours. Stand aside that I may pass on.'

'I cannot; I will not! You are in my path, not I in yours—that is, in the path of my life's happiness.'

Langford looked at him interrogatively.

'Uncle Langford, I must speak to you.'

'I am busy, I have to go to the church. It is the rural dean's visitation. I am churchwarden.'

'I will not detain you long.'

'I will not be detained at all.'

'I must speak to you, uncle. You are too—too cruel! you have come between me and happiness.'

'Get along. Don't think anything you say will make me leave Langford to you.'

'It is not that. I have not given that a thought. But, Honor—'

'What of Honor?' asked Taverner sharply, stopping.

'I love her, uncle—I love her with my whole heart. I always have loved her, more or less, but now I love her as I can love no one else.'

'Oh, that is it!' exclaimed the old man, bending his brows, and disguising his agitation and annoyance by striking the stones out of the road with the end of his stick. 'A boy's fancy, light as thistle-seed; and a boy's head is as full of fancies as a thistle is of seed.'

'Nothing of the sort,' said the young man vehemently. 'There is no one but Honor can make me what I know I ought to become. I have never had a mother or a sister to guide me. I have grown up unchecked, unadvised, and now I want my dear, dear Honor to help me to be what I should be, and am not. Uncle! you sneer at Chimsworthy because it is full of docks, and thistles, and rushes, but I am like that—worthy land, and none but Honor can weed me. Why do you come cruelly in between us, and kill her happiness as well as mine? Her you cannot make other than noble and true, but me!—me, without her you will ruin. I must have Honor! I cannot live without her. Oh uncle, uncle! what are you doing? It is unworthy of you to use poor Honor's necessity to wring from her her consent. You know she only gives it to save her brother. Why, because she is generous, would you take advantage of her generosity?'

The lad pleaded with earnestness, vehemence, and with tears in his voice. Taverner looked at him, and thought, 'How like he is to his mother! This is Blandina's face and Blandina's voice. He is not a Nanspian, he is a Langford.' But he said roughly, 'Pshaw! let me go by. The rural dean is waiting. Do not you mistake me for a weathercock to be turned by every breath. You must get over your fancy—it is a fancy—or change it to regard for Honor as your aunt. Do not attempt to move me. What is settled is settled.'

As Hillary still interposed himself between Langford and his course the old man raised his stick.

'Come! must I strike you?' he said angrily. 'I've spoken to you more freely than you deserve. Stand aside. I am not to be turned from my way by you or any other.'

He went forward headlong, striking about him with his stick, and was not to be further stayed. He went, as he said, to the church to meet the rural dean, but not only because summoned—he went also to see him as surrogate, and obtain a marriage licence.

'A Langford cannot be married by banns,' he said. 'And I'm not going to have everyone in church sniggering when our names are called.'

As he went along the road, head down, muttering, the face of Hillary haunted him—pale with sickness, refined, spiritualised by suffering, not the suffering of the body but of the mind. He was strangely like Blandina in her last sickness, and there were tones in his voice of entreaty that brought back to Langford memories of his sister and of his mother.

He arrived at the church before the rector and the rural dean. The latter was taking refreshment at the parsonage a mile away. Would Nanspian be there? He did not wish to meet him, but he would not be away lest it should be said he had feared to meet him. Nanspian was not there. He had forgotten all about the visitation.

'He wants a deal of reminding,' said the clerk, who had unlocked the church. 'He forgets most things worse than ever since his stroke.'

Langford disengaged himself from the clerk and entered the church—a noble building of unusual beauty. In the nave at his feet was a long slate stone, and the name Taverner Langford. He knew very well that the stone was there, with its inscription and the date 1635; but as he stood looking at it an uncomfortable feeling came over him, as if he were standing at the edge of his own grave. He was alone in the church. The air was chill and damp, and smelt of decay. The dry-rot was in the pews. The slates were speckled, showing that the church roof was the haunt of bats, who flew about in flights when darkness set in. If it were cold and damp in the church, what must it be in the vault below? He knew what was there—the dust of many Langfords, one or two old lead coffins crushed down by their own weight. And he knew that some day he would lie there, and the 'Taverner Langford' on the stone would apply to him as well as to his ancestor. How horrible to be there at night, with the cold eating into him, and the smell of mildew about him, and the bats fleeting above him! The thought made him uneasy, and he went out of the church into the sunlight, thinking that he would pay a woman to scour the stone of the bat-stains which befouled it. He had never dreamed of doing this before, but when he considered that he must himself lie there, he took a loathing to the bats, and an indignation at the vault-covering stone being disfigured by them.

He walked through the coarse grass to where his sister was laid. She was not buried in the family vault. Nanspian had not wished it.

The clerk came to him.

'Mr. Nanspian had a double-walled grave made,' said the clerk, who was also sexton. 'Folks laughed, I mind, when he ordered it, and said he was sure to marry again—a fine lusty man like he. But they were wrong. He never did. He has bided true to her memory.'

'I would never have forgiven him had he done other,' said Langford.

'I reckon you never forgive him, though he has not,' said the solemn clerk.

Langford frowned and moved his shoulders uneasily.

'The grave is cared for,' said he in a churlish tone.

'Young Larry Nanspian sees to that,' answered the clerk. 'If there be no other good in him there is that—he don't forget what is due to his mother, though she be dead.'

Langford put his stick to the letters on the headstone. 'In loving memory of Blandina Nanspian, only daughter of Moses Langford, of Langford, gent.' 'Oh!' muttered Taverner, 'my father could call himself a gentleman when he had Chimsworthy as well as Langford, but I suppose I can't call myself anything but yeoman on my poor farm. Blandina should never have married, and then Chimsworthy would not have gone out of the family.'

'But to whom would both have gone after your death, Mr. Langford?' asked the clerk. ''Twould be a pity if an old ancient family like yours came to an end, and, I reckon, some day both will be joined again, by Mr. Larry.'

'No, no!—no, no!' growled Taverner, and walked away. He saw the rural dean and the rector coming through the churchyard gate.

An hour later, Taverner was on his way home. He had paid the fee, made the necessary application, and would receive the licence on the morrow. It was too late for him to draw back, even had he been inclined. Taverner was a proud man, and he was obstinate. He flattered himself that when he had once resolved on a thing he always went through with it; no dissuasion, no impediments turned him aside. But he was not easy in mind as he walked home. Never before had he seen the family likeness so strong in Larry; he had caught an occasional look of his mother in the boy's face before, but now that he was ill in mind and body the likeness was striking. Taverner still laid no great weight on Larry's expressed attachment for Honor; he did not know that love was not a fiction, and was unable to conceive of it as anything more than a passing fancy. What really troubled the old man was the prospect of disarrangement of his accustomed mode of life. When he was married his wife would claim entrance into his parlour, and would meddle with what he had there, would use his desk, would come in and out when he was busy, would talk when he wanted quiet. A housekeeper could be kept in order by threat of dismissal, but a wife was tied for life. Then—how about Larry? He might forbid him the house, but would he keep away? Would not he insist on seeing his old friend and companion and love, Honor? That would be dangerous to his own peace of mind, might threaten his happiness. He remembered some words of Mrs. Veale, and his blood rushed through his head like a scalding wave.

When he came to his door Mrs. Veale was there. She seemed to know by instinct his purpose in going to Bratton.

'Have you got it, master?' she asked with husky voice and fluttering eyelids.

'Got what?'

'What you went to get—the licence.'

'It is coming by post to-morrow. Are you satisfied?' he asked sneering, and with a glance of dislike.

'A corpse-light came up the lane and danced on the doorstep last night,' said Mrs. Veale. 'And you are thinking of marrying! "I'd better have left things as they were," said the man who scalded his dog to clear it of fleas. The spider spread for a midget and caught a hornet. "Marry come up," said the mote (tree-stump), "I will wed the flame;" so she took him, embraced him, and——' Mrs. Veale stooped to the hearth, took up a handful of light wood-ash, and blew it in her master's face from her palm, then said, 'Ashes, remain.'

The ensuing night the house was disturbed. Taverner Langford was ill, complaining of violent sickness, cramps, and burning in the throat. He must have a doctor sent for from Okehampton.

'Get a doctor's foot on your floor and he leaves his shoes,' said Mrs. Veale. 'No, wait till morning. If you're no better then we will send.'

'Go out of my room,' shouted Taverner to the farm men and maids who had crowded in. His calls and hammering with the stick had roused everyone in the house. 'Do you think I am going to die because I'm took with spasms? Mrs. Veale is enough. Let her remain.'

'I reckon I caught a chill standing in the damp church with the smell of the vaults in my nose,' said Taverner, sitting in his chair and groaning. 'I felt the cold rise.'

'It is waiting,' remarked Mrs. Veale.

'What is waiting?' he asked irritably.

'The corpse-candle; I see it on the doorstep. And you that should be considering to have the bell tolled ordering a wedding peal! Those who slide on ice must expect falls, and elephants mustn't dance on tight-ropes. Rabbits that burrow in bogs won't have dry quarters. The fox said, "Instead of eating I shall be eaten," when, seeking a hen-roost, he walked into a kennel.'

XXXV
A Warning

THE DAY WAS WET; A warm south-westerly wind was breathing, not blowing, and its breath was steam, a steam that condensed into minute water-drops. The thatch was dripping. The window panes were blind with shiny films of moisture. There had been dry weather for the haysel, glorious weather, and now, just when wanted, the earth was bathed in a cloud. It would be inaccurate to say that it rained. It rained only under the eaves and beneath the trees; the earth was taking a vapour bath.

Honor and Kate were in the cottage, basket-weaving. The children were at school. No wet dismays the Devonian, but east wind throws him on his back, and he shrivels with frost. Kate had recovered her spirits marvellously since her interview with Sam Voaden. She had a buoyant heart; it was like a cork in water, that might be pressed under, but came up with a leap again. She felt keenly for the time, but wounds speedily healed with her. It was other with Honor; she remained depressed, pale, thin-looking, and silent. She said nothing to her sister about Hillary. Kate had some glimmering idea that Honor liked the young man, but did not suppose that there was more in her heart than a liking. But Kate, though she dearly loved her sister, was somewhat in awe of her. She never ventured to peer into her soul, and she understood nothing of what went on there. Honor was scrupulous, precise, close; and Kate, though a good-hearted, true girl, was not close, but open, not precise, but careless, and ready to stretch a point of conscience to suit her pleasure. Kate, in the presence of Honor, was much like an unmathematical boy set over a problem in Euclid. She was sure that all was very true in Honor's mind, but also that the process by which it arrived at its conclusions was beyond her understanding. Honor possessed, what is the prerogative of few women, a just mind. Forced by her position into dividing between the children who looked up to her, obliged to consider their complaints against each other in petty quarrels from opposite sides, and of deciding equably, she had acquired breadth and fairness and self-restraint, against action upon impulse. Kate was eager to take sides, and was partial; Honor never. She was always disposed to consider that there was something to be said on the side opposed to that first presented to her, and was cautious not to pronounce an opinion till she had heard both sides. This Kate could not understand and she regarded her sister as wanting in warmth and enthusiasm.

'No news yet from Sam,' said Kate. 'That is odd. I thought we should have known at once about Charles.'

'How could that be? Plymouth is a large place, and Sam Voaden will not know where to look. It is even possible that Charles may have sailed.'

'If he has sailed you need not be tied to old Langford—that is, not unless you like.'

'I have passed my word. I cannot withdraw.'

'Fiddlesticks-ends! You only promised on condition that Mr. Langford would not proceed against Charles.'

'He has not proceeded.'

'He can't—if Charles is out of England.'

'But he might have done so the day he discovered his loss, before Charles got away. I gave my word to prevent his taking immediate action, and so Charles had time to make his escape from the country.'

'Taverner Langford had no right to ask it of you.'

'He did ask it, and I gave my word. I cannot withdraw now. That would not be fair and right.'

Kate shrugged her shoulders. 'I should pay him out in his own coin.'

'Like Charles at the circus?'

Kate coloured. 'That was another matter altogether. Mr. Langford had no right to put such a price on his forbearance. Besides, I don't believe in Charles's guilt. Sam does not and, thick as some folks think Sam, he has as much brains as are wanted to fill a large skull, and these of first quality. Sam can see into a millstone.'

'Yes, Kate, but what *is* in a millstone?—the same as outside'

'Sam says that he knows Charles is innocent.'

'What reasons does he give?'

'Oh, none at all. I did not ask for any. *He* thinks it, that is enough for me.'

'He *thinks* it, now; he *knows* it, a minute ago.'

'I am quite sure that Charles never took the money.'

'Why?'

'There you are again with your "whys." Because Sam says it.'

'Yes, dear Kate, Sam is a good-hearted fellow, who will not think badly of anyone, and he supposes others are as straightforward as himself.'

'You have a dozen splendid reasons for thinking Charles a thief, and not one of them convinces me. I don't know why, except that Sam is so positive; but I will scratch all the silver off my looking-glass if I am wrong. Charles did not take the money.'

Honor said no more. It was useless arguing with Kate, and nothing was gained if she did convince her. The girls worked on for a few minutes in silence; then Kate burst out with, 'After all, I do not see anything so dreadful in becoming Mrs. Langford. One cannot have everything. Taverner has not the youth and looks of—say Sam Voaden, but Sam Voaden has no money of his own, and Mr. Langford can roll in money when his back itches. Langford is a very fine property still, and the house is first-rate. If I take Sam at any time—I don't say I shall—I shall have to put up with poverty. If you take Taverner Langford you must put up with ugliness. You can't catch herring and hake at one fishing.' Then she burst into a ringing laugh.

'It will be worthwhile marrying him only for the fun of making Larry Nanspian call you aunt.' Honor winced, but Kate was too tickled by the idea to observe her sister's face.

'When is it to be, Honor? It is mean of you to be so secret about the day. I am your sister, and I ought to know.'

'I only do not tell you because you cannot keep a secret, and I wish no one to know till all is over. Some morning when nothing is expected, it——' She shivered and turned her face to the wall.

'I will not blab. I will not, indeed, dear.'

'Some day this week. Well, if you must know, Thursday. Pray be secret; you will only add to my pain, my shame, if it be known, and a crowd of the curious be assembled to see. *He* also wished it to be kept from getting wind. Indeed, he insisted.'

'I don't like a marriage without smart dresses and bridesmaids. Who is to be best man? I don't believe old Taverner has a friend anywhere. Why—Honor, he'll be my brother-in-law. This is a strange prospect. We'll come up to Langford and see you every day, that you may not be dull. What are you going to do with Mrs. Veale? You are surely not going to keep her! Do you know, Honor, in the kitchen is a darling china spaniel, just like ours yonder on the mantelpiece, and he turns his head the opposite way to ours. I'm really glad you are going to marry Mr. Langford, because then the dogs will make a pair. They look so desolate, one here and the other there; they are ordained to keep company.' Honor said nothing; she let her sister rattle on without paying heed to her tattle.

'Honor,' said Kate, 'do you know whence Charles got the notion of putting the five-pound note under the dog? Guess.'

'I cannot guess. It does not matter.'

'Yes, it does matter. Charles got the notion from sweet Mrs. Veale. When I was at Langford looking for you, I saw that she used the dog as a place for putting things away that must not lie about. If you turn one of these china dogs on end, you will see that they are hollow. Well, Mrs. Veale had stuffed a packet of rat poison into the dog. You remember the man at the Revel who sold hones and packets of poison for mice and rats? Do you not recollect the board above his table with the picture on it of the vermin tumbling about as if drunk, and some lying on their backs dead? All his packets were in yellow paper with a picture on them in small like that on the board. It does not seem right to let poison lie about. I should lock it up if I had it; but Mrs. Veale is unlike everyone else in her appearance and in her talk, and, I suppose, in her actions. She keeps the yellow paper of rat poison in the body of the china spaniel. I saw her take it thence, and stow it in there again. The place is not amiss. No one would dream of looking there for it. Who knows? Perhaps Mrs. Veale keeps her money in the same place. Charles may have seen that, and when he came here, and wanted to give us five pounds and escape thanks, he put it under the dog. That is reasonable, is it not, Honor?' Honor did not answer.

'I declare!' exclaimed Kate impatiently. 'You have not been attending to what I said.'

'Yes, I have, Kate.'

'What was I saying? Tell me if you can.'

'You said that Mrs. Veale kept her money in a china dog on the chimneypiece.'

'No, I did not. I said she kept rat poison there in a yellow paper.'

'Yes, Kate, so you did. She hides the poison there lest careless hands should get hold of it.'

'I am glad you have had the civility to listen. You seemed to me to be in a dream. I don't think, after all, Honor, but for Sam, that I should mind being in your place. It must be an experience as charming as new to have money at command. After all, an old man in love is led by the nose, and you, Honor, he must love, so you can take him about, and make him do exactly what you want. I almost envy you. Where is father?'

'Gone to see Frize, the shoemaker. I had a pair of shoes ordered from him two months ago, and father has gone to see if they are done. I shall want them on Thursday.'

'Father is quite pleased at the idea of your marriage. I know he is. He makes sure of getting Coombe Park. He says that Mr. Langford will lend the money; and he expects grand days when we get our own again.

Father don't believe any more in Charles being guilty, after I told him Sam's reasons.'

'What reasons?'

'Well, I mean assertions. Does father know the day on which you are to be married?'

'No, Kate. Mr. Langford wished him not to be told. Father is so obliging, so good-natured that if anyone were to press him to tell, he could not keep the secret, so we thought it best not to let him know till just at the last.'

'Won't father be proud when you are at Langford! Why, the van will not contain all his self-importance. To have his eldest daughter married into one of the best and oldest families of the neighbourhood, to be planted in the best house—after Squire Impey's—in the parish! My dear Honor! an idea strikes me. Shall I throw myself at Squire Impey's head? Father would go stark mad with pride if that were so—that is, if I succeeded. And if he got Coombe back, we three would rule the parish. We might all three become feoffees of Coryndon's Charity, and pass the land round among us. That would be grand! Honor! what, is to be done with Mrs. Veale? I cannot abide the woman. It was a queer idea, was it not, putting the rat poison in the china dog?'

All at once Kate looked up. 'My dear Honor, talk of somebody that be nameless, and he is sure to appear.' She spoke in a whisper, as Mrs. Veale came from the steps in at the door. She had a dark cloak thrown over her pale cotton dress. She stood in the doorway blinking nervously.

Honor stood up, put her light work aside, and, with her usual courtesy to all, went towards her. 'Do you want me, Mrs. Veale? Will you take a chair?'

'No, I will not sit down. So'—she looked about—'you will go from a hovel to a mansion! At least, so you expect. Take care! Take care, lest, in trying to jump into the saddle, you jump over the horse.'

Honor moved a chair towards the woman. Kate looked curiously at her. The pale, faded creature stood looking about her in an inquisitive manner. 'I've come with a message,' she said. 'You are very set on getting into Langford, eh? Oh, Langford is a palace to this cottage.'

Honor did not answer. She drew up her head, and made no further offer of a seat. 'What is your message?' she asked coldly. But Kate fired up in her sister's defence, and, tossing her head, said, 'Don't you suppose, Mrs. Veale, that Honor, or my father, or I, or Joe, or any of us think that a prize has been drawn in your master. Quite the other way—he is in luck. He don't deserve what he has got, for Honor is a treasure.'

'What message have you brought?' asked Honor again.

The vindictiveness against the girl seemed to have disappeared from the woman—at least, she did not look at Honor with the same malevolent glance as formerly; and, indeed, she was not now so full of hate against her as anger against Langford—the deadlier passion had obscured the weaker.

'What is the message?' she repeated.

'Oh, this. You and your father are to come up to Langford as soon as you can. Lawyer Physick be there and waiting.' Then, with quivering voice and eyelids, and trembling hands thrust though her black cloak, 'I—I be sent wi' this message. He had the face to send me! Him that I've served true, and followed as a hound these fifteen years, turns against me now, and drives me from his door! Look here, Miss Honor Luxmore!' She held up her long white finger before her face. 'I've knowed a man as had a dog, and that dog wi' ill-treatment went mad, and when the dog were mad she bit her master, and he died.' She blinked and quivered, and as she quivered the water-drops flew off her cloak over the slate floor, almost as if a poodle had shaken himself. 'Take care!' she said again, 'take care! The man that kicks at me won't spare you. Take care, I say again. Be warned against him. I've given you his message, but don't take it. Don't go to Langford. Let Lawyer Physick go away. The licence has come. Let it go to light a fire. Make no use of it. Stay where you are and let the master find he's been made a fool of. Best so! In the hitting of nails you may hammer your knuckles. I've served him fifteen years as if I were his slave, and now he bids me pack. "I should have thought of my thatch before I fired my chimney," said the man who was burnt out of house and home.'

'Go back to Langford, and say that my father and I will be there shortly.'

'Then take the consequences.' Mrs.Veale's eyes for a moment glittered like steel, then disappeared under her winking white lashes. She turned and left the cottage, muttering, 'When the owl hoots look out for sorrow. When the dog bays he smells death, and I am his dog—and, they say, his blinking owl.'

XXXVI
A Settlement

Oliver Luxmore entered shortly after Mrs. Veale had left. 'Frize promises the shoes by Monday,' he said.

Then Honor told him that he and she were awaited at Langford, and she went upstairs to get herself ready. In the corner of her room was an old oak box, in which she kept her clothes and few treasures. She opened it, and took out the red cloak, her best and brightest pair of red stockings. Then she touched the paper that contained the kerchief Larry had given her. Should she wear it? No; that she could not wear, and yet she felt as if to have it crossed over her bosom would give it warmth and strength. She opened the paper and looked at the white silk, with its pretty moss-rose buds and sprigs of forget-me-not. A tear fell from her eye on it. She folded it up again, and put it away.

Presently she came downstairs, dressed to go with her father. On Sundays she wore a straw bonnet with cherry-coloured ribbons in it, but now that the air was full of moisture she could not risk her pretty bows in the wet. She would draw the hood of her scarlet cloak over her head.

Neither she nor her father spoke much on the way to Langford. He was, as Kate had said, not ill-pleased at the alliance—indeed, but for the trouble about Charles, he would have been exultant.

Honor had been brought to accept what was best for her and for all the family at last. Oliver had easily accepted Kate's assertion that Charles was innocent, but he would not maintain the innocence of Charles before Honor, lest it should cause her to draw back from her engagement.

Even on a fine day, with the sun streaming in at the two windows, Langford's parlour was not cheerful. It was panelled with deal, painted slate-grey; the mouldings were coarse and heavy. There were no curtains to the windows, only blinds, no carpet on the floor, and the furniture was still the chairs and sofa covered with black horsehair. What was in the room was in sound condition and substantial, but tasteless. Even the table was bare of cover. Till Honor entered in her scarlet cloak there was not a speck of pure colour in the room. She removed her cloak, and stood in a dark gown, somewhat short, showing below it a strip of red petticoat and her red stockings. Round her neck was a white handkerchief, of cotton, not silk.

Mr. Physick and Langford were at the table; they were waiting, and had been expecting them. Both rose to receive her and her father, the first with effusion, the latter with some embarrassment.

'What is the matter with you, sir?' asked the carrier of Taverner Langford. 'You don't look yourself to-day.'

'I've been unwell,' answered the yeoman. 'I had to be down at the church t'other day to meet the rural dean, as I'm churchwarden, and Nanspian is too lazy to act; I heated myself with walking, and I had an encounter with the young Merry Andrew on the way.' He glanced at Honor, but she neither stirred nor raised her eyes from the table. 'Some words passed. He was impudent, and I nigh on thrashed him. I would have chastised him, but that he had a broken arm. My blood was up, and I had to stand in the damp church, and I reckon I got a chill there. I was taken bad in the night, and thought I must die—burning pains and cramps, but it passed off. I'm better now. It was an inflammation, but I'm getting right again. I have to be careful what I eat, that is all. Slops—slops. I wouldn't dare touch that,' said he, pointing to a brandy bottle beside the lawyer. 'It would feed the fire and kill me.'

'My opinion is that the affection is of the heart, not of the stomach,' laughed Physick, 'and when I look at Miss Honor I'm not surprised at the burning. Enough to set us all in flames, eh, Langford! Heartburn, man, heartburn!—nothing worse than that, and now you're going to take the best medicine to cure that disorder.'

'Not that at all,' said Taverner surlily. 'I caught a chill across me standing waiting in the church at the visitation; I felt the cold and damp come up out of the vault to me. I was taken ill the same night.'

'You've a nice house here,' said the lively Physick, 'a little cold such a day as this, with the drizzle against the windows, but—love will keep it warm. What do you think, Miss Honor, of the nest, eh? Lined with wool, eh? well, money is better than wool.'

Honor measured him with a haughty glance, and Physick, so disconcerted, turned to the carrier and Mr. Langford to discuss business.

Honor remained standing, cold, composed and resolute, but with a heart weaker than her outward appearance betokened. 'Come,' said Physick, 'next to the parson I'm the most necessary workman to hammer the chain. The parson can do something for the present, I for the future. If you will listen to the settlement, you won't grumble at my part. Little as you may think of me, I've had your interests in eye. I've taken care of you.'

'You have done nothing but what I have bid you,' said Taverner roughly. 'Oliver Luxmore and I talked it over before you, and you have written what we decided.'

'Oh, of course, of course!' exclaimed Physick, 'but there are two ways of doing a thing. A slip of the pen, a turn of expression, and all is spoiled. I've been careful, and I do consider it hard that the parson who blesses the knot should be allowed to claim a kiss, and the lawyer who plaits it should not be allowed even to ask for one.' He glanced at Taverner and Oliver and winked.

'Certainly, certainly,' said the carrier.

'Come,' said Langford, 'to business. I want her'—he pointed with his elbow at Honor—'to see what I have done. I'm a fair man, and I want her to see that I have dealt generously by her, and to know if she be content.'

'I have asked you for one thing, Mr. Langford, and that you have refused. I must needs be content with whatever you have decided for me, but I care for nothing else.'

'Listen, listen, Honor, before you speak,' said Oliver Luxmore. 'I have considered your interests as your father, and I think you will say that I also have dealt handsomely by you.'

'You, dear father!' She wondered what he could have done, he who had nothing, who was in debt.

'Read,' said Luxmore, and coughed a self-complacent, important cough.

The settlement was simple. It provided that in the event of Honor becoming a widow, in accordance with a settlement made in the marriage of Moses Langford and Blandina Hill, the father and mother of Taverner Langford, the property should be charged to the amount of seventy five pounds to be levied annually, and that, in the event of issue arising from the contemplated marriage, in accordance with the aforementioned settlement the property was to go to the eldest son, charged with the seventy-five pounds for his mother, and that every other child was, on its coming of age, to receive one hundred pounds, to be levied out of the estate. And it was further agreed between Taverner Langford and Oliver Luxmore that, in the event of the latter receiving the estates of the Luxmore family, named Coombe Park, in the parish of Bratton Clovelly and other, he, the said Oliver Luxmore, should pay to Taverner Langford, the husband of his daughter, the sum of five hundred pounds to be invested in the Three per cents. for the benefit of the said Honor Langford alias Luxmore, during her lifetime, and to her sole use, and with power of disposal by will. This was the stipulation Oliver had made he insisted on this generous offer being accepted and inserted in the marriage contract. Honor listened attentively to every word. She was indifferent what provision was made for herself, but she hoped against conviction that Langford would bind himself to do something for her father. Instead of that her father had bound himself to pay five hundred pounds in the improbable event of his getting Coombe Park. Poor father! poor father!

'You have done nothing of what I asked,' said Honor.

'I have no wish to act ungenerously,' answered Taverner. 'Your request was unreasonable; however, I have acted fairly. I have promised to advance your father a hundred pounds to assist him in the prosecuting of his claims.'

'There,' said Oliver Luxmore, 'you see, Honor, that your marriage is about to help the whole family. We shall come by our rights at last. We shall recover Coombe Park.'

Then Taverner went to the door and called down the passage, 'Mrs. Veale! Come here! You are wanted to witness some signatures.'

The housekeeper came, paler, more trembling than usual, with her eyes fluttering, but with sharp malignant gleams flashing out of them from under the white throbbing lashes.

'I be that nervous,' she said, 'and my hand shakes so I can hardly write.'

She stooped, and indeed her hand did tremble. 'I'm cooking the supper,' she said, 'you must excuse the apron.' As she wrote she turned her head and looked at her master. He was not observing her, and the lawyer was indicating the place where she was to write and was holding down the sheet, but Honor saw the look full of deadly hate, a look that made her heart stand still, and the thought to spring into her brain, 'That woman ought not to remain in the house another hour, she is dangerous.'

When Mrs. Veale had done, she rose, put her hands under her apron, curtsied, and said, 'May I make so bold as to ask if that be the master's will?'

'No, it is not,' said Langford.

'Thank you, sir,' said Mrs. Veale, curtseying again. 'You'll excuse the liberty, but if it had been, I'd have said, remember I've served your honour these fifteen years faithful as a dog, and now in my old age I'm kicked out, though not past work.'

She curtsied again, and went backward out of the room into the passage.

Langford shut, slammed the door in her face.

'Is the woman a little touched here?' asked the lawyer, pointing to his forehead.

'Oh no, not a bit, only disappointed. She has spent fifteen years in laying traps for me, and I have been wise enough to avoid them all.' Then he opened the door suddenly and saw her there, in the dark passage, her face distorted with passion and her fist raised.

'Mrs. Veale,' said the yeoman, 'lay the supper and have done with this nonsense.'

'I beg your pardon,' she said, changing her look and making another curtsey, 'was it the marriage settlement now? I suppose it was. I wish you every happiness, and health to enjoy your new condition. Health and happiness! I'm to leave, and that young chick to take my place. May she enjoy herself. And, Mr. Langford, may you please, as long as you live, to remember me.'

'Go along! Lay the table, and bring in supper.'

'What will you please to take, master?' asked the woman in an altered tone.

'Bring me some broth. I'll take no solids. I'm not right yet. For the rest, the best you have in the house.'

Mrs. Veale laid the table. The lawyer, Langford, the carrier, and Honor were seated round the room, very stiffly, silent, watching the preparations for the meal.

Presently Honor started up. She was unaccustomed to be waited upon, incapable of remaining idle.

'I will go help to prepare the supper,' she said, and went into the passage.

This passage led directly from the front door through the house to the kitchen, It was dark; all the light it got was from the front door, or through the kitchen when one or other door was left open. Originally the front door had opened into a hall or reception room with window and fireplace; but Taverner had battened off the passage, and converted the old hall into a room where he kept saddles and bridles and other things connected with the stables. By shutting off the window by the partition he had darkened the passage, and consequently the kitchen door had invariably to be left open to light it. In this dark passage stood Honor, looking down it to the kitchen which was full of light, whilst she pinned up the skirt of her best gown, so as not to soil it whilst engaged in serving up the supper. As she stood thus she saw Mrs. Veale at the fire stirring the broth for her master in an iron saucepan. She put her hand to the mantel-shelf, took down the china dog, and Honor saw her remove from its inside a packet of yellow paper, empty the contents into the pan, then burn the paper and pour the broth into a bowl. In a moment Kate's story of the rat poison in the body of the dog recurred to Honor, and she stood paralysed, unable to resolve what to do. Then she recalled the look cast at Taverner by Mrs. Veale as she was signing the settlement as witness. Honor reopened the parlour door, went into the room again she had just left, and seated herself, that she might collect her thoughts and determine what to do. Kate was not a reliable authority, and it was not judicious to act on information given by her sister without having proved it. Honor had seen Mrs. Veale thrust the yellow paper into the flames under the pot. She could not therefore be sure by examination that it was the rat poison packet. She remained half in a dream whilst the supper was laid, and woke with a start when Taverner said, 'Come to table, all, and we will ask a blessing.'

Honor slowly drew towards the table; she looked round. Mrs. Veale was not there; before Taverner stood the steaming bowl of soup.

Langford murmured grace, then said, 'Fall to. Oliver Luxmore, you do the honours. I can't eat, I'm forced to take slops. But I'm better, only I must be careful.' He put his spoon into the basin, and would have helped himself, had not Honor snatched the bowl away and removed it to the mantel-shelf.

'You must not touch it,' she said. 'I am not sure—I am afraid—I would not accuse wrongfully—it is poisoned!'

XXXVII
A Bowl of Broth

THE WORDS WERE HARDLY OUT of Honor's mouth before the party were surprised by a noise of voices and feet in the kitchen, and a cry as of dismay or fear. A moment after the tramp was in the passage, the parlour door was flung open, and Sam Voaden, Hillary Nanspian and his father, Piper, Charles Luxmore, and Mrs.Veale came in, the latter gripped firmly by Piper and Charles.

'Here I am,' said young Luxmore, with his usual swagger, and with some elation in his tone, 'here I am, come to know what the deuce you mean, Mr. Langford, charging me—a gentleman to the face but behind the back, with stealing your money? Look here, Sam, produce the box. There is your cash, whether right or not I cannot say. I have taken none of it. I did not remove the case. Tell 'em where you found it, Sam.'

'I found it in Wellon's Mound,' said the young man appealed to. 'I've been to Plymouth after Charles. I didn't believe he was a thief, but I'd hard matter to find him. Howsomedever, I did in the end, and here lie he. He came along ready enough. He was out of money—wanted to go to America, but had not the means of paying his passage, and not inclined to work it.'

'I've lost a finger,' exclaimed Charles. 'How could I work, maimed as I am?—a wounded soldier without a pension! That is shameful of an ungrateful country.'

'He took on badly,' continued Sam, 'when I told him that Mr. Langford said he had stolen his cashbox with a thousand pounds.'

'I'm a Luxmore of Coombe Park,' said Charles, drawing himself up. 'I'm not one of your vulgar thieves, not I. Mrs. Veale did her best to tempt me to take it, but I resisted it manfully. At last I ran away, afraid lest she should over-persuade me and get me into trouble, when I saw she had actually got the box. I ran away from Mrs. Veale, and because nine pence a day wasn't sufficient to detain me. I wasn't over-sure neither that I hadn't, against my intention, broke the neck of Larry Nanspian. Now you know my reasons, and they're good in their way. Mrs. Veale, there, is a reg'lar bad un.'

'As soon as Sam returned with Charles,' said Larry, 'they came on direct to Chimsworthy, and then Charles told us the whole tale, how Mrs. Veale had shown him where Mr. Langford kept his money, then how she'd enticed him out on the moor to Wellon's Cairn, and had let him see that she had carried off the box and had concealed it there. Charles told us that it was then that he ran away, and frightened my horse so that I was thrown and injured.'

'There was nothing ungentlemanly or unsoldierlike in my cutting away,' exclaimed Charles. 'Adam was beguiled by Eve, and I didn't set myself up to be a better man than my great forefather. I'd like to know which of the company would like to be fondled by Mrs. Veale, and made much of, and coaxed to run away with her? She's a bad un. It wasn't like I should reciprocate.'

'When we had heard the story,' continued Larry, 'I persuaded my father and Mr. Piper, who was at our house, to come along with us and see the whole matter cleared up. We went immediately to Wellon's Cairn, and found, as Charles Luxmore said we should, a stone box or coffin, hidden in the hill, with bushes of heather and peat over the hole. That we cleared away, and were able to put our hands in, and extracted from the inside this iron case. It is yours, is it not, Mr. Langford?'

He put the cashbox on the table, taking it into his left hand from his father.

Taverner went to it and examined it. 'Yes,' he said slowly, 'this is the stolen box.'

'The lock is uninjured, it is fast,' said Charles; 'but I can tell you how to open it. "Ebal" is the word this year, and "Onam" was last year's word. Try the letters of the lock and the box will fly open, I know; Mrs. Veale told me. A reg'lar bad un she be, and how she has worreted me the time I've been here!—at nine pence, and Mrs. Veale not even good-looking.'

'How about the five-pound note?' asked Langford, looking hard at Charles from under his contracted heavy brows. 'You can't deny you had that.'

'What five-pound note?—what five-pound note have I had from you?'

'The note you gave us, Charles,' explained his father.

'Oh, that. Did it come from your box? I did not know it; Mrs. Veale gave it me. Now, don't you glow'r at me that way!' This was to the housekeeper, who had turned her white, quivering face towards him. 'Now don't you try to wriggle or shiver yourself out of my hold, for go you don't; as you couldn't catch me, I've caught you, and to justice I'll bring you; a designing, harassing, sweethearting old female, you be!' He gripped her so hard that she exclaimed with pain. 'And to lay it on me when I was gone! To make out I—that am innocent as the angels in heaven—was a thief! And I, a Luxmore of Coombe Park, and a hero of the Afghan war—I, that carried off the sandal-wood gates of Somnath! I, a thief! I, indeed! Mrs. Veale gave me, off and on, money when I was short—I wasn't very flush on nine pence a day. A man of my position and bringing up and military tastes can't put up well with nine pence. I only accepted her money as a loan; and when she let me have a five-pound note, I gave her a promise to pay for it when I came into my property. How was I to know that five-pound note was not hers? I suppose, by the way you ask, it was not?'

'No,' said Langford, 'it was not; it was taken from my box.'

'That is like her—a bad un down to the soles of her feet. Wanted to mix me up with it and have evidence against me. I reckon I've turned the tables on the old woman— considerably.'

'What do you say to this?' asked Taverner, directing his keen eyes on her face. She was flickering so that it was impossible to catch her eyes. Her face was as though seen through the hot air over a kiln.

'I've been in your service fifteen years,' she said, in a voice as vibrating as the muscles of her countenance. 'I've been treated by you no better than a dog, and I've followed you, and been true to you as a dog. Whenever did I take anything from you before? I've watched for you against the mice that eat the corn, watched like an owl!'

'You acknowledge this?'

'What is the good of denying it? Let me go, for my fifteen years' faithful duty.'

'No, no,' said Taverner with a hard voice. 'Not yet; I've something more to ask. Honor Luxmore, what did you say when you took my bowl of broth from me?' Honor drew back.

'I spoke too hastily,' she said. 'I spoke without knowing.'

'You said that the bowl contained poison. Why did you say that?'

'It was fancy. Let me throw the broth away. I am sure of nothing.' Unlike her usual decision, Honor was now doubtful what to say and do.

'I insist on knowing. I made a charge against your brother, and it has proved false, because it has been gone into. You have made a charge—'

'I have charged no one.'

'You have said that this bowl'—he took it from the shelf—'is poisoned. Why, did you say that? No one touched it, no one mixed it, but Mrs. Veale. Therefore, when you said it was poisoned, you charged her with a dreadful crime; you charged her, that is, with an attempted crime.'

'I heard my sister say that she saw a yellow packet of rat poison in the china dog on the shelf in the kitchen,' said Honor nervously, 'which—I do not mean the dog—I mean the poison, which Mrs. Veale had bought at the Revel, and when I was in the passage just now I saw Mrs. Veale put the contents of this packet into the broth she was stirring on the fire, before pouring it out into the basin, in which it now is. But,' continued Honor, drawing a long breath, 'but Kate is not very accurate; she sometimes thinks she sees a thing when she has only imagined it, and she talks at random at times, just because she likes to talk.'

'It was mace,' said Mrs. Veale.

'Follow me,' ordered Taverner Langford taking the basin between his hands, and going to the door. 'Let her go. She will follow me.'

'I've followed at your heel as a dog these fifteen years,' muttered Mrs. Veale, 'and now you know I must follow till you kick me away.'

Charles, however, would not relinquish his hold.

'Don't let her escape,' entreated Charles; 'she's a bad un, and ought to be brought to justice for falsely charging me.'

'Open the door, will you?' said Taverner roughly. 'Mrs. Veale, follow me into the harness-room'—this was the room on the other side of the passage, the room made out of the entrance hall.

Charles drew the woman through the door, and did not relax his hold till he had thrust her into the apartment where Langford wished to speak to her alone.

Taverner and she were now face to face without witnesses. The soft warm mist had changed to rain, that now pattered against the window. The room was wholly unfurnished. There was not a chair in it nor a table. Taverner had originally intended it as an office, but as he received few visitors he had come to use the parlour as reception room and office, and had made this apartment, cut from the hall, into a receptacle for lumber. A range of pegs on the wall supported old saddles and the gear of cart-horses, and branches of bean-stalks, that had been hung there to dry for the preservation of seed. An unpleasant, stale odour hung about the room. The grate had not been used for many years, and was rusty; rain had brought the soot down the chimney, and, as there was no fender, had spluttered it over the floor. The window panes were dirty, and cobwebs hung in the corners of the room from the ceiling—old cobwebs thick with dust. Moths had eaten into the stuffing of the saddles, and, disturbed by the current of air from the door, fluttered about. In the corner was a heap of sacks, with nothing in them, smelling of earth and tar.

'I've served you faithful as a dog,' said Mrs. Veale. 'Faithful as a dog,' she repeated; 'watched for you, wakeful as an owl.'

'And like a dog snarl and snap at me with poisoned fangs,' retorted Mr. Langford. 'Stand there!' He pointed to a place opposite him, so that the light from the window fell on her, and his own face was in darkness. 'Tell me the truth; what have you done to this broth?'

'If you think there's harm in it, throw it away,' said Mrs. Veale.

'No, I will not. I will send it to Okehampton and have it analysed. Do you know what that means? Examined whether there be anything in it but good juice of meat and water and toast.'

'There's mace,' said the woman; 'I put in mace to spice it, and pepper and salt.'

'Anything else? What do you keep in yellow paper, and in the china dog?'

'Mace—every cook puts mace in soup. If you don't like it throw it away, and I will make you some without.'

'Mrs. Veale, so there's nothing further in the soup?'

'Nothing.'

'You warned me that a corpse-candle was coming to the door—nay, you said you had seen it travel up the road and dance on the step, and that same night I was taken ill.'

'Well, did I bring the corpse-light? It came of itself.'

'Mrs. Veale, I am not generally accounted a generous man, but I pride myself on being a just man. You have told me over and over again that you have served me faithfully for fifteen years. Well, you have had your way. You served me in your own fashion, with your head full of your own plans. You wanted to catch me, but the wary bird don't hop on the limed twig, to use your own expressions. I don't see that I'm much in your debt; if you are disappointed in the failure of your plans, that's your look-out; you should have seen earlier that nothing was to be made out of me. Now I am ready to stretch a point with you. You have robbed me. Fortunately for me, I've got my money and box back before you have been able to make off with it. What were you waiting for? For my death? For my marriage? Were you going to finish me because I had not been snared by your blandishments? I believe you intended to poison me.'

'It's a lie!' said Mrs. Veale hoarsely, trembling in every limb and with flickering lips and eyes and nostrils and fluttering hair.

'Very well. I am content to believe so. I can, if I choose, proceed against you at once—have you locked up this very night for your theft. But I am willing to deal even generously with you. It may be I have overlooked your many services; I may have repaid them scantily. You may be bitterly disappointed because I have not made you mistress of this house, and I will allow that I didn't keep you at arm's length as I should, finding you useful. Very well. The door is open. You shall go away and none shall follow, on one condition.'

He looked fixedly at her, and her quivering became more violent. She did not ask what his condition was. She knew.

'Finish this bowl, and convince me you were not bent on my murder.'

She put out her hands to cover her face, but they trembled so that she could not hold them over her eyes.

'If you refuse, I shall know the whole depth of your wickedness, and you shall only leave this room under arrest. If you accept, the moor is before you; go over it where you will.'

He held the bowl to her. Then her trembling ceased—ceased as by a sudden spasm. She was still, set in face as if frozen; and her eyes, that glared on her master, were like pieces of ice. She said nothing, but took the bowl and put it to her lips, and, with her eyes on him, she drained it to the dregs.

Then the shivering, like a palsy, came over her again. 'Let me go,' she said huskily. 'Let none follow. Leave me in peace.' Langford opened the door and went back into the parlour. Mrs. Veale stole out after him, and those in the sitting-room heard her going down the passage like a bird, flapping against the walls on each side.

'Where is she going?' asked Charles. 'She is not to escape us. She's such a bad un, trying to involve me.'

'I've forgiven her,' answered Langford in a surly tone. 'I mayn't be over-generous, but I'm just.'

'And now, Taverner, one word wi' you,' said old Nanspian. 'I reckon you thought to sloke away this Red Spider, as you did the first; but there you are mistaken. As I've heard, you have tried to force her to accept you—who are old enough to be her father—shame be to you! But this is your own house, and I'll say no more on what I think. Now, Taverner, I venture to declare you have no more hold on the girl. Her brother never took your money; you were robbed by your own housekeeper. You say you've forgiven her because you are just. What the justice is, in that, I don't see, but I do see one thing clear as daylight, and that is, you've no right any more to insist on Honor coming here as your wife, not unless by her free will and consent, and that, I reckon, you won't have, as Larry, my boy, has secured her heart.'

Langford looked at Nanspian, then at Honor and Larry; at the latter he looked long.

'I suppose it is so,' he said. 'Give me the settlement.' He tore it to pieces. 'I'll have nothing more to do with women, old or young. They're all vexatious.'

'Hark!' They heard a wailing cry.

'Go and see what is the matter,' said Langford to Piper; then, turning to Oliver, he said, 'I tear up the settlement, but I'll not lend the hundred pounds.'

'Larry!' said old Nanspian, 'she shan't be sloked away any more. Take the maid's hand, and may the Lord bless and unite you.' Then to Langford, 'Now look y' here, Taverner. Us have been quarrelling long enough, I reckon. You've tried your worst against us and you've failed. I've made the first advance on my side, and uninvited come over your doorstep, a thing I swore I never would do. Give me your hand, brother-in-law, and let us forget the past, or rather let us go back to a past before we squabbled over a little Red Spider. You can't help it now; Langford and Chimsworthy will be united, but not whilst we old folk are alive, and Honor will be a queen o' managers. She'll rake the maidens out of their beds at five o'clock in the morning to make the butter, and——'

Piper burst into the room. 'Mrs. Veale!' he exclaimed.

'Well, what of Mrs. Veale?' asked Langford sharply.

'She has run out, crying like an owl and flapping her arms, over the moor, till she came to Wellon's Hill.'

'Let her go,' said Langford.

'She went right into the mound,' continued Piper breathlessly, 'and when I came up she had crawled into the stone coffin inside, and had only her arm out, and she was tearing and scraping at the earth and drawing it down over the hole by which she'd gone in—burying herself alive, and wailing like an owl.'

'Is there any money still hid there?' asked Langford.

'She screamed at me when I came up, "Will you not leave me alone? I be poisoned! I be dying! Let me die in peace!" Whatever shall us do?'

XXXVIII
The Look-out Stone

One Sunday evening, a year after the events just related, Taverner Langford and Hillary Nanspian, senior, were seated in the sun on the Look-out stone, in friendly conversation. Nanspian was looking happier, more hale, and prosperous than he had appeared since his stroke. He wore the badger-skin waistcoat, and his shirt-sleeves. The waistcoat had been relined with brilliant crimson stuff; bright was the hue of the lining displayed by the lappets. Taverner Langford had not a cheerful expression; his hair was more grizzled than it was twelve months ago, and his face more livid. There was, however, a gentler light in his eyes.

'It is a great change in Larry,' said Nanspian. 'Though I say it, there never was a steadier and better son. He is at work from morning to night, and is getting the farm into first-rate order—you'll allow that?'

'Yes,' answered Langford, 'I'll allow he begins well; I hope it will last. As for first-rate order, that I will not admit. "One year's seeds, three years' weeds," as Mrs. Veale——' He checked himself.

'That were a queer creature,' observed Nanspian, taking the pipe from his mouth, and blowing a long puff. 'That was the queerest thing of all, her burying herself; when she felt she was dying, in old Wellon's grave.'

'It was not his grave. It was a grave of the old ancient Britons.'

'Well, it don't matter exactly whose the grave was. Mrs. Veale seemed mighty set on making it her own.' He continued puffing, looking before him. 'I'm not sure you acted right about her,' he said after a while. 'I suppose you didn't really suppose there was any poison in the broth.'

'I'm a just man,' said Langford. 'To do as you were to be done by is my maxim. And—it's Gospel.'

'But you didn't think it would kill her?'

'I don't know what I thought. I wasn't sure.'

Another pause.

'Swaddledown ain't coming to the hammer after all,' said Nanspian.

'No, I'm glad the Voadens remain on.'

'Ah! and Sam is a good lad. I reckon before Michaelmas he and Kate will make a pair. They'd have done that afore if it had been settled whether Swaddledown would be sold, and they have to leave.'

'Kate is too giddy to be any use in a farm.'

'Oh, wait till she has responsibilities. See how well she has managed since Honor has been here—how she has kept the children, and made her father comfortable.'

'The children are half their time at Chimsworthy.'

'Well, well, I like to hear their voices.'

'And you see more than you like of Luxmore.'

'Oh no, I like to see a neighbour. I allow I'm a bit weary of Coombe Park; but bless you, now you and I let him have a trifle, he is most of his time when not in the van rambling about from one parish to another looking at the registers, and trying to find whether his grandfather were James, or John, or Joseph, or Jonah. It amuses him, and it don't cost much.'

'He'll never establish his claim.'

'I reckon he won't. But it's an occupation, and the carrying don't bring him much money—just enough to keep the children alive on.'

'Have you heard of Charles lately?'

'Oh, he is on the road. That was a fine idea, making a carrier of him between Exeter and Launceston There are so many stations on the way—there's Tap House, and Crockernwell, and Sticklepath, and

Okehampton, and Sourton Down Inn, and Bridestowe, and Lew Down, and Lifton; and he can talk to his heart's content at each about what he did in Afghanistan, and what he might be if his father could prove his claim to Coombe Park. Then he's so occupied with his horses on Sundays at Launceston that he can't possibly get over here to see his relations, which is a mercy.'

'I've been thinking,' said Langford, 'as we've got Larry in for third feoffee in Coryndon's Charity, couldn't we get the baby in for the fourth now there's a vacancy?'

'But the baby ain't come yet, and I don't know whether it'll be a boy or a maid.'

'It would be a satisfaction, and a further bond of union,' argued Langford. 'The Coryndon trust land comes in very fitting with Langford and Chimsworthy, and I thought that when you and I are gone, Larry might absorb our feoffeeships into himself; as a snail draws in his horns, and then there'd be only he and his son, and when he himself goes, his son would be sole feoffee and responsible to no one. Coryndon's land comes in very fitly.'

'I don't think it can be done,' said Nanspian, shaking his head. 'There's such a lot of ramping and roaring radicalism about. I thought we'd better put in Sam Voaden. Thus it will be in the family.'

'In the Luxmore, not in ours.'

'We can't have everything,' argued Nanspian. Then both were silent again. Langford sighed. Presently he said, 'I'm a just man, and do like to see the property rounded shapely on all sides. That is why I proposed it.'

Then another pause.

Presently Hillary Nanspian drew a long pull at his pipe, and sent two little shoots of smoke through his nostrils. 'Taverner,' said he, when all the smoke was expended, 'going back to that woman, Mrs. Veale. I don't think you ought to have taken me up so mighty sharp about her. After all this is sifted and said, you must allow you stood afraid of her, and I allow that you had a right to be so. A woman as would steal your cashbox, and make attempts on your heart, and poison your gruel, no man need blush and hang his head to admit that he was a bit afraid of.'

'And, Nanspian,' said Langford with solemnity, 'you will excuse my remarking that I think you took me up far too testily when I said you was a long-tailed ourang-outang, for it so happens that the ourang-outang is a tailless ape. Consequently, no offence could have been meant, and should not ha' been taken.'

'You don't mean to say so?'

'It is true. I have it in print in a Nature History, and, what is more, I've got a picture of an ourang-outang, holding a torn-off bough in his hand, and showing just enough of his back to let folks understand he's very like a man. Well, I've a mind, as the expression I used about you was repeated in the long room of the "Ring of Bells," to have that picture framed and hung up there. Besides, under it stands in print, "The ourang-outang, or *tailless* ape."'

'You will? Well, I always said you were a just man; now I will add you're generous.' The brothers-in-law shook hands. After a moment's consideration Nanspian said, 'I don't like to be outdone in generosity by you, much as I respect you. If it would be any satisfaction to the parish of Bratton Clovelly, the weather being warm, and for the quieting of minds and setting at rest all disputes, I don't object to bathing once in the river Thrustle before the feoffees of Coryndon's Charity, excepting Larry, whom from motives of delicacy I exclude.'

'Well,' said Langford, 'I won't deny you're a liberal-minded man.'

Taverner sprang to his feet, and Nanspian also rose. Over the stile from the lane came Honor, in her red stockings and scarlet cloak, the latter drawn closely round her.

'Why didn't you call us?' said Nanspian. 'We'd have come and helped you over.'

'You shouldn't be climbing about now,' said Taverner.

'Come and sit between us on the Look-out stone' said Nanspian.

So the two old men reseated themselves on the granite slab, with Honor between them.

'You tried hard to sloke her away,' remarked Nanspian, shaking his head.

'Let bygones be bygones,' said Langford. 'She may be here at Chimsworthy now, but she'll be at Langford some day, I'm proud and happy to think.'

'Ah!' said Nanspian, 'she's made a mighty change in Larry, and, faith, in me also. I'm a happier man than I was.' He put his arm round behind Honor.

'I may say that of myself,' said Langford. 'I can know that Langford will be made the most of after I'm gone.' He put his arm round her, and clasped that of Nanspian.

'Ah!' said Nanspian, in his old soft, furry, pleasant voice, 'if I'd a many score of faces in front of me, and I were addressing a political meeting, I'd say the same as I says now. Never you argue that what we was taught as children is gammon and superstition, it's no such thing. It has always been said that he who lays hold of red spider secures good luck, and we've proved it. Taverner and I, we've proved it. Us have got hold of the very best and biggest and reddest of money-spinners between us—us don't try to sloke her away to this side or to that. Her belongs ekally to Chimsworthy and to Langford, to myself and to Taverner, and blessed if there be a chance for any man all over England of getting such another treasure as this Red Spider which Taverner and I be holding atween us—ekally belonging to each.'

THE END

ALSO AVAILABLE IN THE NONSUCH CLASSICS SERIES

Balzac, Honoré de	*At the Sign of the Cat and Racket*	1 84588 051 X
Balzac, Honoré de	*The Seamy Side of History*	1 84588 052 8
Beckford, William	*Vathek*	1 84588 060 9
Bede, Cuthbert , B.A.	*Mr Verdant Green*	1 84588 197 4
Caldwell, Anne Marsh	*Chronicles of Dartmoor*	1 84588 071 4
Caldwell, Anne Marsh	*Two Old Men's Tales*	1 84588 081 1
Clarke, William	*Three Courses and a Dessert*	1 84588 072 2
Clarke, Marcus	*For the Term of His Natural Life*	1 84588 082 X
Clarke, Percy	*Three Diggers*	1 84588 084 6
Cooper, James Fenimore	*The Spy*	1 84588 055 2
Craik, Dinah	*John Halifax, Gentleman*	1 84588 027 7
Dickens, Charles	*Christmas Books*	1 84588 195 8
Galsworthy, John	*The Apple Tree*	1 84588 013 7
Galsworthy, John	*A Long-Ago Affair*	1 84588 105 2
Galsworthy, John	*The White Monkey*	1 84588 058 7
Gosse, Edmund	*Father and Son*	1 84588 018 8
Haliburton, Thomas Chandler	*The Attaché*	1 84588 049 8
Haliburton, Thomas Chandler	*The Clockmaker*	1 84588 050 1
Hardy, Thomas	*Desperate Remedies*	1 84588 099 4
Howells, William Dean	*Suburban Sketches*	1 84588 083 8
Poe, Edgar Allan	*Tales*	1 84588 036 6
Radcliffe, Ann	*The Romance of the Forest*	1 84588 073 0
Surtees, Robert S.	*"Ask Mamma"*	1 84588 002 1
Trollope, Anthony	*The Vicar of Bullhampton*	1 84588 097 8
Wilkins, Mrs William Noy	*The Slave Son*	1 84588 086 2